ONCE FOR LOVE,
THEN
POWER AND PASSION

by

John H. Johnson, Ph.D

Published by:
Voices Books & Publishing
P.O. Box 3007
Bridgeton, MO 63044
www.voicesbooks.homestead.com

Printed in the United States of America

Library of Congress Catalog Card No.: Pending

ISBN: 0-9779375-8-5

A VERY SPECIAL DEDICATION

I dedicate this entire book to my loving daughter LaVena Lynn Johnson, who mysteriously died in Balad, Iraq on July 19, 2005, at the tender age of 19, and while serving in the US Army. The character portrayed in this story as Vena, reflects her character at home prior to her going into the Army. She was smart, ambitious, and a very unselfish young woman. The life of Vena, as I have prescribed in this book, is how LaVena, A.K.A. SQEAKY, I believe would have turned out, had she been allowed to live out her life to its fullness.

To a daughter, who was a living angel to her mother, to a sister, who meant the world to her baby sister and three brothers, to a niece who was dear to her aunts and uncles, to a cousin who so many of her cousins loved and admired, to a daughter who was so very close and special to me, you are desperately missed and sincerely loved.

LOVINGLY from: The JOHNSON/CARTER/JOHNSON-MOORE/GIVENS FAMILIES.

A MESSAGE TO MY LOVELY WIFE, LINDA CARTER-JOHNSON

Between us we produced five wonderful children. After having three boys, you prayed for an angel. This book is a tribute to the one you prayed for and God gave us, LaVena. Now I want to thank you for being wonderful mother to our five children. As of June 4, 2006, we will be married for twenty-nine years. It has been a wonderful ride. Thank you very much!

With All My Love
Your husband
John

ACKNOWLEDGMENTS

Title concept developed by
Dr. John H. Johnson and LaKesha F. Johnson

Cover Concept by
Dr. John H. Johnson

Cover Illustration and Original Drawing by
17 year old
LaKesha Floreece Johnson

Cover Artwork and Innovations by
Mr. Antonio A Bread

INTRODUCTION

There is an old saying that goes behind every good man there is a great woman. I use to have a difficult time trying to figure out what the prevailing factors were in this particular scenario. Did it mean that no man could reach a high level of success without the backing of a great woman? Or was it possibly, a man with potential will never reach that potential, unless he has a good woman to bring that potential to the forefront. I found the validity of the meaning of this statement would depend on the values such a woman has.

So the question then becomes how much value can be placed on a woman's who knows how to support a man's effort. If she works to help support the man and their family and her income is let's say, $40,000 a year, how much value does that assumes other then the income she brings into the household? On the other hand, what if she was a stay home mom, and that was her contribution to a man's effort of success? According to the 21st century version on this scenario, her value might be estimated to be over $100,000.00 a year.

But what if a woman with values is also an aggressive female in either of the above scenarios and understands the power of her sexuality? She will also understand the potential power she has over a man. She also has to understand her sexuality is too valuable to be given to just any man just for the mere sake of intimacy. Otherwise, it has a tendency to lose some of its value and the power. If a man has no potential, and she uses her sexuality to merely please him, sooner or later she will have to come to grips with what she is really getting out of her action. Any woman can sacrifice her sexuality. The questions are, why? And what ultimate goal can be accomplished by doing so.

But what if a woman shows that she has no values? Shows she has no morals, particularly when it comes to dealing with a man? How then can her value to a man be estimated? Another question might be, how does he see her as a value to him?

History might suggest a woman had absolutely nothing to do with a man achieving success in his life and that the sexuality of the woman behind him is merely for his benefit. He might be best served if he realizes there may still be a good woman behind his achievements. But that woman just might be his, MOTHER!

CHAPTER ONE

AT FIRST GLANCE

The year was 2005. It was a brisk, windy fall morning in St. Louis. Old man Jenkins had been dead and buried for a couple of months and it was time for his will to finally be read, something his family knew would come but something they had not looked forwards towards. For Floreese Jenkins, his daughter, it was to be a day she would not soon forget just as the memories she had of a father who meant so much to her.

When the elevator door opened, she got off and walked past several doors reading as she did, until she found the one marked 'Myron Jenkins, Attorney At Law'. She walked into the lawyer's, office. When she peeped into the conference room, she became somewhat confused. She had assumed the entire family would already be there. She was also surprised to see his secretary not at work in lieu of it already being nine in the morning.

"I'll be with you in a minute! Have a seat!" came a male voice from the inner office.

Rather then sit, she walked over and looked out of one of the side windows. She could see the park from where she stood. She couldn't help but notice the trees with their red, brown, orange and faded dark green leaves. From where she stood, the trees put her in mind of a rainbow. But when she looked beyond the trees, she could see some of those same leaves lying on the ground. It was then the true meaning of the hue of color leaves reminded her they were dead, all of them, just as her father was dead. But the leaves she thought would come back and she would see them alive again when the spring sun blasted through the rainy clouds. As for her father, he was dead forever and she would never see his smiling face again.

The depressive thought caused her to walk away from the window. This time she did sit down in one of the chairs lined up against the wall. Before she was in the least bit comfortable, she heard the office door open. She looked up just as Mr. Thomas was walking out to greet her.

"Floreese, how are you?" he asked as he held out his hand.

"I'm doing fine Mr. Thomas. I thought you were retired?" she asked as she shook his hand.

"I am, but there's no way I would have missed this day," he chuckled.

"Oh really? Where is everybody?" she asked.

"I asked them to come later. I needed to see you alone."

"Alone? Why?"

"Come on into your brother's office, I'll explain."

She got up and followed Thomas into her brother's office. Once inside, she could see he had a tape cassette player sitting on a conference table.

"Have a sit down," he requested.

She pulled out a chair and sat down at the conference table. She then looked to him to explain what was happening.

"I made several visits to the hospital to see your father before he died. He made this tape and asked if I would ask you to listen to it before the others got here."

"What's on it?"

"It's personal and only for you."

"Okay," said a curious young female.

She turned on the cassette players and listened. It was obvious it was her father and what he had to say on the tape was quite interesting:

"Dear Flo, if you're listening to this tape, it means I have gone to be with God. I don't need to tell you now much I am going to miss all of you. You have all been such a joy in my life and I wish I could have lived forever to enjoy you. But the Bible says 'Every man is appointed to die once' and I guess it was just my appointed time. At any rate, I made this tape especially for you to hear. Mostly because of all the kids, you seemed to have the most problem adjusting to losing your mother and to me marrying Menzie. But you don't understand what she has meant to me, to us as a family. Now that I am gone, she will need all of you. So I thought I'd give you an understanding of how things were between us."

Floreese listened, but not without shading tears as she did so.

"It all kind of started, the first time I caught my first glance of her. I was conducted management training class in the conference room located on the main floor of our building. Suddenly, there was this uncontrollable commotion outside the conference room. When I looked up, I saw her through the training room glass door, though only for a brief moments. She was tall for a woman and very pretty. As she walked she seemed to move in slow motion, her hair seemly bouncing with every step she took. I thought I saw her glance over at me if only for a brief second and smiled. On the other hand, I was surprised of the reaction of my students, who seemed to have a total disregard for my status as their teacher, and jumped up and immediately rushed out of my class to go see her and join in on the mass hysteria.

If I had not been so upset, I would have recognized her although I would not have panicked like the others just to get a look at her. To say I was upset would be a gross understatement. I just stood in the classroom, aggravated over the entire affair. After I gathered myself, I walked over to the doorway, stood and watched. The only other person, who didn't seem all caught up in the excited of seeing her was Sara Tillsberge, who stood just outside the classroom door and looked on.

"Oh God, why don't they just kiss her butt and be done with it!" she snapped.

"Who in the world is she?" I asked.

"Some broad who starred in a few low budget films!" remarked Sara.

It wasn't until later I found out why Sara had the attitude she had. As for me, I still didn't recognize her and for that matter, I didn't care who she was. Just having lost my whole class was so aggravating, I walked out of the classroom and stood just outside the classroom door and listened as old man Cecil Robinstein, the owner of the firm, introduced her to an already hysterical crowd.

"Lady and gentlemen, it is obvious most of you recognize this young lady," he said. "If not, she is Miss Menzie Ferguson, the movie star."

"Please Mr. Robinstein, you don't have to--"

"Come now, let's not be too modest," he interrupted. "This lady starred in several movies. To include, 'Unmarried Women', 'Bobby Jean's Hot Book' and a few others I can't recall at this time."

"Well, don't worry about it now! You've already named the two worst films I've ever been in!" joked Menzie, which drew a chuckled from the staff.

"Oh, I don't know about that! I thought one film was just as bad as the next!" whispered Sara to me.

"Sorry about that!" snickered old man Robinstein. "But I am happy to announce that Miss Ferguson will be joining our staff as head of our Promotion and Publicity Department, isn't that wonderful?" snickered an overly excited Cecil Robinstein.

"Goodness! I hope he don't get a heart attack over her!" instigated Sara.

"Miss Ferguson, would you like to say something?"

"No, it looks like you've said it all!" she joked.

"Thank God!" mumbled Sara.

Nearly the entire staff clapped and cheered as if she was some kind of savior or something. In fact it was one of the few days old man Robinstein didn't seem to mind people standing around not getting any work done. Instead, they hovered over her like a buzzard over a dying bulldog.

But savior or not, she started to make the right moves the moment she settled in her office. Her first official duty was to invite Sara Tillsberge to her office.

"You sent for me?" she asked as she entered Ferguson's new constructed office.

"Yes...Have a seat," she responded.

"Oh my!" she uttered as she closed the door behind her.

"What's the matter?" asked Menzie.

"This is a nice office. Everything looks so brand new. Come to think of it I believe is the first time I've been in any of the offices on this floor without being in trouble! Or did I assume too much?" snickered Tillsberge.

"You're not in trouble if that's what you mean. Go on, have a seat. Trust me, I won't bite you!"

Sara walked over near her desk and sat down. Then watched as she thumbed through a stack of papers she had on her desk. She pulled out a sheet, read it, then looked up at Sara and smiled.

"Are you sure I'm not in trouble?" asked a suspicious Tillsberge.

"No, and why would you ask me that?" responded Menzie.

"The last time I saw a smile like that, I was being kicked out of Junior High for throwing a stink bomb in the cafeteria!" joked Sara.

"Really?" chuckled Menzie Ferguson.

"Really!" responded a chuckling Sara.

The two of them got a good laugh out of Sara's little remark. Once Menzie composed herself, she got to why she had sent for Sara.

"I've been going through your work record. From what I've seen, you're a excellent worker," she commented.

"Well, I've been called worse!" joked Sara.

Ferguson didn't comment, just sat and peered over at the wanted to be comedian. Sara attempted to smile her way though the look she was getting but couldn't.

"Sorry! That was a try at a little humor!" she remarked after clearing her throat.

"Well, at best it was very little!" chuckled Feguson.

"Huh, the woman has a sense of humor! I think I like you already!" chuckled Sara Tilleberge.

Again, Ferguson didn't crack a smile, but just peered at Sara for a second time. This time Sara realized something about her hopefully potential boss. She did not mix business with pleasure, or so she assumed. She cleared her throat a second time. She then continued the conversation with Ferguson.

"You were saying? I mean about the job?" she asked.

"Thank You...Now, I understand you most likely would have gotten this job had I not come along?"

"Ahh that depends!"

"Depends on what?"

"Old man Robinstein tries to be a fair enough man. But there are times when the old guy's mind goes south. When that happens, he has a tendency to go to his kinfolks for advice. You know, ask his family members to help him make important decisions on business matters. When that happens, fairplay goes right out the window and is replaced by stupidity, prejudice and narrow mindedness!"

Ferguson chuckled.

"Let's suppose he was in his fair state of mind. You being the best person for this job, what are the chances he may have selected you?"

"I'm sure I would have gotten this job! Although, I will admit, hiring you was a pretty smooth move on the part of old man Robinstein. You' re a movie star, singer, and model. I mean your name alone is a gold mind to this firm and will no doubt draw clients and business here."

"You're kind of frank about things aren't you?"

"So I'm been told. Although I have been call worse," said Sara with a friendly frown on her face.

Ferguson laughed at her remark.

"Tell you what, there's going to be a lot of work around here that needs to be done and I'll need a good Administrative Assistant. I'm a bit of a perfectionist and want nothing but the best working for me. You interested?"

"Am I to assume, I'm going to get a pay raise?"

"Indeed. In fact, I'll see to it that you get the same pay you would have received if you had gotten this position."

"Really? Now I feel guilty!"

"Guilty? About what?"

"When I heard the firm had hired you, I got a little upset!" confessed Sara.

"You mean jealous?"

"Well yeah, jealous works!" snickered Sara.

"That's okay, I understand."

"You mean it's okay that I talked about you behind your back? Made little sneaky remarks about you? And told people you were a snob and a big showoff?"

"Now I didn't say all that!"

"Oh, sorry!" uttered Sara.

"Besides, all those people you talked to about me, now you have to walk around here with them knowing you now work for me," retorted Menzie.

"Oh yeah!" murmured Sara as she rubbed the back of her neck. "I never thought about that! You know, you're a pretty smart cookie!" snickered Sara. "And I've got a feeling things around here are never going to be the same."

"You're right. So, does that mean you will take the job?"

"I made have a big mouth, but I'm not stupid! Of course I accept!"

"Good, as of now, you work for me. I've already given them a work order to start working on building your new office."

"So you already knew I was going to accept your job?"

"Yes I did, Mr. Robinstein told me you had a big mouth, but that you were no fool."

"Oh he did, did he?" chuckled Tillsberge "And what else did that old goat say about me?"

"I don't think I should repeat the rest of it!" snickered Menzie.

Tillsberge laughed, "That was cold, boss!"

"Now here's your first official duty. I need to have an organizational chart of every department in this firm, plus job descriptions. Can you get them for me?"

"No problem! But ahh, what are you going to try and do, reorganize this place?

"It depends on whether the current structure is getting the job done."

"Good point! Is there anything else?"

"Yes, but this is sort of an unofficial duty."

"From what you're paying me, there is no such thing as an unofficial duty!"

"Good! I ahh, saw a man yesterday. About five nine, five ten, seemed well built, good looking, dressed nice."

"You mean Dr. James Jenkins, very intelligent and a very nice man!"

"Oh, he is?"

"Yeah! But forget it!"

"Meaning?"

"Meaning he's also very married and have five kids."

"Wow! Big family...Faithful husband, huh?"

"Yeah, husband, faith father and a faithful church going brother. It has been rumored that this woman, Gladis Henley is her name, who looks okay, but thinks she God's gift to men. Well, she got him cornered in one of the empty offices last year. I'm told all she got for her trouble was a hot booty and a lecture on fornication or the lack of there of."

Both she Ferguson laughed.

"Well, that's okay. I just thought I'd ask," said Ferguson.

"While we're on the subject, here's my second unofficial duty for you. He's pissed with you because you emptied out his class yesterday when you made your grand entrance. If I were you, I'd go to him and make up. Give him a peace offering."

"Any suggestions?"

"Try anything short of a kiss on the cheek. That will get your feeling hurt!"

Later that day, Ferguson walked into Dr. James Jenkins' office. His secretary announced her and he asked her to come in. But once she was close to him, she became extremely nervous as she watched him sitting at his desk. But she gathered herself long enough to say what it was she wanted to say.

"I understand, I owe you an apology?" she asked.

"Really? And who told you that?" he asked as he stopped working and leaned back in his executive chair.

"Let's just say, a little birdie told me," snickered Ferguson.

"Sara Tillsberge, huh?"

"Well, yes!" chuckled Menzie. "It's about me empting out your class yesterday when I first got here, I'm sorry. Believe or not, I asked Mr. Robinstein not to make a big deal out of me taking a job here, but he did it anyway."

"Yeah, he gets excited about things like that!"

"Things like what?"

"Things he feels will make this firm a few bucks!" suggested Jenkins.

"I hear ya!" chuckled Menzie. "Well, I'd like to make it up to you by buying you lunch."

"Why would you want to do that?"

"I just told you why!"

"Look Miss Ferguson, I understand you are a big time movie star and all that. I've even heard about your new hatchback Cadillac. And everybody here thinks you're a big shot with plenty of money. Now me, I don't care about things like that. You are now a part of this firm and I will treat you with respect accordingly. I've been here a long time. If you need help with anything, I'll do what I can to help you out. But please, don't start out by trying to buy me off."

"Well I wasn't--"

"If you weren't, then I apologize," interrupted Jenkins. "Having said that, I have a lot of work to do and I am sure you do too."

"Well, I'm sorry I bothered you!" said an angry Menzie Ferguson.

"Trust me, you were no bother!" retorted Jenkins.

Later during lunch, Menzie and Sara were having lunch in the cafeteria, when they saw Jenkins past by them carrying a tray of food.

"You know, that brother shoo think he's fine!" scolded Menzie.

"I take it things didn't go well with you and the good doctor!" said Sara as she ate a fork full of food.

"The man has the disposition on a runaway train!" suggested Ferguson as she slowly ate a fork of food.

"Him? Noh, he's good people!"

"Well, I don't think so!" snapped Ferguson.

"The man has the respect of everybody here. How is it that you two started off on the wrong foot? Or could there be something else going on here?"

"I doubt it. But I went to see him like you suggested. I offered to buy him lunch as a gesture of an apologizing. He accused me of trying to buy him off. The nerves of that bone head!" remarked Menzie as she peered over at him.

Sara noticed how she was looking at him, so she offered her more advise on how to deal with Jenkins.

"Well don't say I didn't ware you."

"Yeah but you suggested I should take a peace offering! You should have told me to take a brick with me...That jug head!" she snapped.

"Okaaaay! Just what are you angry about? Him talking to you the way he did? Or him refusing to have lunch with you?" asked Sara as she ate another fork full of food and rolled her eyes around as a gesture of sarcasm.

"It was his attitude...I think."

"Are you sure about that?"

"Yes I'm sure...No, I'm not sure," chuckled Ferguson. "But I see where you're headed with this," she continued.

"And just where is that?"

"You're thinking I don't take rejection too well, right?"

"You said it, I didn't!"

"Well...maybe a little," chuckled Menzie. "But I just wanted to make it up to him for interrupting his class, not sleep with the man!" she snapped.

"That may be. But you sure he didn't damage your ego a little when he rejected you?"

"Look, you're inferring that I find the man attractive."

"And of course, I'm wrong about that, right?"

"Okay, so the man is handsome, dresses nice, and has a fine butt...Plus he's packing a little bit, if you know what I mean?"

"You see that's your problem."

"What's my problem?"

"Jumping the gun a bit. With him, you can't make it look like you're interested in sex. Many have tried and failed. Now if you just want to be his friend, you can do that."

"And how is that Miss know it all?"

"Didn't I hear you were trying out for the symphony?"

"So?"

"Well, if you make the symphony, I was thinking you should offer him free tickets to one of the concerts."

"I offered the man lunch, and he turned me down. Why would I be glutting for more punishment by now asking him to go to a symphony? I don't think so."

"Well, it was only a suggestion."

Yeah, I know...Beside, how do you know the man even likes symphony music?"

"Boss, I heard it through the grapevine that the man goes to the Handle's Messiah concert every year!"

"Really! Interesting! Well, it's too late now. Beside, I don't even like him!"

Tillsberge snickered. "You sound like a little girl, who just had her doll taken away from her, poor baby."

"Look, get off that rejection kick!" snapped Ferguson.

"My, now we're getting defensive."

"Okay, so now you're the resident shrink, huh?"

"I wouldn't have to be to figure you out."

"Well, don't under estimate me when it comes to men. I can more than hold my own. Beside, he's the type you have to wait and make him come to you," uttered Ferguson as she ate a fork of food.

"Yeah, well I wouldn't hold my breath if I were you."

"Meaning what?"

"Meaning Miss prissy! You watch! You'll change that tone and soon. You think you have some feeling now, you just wait, you'll have plenty later."

The moment Menzie stopped talking, she glared over at the handsome Jenkins as she lifted an empty fork to her mouth and sucked on it for several seconds.

"You ah, going to eat food with that fork? Or are you going to suck all of the silver out of it?" asked an observant Sara Tillsberge.

"What? Ah, sorry!" said Menzie as she continued to eat her lunch.

"Look, he is a very handsome man and you are not the first women who liked him at first glance. But he carries himself well around here. And he's smart, very smart. And has a lot on influence around here because of the education he has. And in time he'll charm you just like he has everybody here. So, don't feel bad if you find yourself running to him for help."

"Well, that ain't gonna happen. But you're right he is one fine brother, just stuck on himself. And if he thinks I'm going to kiss his ass, he got another think coming."

Sara Tillsberge laughed. "Take my advice. Because he's well liked and respected around here, you need to be careful what you say and how you act around him. Rumors around here spread very fast. You're a famous person. Right now people think you are hot stuff, but you're new. And after you've been here for a while, they tend to forget about things like that, and will talk about you like a dog."

"Look, I don't care about the grapevine and all that other crap that goes on around here."

"I hear ya. All I'm saying is, if the two of you don't get along, people will wonder why. That could make your time around here miserable."

"You're saying that to say what?"

"Cut the man some slack. Get to know him like a friend like the rest of us. Be careful how you act around him, what you say to him. You might find him to be quite a friend to have."

Menzie stopped eating and looked directly at Sara as she talked. And she was listening to every word and thought about them as well.

"And I'll tell you something else," she continued. "Old man Robinstein likes him. If you have something you want him to listen too, he'll tell you he's interested and he'll get back with you. Then he'll go behind your back and ask the good doctor for his opinion."

"What are you, an Ann Landers helper or something?"

"No silly!" chuckled Sara as she ate another fork of food.

"Well, what you've told me is good to know...And you must keep your ears to the walls to know so much about what goes on around here?"

"Well, people around here think because I talk so much, I don't listen. But sometimes I talk, just to get them to tell me stuff."

"Well, remind me not to confide in you!" insisted Menzie.

"I'll remind you all you want! But you'll do it anyway...Everyone does!"

CHAPTER TWO

A PERFECT TEAM

After Ferguson had been on the job for six months, she had worked hard. And just as old man Robinstein had projected, business picked up slightly because of him hiring her. But him hiring her was just the beginning. She had learned more about the firm and was now about to put the firm in a position to make history and a lot of money. And to show how tactful she was, she went to the one source she knew would be of some help to her, in lieu of them barely speaking to one another during her time there.

"Is Dr. Jenkins in?" she asked once she had walked into his office.

"Oh, hi Ms. Ferguson!" said his secretary. "He's in, I'll let him know you're here!" said an excited secretary.

She then called Dr. Ferguson on the intercom and announced Menzie Ferguson. As she talked to her boss, she started to trembling a bit, although she wasn't quite sure why. He asked his secretary to ask her to come in. She took several deep breaths then went into his office. He was sitting at his desk working, when she walked in.

"Good afternoon, Miss Ferguson," he said as he stopped working. "Have a seat."

"Thank you," she responded as she sat down in the chair next to his desk.

"How can I help you?"

"I have something I want you to take a look at," she said.

She handed him a spreadsheet and what looked to be an outline of the locations of the offices at the firm. He took and looked them over. While he looked at the outlines, she couldn't take her eyes off him. When he looked at her, she was sure he had seen her starring at him, but he didn't let on that he had.

"Well, what do you think?" she asked

"Interesting!" he uttered.

"As you can see, by the spreadsheet, business has picked up significantly. And as you can see, our profits are on the raise."

"Yeah, I can see that. Why are you here to see me?"

"I've checked the qualifications of every person working here. I found yours to be quite impressive."

"Oh really?"

"Really? Are you interested in what I have to say?" asked Ferguson in a snappy tone of voice.

"Let's say that I am, why are you here?" he asked in a suspicious tone of voice.

"Look, if you are not going to listen to me with an opened mind, forget it!" she snapped in an angry tone of voice.

He sat and watched as she attempted to pick up all of the information she had brought with her. He could see how angry she was because she kept fumbling with trying to pick the information, while dropping it back on his desk just as fast as she could pick it up. Finally, she gathered most of it, then peered over at him with a look of contempt.

"Why don't you leave all that here. I'll go over it then get with you later," he suggested.

"Fine!" she snapped.

She dropped all of the information back onto his desk, then turned and hurried headed towards the door. Once she had opened the door, he gave her some last minute advice.

"You might work on controlling your temper a bit," he suggested.

"What eveeerr!" snapped Ferguson as closed the door behind her.

Once she was back in her office, she rushed right past the secretary, then Sara Tillsberge's office, and without saying a word. Sara obviously knew she was upset, so she immediately followed her into her office. Once there she could see her boss sitting at her desk with her arms crossed, this angry look on her face.

"What's wrong with you?" she asked.

"It's that knucklehead!" she snapped. "I can't stand him!"

"By him, I'm assuming you mean the good Dr. Jenkins."

"That's right! The man has the charisma of a pit bull!" she scolded as she sat there her arms locked against her body.

Sara started to chuckle.

"I don't see anything funny!" she bellowed.

"I do. Look at you. Just a huffing and a puffing like a big bad wolf ready to blow his brains out."

"Well, it was a good thing I didn't have a gun, don't I would have."

Sara laughed at her remark.

"Suppose you tell me what happened."

"I went to that birdbrain, and attempted to show him the plans I had for this firm. He acted like he had his head up his ass!" she snapped.

"Ohhh now I see. You went to his office, with your big plans to change things around here?"

"That's right. The man has good potential if he could stop being stuck on himself for a few moments."

"Is it him or is it you?" asked Sara with a serious tone to her voice.

"Watch it! Don't forget whose the boss around here!"

"You see that's part of your problem. You are trying to be too bossy. Look you're new around here. He's been around here awhile. Did you really think he was going to jump because you say so? You sure there's nothing else going on?"

"Like what?"

"Well, look at you. You are very pretty and have a body to die for. What you expected was for him to jump all over you like I guess other men have tried. But he didn't, so you are trying to push the issue and doing a lousy job of it."

"What if I told you, you were fired?"

"I'm afraid that wouldn't change anything between the two of you. Besides, that would only show how mad you are."

Menzie started to chuckle at her remark.

"Now, that's better."

"As I was leaving that numb heads office, he said, I needed to control my temper," she chuckled.

"Of course, you didn't pay any attention to that," chuckled Sara. "Hey! I did try and warn you about him? He's different, not a run of the mill man."

"Okay Miss know it all, what do you suggest?"

"You are use to men coming to you, give him that same courtesy. He is smart. If what you left with him has any merit, he will come to you."

Later in the day, Dr. Jenkins walked into Ferguson's office carrying the information she left with him.

"Oh hi Dr. Jenkins," said the secretary.

"Hi Lucy, is Miss Ferguson in?"

"Yes, I'll buss her for you...Miss Ferguson, Dr. Jenkins is here to see you."

"Oh really? Tell him to come in said Ferguson as she attempted to compose herself.

"Good afternoon," said Jenkins as he walked into her private office.

"Hi Dr. Jenkins," she responded in a pleasant tone of voice.

"I've been looking over the information you left with me, and you're right. There are a lot of possibilities going on here. Where do we start?"

"I think we should start with you. You have a lot to offer this firm. You are well educated, well liked and have leadership potential and I've heard, a tremendous ability to motivate people. Just doing it for the staff here, makes you way under utilized. Do you agree?"

"I've always felt I was!" remarked Jenkins without apprehension.

"Well, with your qualifications, they are lucky to have you here. So, as for that part of this proposal, I'm recommending that change. Instead of you sitting back in this small office, I'm thinking you should be head of a department. I think the Marketing Department and Human Resources should be combined and put under a newly formed Public Relations Department, with you as Department Head. But more importantly, you need to be making presentations outside of this firm. That will enhance the firm's reputation, plus bringing in more clients, not to mention more revenue. So, you do see the possibilities?"

"In deed," remarked Jenkins.

"Of course the personal benefit to you is, you will still be paid your salary for the work you do here, plus a percentage of the outside contractual agreements when you do presentation outside the firm. You interested?"

"Very much so," responded Jenkins.

"How then can we work out all the details?"

"Maybe we should work together on this," suggested Jenkins.

"I would like that. But before we start to work together, I would like to clear the air between us."

"Actually, I owe you an apology. I was still upset because of what happened your first day here."

"Well, are you over that now?" chuckled Ferguson.

"I believe so," chuckled Jenkins.

"I haven't been diplomatic in approaching you. So, I apologize and I promise, I won't be as difficult to work with."

For an entire week, the two worked diligently on the realigning of the firm to include a drawing up of the format for the contractual outside agreements. Once they had all the details worked out, then came the hard part and that was getting old man Robinstein to accept it. To increase their odds, they both went to his office and made their proposals.

"As you can see, the purpose of this realignment is to make more people contacts, and increase business clientele, not to mention to draw new revenue by using Dr. Jenkins' expertise outside of the firm," said Menzie.

"The realignment for awhile will create a very minimal increase in our doing business. Each department's increases of clientele will automatically increase their profits," interjected Jenkins. "Our perspective departments will indicate the largest increase because of Miss Ferguson's personal appearances in the promoting of the firm and our products and me with public appearances and outreach motivational talks, as another product. We will being in more clientele and more profits."

"This is very impressive!" said old man Robinstein as he sat and looked over the realignment plans. "Very impressive in deed! What about Burns and Jones? How do you think they are going to like having their departments combined and put under a third entity?"

"Well, this is business and the purpose of business is to make money. If they have a problem with it, they can leave," insisted Menzie.

"My guess is, they will be so busy, they won't have time to think of that kind of foolishness," added Jenkins.

"Well, it seems you two have worked everything out. Which one of you came up with this idea?" asked Robinstein.

"The two of us have been working on it together all week," responded Ferguson.

"Good...I think you two make a hell of a team!" he confirmed.

For the next few weeks Ferguson and Jenkins worked on getting the new structure underway. They had mapped out office space, location of desks, reassignment of personnel, everything. Before long, everything was in place. Menzie Ferguson, when she made personal appearances, drew huge crowds. Jenkins started out slow, but as his reputation increased, so did the size of his audiences. And as projected, the firm started to make huge sums of money.

When people are busy, working overtime and making money, they are happy. In fact other than a few personal problems, the morale of the firm had gone up. But one personal problem that surfaced had to do with Gladis Henley, who liked Jenkins but hated Ferguson. She also had the reputation of being a nosey busy body and for being the root of the firm's rumor mill. It was she who started a rumor of Ferguson and Jenkins having an affair. The fact they were spending a lot of time together, sure didn't help matters much. Once Sara Tillsberg got wind of it, she came to her boss with it.

"These are requests from D.J. Farmers' group and The Coleman Corporation," said her boss as she handed the paper work to Sara. "They want us to provide them with consulting services. Do two separate business contracts. Do the first one for the realignment consultation service and one for the motivational consultation."

"Are you and Dr. J. going in to do the organization realignment?" asked Sara.

"I'll check with him, but I'm sure he'll want us to work on it together."

"Don't you think you two are working together a little bit too much?"

"I don't quite understand what you mean!" said a surprised lady boss.

"Be it for me to listen to rumors, but--"

"Yeah! Right!" interrupted Menzie.

"Well, maybe some. But there's a rumor going around that you two are an item."

"Oh, is that right?"

"You don't seem concerned about it, are you?"

"Sara, he and I make a good team. Because of our working together, the people here are making lots of money. They shouldn't even have time to sit around and gossip."

"That may be, but money isn't the issue, it's appearance."

"Okay Sara, obviously you have something on your mind. What is it?"

"I know how you feel about him."

"And how do you think I feel?"

"You remember, I told you sooner or later he would charm you? Well, I think that has already happened."

"Least you forget you are talking to your boss."

"There you go again, playing hard ball with me and I'm trying to help you out. I'm just saying when he's around you act differently, and I am not the only one who has noticed it. That's why they think you are messing around. "

"I can't do anything about how people think!" snapped Menzie.

"Well, snapping at me, ain't gonna change anything!" retorted Sara.

"Okay! I'm sorry. But what can I do about it?"

"The fact that you like him, tells me you are a healthy, vibrate woman. Maybe you should get a man of your own."

"Sara, I don't need a man right now!"

"Right now?"

"Look! Now we have work to do. You say what you have to say and get back to work!"

"My, you can be a bitch when you want to!"

"Sara!"

"Okay! Okay! You know George Blackshere?"

"Everybody knows about George Blackshere. They say he's a ladies man."

"He's actually more of a cock hound!" chuckled Sara.

"What's your point?"

"He's not that bad looking and he is one of the most eligible bachelors around here. Maybe, well you know?"

"Well, if he's all that, then why don't you date him?"

"Well, now I like this salt and pepper thing, but I heard he likes you."

"Are you suggesting I sleep with him?"

"Well, rumor has it he cherishes the ground you walk on."

"Well, he's not my type!" she snapped.

"What is your type?"

"Intelligent, smooth, handsome, dress nice and smell good."

"That sounds like James Jenkins to me."

"Now there's a man that literally turns me on," uttered Ferguson.

"Well he might turn you on, but keep in mind, he has a wife who might turn you out," chuckled Sara.

"Somehow, I doubt that!" snapped Ferguson. “Okay nosey Rosie! You want to know something? He is the kind of man I like. No, he isn't just the kind of man I like he is the man I want. But I know he's married. And I know there no chance of us ever being together. But that doesn't mean I can't be around him. I admire him, I adore him, I --"

"You want to sleep with him," interrupted Sara Tillsberger.

"I might, but I won't even try. I respect him too much. And I respect his wife. Besides, I'm not desperate enough to mess around with a married man or the likes of George Blackshere for that matter."

"I'm not saying sleep with him. Just date him. Besides, you might like him."

"I doubt that...But for the sake of argument, let's say I go out with him, what would that prove?"

"It might not prove anything, but it least it might stop the rumors going on."

"Well, we'll see," said an apprehensive advertising executive.

As soon as Menzie made the commitment to go out with George Blackshere, that rumor spread just as fast as the rumor about her and James Jenkins. Only this time it was James Jenkins who heard about it. So, after work, he ran into her on her way to her car. It was then they walked and talked to one another.

"I heard you are going out with George Blackshere, is it true?"

"Man, the rumors around here spread quicker than jelly on bread!"

"Well, this wasn't really a rumor. He made it a point of telling me personally."

"Why would he do that?"

"Because he thinks you're hot to trot and he hates me over something that happened when we were in college together."

"So, sounds like he's been listening to the rumor floating around here."

"I don't think he believed the rumor about us. This was just his way of letting me know he has beaten my time with you."

"Ahh, so you've heard we were suppose to be sleeping together?"

"Yeah, I heard that!" chuckled Jenkins.

"And you thought it was funny?"

"Yeah, I do. One thing I've learned about life and that is you can't stop people from talking. Besides, I thought it was flattering for them to think I had a chance with a woman like you. I've been married almost fifteen years. Everybody knows I try and be a faithful husband and to some, that's considered square. But then to think I was tripping with you, well that's almost like a badge of honor."

"Well, if it's any consolation, I felt honored when I first heard it. Anyway, you keep on being a faithful husband. It makes me like and respect you the more," she said as they reached her Cadillac and she remotely unlocked the door and got in.

"Look, be careful of Blackshere," he said as he closed her car door for her. "I knew a woman who said he attempted to rape her after a date. I wouldn't want him to try that with you."

"Thank you for the warning. If he tries that with me, he's in for a rude awakening," she chuckled.

Later that Friday evening, George and Menzie were out and having dinner. So far he had been nothing short of being a gentleman. He even offered to pay for dinner once they were finished, but she refused. In fact to be on the safe side, she paid for dinner, which did upset him quite a bit, which he conceited once they were outside the door to her apartment.

"Well, thanks George for a wonderful evening," she said.

"You asked me to go out, but I wanted to pay for dinner!" he snapped.

"Does it bother you that I paid for dinner?"

"Well, yes!"

"Why?

"Because it's the man's responsibility to pay for dates. It's the first signal to let him know when two people are getting close."

"Close?"

"Yeah! You know what I mean!"

"No, I don't. What does you buying me dinner have to do with our getting close?"

"Come on Menzie, you've been around."

"Ohhhhh! We're talking about close as in sex close, aren't we?"

"Okay Menzie! Stop playing these games! You are about the finest women I have ever seen."

"Excuse me! About the finest?"

"Okay, you are the finest!" he uttered. "And I have never see a woman I desire as much as I desire you."

"Desire? You mean desire as in wanting to get laid?"

"Whatever you want to call it. All I know is, I want you...Well, how about it?" he asked as he backed her up and pinned her up and against the corridor wall.

"Now, what is this suppose to do?"

"Oh, I'm just beginning," he said as he started to roll his body against hers.

"Wait a minute! I think you better get off me!" she insisted.

"Look, I know you want it! That's why you ask me out on this date," he whispered as he continued to roll his body against hers. "So let's stop wasting time!" he said as he attempted to kiss her.

"Wait a minute!" she insisted. "Me asking you out on a date had nothing to do with me wanting to have sex with you. Now get off me and I mean right now!" she said as she struggled to push him away from her.

"Come on Menzie! Stop fooling around, you know you want some."

"Man, if you don't get off me, you'll be sorry," she warned.

"Not until I at least get me a little kiss," he insisted.

"Okay, you ask for it!" she warned.

She quickly snatched away one of her hands and grabbed him by the throat, cutting off his breath causing his eye to cross. Once he was far enough from her, she quickly kneed him in his crouch, then flipped him over causing him to land on his buttocks.

"Ahhhhhhhhhhhh!" he squawked in pain as he laid on the floor, holding his crouch with both hands.

"I forgot to tell you, I know marshal arts."

He struggled getting to his feet. Once he did, his knees seemed locked together as he attempted to stumble away from her.

"Was that close enough for ya?" she whispered in his ear.

"Ahhhhhhhhhhhh!" he squawked as he stumbled around trying to catch his breath.

She watched as he struggled down the hallway on his way to the elevator. When the door opened, a man got out and saw him bent over and holding his crouch.

"You okay fellow?" asked the man.

"Screw you! Ahhhhhhhhhhhhh!" He moaned as he got on the elevator.

"The man has a one track mind!" Menzie mumbled to herself.

Blackshere stumbled to his car, struggled to open the door. Once he did, he struggled with getting in.

"Ahhhhhhhhhhhhh!" he moaned in pain and agony as he climbed into his car and drove off. Because he was feeling pain, he stopped and started, stopped and started as he attempted to drive home.

Early that Monday morning, Sara was in her boss' office, picking up the weekly contracts they were to start working on for the week.

"These are all signed and ready to go," remarked Menzie as she handed her a hand full of contracts. "Send Doug Larson his contracts back and tell him he forgot to date them," she reminded.

"What if he wants to come in today and date them, what do I tell him?" asked Sara.

"If he prefers coming in and dating them personally, tell him to give you a definite time to work with. Once he lets you know, you advice me."

"Okay Miss Boss!"

Once Sara received the week's work from Ferguson, she was expected to rush right out and get busy. But instead, she just stood there peering at her boss.

"Is there something else you needed?" asked Ferguson.

"Yeah! I'm waiting for you to tell me how it was " cited Sara in an excited tone of voice.

"How what was?"

"You and George hitting it off so well."

"Oh we hit if off, alright!" bragged Menzie.

"I could tell, the poor man can barely walk. Rumor has it, you hadn't had any for a while and you tried to get it all this weekend."

"You're kidding me," laughed Menzie.

"What so funny?"

"He walking around like he is because he got too rough with me and I had to kneed him in the nuts!"

"Ouch! That must have hurt!" instigated Sara.

"So what, he's the one saying we had sex?"

"Not quite, you could say he's more like insinuating you did. People who know you two went out, assumed that's what happened."

"Huh, so he wants to play games. Well, two can play that game. Let me know when you want to go to lunch."

"Okay! I like to see a good fight!"

On their way to lunch, Ferguson and Sara stopped by Jenkins' office to tell him what they had in mind.

"We were on our way to lunch, want to join us?" asked Menzie.

"Yeah, did you guys want to go out? Treats on me," insisted Jenkins.

"Sounds good to me," snapped Tillsberge.

"Okay, you're on. But we need to stop by Tony's Cafeteria and pay a little visit to an old friend of yours."

"We wouldn't be talking about your new boyfriend, would we?"

"Now look!" she snapped. "He is not my boyfriend, and yes, we would be talking about George Blackshere."

"She wants to thank him again for his bad manners on Friday," interjected Sara.

"Are you here to solicit my help?" asked Jenkins.

"As a matter of fact, we are!" uttered Ferguson.

As the three of them headed for Tony's Cafeteria and George Blackshere, they updated Jenkins and told him how he could help out. He thought it would be fun, so he volunteered his services. On their way there, Menzie stopped at a quick food place and bought a salad. When the three of them reached the outside of Tony's, they could see Blackshere sitting with Gladis Henley and two other co-workers in a booth. Jenkins came into the cafeteria through one door as Menzie and Sara waited outside of the cafeteria, waiting for their cue to come in the door on his blind side. As Jenkins approached the booth, Gladis Henley saw him.

"Hi James!" she flirted.

"Hi Gladis, you doing okay?"

"Yeah, but I'd do a little better is you wasn't so stuck up!" she responded.

Instead of responding to Gladis' remark, Jenkins cleared his thoart, then started to deal with the issue of Blackshere.

"George, my man!" bellowed Jenkins as he put his hands on his shoulders.

"Jimmy my boy! How are tricks?" snickered Blackshere.

"I should be asking you that," responded Jenkins.

"You know me, I'm just a squirrel trying to get a nut!" bragged George as he threw out both of his hands.

"Well, a squirrel can still be a dirty rat, you know!" retorted Jenkins.

Blackshere chuckled. "You have to admit, this man does have a sense of humor. That's the thing I like about you. In fact, that's the only thing I like about you."

"How that is funny! Because there's nothing about you I like," chuckled Jenkins "By the way, how was your date with Menzie Ferguson on Friday?"

"Ahh, it was okay!" snapped Blackshere.

"From what I've heard, you were all over that stuff the whole weekend."

"Well, you know me?" bragged Blackshere as he bobbed his head around.

"How was it?"

"Jimmy my boy, my motto is, if you've had one, you've had them all!" boosted Blackshere.

"Are you saying, you didn't think she was special?" asked Jenkins.

"Well, the woman didn't really throw down, so I had to show her how a real man gets down, you know what I mean?" he bragged.

"Did you make her moan and groan, like a real man would do, George?"

"Man, I was putting it to her so hard and good, she started calling my name. Oh Georgie! Oh Georgie!"

"Georgie," moaned Menzie as she sneaked up on his blind side.

"Ahhhh!" he abruptly flinched and bellowed when he saw it was her standing right next to him.

"Oh Georgie!" she mocked as she sat down next to him.

She then attempted to move in close to him. He tried to move away from her but Gladis and the other co-workers had taken up the rest of the room in the booth and were not about to give him any more space.

"Gee, get away from me!" murmured a nervous Blackshere.

"Get away from you! Now, that's funny! On Friday you said you wanted to get real close to me. Now look at you, trying to find a hole to crawl into. When you want some more of what you got this weekend, you just give me a call. You do want to go out with me again, don't you, Georgie?"

"Ah ah!" he mumbled in the negative, his eyes rolling around.

"Ahh, what was that Georgie? I didn't understand you!"

"Ah ah!" he mumbled again as she shook his head back and forth.

"I think he said, ah ah," repeated Sara.

"Ohhhhhhh, that's too bad! I thought you might want to get down again. Give it to me hard and good," she mocked. "Tell you what, I brought something for ya," she said as Sara handed her the salad. "I want to toss a little somein, somein at you," she said as she dumped the salad over his head.

"How you've had both of your heads taken care of!" cracked Sara.

Menzie got up and joined Jenkins and Sara as they started to walk away from the booth, snickering as they did.

"You are one crazy bitch! You know that?" shouted Blackshere.

The three of them stopped and turned and looked back at the table. The sight of George the great lover sitting there with a salad bowl draped over his head and salad in his lap was funny. But Menzie wasn't done yet.

"What did you just call me?" she asked as she pretended she was coming after him.

In his effort to quickly get away from her, he abruptly knocked Gladis and the other two co-workers to the floor as he ran out of the cafeteria to get away from her, leaving the bowl and a trail of salad behind him. Being it was hilarious, the entire crowd started to laugh at his exit, while pointing their fingers at the three employees sitting on the floor.

"Man, the man really knows how to get up and get away," mocked Tillsberge.

"You should of seen how up he was when he had me against the wall the other night," chuckled Ferguson.

"Well, I'm sure there won't be any getting close, now," insinuated Jenkins.

"You're right, what about the three of them?" asked Sara.

"Oh, they're just sitting in. And I'm afraid I don't have any more salad to toss their way," chuckled Menzie.

The three of them turned and walked away laughing their fool heads off. And so did the other people in Tony's Cafeteria who witnessed what happened. And much to the embarrassment of Gladis Henley and her two co-workers as they sat on the floor seemly too embarrassed to make a move getting up off the floor.

CHAPTER THREE

FAMILY CONCERNS

It was nearing the Thanksgiving holidays. Old man Robinstein was glad to hand out turkeys considering how much money his firm had made during the year. Menzie was finishing up some last minute work and was about to leave to visit her parents in Atlanta, when the carrier bought a turkey for her and Sara, and sat them on her desk. It was she who took her boss' turkey to her in her office.

"You just about finished with those reports?" she asked as she sat the box on her desk.

"Yeah, I'm just finishing up with the last one."

"So, you're going to Atlanta for the holidays?"

"Yes I'm anxious to see my family."

"How long has it been since you've seem them?"

"Almost five years, plus my family has increases since then. My oldest sister, Barbara and her husband just had their second child and I'll get a chance to see him."

"Sounds like you are going to have an excited holiday."

"I hope so. Okay, that's the last report," she said as she handed Sara a folder. "Have fun with it," she joked.

"Gee, thanks boss" uttered Sara.

"What's in that box?"

"It's your turkey from old man Robinstein. He gives us turkeys every year about this time."

"Do you have someone who would like to have a free turkey?"

"Yeah, lots of people...Man, these are the biggest turkeys I have ever seen!" commented Sara as she took a look inside the box.

"Yeah, but there's no money stuffed inside," said Menzie.

"You didn't really expect to find money stuffed in your turkey, did you?"

"No Sara, I was being facetious!" snapped Menzie. "But you would think he would give his employees something extra for all the work they've done these last nine months."

"You don't know that old tight skinflint! He can squeeze a nickel so tight, it will make George Washington's head pop out of the buffalo's butt hole!" joked Sara.

Menzie laughed. "What about Christmas?"

"Oh now Christmas is usually better. Last year we got a turkey and a gift certificate worth fifteen bucks. My guess is he spent every bit of twenty-five bucks on each of us."

"You do have a Christmas party, don't you?"

"Oh yeah, every year."

"Huh! Where do you have your parties?"

"Boss, they're called office parties, where do you think we have them?"

"Well, all of that is about to change. This is now a major corporation and is going to be bigger next year. It's time we stop acting and being treated like slaves and demand our fair share."

"Okay Joan Of Arc! What do you have in mind?"

"I'm not sure yet! Whose responsible for setting up the party?"

"Old man Robinstein's nephew, Horence Robinstein. And he looks forward towards it every year."

"Sounds like Horence needs a life," said Menzie with a chuckle.

"Nobody in their right mind would share a life with that Yahoo!"

"I hear ya," chuckled Ferguson. "Tell ya what, I'll give it some thought while I'm at home in Atlanta. Meanwhile, enjoy your turkey dinner."

When Dr. Jenkins brought his turkey home and sat in on the kitchen counter, his wife was delighted. As for his mother, her ears were pricked for another subject.

"Man, this is a big turkey," commented Mrs. Jenkins. "Mr. Robinstein must have gone all out to get these babies. How much do you think he paid for them?"

"My guess would be he got them for pennies on the dollar, the old tightwad," chuckled Jenkins. "I wonder what Menzie thought when she saw her turkey," snickered Jenkins.

"I take it you don't approve of getting this turkey?" asked his mother?"

"As much money as Menzie and me help him make, you would think he would have given us some of that money."

"Well, maybe he'll make it up at Christmas time," added his wife.

"Some how I doubt that," chuckled Jenkins. "But if I know Menzie, she'll address that, and soon."

"Who is Menzie?" asked his mother.

"The firm hired this ex-film star as head of our advertising department. She's real sharp and has helped the firm improve its quality of service and earn lots more money."

"Now dear, don't be modest. Let your mother know you worked hard, day and night, helping her put all that stuff at work together," said his wife.

"Yeah, I did. She and I make a tremendous team."

"Menzie, what's her last name?" asked his mother.

"Her name is Menzie Ferguson," said Mr. Jenkins.

"Oh yeah, I remember her. She's very pretty," said Mamma Jenkins.

"Yeah, she sure is," responded James Jenkins.

"If she's a movie star, how is it that she's working with you?"

"I believe she said she didn't like being a movie star, so she quit. Now she's working with us, and really has a good head for business."

"Oh really? Is she married?"

"No mamma, she's not married."

"This Menzie I saw in the movies, was also very sexy. Does she look sexy to you Jimmy?" asked his mother in a sarcastic tone of voice.

"I guess you could call her sexy, I don't notice that about her. I just know she's awful sharp when it come to business," remarked Jenkins.

"Well now James, you are not blind. You know she is a well put together woman."

"Mamma Jenkins, James said he didn't notice that about her, and I believe him."

"Well, I've got some land in Florida I would like to sell you," chuckled Mrs. Jenkins.

"There's no need to get nasty Mamma," said Jenkins. "I said she's a real sharp woman when it comes to business. And she and I make a good team. You know, a good working team? Don't go making something else out of it."

"Well, I think she sounds wonderful."

"Yeah, she is. She's the best thing to happen to our firm," said Jenkins as he turned to leave the kitchen.

"Sounds like he's really taken with this Menzie, woman."

"Now Mamma Jenkins, you heard James. Don't go making something out of it."

"Out of what?" Him seemly thinking this woman is all that."

"He's mentioned her to me before. I think he likes working with her. Beside, she seems to be all business."

"I just bet she is," uttered Mother Jenkins.

"What was that?" asked her daughter in law as she unboxed the turkey.

"Nothing, just thinking out loud...Are you sure that is all that's going on?"

"What do you mean by that?" snapped Marian Jenkins.

"Pretty, smart and sexy and working with your husband. I don't like that."

"What is there to like? They work together."

"That don't make you nervous?"

"Why should it?"

"Of course, you're right. I'm sure it's all innocence," said Mrs. Jenkins as she picked up the turkey to walked over to the refrigerator and opened it.

"I'm sure it is too," responded Mrs. Jenkins as she watched her mother-in-law stuffed the turkey into the refrigerator and closed the door.

In Atlanta Menzie's older brother, Dr. Ted Ferguson, announced he was getting married and brought his wife to be to meet the family. Not only did she get a chance to meet her sister in law to be, she also met her new nephew. Now with her oldest sister,

Barbara, married with two kids and Ted now getting married. That only left her and her youngest sister, Tomaria, unmarried. But then Tomaria was eleven and she was twenty-eight. So after Thanksgiving dinner, Menzie was sitting in the swing on the back porch relaxing and with her head resting on the back of the swing. Her mother, Pat Ferguson, came out sat down on the porch steps and started a conversation with her. The subject? Marriage.

"My you kids are growing up so fast," she commented.

"Yeah, it sure seems that way," responded Menzie.

"How do you like Teddy's wife to be?"

"She seems nice enough."

"What? Is there something about her you don't like?"

"What is there for me to like? Ted is the one marrying her."

"I know, but you know how you are? No one is good enough to marry your brother and sister."

"What are you talking about, I like Mark."

"You do now. But you remember how you were when you first met him. Gave him the third degree like he was a criminal and you were Thurgood Marshall."

"Yeah, I did do that didn't I," chuckled Menzie. "I had him nervous there for awhile, didn't I?" she continued to chuckle.

"You had poor Bobbie nervous. She was afraid you weren't going to disapprove of him...You know how she has always respected your opinion?"

"Mamma, Bobbie would have married Mark whether I approved of him or not."

"Well, you never know...First, Bobbie got married and now Teddy. Well, that leaves you...When do you think you'll be getting married?"

"I knew we were going to get to the subject of me and marriage sooner or later."

"Well, what's your answer?"

"I don't know mamma!" snapped Menzie. "Why do you keep asking me that?"

"Because you are almost twenty-eight years old and I have never heard you talk about a man...You do like men, don't you Menz?"

"Mamma, there's no need to get insulting. You already know the answer to that."

"Yeah, I do...You haven't seen anybody in St. Louis you like?"

"Not well enough to marry. Why? You getting worried about me?"

"No, worried is not the word. You are a good daughter. You were always a disciplined child and the most helpful child we've had and the smartest too. You deserve to be happy."

"Well, you're assuming I'm not happy because I'm single."

"Are you?"

"I guess so...To be honest, I don't think about it much."

"Well, maybe you should."

"Why?"

"Because I don't want you to focus so much on your career and money, that you don't get to share your life with somebody. You know what I mean?"

"Yes ma'am. I wouldn't mind being married. It's just that I want the man to be perfect for me."

"Nobody is perfect and you know that."

"Well, I didn't say he had to be perfect, just perfect for me."

"As long as you know what you want in a man...You do know that, don't you?"

"Mamma, why are you talking to me about marriage, again?"

"Because you won't talk to me about it. Beside, the man who gets you will get a perfect wife."

"I though you just said nobody was perfect?"

"I didn't say you were perfect, I said you would be a perfect wife."

Menzie chuckled. "You got me there, Mamma."

Her mother laughed. "You're a good person, never regret being a good person. I just hope you get married so that you can have children and before I die," insinuated Mrs. Ferguson.

"Mamma, don't go there with me, okay?"

"Okay," snickered Mrs. Ferguson. "It's just that I would like to see you as a mother. You will make a good mother."

"You don't have to be married to have children, you know?"

"Yeah I know that. But I don't think you will put the horse before the cart. Besides, I know you are still a virgin."

"And how do you know that, Mamma?"

"I just know that's all. But when you do get married, some guy is really going to be lucky having you for a wife."

"I know Mamma. And if I decide to give up my virginity before I get married, you're be the first to know."

"Somehow, I doubt that," chuckled Mrs. Ferguson.

After being home for a couple of days, Ferguson was having a good time. She did however, have a problem and that was the thought of Dr. Jenkins popping in her head. She sat in the bedroom, watching her sister, Barbara, breastfeed her young baby.

"What made you decide to breast feed your baby?" she asked.

"Because it helps with the bonding process...Look at him. He's looking in his mama's eyes as I'm satisfy his basic need for hunger."

"Oh God!" bellowed Menzie. "What medical journal did you get that old crap out of?" she chuckled.

"Laugh all you want, but it works."

"Yeah right...How's Tonie taking to having a little brother?"

"Funny you should ask. She's a lot like you were with Teddy, over protective, bosses, and possessive."

"You trying to say, she's like me?" asked Menzie.

"Yeah and I'm glad."

"Really?"

"Oh yeah...Menzie you know I've always admired you. You are famous, talented, smart, all the things I want her to be. If she's that way, then I don't have to worry about him. She'll help me take care of him, just like you helped mamma take care of us. Even me and I'm the oldest," snickered Barbara.

"Wow, thanks, I needed to hear that."

"Why?" said Barbara as she positioned her baby on her shoulder to burp him.

"It's mamma. She got back on that marriage kick again."

"Well, you understand, she only wants the best for us, specially you."

"I know that's the way parents are, but she makes me feel bad when we talks."

"Burp," went the baby.

"That's a good boy," commented Barbara as she then laid her son in his crib. "Menzie, mom knows you are a kind hearted person. You have spent so much of your life giving to other people. Remember when you were about nine, and daddy bought you that real expensive Pam Grier jacket?"

"Yeah, I remember that."

"Do you remember what you did with it?"

"I remember somebody stole it."

"Noh they didn't. You exchanged it to a strange woman who was standing on the bus stop wearing this thin jacket and freezing. Then you made me promise to tell daddy somebody stole it."

"Now I remember. You told him the truth anyway," chuckled Menzie.

"Yeah, but that was the next winter when he asked you what happened to it. I remember he was upset until he realized that was just the way you were."

"Yeah, I remember him talking to me about it later," said Menzie as they stood and watched Barbara's new son as he slept. "Look at that, new life, sleeping like he doesn't have a care in this world...Bobbie, you said you admire me, well I admire you. I mean you have a husband, two great kids, the things I would like to have someday. Before you got married, did you think about it a lot?"

"There were times I did. But when I was a junior in college, Mark just sort of showed up when I least expected a husband. We were friends at first, but that didn't last long. Before you knew it, we were talking marriage."

"What made you do it? Get married I mean?"

"I guess you could say I was looking for a man like daddy and he was the closes I thought I would get. You just do it because you fall in love and you want to. And at that point in time, nothing else matters. You ever think you will actually get married and have kids?" she asked as the two of them left the room.

"I sure hope so. But when I do, I want the kind of man with the same kind of passion that I have."

"A man with your kind of passion. Is that possible?"

"It better be. Otherwise I'm going to be a lonely old maid, with unfulfilled love but with plenty of money," indicated Menzie as the two of them left the room hugging and chuckling with one another.

In the Jenkins' home, the conversation of Menzie Ferguson just wouldn't go away.

"My, what a nice dinner," complimented Mother Jenkins as she helped pick up the dishes from the table.

"It sure was. Be sure and tell your boss thanks for that big old turkey."

"I sure will," remarked Dr. Jenkins. "And I'm going to ask him for a Christmas bonus," he chuckled.

"Maybe you won't have to. Maybe Menzie Ferguson will ask him," said his mother. "She seems to have all the pull around your company."

"Most likely if she does, she'll ask me to go to his office with her."

"Why?"

"Because that's the way we roll, Mamma, "remarked Jenkins.

"What does that mean?"

"He means, that's the way they do business," chuckled Mrs. Jenkins.

"Oh Yeah, I get it," chuckled Mother Jenkins.

"Who is Menzie Ferguson asked John Jenkins, husband of Lynnett Jenkins, as he was getting up from the diner table.

"She's this movie star who works at the same company as Jimmy."

"Really? Is that right Jimmy? You work with a movie star?"

"Dad, Mom is being facetious," chuckled James Jenkins.

"Oh no I'm not!" snapped Lynnett Jenkins. "Tell your father who this woman is."

"Dad, this lady is a former movie star, who is now a business woman and working with us. For some reason, Mom seems to be making more out of it then there is."

"Lynnett, it sounds to me like you need some business."

"Look you two, don't start," said Marian Jenkins

"What's the big deal?" asked Lona Johnson, Jenkins's sister.

"I don't think it's a big deal myself," stated James Jenkins.

"Well, the way I've heard you talk about her before, she must be something special," shouted Mother Jenkins.

"Marian, does James talk about this woman a lot?" asked Lona.

"Look, keep me out of this," responded Marian Jenkins as she turned and left for the kitchen.

"Yeah, and me too," said James Jenkins as he got up and left the diner table.

"Mamma, what's going on with you?" asked Lona Johnson.

"I don't have any more to say about the subject!" snapped Lynnett Jenkins as she took a hand full of dishes into the kitchen."

"Lona, you know how your mother can be at times. She can smell trouble in a Priest convention," chuckled John Jenkins.

"I heard that!" insisted Lynnett Jenkins. "And sometimes this nose can smell a dirty rat hiding in the walls," she fussed.

"What was that you said Mom?" asked Dr. Jenkins from the living room.

"Nothing, just thinking out loud again...Have you met this Jezebel?" whispered Lynnett Jenkins.

"No I haven't met her. And why should I have to?"

"Yeah, why does she have to?" asked Lona as she walked into the kitchen.

"You heard him talking about her. The man is fascinated with this woman," said Lynnett Jenkins.

"I don't think so. It seems you are the one who seems to be having a problem with her," said Lona.

"I agree," said Marian. Jenkins. "I think he just respects her work."

"Respects her work today, inspect her works tomorrow," quoted his mother.

"What," chuckled Mrs. Jenkins and Lona.

"Mother Jenkins, what are you saying about this woman?"

"All I'm saying is, you just better mark my word. Keep an eye on your husband because I don't trust this woman around him."

"Mother Jenkins, you don't even know this woman."

"I don't need to know her. It's him knowing her that worries me."

CHAPTER FOUR

THE CHRISTMAS PARTY

The entire Thanksgiving weekend passed pretty quickly and everyone was back at work, busy but thinking about the up coming Christmas holidays. Obviously, the one who thought about it the most was Menzie Ferguson. So much in fact, she personally sat out to fix it. And of course, when she wanted to come up with a plan, she called upon her partner in crime.

Hello Sara!" bellowed Jenkins as he walked into their newly built office and closed the door behind him. "Miss Ferguson called for me?" he explained.

"Don't worry, your secret is safe with me!" teased Sara.

"What secret?" he asked.

"Cool it Doc. I was just kidding!" said Sara. "She told me you were coming. Go on in!"

"Thanks," he said as he walked into the office and closed the door behind him.

"Hi, how was your Thanksgiving?" asked Menzie.

"Same old same old! Some of my relatives were over and they invaded the food table just like they always do," chuckled Jenkins. "On the other hand, my mother was over and she was just as nosey as ever. She asked me a lot of questions about you," said Jenkins as he sat down in the chair next to her desk.

"Really? Why me?"

"She got this crazy notion that you might be a husband stealer."

"Huh, how did she come to that concussion about me?"

"Well, she claims I talk a little too much about you to my wife."

"Do you?"

"I don't think so. But don't worry about it, it's only because you are new and they don't know you as well as I do."

"And how do you know me?"

"I know you to be very intelligent, ambitious and a hard workers who knows how to get things done around here."

"Is that all you think?"

"That's enough to get me in trouble at the crib," chuckled Jenkins.

"Well, we wouldn't want you in trouble at the crib, would we?"

"No we wouldn't," he laughed.

"Other then your mother who else was there?"

"My Dad and he was my mother's super ego, just as always," he chuckled. "My sister, Lona was there and she was as opinionated as ever. And her husband, Robert was there, who seems to be the only member in the family who knows how to keep his mouth shut," snickered Jenkins.

"Sounds like a fun family," chuckled Menzie.

"You don't know the half of it."

"Well, maybe I will get a chance to meet them."

"Sounds to me like you might be glutton for punishment," chuckled Jenkins.

"Well, I think I might have the perfect solution."

"Oh really? And do tell how you plan on working this miracle."

"Would you stop that," chuckled Menzie. “I'm serious and I need your input."

"Okay, you have my undivided attention."

“I'm trying to work something out so we can have a Christmas party this year."

"Haven't you heard, we have a Christmas party every year."

"But you have an office party and for staff members. I'm talking about something big enough for our firm's families to attend. Get to know one another."

"Should I be asking what you have in mind?"

"Yes you should!" snickered Menzie. "I've been going through our list of client possibilities. What do you think about us incorporating a customer referral section into our corporate structure?"

"Depends on how you use it. And I thought we were talking about Christmas?"

"We are. Let me tell you what I have in mind. Let's take the new Millennium Crown Hotel. Good location, centrally located, luxury accommodation--"

"And very expensive!" interrupted Jenkins.

"Okay, but hear me out first. What would you think of us going to them and asking if we could have our Christmas party there?"

"I would say old man Cecil would have a stroke once he got the bill," he chuckled Jenkins.

"Stop it silly! Will you be serious?" chuckled Menzie.

"I am," responded Jenkins.

"Okay, listen to this. What if, instead of them charging us a rental or leasing fee, we provide them with a referral service?"

"You mean, we use their facility for our party in exchange for us recommending their hotel to our out of town clients when they come here?"

"Right...What do you think?"

"If we could swing it with them, that could be right on!" expressed Jenkins. "But why limit it to just our clientele? Why don't we extend the service to any out of town business guests? I'm sure the owners will welcome the additional revenue."

"Good point. We could make them part of our new publicity campaign."

"Yeah, you know, that'll work. And we can use them when we have our local conferences. In fact, we could use them for all of our major events? Old man Robinstein has been complaining about having to spend the money to build more conference rooms. This way we can show him a no cost item, which I'm sure he'll go for."

"Okay, I've worked out the details. What do you suggest we do first?"

"Let's go visit the hotel and talk with the local owner. If we can get it all arranged, old man Robinstein will have no problems biting the bullet."

Sara called the Millennium Crown Hotel and arranged a meeting between the hotel manager, to include Ferguson and Jenkins. They met in the General Manager's office and the moment they walked in, the atmosphere was right for business.

"Mr. Meyers, it was so nice for you to meet us on such short notice," apologized Jenkins as he shook the owner's hand. "I'm Dr. James Jenkins, this is my colleague, Miss Menzie Ferguson, perhaps you have heard of her?" he asked in a tactful manner.

"Not unless she is the Menzie Ferguson I've seen in the movie," commented the hotel general manager as he shook her hand.

"Guilty!" chuckled Ferguson as she returned his handshake.

"A Ph. D and a movie star on its corporate staff. I'm sure that's why Corrall International Network Incorporated is fast becoming a firm to be reckoned with!" said an impressed Mr. Robert Meyers.

"Well, we hope you don't hold that against us!" snickered Ferguson.

"I'll try not to," snickered Meyers with a sly grin on his face."

He led the two executives to a huge conference room, where they are sat.

"Would you like to have coffee?" asked Meyers.

"I'm fine," responded Ferguson.

"So am I," said Jenkins. "Will the owners be joining us?" he asked.

"No, the owners have asked me to conduct this business on their behalf. Let's get started."

The representatives from Corrall International Network Incorporated presented an impressive proposal to Mr. Meyers. He was so impressed with the projected profits for the hotel he wasted no time in contacting the owners and advising them accordingly. They too were impressed. Once the details had been worked out, they had a deal.

After visiting with Meyers, the team was on their way out of the hotel, when Gladis Henley and another co-worker drove by and spotted them.

"Ah ah!" she bellowed. "What did I tell you?" she asked the co-worked in a I told you so tone of voice. "Didn't I tell you he was screwing her? And on company time...That no good hypocrite!"

By the time the team reached the firm, Gladis had already started spreading the rumor about seeing them coming out of the hotel. Since neither, Menzie or Jenkins had had time to hear the rumor, they went on with the next phase of their proposal, presenting it to Mr. Robinstein, who sat in Ferguson's office listening to the phase of that proposal concerning the Christmas party arrangements. Sara was involved in the meeting in support of the team. Horence Robinstein was there as usual with his own agenda.

"So you've already worked this out with the hotel?" asked the senior Robinstein.

"Yes we have," responded Ferguson. "In fact Mr. Meyers and the owners of the hotel, were all impressed with our proposal and arrangements where we provide corporate management training not only for his hotel, but for their chain of hotels nation wide. Which means, we're in the process of gaining more clients, which means more money," she continued.

"Excuse me, but no one told you I am already responsible for arranging our yearly Christmas party?" asked Horence.

"Yes they did," responded Jenkins. "Why are you asking?"

"Because, you should have checked with me before you took on this task without my permission."

"What task? We're talking about a Christmas function not a company office party," uttered Jenkins.

"They are one of the same!" insisted Horence Robinstein.

"Is there any air on that planet that you're on?" insinuated Sara.

"I'm afraid you are mistaken," responded Ferguson. "Our proposal has to do with business. And I wasn't aware we had to consult with you on matters of company business."

"You're missing the point. It has been my responsibility for the last five years to schedule our Christmas party and we've always had a good enough time!"

"No we haven't!" belted out Sara. "The parties have been dull and the music boring! If it was not for the free food, you wouldn't have had anyone at your party."

"No one asked you, misses!" snapped Horence.

"Well maybe you should have," responded Ferguson.

"What is that suppose to mean?" asked a defensive young Robinstein.

"Then we would have told you to give us our food and let us go home," snickered Sara Tillsberge.

Her remark got a chuckled from the rest of the group, to include the senior Robinstein. Of course, his nephew had had his feeling hurt.

"You people think you are so smart, so funny. But, do you know how much that kind of function will cost this company?"

"Yeah, nothing!" bellowed Ferguson.

"There is no free lunch. So, what is this costing the company?"

"Why do you want to know?"

"Look you, Dr. Jenkins and I are both senior members of this staff. You are one of the Accountants in the Accounting Department. And for you to insist we should check with you about conducting business is absurd!"

"We're not talking about business, we're talking about a Christmas party!" insisted Horence.

"Helloooo! Have you been paying attention?" asked Sara.

"Now, what does that suppose to mean?"

"She means we are not talking about an office party for staff!" bellowed Menzie. "We are talking about a Christmas function for the entire staff and their families, in the ball room of a major client."

"I fail to see the difference!" said Horence.

"I believe you!" chuckled Sara.

"I give up! What do you say CR?" asked Jenkins.

"This looks like good business to me," said Cecil Robinstein. "And a nice Christmas get together for the staff and their families would be good considering how hard everyone has worked...I say let's go with it!" shouted an enthusiastic Cecil Robinstein.

"What? What about the party I schedule every year?"

"If it makes you feel better, go on and have it!" suggested Jenkins.

On their way back to their perspective offices, Horence Robinstein attempted to appeal to his uncle.

"Uncle Cecil, I must protest the actions of your subordinates!"

"Exactly what are you protesting, Horence?"

"They seem to take it upon themselves to do whatever they want to do."

"Horence, how much money did you make last year?"

"About seventeen thousand dollars."

"How much have you earned so far this year?"

"Close nearly twenty-seven thousand dollars."

"That's a ten thousand dollar raise. You've earned that much because of them doing what it takes to make money! And while we're at it, you schedule that dull ass Christmas office party and I'll see to it that you get a new position with the clean up crew!" said Cecil Robinstein as he walked off from his nephew.

Back in Menzie office, Sara, Menzie and Jenkins were elated over scheduling of the new revised Christmas function.

"I finally got a chance to see you two in actions!" commented an excited Sara. "Remind me not to ever buy a car from you!" she continued.

"That was actually easier then I thought it would be," expressed Menzie.

"It's like I told, that old man understands anything that will make him a buck!"

"Well, you don't have to convince me, I saw it with my own eyes," snickered Sara...Not to change the subject, but did you tell the good doctor your good news?" she asked.

"What news is that?" asked Jenkins.

"My boss has been practicing with the St. Louis Symphony," announced Sara.

"Really? I didn't know you played an instrument!" said a surprised Jenkins.

"I've been playing the violin since I was in the forth grade. I'll have you to know, I minored in music in college and played the violin in the university concert orchestra for four years," bragged Menzie. "In fact I was the first freshman they ever had play at that level."

"Man! That's great! How many Blacks do they have in the symphony?"

"I'm only the third, but it will be better in a few years."

"When will you have the opportunity to play in a concert?"

"I'm playing in Handel's Messiah in two weeks. Do you like classical music?"

"I sure do. In fact, I have a daughter who plays the violin, and she would love to come to that concert. Is it too late to get tickets?"

"Boss, don't you owe the man a peace offering?" asked Sara

"I was getting to that, big mouth!" uttered Menzie. "How many tickets would you like to have?" she asked as she reached for her purse.

"I think two might be enough."

"Here!" she said. "Here are three tickets. One for you and your wife, the other one is for your daughter. I owe them to you for emptying out your class the first day I started here. Now we're even."

"Yeah, I guess so," chuckled Jenkins. "But I'll only need two tickets. I don't think my wife will come. But my daughter would love to come to the concert."

"Ahh, don't your wife like classical music?"

"The only music my wife like is gospel."

"That's too bad, she could really enjoy the concert. But, those are your tickets and you can bring whomever you please! But please, come. I want you to see how talented I am."

"I wouldn't miss it for the world, thanks," said Jenkins as he started towards the door.

"Anything for you," whispered Menzie as she watched him close the door behind him. "Man! Now might be a good time for me to go change my panties," she chuckled.

When Menzie peered over at Sara, she could see her holding her hand over her mouth and chuckling.

"What's funny?" she asked her subordinate.

"I was just thinking, the man already knows how talented you are," insinuated Sara. "When he's around, you can't keep still," she continued to snicker.

"Well he has no idea what's going on with me. And if I told you, you would die from laughing, "she chuckled.

The night of the concert came quickly. Dr. Jenkins did come but not with his Wife, but he did escorted his dressed up thirteen year old daughter, Vena, to the concert. This was her first live concert, so she was really excited from the moment she stepped into Powell Symphony Hall.

"This is a beautiful hall, isn't it Dad?" she asked as they walked into the mezzanine of the concert hall.

"It sure is," responded Jenkins as he handed the attendant their tickets.

"You are located three rolls from the front to your right," said the attendant as she handed him the ticket subs.

"Have you ever been here before dad?" asked Vena as they started towards their seats. "I have," she stated.

"Yeah several times. And I remember when you come here with your junior high orchestra. Our seats are in this roll."

"Wow, these are great seats," said Vena as they made it to their seats.

Once they were seated, she looked around at the magnificence of the concert hall, then peered over at her father and smiled with excitement. When the performers came out and took their seats, Jenkins pointed out Menzie Ferguson, who was toning up her violin. The fact that she also played a violin impressed her even the more.

During the performance, Vena kept her eyes on her as she performed during the entire concert. When it was over, she stood and clapped. To make her night out to be even more special, her father introduced her to Menzie Ferguson, who then signed her program, which made it even more exciting. She was so worked up when she got home from the concert she immediately went into her parent's bedroom to share her excitement with her mother, as she explained each movement to her. Once she was burnt out, she kissed her father goodnight and went to bed. Mrs. Jenkins watched as her husband walked into the closet to get undressed.

"Obviously, the concert went great," she said as she sat with her arms crossed.

"Yeah, it was," he responded.

"Naturally your friend did great."

"If you mean Menzie, she sure did...But then, that didn't surprise me."

"Is there anything this woman can't do?"

"What was that?" asked Jenkins from the closet.

"She seem to be quite talented, this Menzie. Is there anything she can't do?"

"You name it, it seems she can do it," remarked Jenkins as he walked out of the closet, closing the door behind him.

"Well Vena seems to have had a good time."

"She had a wonderful time. I even introduced her to her after the concert. That was when she autographed her program."

"She show me that...That was really nice of her."

"Yeah, I thought so," said Jenkins as he got into to bed.

"She sign your too?"

"Yeah, she did. Good night dear," he said as kissed his wife, pulled the covers over himself, and drifted off to sleep.

"Huh, good night to you too dear," she remarked with a jealous tone to her voice.

On the evening of December 22, 1970, the Christmas function at the Millennium Crown Hotel was in full swing. Every staff member of the Corrall International Network Incorporated was either there, coming in or on their way there. A small professional ensemble played the music and at that moment, it was the instrumental 'Sleigh Bell'. Menzie was there dressed in a sexy red dress and holding a paper cup of punch, while she talked to Sara Tillsberge.

"Wow, would you look at this. I mean all of these beautiful people work for us?" asked Sara over the music. "And look how nice these children are acting."

"Yeah, this is nice. I'm looking forward towards meeting Dr. Jenkins' wife."

"His wife or his family?" asked Sara.

"I meant his family...What did you think I meant?"

"His family, like you said...I've met his wife before. She's very pretty, very smart and a very nice lady."

"She has to be to keep a man like him happy!"

"Watch it boss! Your subconscious desire is showing!"

"Thank you, Dr. Sigmund Freud!" chuckled Menzie.

"Oh Oh! Here comes trouble," murmured Sara when she saw Gladis Henley headed their way.

"Hi Gladis, you look descent tonight," remarked Menzie.

"Don't let those closes fool you. There's nothing decent about this woman!" insinuated Sara.

"Cool it Miss berger queen, I'm not in the mood," snapped Henley.

"See? The Grinch is still among us," snickered Sara.

"What eveeeeer!" snapped Henley as she threw up her hand to her face. "Well if it ain't Miss Ferguson, walking around like she is Miss congeniality, Miss big shot! Miss piranha. Look at you. Just a peeping and a creeping, waiting to bite somebody in the back. Well, Miss, I can't act, we'll see how you handle the first lady when she gets here" she said as she turned and walked away from them.

"Jesus, what is her problem?" asked Ferguson.

"She's suffering from a mild case of neurosis arising from feelings of envy, prolonged jealousy and or bitter hostility," recited Sara.

"What?" chuckled Menzie.

"In other words, who cares?" said Sara as she took a sip of her punch.

Once the function was in full bloom, Dr. James Jenkins and his wife, Marian, walked in accompanied by his mother Lynnett Jenkins and her husband John Jenkins, his sister Lona and her husband Robert Johnson. He also had two of his sons, and Vena with him. Mr. Robinstein and his wife met them at the door and introduced themselves and while Menzie and Sara looked on.

"Wow!" he looks so handsome," uttered Menzie Ferguson. "So, that's his wife?"

"Yes, that's his wife," remarked Sara.

"She is very pretty! Just as I thought she would be."

"Be careful boss, your valentine face is showing," insinuated Sara.

"Shut up!" snapped Menzie.

She waited until the Robinsteins started back towards their seats. She sat her cup down and started to walk over to meet Jenkins and his family. She was nervous at meeting his wife, but felt compelled to do so if for no other reason but to prove she respected him, his wife and his marriage.

"Oh, here she is!" remarked Jenkins as he saw her walking towards them.

"Hi Miss Ferguson. You sure look pretty," commented Vena.

"Hi Vena and so do you," she responded as they hugged one another.

Neither of the Jenkins women said anything but did peer at one another as they waited for Dr. Jenkins to introduce them.

"Menzie, this is my wife, Marian, Marian, this is Menzie Ferguson."

"Mrs. Jenkins, I am so happy to finally meet you," she said as she hugged Jenkins' wife.

"Miss Ferguson. I've heard some wonderful things about you from my husband," insinuated Marian Jenkins as she shook Ferguson's hand. "And my daughter obviously admires you and cherries the autographed program you signed for her. That was very nice of you," she added.

"Thank you! And it is such a honor to finally get the chance to meet you," responded Menzie. "Your husband pleasantly talks about you all the time."

"I'm sure he does and you are very gracious. No wonder he has you up on a pedestal...For putting the firm on the map, I mean."

"Well, I wouldn't have been able to do that without the brilliance of your husband. We make a good team."

"So I'm told," said Mrs. Jenkins with phony smile on her face.

"Excuse me!" bellowed Mrs. Lynnett Jenkins. "I'm James' mother...Has he mentioned me to you?" she insinuated.

"Not if he cherries his privacy," snapped John Jenkins.

Menzie chuckled. "He sure has and it is such a pleasure to finally meet you too," she said as she shook her hand.

"I'm sure it is," mocked Mrs. Jenkins as she shook her hand as she peered over to her daughter in law.

"My name is John Jenkins. I'm James' father and his Mother's gag piece."

"And I am sure you do a wonderful job of it," chuckled Menzie.

"Noh he doesn't," retorted Mrs. Jenkins.

"Menzie, this is my sister, Lona and her husband, Robert. Folks this is Menzie Ferguson.

"It is such an honor to meet you," said Menzie as she shook each person's hand.

"I would like for you to meet some of my other kids, this is Marcus, my oldest son and this is Javey. Boys, this is Miss Ferguson," said Dr. Jenkins.

Let's see, she is a movie star, a violin player, and an extremely bright businesswoman. Did I cover just about everything?" said Lynnett Jenkins in a sarcastic tone of voice.

"Just about," remarked Menzie trying to keep her cool about the whole situation.

"Oh my," remarked Lynnett Jenkins.

"My such handsome young men...I would say you got your looks from your father but your mother is so pretty, it's hard to tell," complimented Menzie Ferguson.

"Well as you can see Vena looks just like her father. The rest seems to be a combination of both of us," remarked Mrs. Marian Jenkins.

"You did know that he had five kids didn't you?" asked Lynnett Jenkins.

"Yes, I did. I think that is so wonderful to have a large family," said Menzie as she started to escort the Jenkins family to where the tables were located.

"Lynnett, behave yourself tonight," warned Mr. Jenkins.

"Man, I'm here to eat and that's all," she snapped.

"Somehow, I doubt that," snickered John Jenkins.

Later during the party, the ensemble was hot playing the instrumental jazz version of 'The Christmas Song'. Marian and Menzie had started to talk to one another and seemed to be getting along, much to the dismay of his mother, who seemed to resent the fact that they were even talking to one another. Then there was Gladis Henley, who sat at one of the tables eating dinner with George Blackshere and Sara Tillsberge. And it could be said she was being just as hateful and nosy as ever.

"Why is she up in that woman's face?" she asked in an irate tone of voice. "Don't she know that woman can feel the vibes of how bad she wants her husband?"

"You know it's a long time since I've seen a woman's fight. You know thighs showing, breast flopping, hair pulling, all that good stuff," instigated George Blackshere.

"Yeah, much like the kind of fights you use to see back in the hood?"

"Well, you are not back in the hood," insisted Sara.

"You don't know nothing about that," Show White," mocked Henley.

"Why don't you people grow up," said Sara Tillsberge.

"George is right. And we might have one at this table if hamburger don't keep her mouth shut," threaten Henley.

"So what did you people come here to do, see a fight or to get the free food?" asked Sara in a chuckling tone of voice.

"I'm going to ignore you!" bellowed Henley.

"Now, that's the best news I have had all night," chuckled Sara.

"Well, they might be getting along right now, but sooner or later, the shit will hit the fan!" insinuated Henley

"Why, because they both seem to be intelligent people, and are getting along so well right now? What is the problem with you people?" asked Sara. "It's Christmas and you're suppose to be having fun."

"I haven't seen you get caught under the mistletoe tonight," mocked Gladis.

"Well, my boss has a better chance of getting her butt kissed than you two have getting a kiss on the cheek. Besides, when was the last time you had a man?" recanted Sara.

"Why do you keep defending her? "And it's none of your business the last time I had a man."

"Huh, you can't count that high, can you?" snickered Sara.

"Look at his wife grinning...I bet you she knows what that hussy is up to."

"Let's see, so far I've seen her talking, dancing and eating dinner and having fun, just like all the other human beings here!" mocked Sara.

"Yeah, all part of her conning, sneaky game," commented Henley.

"I think the heifer is crazy if you ask me," commented Blackshere.

"Well, nobody asked you birdbrain," retorted Sara.

"Who you calling birdbrain, nitwit?"

"You better bit your filthy tongue, or I ask her to give you more of what you got when you took her out on that date," snickered Tilleberge.

"For your information, I didn't take her out on a date, she took me and she paid for everything," defended Blackshere.

"Well, I heard about what you had to pay that night...By the way, how are your family jewels?" chuckled Sara.

"Yeah, well she better not try that again," threatened Blackshere.

"Be quiet George!" bellowed Henley. "The last time she even talked to you, she had you shaking like a punk in prison and she dumped salad all over your head."

"Yeah, that's what I'm saying, she better not try that again," he reiterated.

"Yeah right!" uttered Henley as she continued to watch her enemy in action.

While George Blackshere and Gladis Henley seemed to be teaming up on Sare

Tilliberge, Menzie Ferguson was getting much the same treatment from the Jenkins women once Dr. Jenkins left them to fraternize with some of the other employees.

"Miss Ferguson, I must admit I was surprised when my husband came home and told me you had started to work for the firm," remarked Marian Jenkins.

"There are a lot of women in high positions at some of the largest firms."

"I know, but aren't you a movie star?" ask Lynnett Ferguson of Menzie.

"Well, you can say I played in a couple of movies, but I was never a major star. And I didn't want to be like a lot of other Black women sitting around waiting for movies that feature very few thirty year old Black women and when they do, their either whores, servants or drug addict," she responded.

"You're in business and play the violin, why is that?" Marian.

"On a regular job you are judged by factors other than your skills. The color of your skin, your sexual gender, things like that. In this business I am seen as a professions woman, and I like that. Being a Black woman, playing the violin and being in the orchestra, just helps me prove how talent a Black woman can be. We need to work hard to eliminate some of the stereotypes concerning Black people and their abilities."

"Doesn't that make you like, bourgeoisie?" asked Lona Johnson.

"Not at all, because the opposite of that would be to accept our faint and culture as Black people to be the low of the lowest and predetermined to be that way. We are a great people. It's time for us to start acting like it. At home I was always taught, that some times it takes one person to make the difference. I would like to think I am at least one of those persons."

"That was a good answer," responded John Jenkins.

"Thank you," responded Menzie.

"When you were in college, did you major in business?" asked Lone.

"I actually had a double major. I majored in business with emphases in pre law. And believe it or not, I was valedictorian of my class."

"I'm surprised you didn't go into law. From what I'm hearing, you would have made an excellent lawyer," commented Lynnett Jenkins.

"Thank you, but I think there are more challenges in business for a woman and I like that. And who knows, my knowledge in law may come in handy someday."

"You three are asking Miss Ferguson questions like she stole something," said John Jenkins.

"Oh, I don't mind," responded Menzie. "I'm assuming they are trying to understand me better."

"Yeah, that's what we're trying to do. Getting to know her better," remarked Lynnett Jenkins.

"Would I be too presumptuous if I believe your intent is to have your own business some day?" asked Lona Johnson.

"Not at all. But, what made you ask?"

"You just don't seem like the type of woman who would work for somebody all your life."

"True...let's just say, I'm in the training phase of my career. When the time is right, I'll start my own business."

"Will you be asking my brother to join you?" asked Lona Johnson.

"I haven't thought that far ahead yet. Why did you ask me that?"

"You two seemed to have so much in common, to include being valedictorian of your graduating classes."

"I didn't know that, although that really doesn't surprise me, he is awful smart."

"Of course he's smart! He's my son!" snapped Lynnett Jenkins.

"And she made him all by herself," chuckled John Jenkins.

"Well, I have heard him often say he might start his own business someday," interjected Marian Jenkins.

"Well, that doesn't surprise me either, he could, and would do quite well. Of course, the thought of him and I in business together could prove to be quite interesting," said Ferguson, just to provoke the Jenkins women a bit.

"Why interesting?" asked Lynnett Jenkins, who obviously fail for the bait.

"Two brilliant minds like ours, working for one common cause, has got to produce some real tangible and powerful results."

"Huh!" uttered Lynnett Jenkins as she conceded she was dealing with a very cleaver woman, too cleaver for her.

Meanwhile, Henley seemed beside herself as she continued to watch the three of them talking soberly between them, as Dr. Jenkins continued to made his rounds wishing the other employees a Merry Christmas.

"Look at her, all up in that woman's face!" she scolded.

"So what?" asked the other co-worker.

"Oh don't pretend you don't know!" said Gladis to the co-worker.

"Know what?" asked Sara.

"Well, I didn't want to be the one to spread rumors, but we saw her and James Jenkins come out of this very same hotel a few weeks ago."

Sara couldn't help but laugh.

"Well, it wouldn't be so funny if his wife knew about it!" bragged Gladis.

"You're a moron, you know that?" retorted Sara. "They were here setting up this Christmas function for us, you dip stick!" chuckled Sara.

"She help set up this party? I thought Mr. Robinstein's nephew did it!"

"Ah come on! You couldn't really think the choir boy would have enough soul to throw a big time jam session like this!"

"When you think about it, hell no!" chuckled Henley. "Yeah, well that don't change the fact that she does have a thing for that woman's husband!"

"So do you! So what?" asked Sara.

"I'm not all up in her face, that's what! Besides, she can't fool that woman. She probably already knows how she feels about her husband. Women get this feeling in their gut about these kind of things."

"Well, don't you go anywhere near her, or she'll have a bleeding ulcer!" instigated Sara as she ate a spoon full of desert.

Much to Henley's embarrassment, the others got a good laugh on her.

In lieu of the Christmas party being packed with employees and their family members, it seemed everyone was having a good time. Even as the party seemed to be winding down, no one seemed to want to go home. The ensemble was still hot, as they played an instrumental version of Stevie Wonder's 'Caroling Through The Night'. Then Mr. Robinstein got up from his table and made a couple of requests.

"Excuse me," he asked as he got everyone's attention. "As you know we've had a remarkable year and it was all because of Menzie Ferguson and Dr. James Jenkins. Will you two stand and be acknowledged?" he requested and they responded. "I can't thank you two enough for all you have done for our company in such a short time. I guess it must have been God who put you two among us at this point in time. As each employee leaves here tonight, make sure you pick up an envelope from me. I have a little something for you for all of your hard work. Again Menzie, Dr. Jenkins, thank you so very much," said Rodinstein as he threw each of them a kiss, as the guests clapped. He then continued. "I would like to ask one more favor," he said as the two of them sat down. "Menzie has a tremendous voice. I would like to hear her sing something for us before we close out the year. Let's encourage her," he requested as he started to clap.

The crowd started to clap as she got up, walked over to the ensemble, whispered a few words then took center stage. The ensemble played and she song, 'Bless This House.' As she song, the crowd was extremely silent. It was a time for reflecting and being grateful of the old year and focus and rejoicing in expectations on the New Year to come.

As she continued to sing, it was the only time when everyone there felt something special. The weak thought about trying to strong, the lazy remembered to try and be more productive. The less then enthusiastic thought more of being ambitious and the mean and ugly to see more beauty in the world. At least for those few fleeing moments as she ended her song on a note of peace and good will towards all.

Just as the function was dissipating and families were starting to leave for home, even the parting was emotionally charged for most people, who had felt the love and caring so profoundly demonstrated during the entire holiday function. Marian Jenkins turned to Menzie and whispered to her.

"Excuse me Miss Ferguson, which way is the rest room?" she asked

"I'll show you, come on!" said Mendie.

The two of them got up and she led Mrs. Jenkins to the rest room pulling her along by her hand. Once there, they went in together.

"Oh good, free stales!" joked Mrs. Jenkins as she went into one of the stalls and locked the door behind her.

Menzie walked over, looked into the mirror for several seconds, as she tossed her hair around a bit. There was something on her mind, so she started a conversation with Marian Jenkins although she couldn't see her.

"How did you enjoy yourself tonight?" she asked.

"Oh, I've had a nice time. The food was good, the music the atmosphere, all just excellent. And so was your singing."

"Thanks...You know, I shouldn't have been surprised with what I was told about Dr. Jenkins," she said.

"What was that?" asked Marian.

"I said I shouldn't have been surprised about Dr. Jenkins being valedictorian of his class. He is really a very smart man and he is good with people, you know motivating them and all?"

"Yeah, he is. He keeps me motivated and that's for sure."

"I just bet he does," uttered Menzie.

"What was that?"

"I just said I can believe he does, he motivates everybody around the firm and everybody really respects him, and so do I!"

"That's good," good said Marian as she flushed the stool, and walked out of the stale.

"You mind if I make a personal observation?"

"I get the feeling you will regardless to what I say," snickered Mrs. Jenkins as she started to wash her hands.

"I guess you're right...I think you have a wonderful husband! I hope you realize how lucky you are to have a man like him!"

"A man like him?" asked Mrs. Jenkins as she pulled paper towels from the dispenser.

"Yes! Intelligent, caring, successful, loves his family, what more could you ask of a man?"

"I guess you're right! I am very lucky," said Marian as she dried her hands while peering as Ferguson with this suspicious look on her face.

Once back home, Jenkins was dressed for bed and was in the bathroom bushing his teeth, while his wife sat on the bed taking off her shoes.

"That was a real nice party! I had a wonderful time!" she expressed.

"Good, so did I."

"Wasn't it nice of you boss to give out bonuses?"

"Yeah, that was nice of him."

"Did you know he was going to do that?"

"No, nobody did. Especially two hundred dollars."

"So Miss Ferguson arranged all that?"

"Yeah, she went all out just like she does with everything she's involved in."

"That's the second time you've said that...She is one smart lady and a very pretty woman!" she said as she pulled off a stocking.

"Yeah!" said Jenkins as he rinsed out his mouth with mouthwash.

"What did you say?" she asked as she got up and walked over to the bathroom door.

"I said yes, she is smart and yes, she's a very pretty girl," he repeated.

"You know she likes you?" she said as she watched him spate in the toilet bowl.

"Yeah, she like everybody!" said Jenkins as he walked out of the bathroom and over towards the bed.

"I wonder why a woman like that isn't married?" she asked as she walked over and sat down on the bed.

"Too picky would be my guess," said Jenkins as he got into bed.

"Well, as long as she doesn't pick my husband!"

Jenkins chuckled as he peered over at her.

"I mean she could probably have any man she wants, but not you, huh?"

"Was that a question?"

"No, just an observation as she put it."

"Well, I'm not sure what that means, but you don't have to worry about anything like that happening."

"I don't? Why?"

"First of all, she's not my type. Secondly, she knows I already have a woman and one that I love very much!" said Jenkins as he leaned over and looked her in her eyes. "I love you very much," he repeated.

He then gave his wife a long goodnight kiss.

CHAPTER FIVE

THE NEW YEAR BLUES

It was two days before the start of the New Year. To not be out done, young Horence Robinstein arranged an office New Years party and on office work hours. Of course, everyone showed up for his party, but only because old man Robinstein had the affair catered. After all, it was the least he could do considering how much money his company had mad over the last several months and he had already given out bonuses. As it turned out, the party was some fun, it was the company that spoiled the atmosphere. You guessed it, Gladis Henley. She stood with another co-worker watching as James Jenkins and Menzie Ferguson sat eating and talking with Sara and another co-worker.

"Will you look at that...She don't give that man no room to breath. Did you see their picture in the company paper?"

"Yeah I saw it," said the co-worker.

"I bet she ask them to do that. I wonder if his wife have seen it?"

"I sure she did. It was only a picture."

"Yeah right! I wonder how come his wife didn't see right through her?"

"Maybe his wife don't think there's anything going on," said the co-worker.

"Don't be naive. Of course there is! I know it and you know it!" she insisted.

"No I don't," responded the co-worker.

"Yes you do, I told you."

"That's the point? You told me? I haven't seen them doing anything but talking."

"Oh, I see what's going on here, you punkin out on me!" snapped Henley.

"Call it what you want. But according to what I read in the paper, if it hadn't been for the two of them working together, we wouldn't have made the money we got this year and we wouldn't have been given a bonus."

"What's your point?"

"You know I came here to have a nice time. I am not going to start off my new year by listening to you put them down. Besides, I like them," said the co-worker as she started to walk away from Gladis.

"Go to hell!" snapped Henley.

"Yeah, yeah, yeah," uttered the co-worker as she walked away from her.

"What is wrong with you people? Can't they see what I'm seeing?" she asked herself.

While the party was in full bloom, young Robinstein walked around soliciting comments on how well his party was going. His mistake was walking over to the group of which Sara Tillsberge was.

"Well, how are you folks enjoying the party" he asked.

"The food is good," responded Sara.

"Yeah, but how are you enjoying the party?" he repeated.

"The food is good," repeated Sara in a sarcastic tone of voice.

"You know what I mean," scolded Robinstein.

"Oh I see, you mean not having to work, standing around talking and enjoying good food. I could do this everyday. Or course, we could breakout with an old rendition of 'Annusmirabilis', and make is more official," snickered Sara Tillsberge.

"Why do I waste my time trying to talk to you people?" asked Robinstein.

"That's what I've been trying to figure out, Horence," insinuated Sara.

"Happy New Year," he snapped as he stormed away from them.

The four of them laughed.

"That was mean," said Menzie.

"Well, he desired that. Trying to prove he could do just as well as you two when it comes to scheduling events."

"Well, at least he tries," chuckled Jenkins.

As the event was coming to an end, the workers started parting company while wishing each other Happy New Year. When there were only a few people left, Gladis Henley finally got a chance to talk with Menzie Ferguson.

"Well, you did okay for the short time you have been here," she snapped.

"I'm I suppose to take that to be a compliment?"

"No, it was more of an implication."

"Well, that's something you are good at. What are you implying about me now?"

"What do you think? You got the boss eating out of your hands, got the employees kissing your butt and even got James acting like a love sick puppy."

"What are you talking about?"

"Oh come on Ferguson! Everybody around here knows you are his whore."

"I think you've got me confused with a wanna be, you. I heard about you getting him trapped and trying to seduce him. I was told he put you in your place."

"Who told you that lie, Tilliberge?"

"No, it common knowledge around here about you having a thing for him. In fact, while I'm at it, you talk about your wanting to let him get into your stuff too much. "

"So, you saying I should be sneaky like you. I know you've been screwing that man every since you got here, admit it," she demanded.

"I won't admit to such a thing, but I will say this. You better get off my ass don't you will find out just how much pull I do have around here."

"So, what are you saying? You'll get me fired."

"I'm saying get off my ass or I will fire you up! Did that make it clearer for you?" implied Ferguson as she walked away from her.

"Bitch!" snapped Henley.

Later that evening, Ferguson walked into her well, furnished apartment. After closing the door and setting down her purse, she picked up the mail and sorted through it.

"Junk," she muttered.

Later that night, she had showered and was dressed in a sexy blue, two piece tranquillity set, as she sat reading a book. She had a difficult time concentrating. She laid down on her bed and attempted to sleep, but she kept remembering what Gladis Henley had said to her. It wasn't so much of what she said about the two of them that bothered her. She was wondering how well she was able hide her feeling for him from other people. She didn't want anybody to know, and that did bother her.

"Menzie, what is wrong with you?" she asked herself. "Why are you tripping over this one man," she uttered.

She kept reminding herself that Jenkins was married, and she knew he loved his wife and had not given as much as a thought to them being together. She got up and decided to put on some music to help cheer her up. But she ended up playing, 'Just My Imagination,' by the Temptations. The only thing that did for her state of mind was to make her more sensitive. In fact, all she felt like doing was cry and cry she did.

"Ohhhhhhhh, God, help me!" she uttered.

"Ahhhhhhhhhhhhhhhhh."

It was early New Years day, 1971. Menzie was relieved to see daylight because she had had a difficult time sleeping. She needed desperately to talk to somebody, so she called her sister, Barbara.

"Bobbie, happy new year," she greeted.

"Menz, happy new years to you too."

"How are the hubbie and the kids?"

"Everyone is doing great. How is your New Year going so far?"

"Oh, I'm having just a wonderful time," she mumbled in a sarcastic tone of voice.

"Menz, is something wrong?"

"Nothing more than usual. Why do you ask?"

"You sound a little tired.

"I am, I didn't get enough sleep last night. I've got myself a little problem."

"Oh no, you're pregnant!" bellowed her sister.

"Don't be ridiculous," snickered Menzie.

"Well, if you don't have cancer, then it can't be that bad," snickered her sister.

"Look, I'm serious. My problem is serious...There's this guy that I met and I just adore him."

"Really? Well, what's the problem?"

"He's older, he's married and he has five kids."

"You've got to be kidding me!" bellowed Barbara.

"No, I ain't kidding...And I've got it bad."

"Menzie you're not messing around with this guy, are you?"

"No I'm not messing around with him!" she defended.

"Is this someone you work with?"

"Yes."

"Does he know how you feel?"

"No, and I am not going to tell him."

"What are you going to do?"

"Nothing...I've met his wife and she is an awful sweet person and he loves her very much."

"Maybe you should change job."

"No I'm not going to do that either. Beside, I like my job."

"So, how are you going to handle being around him?"

"I'm going to work with him and keep my feeling to myself, just as I've always done."

"So, of all the men in St. Louis, you pick the one that's married and with a house full of kids?"

"I didn't call you to have you beat me up."

"I know you didn't and I'm sorry," apologized Barbara. "I'm just surprised at you. I mean you are such a good judge of character."

"His character is only part of my problem. He's smart, good looking, sexy and he has makes me wet my panties just being around him."

"He makes you pee on yourself?" asked her sister in a surprised tone of voice

"No, he makes me wet my panties. You know? Makes me horny?"

"Menzie, I hope you're not saying he makes you have an orgasm."

"Girl, I ain't lying. I have literally wet my panties, just being around the man and it has happened more than once. Here's what's weird, I enjoyed myself."

"That is weird and it sounds like you need professional help."

"Yeah, like maybe a sex theorist," chuckled Menzie.

Barbara laughed. "Well, maybe you just need a man to tap that stuff up a little bit for you, cool that stuff down."

"The man who gets to tap this stuff, will have to do an awful lot of tapping to cool down this stuff and satisfy me at the same time," chuckled Menzie.

"Girl, you are crazy," snickered Barbara. "Well, let's not let lover boy tap it. Because if he does and you like it, somebody is going to get hurt, and bad."

"Don't worry, I wouldn't do that. Besides, he has no idea what he does to me and he will never find out. In fact, it's our little secret."

"Well, I am glad I'm not in your shoes."

"And why is that?"

"That means I would have to carry around several pairs of panties in my purse," chuckled Barbara.

"Girl, you're right. I'm already up to my Saturday draws, and today is just Wednesday," she chuckled as she and her sister had a good laugh.

Once the New Years was in full swing, she was one person who was glad to back at work. She needed to stay busy, which kept her mind off things. That is until she got a surprise visitor.

"Miss Ferguson, you have a visitor," said her secretary over the intercom.

"I didn't know I had an appointment. Who is it?"

"It's Mrs. Jenkins?"

"Oh, Marian?"

"No ma'am, it's Dr. Jenkins' mother."

"Oh really...Ask her to come in."

"You can go in Mrs. Jenkins," said Sara as she turned off the intercom.

"Well, happy New Year," said Menzie as Mrs. Jenkins walked into her office and closed the door behind her.

"Well, I hope so!" snapped Mrs. Jenkins.

"Have a seat," requested Menzie as she gestured towards the chair which sat next to her desk.

"I'm here to discuss our little situation," said Jenkins as she sat down.

"Our situation? What situation would that be?" asked Menzie.

"You and my son."

"I'm afraid I don't know what you mean."

"Look, let's not play games here. I know how you feel about him."

"And how can you possibly know that?"

"Before I even met you, I could tell he had this admiration for you. He talked about you like he use to talk about my daughter in law before he married her."

"I don't see what one has to do with the other. I'm sure he was dating her. Me, we have a working relationship, a productive working relationship."

"Look, you have feeling for my son and I know you do. And so does his wife."

"What does me having feeling for him have to do with anything?"

"So, you admit that you do?"

"Look, Mrs. Jenkins, why don't you come right out and tell me why you are here?"

"Okay, you are everything my son admires in a woman. You are pretty, smart, and aggressive. And the way he talks about you has my daughter in law scared."

"Scared?"

"She's afraid you could try and take him away from her."

"I don't know why she would feel like that."

"Well, you could call it women's intuition, acute observation, anything you want to call it."

"In that case, I call it having a lack of confidence. The feeling you and your daughter in law have has nothing to do with me personally. It has to do with her feeling insecure about herself and her ability to keep her man from other women."

"Funny, she didn't have these feeling until you got here."

"Did she send you here to fight her battle for her?"

"No, she has no idea I am here."

"So this is your own personal war?"

"I'm not fighting a war, but I am fighting this battle on my own."

"Good, because if she was so concerned with me taking him away from her, she would be woman enough to confront me, then do what she has to do to keep him."

"You don't understand do you? He's been around other women before. Attractive women at church, in our neighborhood, even around here. But you, there is something about you, something I can't quite put my finger on. So, I'm asking you...I'm begging you for the sake of him and his family. Stay away from him, please."

"We work together, so staying away from him is an impossibility."

"Don't play mind games with me," snapped Mrs. Jenkins. "You know what I mean."

"Look, I'm going to be honest with you. I adore the man. If I wanted him, there's no doubt in my mind, I could take him away from her. But I will tell you this, other then a working relationship we don't have any other interest in one another. So you can tell your daughter in law, I said I don't want her man. And even if I did, I won't try and get him because he loves her. He loves his family and that would be too much of a disruption for him and would destroy everything I admire about him being a Black man. I've already told her how lucky she is. Let's leave it at that."

"What about your feelings?"

"My feelings are personal. And I will not share them with anyone. Not you and surely, not him."

"Do I have your word on that?"

"Mrs. Jenkins, you--"

"Do I have your word on that?" interrupted Mrs. Jenkins.

"Yes, as God be my witness, I give you my word."

"Okay, I believe you are a woman of integrity and I will take you at your word."

"But that's because you have no choice."

Mrs. Jenkins didn't respond to the remark she made. She peered at her for several seconds. It was as if she was trying to read her sincerity in the blank expression she had on her face. She got up and walked towards the door. Once there, she opened it, then peered back at her, a slight grin on her face.

"Have a Happy New Year," she recited, then left, closing the door behind her.

"And the same to you," Ferguson whispered to herself.

CHAPTER SIX

SOME TROUBLED TIMES

Two years later, Corrall International Network Incorporated had become one of the busiest company in the Midwest. It had started to appear on the Fortune 500 list and steadily climbed each year. It was also known as one of the few companies where any qualified person, particularly Black, and females, could come and get a descent paying job. With all that Ferguson had done to put the company on top, she was not finished yet.

It was the summer and the time when most people were thinking about where they might be going on vacation, but not her. She was on her way to Jenkins' office with another proposal. When she got there, his secretary was already gone for the weekend, but he was still working in his office when she peeped in on her.

"Hey, handsome, you got a few minutes?" she asked.

"I always have time for you, what's up?"

"I have another project for us, but it can wait until Monday."

"You know if you don't tell me what it is, I'll be thinking about it all weekend. Come in," chuckled Jenkins.

An excited Menzie Ferguson came in, closed the door behind her, then rushed over to his desk and sat down in the chair next to his desk. He could see she had a hand full of papers.

"Have you read your quarterly reports yet?" she asked.

"No, I haven't" said Jenkins as he reached into his in box and pulled out the report and looked it over. "Man!" he bellowed when he read it.

"I have the quarterly reports for the last year and a half," she said as she spread them over his desk. "They show me that profits are way though the roof."

"You're not thinking, what I'm thinking, are you?"

"Depends, hit me!" she bellowed.

"Profit sharing!"

"Bingo!" she shouted. "We are postured as a major cooperation and we have a lot more revenue coming in for the company to start putting some of it into investments and allowing the employees to buy stocks in the profits made."

"You know, we could be talking major bucks!"

"That's what I thought!"

"Okay, the problem is how to approach old man Robinstein with it."

"Here's how we can handle him. As you know we provide major training and consulting services for three major brokerage firms. Since they are already our clients, we're in a position to recommend a co-op arrangement. We provide them a percentage off the training at a produced rate, they then could determine some the best commodities and hold them in escrow as a company entity. That way we still make money, they provide us with a service that's profitable for them."

"Yeah, then we could let the employees make their own decision about where and how much they what to invest in those commodities. Even that old skinflint can appreciate a deal like that."

"I would think so."

"Man, just thinking about the possibilities got my blood boiling, over time!"

"So, now you know how I felt when I started to carefully monitor these reports."

"Okay, first thing Monday morning let's set up a meetings with those brokerage firms and get the ball to rolling."

"You know, this is going to be big. I--"

Menzie was interrupted when Jenkins' phone rang. When he picked up the receiver, she could tell something was wrong by the expression on his face.

"Marcus, calm down!" he yelled. "What are you talking about?...Oh my God! I'll be right there!" he said as he slammed down the phone

She watched as he fumbled around looking for his car keys.

"Dr. Jenkins, what's wrong?" she asked as she helped him look for his keys.

"It's Marian, she's...Where in the hell are my keys!" he shouted as he continued to shuffle around the papers on his desk and with her help.

"Here they are!" she shouted as she found them under the quarterly reports and handed them to him.

"I've got to go!" he said as he headed towards the doorway to his office.

"Yes! Yes! Go! See about your wife!" she said as she rushed him towards the doorway.

Once he was out of the office, she covered her mouth with both hands. She stood and watched him rush out of the building and towards his car.

"Oh God! Please don't let it be bad! Please God!" she uttered though her hands as tears started to trickle down her cheeks.

Later that night, Jenkins sat in the hospital waiting room with his head hung down, waiting to hear the news on the condition of his wife. Lying across from him sleeping on two chairs he had put together was his sixteen year old daughter, Vena. It was she who had road in the ambulance with her mother on the way to the hospital. They were there for hours before Jenkins saw a doctor headed towards them taking off a blood soaked surgery cap and wearing a blood soaked surgery suit. He jumped up and met him before he got to the waiting room.

"Are you, Mr. Jenkins?" asked the Surgeon.

"Yes, I am!"

"Would you like to have a seat, sir?" he requested.

"No, just tell what's wrong!" snapped Jenkins.

"I'm sorry to tell you, sir, but your wife passed a few minutes ago!"

"She's dead? How? She was a healthy, young woman!"

"Yes sir and she died of an aneurysm. The entire blood vessel near her brain was so badly dilated, when we were able to shrink one area, another would puff up, and we just couldn't keep up with the trauma! I'm sorry, we did all we could!"

Jenkins didn't say anything. He slowly turned around thinking how he was going to tell Vena. When he turned towards the waiting room, he could see her standing in the doorway, with this scared look on her face. He slowly walked towards her. But before he took three steps, his legs gave out and he started to fall to the floor.

"Daddy!" she shouted.

She rushed over and grabbed him and lowered him to his knees. She wrapped her arms around him tightly, as they then hugged and wept together.

Later that night, Ferguson was at home reading a book when her phone rang. She was hoping it was good news. When she slowly picked up the receiver, it was old man Cecil Robinstein.

"Menzie, I called the hospital to see how Marian Jenkins was doing. I was told she died a couple of hours ago. I need you to help in our prayers for James and his family. I know he's hurt. He thought the world of her."

"I know he did and thanks for calling me...Good night!" she muttered.

She slowly hung up the phone, and just sat there numb for several moments.

"Ohhhhhhhhhhhh!" she painfully sobbed as she laid across her bed.

Several days later, they had Marian's funeral and took her body to the burial sight the same afternoon. There the minister quoted Psalms 23:

"The Lord is my shepherd; I shall not want. He maketh me to lie down in green pastures: he leadeth me beside the still waters. He restoreth my soul: he leadeth me in the paths of righteousness for his namesake. Yea, though I walk through the valley of the shadow of death, I will fear no evil: for thou art with me; thy rod and thy staff they comfort me."

As the minister continued to read from the Bible, Ferguson wearing black, eyes all puffy and red briefly peered over at Jenkins. He sat with his head hung. She could see he was still sobbing, desperately by the posture of his body language. In fact the children seemed to be more composed than he. Regardless, it grieved her to see the family going through these real troubled times. She then looked back at the minister.

"Surely goodness and mercy shall follow me all the days of my life: and I shall dwell in the house of the Lord for ever."

After the reading of the scripture, Jenkins sat, quietly, still as scores of people passed by and touched him on the shoulders as a way of showing their condolences. Old man Robinson and his wife were there and so was his nephew, Horence. Sara Tillsberge was there with a friend as was Gladis Henley, George Blackshere and a host of the firm's other employees.

Once everyone had passed, some of the relatives took the children while James Jenkins sat in his chair almost motionless as he peered at the casket. Ferguson stood quite a distance from him watching him as he just sat there. She looked on as Vena, walked over and got down on her knees in front of her father, leaned on his lap and looked into his eyes.

"Daddy, it's time for us to go," she said. "Don't worry Daddy, I'll take care of you!" she sobbed.

She watched as he bent down to his daughter and the two of them embraced and they both sobbed. The scene was too touching for her to watch and bare, so he turned and walked away, sobbing into a handkerchief.

After the service the Jenkins' went out of town to visit relatives. It was two weeks before Jenkins came back to work. His first day back, he sat at his desk working diligently trying to catch up. Ferguson came down to see him. When she walked into his department, the entire atmosphere was different than she had ever seen it before.

"Hi Miss Ferguson," said his secretary.

"Hi Maria, how's he doing?" she asked.

"Oh Miss Ferguson, he is still taking it hard! Nobody knows what to say to him, what to do! I'm really scared for him!" baffled a terrified secretary.

"You think it's okay if I go in and see him?"

"Please! And see if you can cheer him up!" she plead. "Tell him if he needs help, we will all do what we can to help him out."

"I'm sure he will appreciate that. And I'll let him know."

"Thanks."

She walked over, opened the door and poked her head in his door. He was busy working he didn't notice her doing so.

"Hi!" she bellowed out so he could hear her.

"Oh, hi!"

"How ya doing?"

"Just trying to catch up. It seems like there's so much work to do!"

"Is there something I can do to help?"

"No, you've got your own problems!" he snapped.

"Problems?"

"I didn't mean problems, I meant work!"

"I know what you meant...I'll tell you what, why don't I help you sort through some of this stuff."

"You sure you have the time to help me out?"

"I'll make time. I know one thing we can do! It's called delegating. And your staff is anxious to help you out, so let them."

She began to help Jenkins prioritize his work. Some of the most important stuff, they worked on and some of the lesser work was divided among his senior administrative staff. Before long, thing were caught up and Jenkins seemed more relaxed, although not much. Those times he and she worked together, he never seemed to get back to his old self. And she was worried about him. One thing was he didn't talk much and that alone was enough for concern.

After she helped him get caught up on his work, she visited him with good news in hopes it would cheer him up.

"While you were out, I worked on the proposal we had talked about. I've got all of the details worked out. The three Brokerage firms are participating and have identified the most profitable commodities. We've even identified the training the employees will need to be able to make good investment decisions. All we have to do is present it to Mr. Robinstein, You up to it?"

"What proposal was that?"

"Oh, I'm sorry, it was about the profit sharing, remember?"

"Oh yeah, I remember. Why didn't you go forward with the presentation?"

"Because we developed this ideal together and we agreed to present it as a team. Besides, you are better at handling him when it comes to the subject of money."

Jenkins gathered himself well enough to assist Menzie in presenting the profit sharing proposal to Cecil Robinstein. Since he was clearly shown it couldn't cost him any money, and that he too could invest money and earn additional profit, he had no problems accepting the proposal. After a couple of pay periods, it went into effect. All of the employees participated and the morale of the company sword to an all time high. And again, the team of Ferguson and Jenkins, helped excel Corrall International Network Incorporated to the forefront of the place to do business.

It had been almost a year since Marian Jenkins death. Jenkins had made it to a point where he didn't talk about it a lot, but occasionally but only to a few people. It was a Tuesday and lunchtime, and Jenkins was standing in line getting a bowl of soup for his lunch when Menzie walked into the cafeteria.

"Hi handsome!" she said as she walked up to him.

"Oh hi Menzie!" he responded in less than an enthusiastic tone of voice.

She didn't say anything at first, just took a good look at him. Once the two of them got their lunches and sat down, she watched as he picked through his soup with his spoon.

"James, are you okay?" she asked.

"Oh sure, everything is honky dory!" he sort of mumbled.

"You sure? You look a little, tired."

"Yeah, I guess so."

"Try to eat your soup, maybe it will make you feel better."

"I'm really not that hungry. I think I'll go back to my office. I've got a lot of work to do."

"Well wait! I'll walk back with you!" she said in a concerned tone of voice.

Just as Jenkins stood up, he lost his balance and fell back towards the table. Before he could hit the table she caught him and lowered him back in his seat.

"Oh God!" she uttered.

"I feel dizzy! I can't breath!" uttered Jenkins.

"Whose got aspirins?" she shouted.

"I do! I'll give you a couple said the female as she took out aspirin from her apron pocket and attempted to open the box.

"Give me those!" she snapped.

She snatched the box of aspirin, banged the box on the table. When the aspirins fell out, she grabbed two and stuffed them in Jenkins' mouth.

"Take these!" she insisted as she picked up the glass of water to help him force the aspirin down. "You, she said to one of the cafeteria workers. "Go to the nurse, tell her to call the hospital and ask for an ambulance!"

"I am the nurse, but I don't know the number off hand, it's in my office!"

"Oh great!" she bellowed. "You, with the phone, call the 911 operator and ask them to send an ambulance!" she shouted. "Hurry! Hold on James, we're going to get you to a hospital," she said as she held onto his hand.

Later a huge crowd of worried co-workers and onlookers stood and watched while the orderlies worked on Jenkins right there on the cafeteria floor. Once they had him stable, they quickly prepared to rush him to the ambulance and on to the hospital.

"Can I go with him?" she asked.

"You a relative?"

"I am now, let's go!" she demanded as she hopped into the ambulance.

"Hold on James, you're going to be all right. You're going to be all right," she insisted as she held his hand.

Later in the hospital waiting room, she pranced back and forth, from the door and back praying.

"Oh please God! Those poor kids need their father!" she said as she continued to prance back and forth, and pray.

After what seemed like forever, she could see the same doctor who had rushed in with Jenkins and he approached her concerning Jenkins.

"You the lady who came in with Mr. James Jenkins?"

"Yes, I am!"

"Well, he's doing fine."

"Thank God!" she uttered as she held her hands over her heart. "Was he having a heart attack?"

"Not really. But if was a good thing you gave him those aspirins or he might have. He did have a sugar count over four hundred when he first got here. We've gotten it down a lot and should have it close to normal by morning. The good news is he's in good shape otherwise. He seems to be under a lot of stress, you know why?"

"Yes, he lost his wife about a year ago,"

"That might explain a lot about what brought on his condition. Anyway, we're going to keep him here a couple of days, then he can go home."

"That is good new! Can I see him?"

"Sure, but I wouldn't stay too long, I gave him something to relax him."

"Thank you."

A nervous Menzie slowly walked into Jenkins' room. He was lying down with several intravenous tubes running out of his arms. The sight of him lying there, looking so helpless, didn't do much to calm her nerves. Still, she felt compelled to seem calm to him, in lieu of her true feelings.

"Hey handsome!" she said. "How you doing?"

"I lot better thanks to you."

"I'm just glad I decided to come to lunch early...Did they tell you, you were going to be alright?"

"Yeah, it looks as if I'm going to be on medication for high blood pressure. And I have to keep my blood sugar under control. Here I'm just in my forties and I'm on two medications already."

"That may be!" she said. "But be grateful you are still alive and that is the most important thing!"

"I suppose you're right. Anyway, the doctor said I could go home in a couple of days if I'm a good boy!" joked Jenkins.

Menzie chuckled a bit.

"Joking already, now that's the James Jenkins I know and love."

"Oh Gees! Did anybody call my kids, they must be worried sick!"

"I called them and told them I was here with you. Vena told me Lona was with them!"

"Good, they're in good hands," sighed Jenkins in a relieved tone of voice.

"My poor kids! What they must be going through! I mean suddenly loosing their mother one year and almost loosing their father the next!" said Jenkins as he took a deep breath and peered over at her.

"Yeah, my heart really goes out to them. But I don't think you can help them by worrying. They really need you and you having a good attitude will mean more to them than anything."

"Yeah, I know...But I can't help but have some concerns."

"Yeah...Look, I'm going to get out of here and let you get some sleep."

"Sleep, I can't sleep! I'm too whined up!"

"They told me they gave you something to calm you down."

"Well, it haven't kicked in yet!" snickered Jenkins.

"Maybe it's me!"

"What do you mean?"

"I mean, I'm keeping you awake."

"I doubt that."

"Tell you what, you have my number, if you need anything, need to talk, you call me!"

"What if I just want to talk, can I call you?"

"Sure you can. But I would try and get some sleep if I were you. I'll call you tomorrow."

"Okay and thanks."

"Don't mention it, good night."

"Good night Menzie."

Once she was back at her apartment, she was completely exhausted as she threw her keys and her purse on her bed. She continued on to the kitchen, where she opened her refrigerator, took out a carton of orange juice, took a glass from the cabinet and pour herself a tall glass. After putting the carton back into the refrigerator, she walked back into the bedroom carrying the glass of orange juice.

"What a day," she uttered.

She sat on her sofa, then picked up the phone and dialed. After the second ring, a female answered the phone.

"Hello," she said.

"Hello, is this Lona?"

"Yes it is, whose this?"

"This is Menzie Ferguson again."

"Oh hello Miss Ferguson," she said in a happy tone of voice.

"I'm glad to hear you are in a good mood in lieu of you knowing it was me. How is Mrs. Jenkins holding out?"

"She's fine," chuckled Lona. "She's on her way to the hospital. Are you still there?"

"No, I'm home. I don't think I could have taken her tonight," she chuckled.

"And I don't think my brother could have taken hearing the two of you," implicated Lona with a chuckle in her voice.

"You seem in a good mood. Can I assume you have heard about James?"

"Yes, I've already talked with the hospital and they told me he was doing fine. But I'm also laughing because of my mother. You do understand she is somewhat of an alarmist?"

"Yeah, she sure is...At any rate, I'm glad Dr. Jenkins is doing fine. Did you understand he should be out of the hospital in a couple of days."

"Yes, and that was good news. His kids were really concerned about him."

"Well, he's a fighter, tell them that for me."

"I sure will, and thank you."

"You're welcome, goodbye."

After hanging up the phone, she walked over the entertainment center, sorted through a stack of cassette tapes until she found the one she wanted. She put the tape in the cassette player, turned it on and listened to Dione Warrick singing 'A House Is Not A Home'.

At first, she stood and listened to the melody of the song as it played. She took a sip from her orange juice and stood there. As she listened closely, the lyrics started to hit her hard. The more she listened the more affected she became. Here she was, a very successful woman, the best at what she does. Yet, here she was alone in her huge apartment, drinking orange juice and listening to a song that was pricking at her heart.

She walked over to her bed and sat down on the edge of it. She took another sip of her orange juice as she continued to listen to the lyrics of the song. She look a long drink and nearly finishing off all of the orange juice before sitting down the glass. She pulled out her pillow, laid it sideways across her bed and rested her head on it. She laid and looked at the bare walls as she listened to Miss Warrick finish off the song. And by the time she had hit her last note, Ferguson was sobbing desperately again. This time she didn't really know why, other then she just felt like it.

CHAPTER SEVEN

FEAR ON THE UNKNOWN

It was the second day of Jenkins' hospital stay and the doctor had given him permission to go home the next day. He was sitting in his room reading a box, when Ferguson opened the door and peeped in, only to see him not hocked up to any type of hospital equipment.

"Well, look at you!" she bellowed in a surprised tone of voice.

"Hey! Come on in!" said an excited Jenkins.

"You're looking good!" she said as she came into the room closing the door behind her. "I hear you can go home tomorrow?"

"That's what they say!"

"Here, this is for you!" she said as she sat a plant on the table in his room.

"Thanks, it's pretty."

"You seem a lot more relaxed, are you?"

" Well, I didn't have much of a choice. My kids really need me now!"

"Yeah, I know. I've been checking with them, to see how they were doing. Vena seems to have everything under control."

Jenkins laughed. "She's quite the young lady isn't she...They're all great kids."

"They had two wonderful parents...You know what I mean?"

"Yeah, I do!" sighed Jenkins.

Suddenly, he started to roll his shoulders around, then up and down. Then he started to roll his head around.

"What's the matter?" asked a concerned Menzie Ferguson.

"I think all this lying around has made me stiff. I think I'll asked for a massage."

"Would you like for me to rub you down?"

"Noh, I don't want you to go through any trouble."

"Don't be ridiculous, it's no trouble at all. In fact I am going to make you feel wonderful," she bragged.

"Okay!" sighed Jenkins.

She walked behind his chair, and helped him to the bed where he laid down on his stomach. She stood over his head, and undraped his robe from his shoulders and started to massage his shoulders. As she did so, it must have started to feel good to him, because he started to respond accordingly.

"Ahhhhhhhh!" he moaned. "That feels good!"

"Huh! You are so tight!" she uttered as she continued to massage his neck and shoulders, occasionally rotating his neck around.

She then worked her way down to the middle of his back. As she massaged, he rotated his hands from the center of his back, then up and down his back. She slowly worked back up to his shoulders and continued to massage them as she moved down his back again, and massaged up, down, then around and around..

"Ohhhhhhhhhh!" moaned Jenkins.

"That's right baby, relax," she uttered.

The more he moaned and groaned, the more she worked her hands. She then slowly worked her way down his back again, stopping short of the top portion of his buttock. At that point she closed her eyes and worked her hands firmly in the lower portion of his back.

"Ohhhhhhhhhh, man!" That feels good!" he moaned.

"You like that, huh?" She whispered as she stood there massaging the lower portions of his back and still with her eyes closed. "Yeah relax!" she passionately uttered.

"Oh yeah, do it!" expressed Jenkins as he too closed his eyes

She then lowered her hands so she was now massaging the tops of the cheeks of his buttock. The more she worked her hands, the more she got into it. The more she got into it, the more he enjoyed it. The more he enjoyed it, the more he responded.

"Ohhhhhhh, sssssssss, ohhh, that feels good!" he moaned.

"Daddy!" echoed a young female voice.

When they both opened their eyes and looked towards the door of his room, they faced all five of Jenkins' children who were standing in the doorway and peering at them. She snatched her hands in a gesture of innocence. She then pulled up Jenkins's robe as he got up to sit back down in the chair.

"I was just, giving him a rub down!" she explained as she walked around and helped him pull his robe back over his shoulders. She then walked from behind his chair and headed towards the bed.

"Oh, we saw what you were doing all right!" insinuated Marcus.

Ferguson snickered, before cleaning her throat.

The five Jenkins kids slowly walked into the room, with Javey closing the door behind them. They all suspiciously peered at her as they walked passed her on their way towards the chair where their father was now sitting. She then sat down on the other side of the bed as the kids came over and hugged their father, one at a time.

"We came here to see how you were doing!" said Vena. "But it seems you are really doing a lot better then we thought!"

"Vena!" bellowed Jenkins.

"Well, Miss Menzie, it is so nice to see you again. And still playing the fiddle I see," she chuckled

"Oh is wasn't like that. He was stiff and I was just helping him out...You know?" explained Ferguson.

"Oh really! You were stiff Daddy and she was just helping you out, how nice," snickered the sixteen years old female.

"No, I didn't mean it like that either," apologized Ferguson.

"She knows what you meant, she just trying to tease you."

"Tease, that's an interesting word," snickered Vena.

"Vena, behave yourself and apologist to Miss Ferguson."

"Oh, I'm sorry! Miss Ferguson," said the sixteen year old. "I just got the wrong impression. I mean, you with your hands all over my Daddy, him sitting there and enjoying every moment of it. But, what do I know? I'm a naïve, sixteen year old teenager," she insinuated.

"Somehow, I doubt that," mumbled Ferguson.

"What was that, Miss Ferguson?" asked Vena.

"Something," she uttered.

She then started to notice the children seemed to spread out all over the room like a military attack unit. His ten year old sat in a chair near the bed. His seven years old son leaned against a nearby wall, his oldest daughter, Vena, leaned against the windowsill in back of the chair where her father was sitting, while his oldest son stood next to him. She watched as his youngest daughter walked behind her and to the other side of the bed and leaned on it.

"Miss Ferguson, you've met Javey, Marcus and Vena. This is Myron, my youngest son, and that's Floreese leaning on the bed."

Ferguson nodded to each of the kids as they were being introduced. When she peered back at Floreese, who was behind her and on the bed, she could see she was lying with her elbows resting on the bed, with her chin resting in the palms of her hands and peering at her without blinking an eye.

"Hello, all of you," she said as she looked from one child to the next they were all peering at her with this suspicious looks on their faces. Feeling like she was under a microscope, she bailed out in good style.

"You three have grown so much since I last saw you. And you are all so good looking. Of course, you do have two extremely handsome parents."

"Women are not handsome, only men!" bellowed Floreese.

"Yes ma'am!" remarked Ferguson, who then cleared her throat again.

"How did you guys get here?" asked Jenkins.

"Aunt Lona brought us," responded Marcus.

"She thought we might wanted to be alone with our father," insinuated Javey.

"I guess I can take a hint!" said Ferguson in an apologetic tone of voice.

"Oh, they weren't asking you to leave, were you children?" asked Jenkins.

But the children did not respond to his question, just peered from one to the other. It Ferguson hadn't gotten the hint the first time she certainly took the hint that time.

"I'll call you at home! Goodbye kids!" she said as she started out the door.

"Goodbye!" said the children in unisons, a bit of sarcasm in their voices.

On her way out of the room, she ran into Lona Johnson, Jenkins' sister standing by the lobby desk. They recognized each other right away.

"Hi Miss Ferguson," said Johnson.

"How much do I need to pay you to call me Menzie?" she joked.

"Okay Menzie," chuckled Johnson. "I didn't know you were here."

"Trust me, a few seconds ago, I wished I had a hole I could have crawled into," she chuckled.

"Oh, the kids," chuckled Johnson. "By the way, I've seen one of your movies."

"Tell me, did I have on clothes or not?" snickered Ferguson.

"You had on clothes, Well, most of the time," chuckled Johnson. "James told me you were the one who got him to the hospital?"

"Yes, I was. We were having lunch together when he got sick."

"I guess we were lucky you were there to help him out."

"I guess."

"Well, let me get in there and see how he's doing...May I ask you a question?"

"You just did," teased Ferguson.

"Oh, I guess I did," chuckled Johnson. "Will you be seeing my brother?"

"Why do you ask?"

"Just curious."

"Well, we work together, and that's as far as our relationship will go, if that's what you're asking."

The next morning Ferguson was at work in her office working, when Sara walked in, picked up the work from the work slots and started out the door with it piled in her arms. Before she made it clear of the door, she stopped in the doorway.

"I'm sorry to disturb you, boss, but do you know when Dr. Jenkins is coming back to work?"

"My guess would be soon. He's going home from the hospital today. Why do you ask?"

"His office has been calling me because he has pile of requests on his desk from people asking for him to come and speak for them. Some are several weeks old."

"Huh!" moaned Ferguson as took a quick glance at her watch.

She then seemed to contemplate for several seconds like she was trying to figure out what to do next.

"He should be home by now. I think I'll give him a call and find out."

She picked up the phone, put it to her ear, and dialed several numbers. But before she had completed dialing all of the numbers, she hesitated then abruptly hung up the phone.

"What's the matter?" asked Sara.

Instead of responding to Sara, Ferguson started to laugh out loud.

"Christ! What's so funny?" asked Sara.

"Yesterday I was giving him a massage, when--"

"Giving who a massage?" interrupted Sara.

"Would you let me finish my statement!" chuckled Ferguson.

"Are you sure you can? I mean, whatever it is must really be funny!"

"Never you mind" she chuckled. "Yesterday, I was in Dr. Jenkins' room giving him a massage. We were really into it, when his kids walked in and caught us."

"Caught us?" asked Sara, who then started to laugh. "And ahh, where were you massaging him, when they caught us?" she mocked. "Or do I really need to know?"

"He was tight. You know, up tight? So I was just massaging him all over."

"So what was funny about it?"

"Weeeell," chuckled Ferguson. "They thought they caught us doing something, sexually," she joked as she held out her hands as a gesture of innocence.

"Let me make sure I understand what you just said. You were, giving him, Dr. Jenkins, a massage, when his kids walked in on you and they thought you were doing something, ah sexually? Why would they think that?"

"Well, I was kind of massaging me a hand full of that butt," chuckled Ferguson.

"Man! That must have been some massage!" snickered Sara.

"Well ahh, it was, nice. I was really into it," said Ferguson as she snickered again. "It was fun having my hands on a man's butt for a change," she gestured as if she was still giving him the massage.

"May I ask you a personal question?"

"Since when did you start asking for permission to be nosy?"

Sara laughed at her remark.

"When was the last time you've had a man?" she asked her.

"If I told you, you wouldn't believe me," she responded.

"Well, you better get you some soon. I think you are strangely horny."

"No, I'm just having fun over what they thought...But man you should have seen them with their father. They hovered over him like I was going to try and steal him away from them. They surrounded me like an army all standing so they could keep an eye on me, " conjectured Ferguson. "I felt like the Pink Panther."

"Well, he was a thief. And of course, you wouldn't try to steal a little of that, would you?"

"Of course not! And why would you ask me something like that?" she snapped

"Okay! Okay! I'd like to keep my head if you don't mind!"

"Sorry!"

"Well, if you're not going to call him and ask when he's coming back to work, how are you going to find out?" asked a curious Administrative Assistant.

"I think I'll stop by his house and see how he's doing."

"I wonder how I knew you were going to say that?"

"Never mind," retorted Ferguson as she stood and picked up her purse.

"Okay! But while you're there, no touching or massages his butt or anything like that. We wouldn't want to give the kids the wrong expression, would we?"

"No, we wouldn't!" snickered Ferguson.

Later she rang the Jenkins' front door bell. She was expecting one of the kids to open the door, so she had already practice on how she was going to respond to them. But instead, James Jenkins opened the door.

"Ah, hi!" she said.

"Hello!"

"You feel up to having some adult company?"

"As long as it's you, I do. Come in and have a seat," he said as he stepped aside and let her in.

She cautiously walked in and again she expected to run into the kids. But again, she didn't encounter any of them. She turned and peered at him as he closed the door behind her.

"It's quiet, where are the children?" she said as she sat down on the couch.

"Their aunt took them to six flags," answered Jenkins as he sat in a chair across from her. "I mean they haven't had a real vacation in two years."

"Yeah, I know what you mean. So, they left you home by your self? What were you doing to keep yourself occupied?"

"Actually, I was just sitting and thinking about my predicament."

"What do you mean?"

"Here I am, a forty-three year old widower, with five kids. You have any idea what that's like?"

"No, I can't start to imagine what's that like!" responded Menzie in a solemn tone of voice.

"Huh! You want to hear what I've always prayed?"

"Yes, I do!" said Ferguson in a sincere tone of voice.

"I've never thought much about going to heaven, or even living until I was an old man. I've just always prayed I'd live long enough to see my kids grown and out on their own. I assumed because Marian was thirty-eight, she would always be there for them.

Looks like I forgot to include her when I prayed," he snickered. "I just thought she would out live me. After she died, I tried hard to convince myself, I could do it all by myself, be mother and father. I worked so hard at it and worried about it so much, I made myself sick. You want to know something? I'm scared! I'm really scared! Thing is, I don't really understand why I feel so much fear."

"I know what you mean. It's the fear of the unknown that scares us all."

"Yeah! That's it! The fear of the unknown! If something happens to me before they are all grown, they don't really have anybody left to really lean on like they can me. What's going to happen to them?" sighed Jenkins as tears rolled his cheeks."

"James, don't! You are going to be fine! And your kids are going to be fine! I'm sure Marian never thought she would die as young as she did. But I am sure she was confident of one important thing, and that was she and her children were in good hands with you as a husband and father. Now, it's time for you to take total control, that's all. A lesser man, I would be concerned about...but, not you."

"Yeah! I know you are right! I need to get myself together if only for the sake of my kids," conceded Jenkins.

"Now, you got it dude!" chuckled Ferguson. "Tell you what, I am glad the children got out of the house today. How do you think they would feel about coming to a concert tomorrow night? I'm playing my first solo performance."

"Yeah, I think they would like that! How do we get tickets?"

"Let's do it in style. You just walk unto the ticket box office and say, 'I'm Dr. James Jenkins, we're guests of Miss Ferguson, please'."

"I have your tickets right here Dr. Jenkins," said the female usher. "Here are your suds," she said as tore off the ends of the tickets. "I'll escort you to your seats."

"We're gonna be escorted to our seats?" asked Floreese.

"Yeah!" bellowed Marcus. "Just like rich White folks!" he bragged.

As the female usher escorted the well, dressed Jenkins family to their seats, the kids felt awful special as members of the audience watched them passing by them. Once they were in their seats, the usher then gave them their programs.

"Are you folks alright?" asked the usher.

"We're fine, thank you!" said Jenkins in his best voice.

As the usher started back up the isles, Marcus and Javey, both looked around bobbing their heads around like they were somebody important.

"Now, this is living," bragged Marcus.

Once the concert was underway it became obvious that the violins were being featured in the first half, as the symphony performed Vivaldi's 'Four Seasons'. As they did so, Menzie was very active.

During the first part of the concert, She and another violinist performed the violins solo parts to the 'Spring' segment. Then Ferguson performed 'Largo' and the 'Winter, Allegro non molto' segment as a solo.

The children sat very intent during the entire concert. It was as if they were completely mesmerized with the music. Sitting where they were, they could see all the hard work that went into performing symphony concert. The fact that Ferguson was featured several times and seemed to work hard at what she was doing, and that helped keep their interest. Then there was the fact of just seeing someone they personally knew performing with the St. Louis Symphony, surely helped a lot.

After the concert, they stood and watched the huge crowd of people attempting to get Ferguson's autograph. After all, she was still known as a movies star. After standing for several minutes, the children got impatient and turned to leave. She saw them and decided to preempt the autograph singing and get to them.

"Wait a minute folks, let me take care of my guests first!" she shouted.

She made her way through the crowd and over to where were now standing.

"How are my guests tonight?" she asked.

"Miss Ferguson, you were terrific!" uttered Vena.

"You sure were!" shouted Javey "Can I have your autograph?" he asked as he held out his program.

"You sure can!" responded Ferguson.

"Use my name, say something special," he requested.

She took the time to write on his program then handed it back to him.

"How's that?" she asked as he took it from her.

"Wow!" he bellowed. 'To Javey a very special guest and a very special guy, love M.J. Ferguson, St. Louis Symphony'," he read out loud.

"Do mine next!" insisted Myron as he handed her his program.

He watched as she wrote on it, smiled, and then handed his program back to him.

"Thanks," he said as he read it to himself.

"Will you do mine Miss Ferguson!" asked Floreese.

"Of course, I'll do yours!"

She autographed her program, and handed it back to her. Then took the time to autographed programs for Dr. Jenkins, Marcus and Vena.

"Okay, we're going to get out of here so you can take care of the other guest, "said James Jenkins.

"Okay, I'll call you tomorrow" she responded.

She watched and listened as the Jenkins family turned and started to walk away from her.

"What does my program say?" asked Floreese as she handed it to her sister.

"It says 'To Floreese, thanks for coming to the concert as my very special guest, love M.J. Ferguson, St. Louis Symphony'," she read as they walked.

"Ahhh! She said I was very special!" bellowed the five years old.

"Ah, that's only because you're the baby!" retorted Javey with a wave of his hand.

"So, what's wrong with that?" she said.

Once they were out of sight, Ferguson turned to continue signing autographs.

"Family?" asked one man after seeking her out for an autograph.

"I should be so lucky!" she responded as she then signed the man's program.

Later that night, she laid in her bed covered with nothing but a sheet and looking up at the ceiling. She turned and gazed out the window and reminisced how rays from the full moon crisscrossed her bed and reflected off her firmly shaped body. She watched the stars as they gathered among themselves. She always thought it was funny that she was taught in school that the stars are in a constant motion and had a short life. But from where she laid, they seemed not to be moving at all.

Then she thought about her life in comparison to the stars. If she only had just those few fleeting moments like stars, she tried to determine now her last moments would be spent. She knew for sure she had accomplished a lot of success in her life. And it seemed she had everything that she has always wanted, with the exception being one thing. That was having the man she has loved since the very first moment she laid eyes on him. She decided what she would do those last few fleeing moments. Make love to the only man she had ever loved in her entire life. Strange she thought to herself. He was now available, but she was afraid to go after him. Mostly because of what people might assume about them. But the fear she seemed to feel the most was the fear of him rejecting her. With her it had become so strong of a fear, the very thought of being rejected caused her to tear, even if it was those few fleeing moment to put here to sleep.

CHAPTER EIGHT

DESPERATE MEANS, DESPERATE MEASURES

Bright and early the next day things started to buzz pretty loud around Corrall International Network Incorporated. The news? That Dr. James Jenkins was coming back to work on Monday. Of course Sara Tillsberg heard it and could not wait to tell her boss that and more, as she stood tapping on her boss' office door.

"Come in Sara!" requested Ferguson.

"Have you heard?" asked an excited Administrative Assistant.

"If you mean about Dr. Jenkins coming back to work on Monday, I have. Cecil Robinstein called and told me."

"Aren't you the least bit excited?"

"Of course I'm excited!"

"Huh! I thought you would be happier than Gladis Henley! But I guess not!"

"What about her?"

"Oh nothing! Except old Gladis seems to think she's got a chance at getting some of his stuff, now that his wife is dead and buried!"

"That's terrible!"

"Well, it may be! I'm only telling you what she's been saying! She thinks the old boy is just about due for an overall and she, being horny as a toad, feels now is the time to whip it on him. Man I'd like to be a fly on the wall if those two get together!"

"Sara, get your mind out of the gutter!" insisted Ferguson.

"It's not my mind you have to worry about! It's her letting him get between her legs. I can hear the moaning and the groaning right now, 'Oh sock it to me Dr. Jimmy boy, sock it to me real good!'" mocked Sara."

"You are a mess, you know that? Look, she obviously has no idea of his real needs. He doesn't need sex! He--"

"He doesn't?" interrupted Sara with a chuckle.

"That's not what I mean!" defended Ferguson. "What I mean is he needs more than just sex. He has needs that only a special woman can give him. Sara, here is a man, who has the potential to be wealthy, powerful, famous. You name it! All he needs is the right woman behind him, encouraging him! Not one who will have him so weak that he can't think straight."

"Ohhhhh! I see. This is one of those behind every great man there's a good woman type thing, huh?"

"Something like that!"

"And do tell, who that woman might be, you?"

"I could be, you never know!"

"Yeah well, you're never get the chance to find out if you don't get moving."

"Look, I can't rush him into anything."

"Rush him into anything like what?"

"Like marriage."

"Who said anything about marriage? Oh, now I get it. So this, behind every successful man thing, has to be marriage?"

"Isn't that what you meant?"

"Not really, I was thinking in terms of him taking care of the little horny feeling you've been carrying around all this time."

Ferguson chuckled at her remark. "Well, with him I'm afraid if he takes on that little chore, it will have to be all or nothing."

"Why?"

"Because it would have to be. The man has five impressionable children. He can't have just any kind of woman around them, especially one like Henley. They have needs also, special needs that only a special woman could provide."

"Or you sure you're talking about their needs or yours?"

"My needs, their needs, that's not the point. The point is what he needs."

"I hear you! But you can't push a man in his position into anything, right?"

"That's right."

"Let's say you are right. Why don't you take your time, have him over to your place for dinner. Afterwards, have all the sex you want. His kids don't have to know," suggested Sara.

"I hear ya, but that wouldn't work with a man in his position."

"The way I see it, his position is single, available, maybe even horny like you. Or have you heard something I haven't?"

"The man has a professional image, a respectable situation with his kids. Besides, I know his needs better than any woman right now. But his wife has only been dead a little over a year."

"So, you expecting her to come back from the dead and haunt you or something?"

"Don't be ridiculous!"

"Okay! But wasn't it Benjamin Franklin who wrote 'Strike While The Fire Is Hot'?"

"I think he wrote 'Strike While The Iron Is Hot', Sara."

"Well I know of a couple of things around here that are hot and need sticking real bad," snickered Sara. "The question is, what are you going to do about it before Monday? You wait until then and Gladis would have already gotten her fire taken care of. You get my meaning?"

"Yeah, but I don't think I should do anything. Maybe I should see how he responds to her. You know, see if nature will take its course."

"Yeah well, nature taking its course, spells a very horny Gladis Henley in action! Trust me, she can get pretty nasty when it comes to men and sex!"

"Now how do you know that?"

"Let's assume I'm dumb as a skunk. But I've heard, just by chance, what she said she would do for him if she got the chance. Now remembering, I'm not to bright. But if I were her, and I got the chance to do all I said I would do, you tell me why I wouldn't?"

"I hate I asked. But I do see what you mean!" said Ferguson as she pondered over the remark made by Sara. "That could make her a bit of an adversary!"

"Correct me if I'm wrong, but don't adversary mean, enemy of God?"

"Yeah, I was taught that."

"Well, I've always consider her as being full of hell, isn't that the same thing?"

"Not quite, but I do get your point," chuckled Ferguson.

"Well, if that devil gets hold of him before you do, that could be a problem."

"And why is that?"

"You may not even want him once she's finished with him."

"Sara, don't you think you're being just a bit over dramatic?"

"Over dramatic? I don't think so. Boss, that woman has wanted to get with the man for years. Don't you see how determined she is? How desperate she is?"

Feguson pretended not to take seriously what Sara had said concerning Gladis Henley. But to be on the safe side, she decided it was time to cultivate the seeds she had planted already. So, later that night, the Jenkins' phone rang. It was Vena who picked it up.

"Jenkins' residents," she said.

"Hi, this is Miss Ferguson."

"Oh hello Miss. Ferguson. This is Vena. I really enjoyed the concert the other night and thanks for the special treatment. It made all of us feel pretty important!"

"Well, from what I'm hearing about you guys, you are special children and deserve to be treated like royalty."

"Thanks, you are really good at playing the violin. And how can you play so fast? I know I'll never be able to play the violin fast like you!"

"Well now, thank you. But you have to work on your speed just like you do everything else. Tell you what, maybe I can come over and bring my violin and work with you sometimes, would you like that?"

"Really! You would do that for me? Why?" asked a suspicious sixteen year old.

"Because I've got a feeling you are a very gifted person and I would like to help you bring that out."

"That sounds great, when?"

"When I get the time, I'll call you and we can get together."

"Okay! You want to talk to my dad?"

"Yes."

"Okay, I'll get him. Dad!" she yelled as she covered the receiver with her free hand.

Ferguson chuckled when she heard her call her father. She could also hear her telling him it was she on the phone.

"Dad, this is Miss Ferguson! She's going to give me violin lessons, how about that?" she asked her father.

"Then get ready for some hard work!" warned Jenkins as he was putting the phone up to his ear.

"I heard that!" she uttered.

"Well, you know how you are!" chuckled Jenkins in response to her remark.

"You got that right!" she chuckled "What's this I hear about you coming back to work on Monday?"

"You heard right! Seems like I've been off forever! I just know the work in my office is knee high."

"Actually, I've had both of our staffs working pretty hard at keeping on top of everything. But I couldn't help but notice you have a stack of speaking engagements waiting for you."

"Then it's a good thing I'm coming back, huh?"

"It sure is...Look, the reason I'm calling is to invite you over for a special dinner tomorrow night, that is if you don't have other plans."

"No, I don't. Are you cooking?"

"I'll have you to know I am an excellent cook. Anything special you want?"

"Surprise me!" snapped Jenkins.

"Okay! Consider yourself surprised."

"Good, then that gives me something to look forward towards. What time shall I be there?"

"Let's say about seven?"

"You've got a date!"

"A date! I like the sound of that!" she hinted.

On Saturday, Jenkins arrived at her apartment door exactly at seven. He felt a little nervous while standing there waiting for her to open the door. When she heard the doorbell, her heart was beating so hard and fast, her only concern was that he would here it. When she opened the door, she could see he was dressed in a sport attire and wearing a huge smile.

"Hi," he said.

"Oh my, look at you! You look good enough to marry!" she excitingly uttered as she held the door opened.

"You don't look half bad your self. That blue becomes you. But then so did the red you had on at the Christmas function." responded Jenkins as he walked into the apartment.

"Well, I'm happy you hear you noticed,' she responded.

"I notice a lot of things about you," he said. "Something smells good."

"You wait until you taste my cooking, it's bound to go straight to your heart!" she hinted.

"Gee, I hope not!" chuckled Jenkins.

"You know what I meant, silly!" snickered Ferguson.

Jenkins laughed.

Later as they sat down at her dinner table to eat, she asked him to bless the food, which he did.

"I hope you like mashed potatoes?" she asked.

"Mash potatoes are my favorite vegetable!" remarked Jenkins as he picked up the bowl of mashed potatoes and put some on his plate.

"Those are made with my own special blend of herb and spices."

"Uhmm! They smell good!" uttered Jenkins. "Huh!! Now that's good he said after eating a fork full of the mashed potatoes.

"Most people cook the skin on the chicken, I don't. This baked chicken was cooked without the skins and seasoned to perfection, taste that!" she said as she broke off a piece of chicken with a fork and fed it to him.

"Man, that's good!" he said after chewing up and swallowing the chicken.

"You know what they say, the way to a man's heart is through his stomach!" she said as she picked up a pitcher and started to pure some of its content in his glass.

"Oh, I don't drink!" said Jenkins thinking it was wine she was pouring.

"Neither do I!" whispered Ferguson. "This is berry juice, sweeten with a bit of equal to give it a sweet taste. It's good for flushing out your kidneys."

After finishing up on the main course, Ferguson brought in deserts and sat them down on the table. She sliced a piece of apple pie and put it on his plate.

"This is my home made apply pie, sweetened with no sugar. I eat yogurt on mine instead of ice cream, less fattening, you know!" she insisted.

Later the two of them sat in the living room drinking berry juice and listening to a recording of Stevie Wonder in the background singing 'Signed. Sealed. Delivered. (I'm Yours Happiness). She was sitting in a chair, he on the couch.

"Dinner was really nice!" commented a contented Jenkins.

"You mind if I sat on the couch next to you? I don't want to have to talk over the music."

"Oh, I sorry if I'm hogging the couch!" said Jenkins as he moved over to make room for her.

She got up and walked over to the couch, sat down next to him and sat her glass on the coffee table. She then locked her fingers together and leaned on the back of the couch right next to him.

"Now, what were you saying?" she asked.

"I was just commenting on the excellent meal you cooked. You're a good cook, although I should not have been surprised!" said Jenkins as he slightly shook his head from side and smiled.

"Why do you say that?"

"Menzie, you are good at everything!" commented Jenkins.

"Ahh, I don't know about that! I seem to be having a hard time getting the man I want!" she hinted.

"I don't see why!"

"You don't?"

"Noh! I mean look at you! You have a lot going for you. You're intelligent, well educated extremely successful and you have to be the prettiest women I've ever seen. Why, you could have any man you wanted!"

"How about you?" she asked.

"Me, ahh! I'm afraid the game is over for me!" snickered Jenkins. "I'm a man with health problems and five young kids to take care of. No woman in her right mind would take on that kind of responsibility."

She was stung at the remark he made. She had thrown out hints all night and all she got for her troubles were a subtle form of rejection. Jenkins must have noticed the look on her face and it did cause him some concern.

"Menzie, is something wrong?"

"No!" she snapped.

"Something is wrong. What is it?"

"I said nothing was wrong!" she snapped.

"You sure? Did I say something to offend you?"

"No!" she said after taking a deep breath.

"Are you feeling okay?"

"Yeah, I'm okay...Maybe you should leave!" she scolded.

"Okay, but I could at least help you with the dishes," he offered as he picked up several dishes.

"I don't need your help!" she snapped.

"Okaaaay!" said Jenkins.

He sat down his dishes, got up and walked over to the door, with an angry Ferguson walking behind him. When he reached the door, he stopped, turned and peered back at her.

"You sure you're alright?" he asked with a concerned look on his face.

"I said I was okay, didn't I?" she snapped.

He stood there for several seconds peering at her as she stood there with her armed crossed and looking down at the floor. She suddenly raised her head and glared into his eyes. He could still see the pensive, angry look on her face.

"A penny for your thoughts," he chuckled.

"Right now my thought is grabbing you by your neck and chocking you until your eyes pop out!" she snickered, still standing there with her arms crossed.

"What?" he snapped.

"Nothing," she uttered as she rolled her eyes around as a gesture of disappointment.

"Wow! I believe this the first time I've seen you really angry!"

"Well, don't worry about it!"

"Menzie, what's wrong?"

"I said nothing! Will you leave!" she demanded.

"Okay, okay. I guess I'll see you on Monday."

She didn't comment on his remark, just peered at him with her cold looking, angry eyes. He opened the door, than peered back at her.

"Thanks for dinner...I really had a nice time."

"I'm glad you did!"

He then walked out of the door, got on the elevator and rode down with a look of confusion on his face.

Meanwhile, she walked over to the window and watched him walk over to his car and unlock the door. He looked up at her and could see she was standing there watching him. He hesitated a few seconds, then got in his car and drove off.

After watching him leave. She walked over and abruptly sat down on her sofa, her arms still crossed.

"That bonehead," she mumbled.

After sitting there for a minute, she picked up the phone and called Sara Tillsberge, who was at home and who was sitting and watching television with a a male friend.

"Hello," said Sara.

"Hi, this is Menzie."

"Oh, hi boss. How did it go with Dr. Jenkins?"

"I bombed out. Big time!"

"Oh, I'm sorry! What happened?"

"The man has no clue what's going on around him!" she snapped.

"Meaning what?"

"I did everything to show him how I felt about him. Tonight, I throw out several hints and all the man did was respond to them by putting his foot in his mouth! Ohh, I could have choked him tonight"

"Miss Ferguson, are you sure he knows how you feel about him?"

"He should have known I went through all this for a reason."

"Why should he have thought it meant anything other then you showing him friendship. I mean you act friendly towards everybody. He might consider your behavior as just being nice because of his situation."

"He couldn't be that dumb!" she snapped.

"We know he's not dumb. Aren't you just a little bit flattered that he doesn't take you for grated?"

"Look, I've been all over him every since we met."

"Now you see, that's my point. To him you're not acting any different."

"Noh, that ain't it. I'm sure that bonehead is just--."

Ferguson stopped before completing her statement. She paused, pondered for several seconds still holding the phone receiver up to her ear.

"Think about it!" said Sara. "How would he really know how you really feel about him? You didn't tell me you told him how you felt, just throw out hints."

"Yeah, but the hints I threw out a five year old child could have picked up on!"

"But we're not talking about a five year old child. We're talking about a grown man, one who has had his heart broken when he lost his wife. You're not going to get him being tactful and coy. You'll get him by being honest and straight. That's because that's the kind of person he knows you to be."

"Could be you're right. As a matter of fact, I know you're right. Remind me to put you in for a raise next month."

"Boss, put me in for a raise next month."

"Good night Sara," snickered Ferguson.

"Good night, boss," chuckled Sara.

Around ten o'clock on Sunday, the Jenkins's doorbell rang. When Jenkins opened the door, it was Menzie Ferguson. He seemed surprised, yet pleased to see her.

"Well, hello!" he said.

"Hi, can I come in?" she asked.

"Please do," snickered Jenkins.

She followed him into the kitchen where he had been sitting and sipping a cup of cappuccino.

"It's always so quiet around here. Where are the children this time?"

"They went to church with our neighbors. Would you like some coffee, tea, or cappuccino?"

"No, I don't want anything, thanks."

"I wasn't sure if I should call you. I wanted to apologize for how lousy our date ended after such a real nice meal!"

"It wasn't you, it was me!" she confessed.

"It couldn't have been you, you were a perfect hostess. But I kept trying to figure out what I did or said that was so horrible, to get you upset like that?"

"It wasn't so much of what you said, it was what you didn't say. James, I need you to listen to me! I have something I want to say and I want it to come out the right way. I've loved you since the very first moment I laid eyes on you. Now, I knew you were married and loved your wife and I was happy to even know a brother who felt about his wife like you did yours. When she died, I tried to shut down my heart. I-"

"Menzie, I had no idea," he interrupted.

"You don't know how hard it was for me to constantly fight even hinting to you how I felt. But in lieu of doing all I could do to keep my feeling to myself, I just couldn't do it any longer. Then I found myself throwing out all these hints, hoping you would take the lead so I won't have to, but that didn't happen."

"Hints?"

"Don't worry! They went right over your head, anyway," she inferred.

"Menzie, I--"

"James, please let me finish!" she interrupted. "The day we talked at the hospital, when you talked about you dying and leaving your kids alone, that...that really got to my heart," she said as she started to tear as she continued to talk.

"I didn't mean to burden you with my problems," apologized Jenkins.

"You didn't, what you said affected me...Since then, I couldn't get it out of my mind. So, I'm coming, I mean, I came with a resolution to our problem."

"Our problem?"

"Yes, I want you very much and you really need a good woman like me! I know you don't love me right now, but marry me and I'll make you three promises," she said as she continued to tear. "First, I'll do all I can to keep you healthy. Secondly, I'll make you the happiest man in the world and you know I can do it! Third, and not least, if something happens to you before your kids are grown and out on their own, I'll make this promise to you. I will take care of them as if they were my own!"

"Menzie, I couldn't, I couldn't ask you to do that!"

"You didn't! I'm asking you to give me the chance to do it!" she sobbed.

"Menzie, you're young, you'll find somebody, have a family of your very own someday!" said Jenkins as he then began to tear. "I couldn't--," he hesitated as he held down his head and sobbed. "I couldn't do that to you!"

"James, the only thing you would be doing for me is making me happy! And I already know the family I want, the man I want."

"But what do you get out of it?" I mean there has to be something you want?"

"There is a catch! There's always a catch!"

"What is it?"

"We'll have to agree that we will try and get me pregnant."

"Pregnant? But why would you want that?"

"I just want to know how it feels to have a child, just once. I'll already have my hands full with the children we have."

"Menzie, you sure this is what you want?"

"Right now, more than anything in this world," she emphasized.

"I know I should be agreeing to this, but I'm just not sure if it's fair to you!"

"Don't you want me? I mean want to marry me?"

"A man would have to be crazy not to want to marry you!"

"I didn't ask about any man, I'm asking about you," she insisted.

"Menzie, I--"

"Look," she interrupted. "You don't have to give me an answer right now, just think about it."

"I'm thinking about it right now, but I don't know what to say."

"That's okay, when you have decided, let me know, okay?"

"Menzie, you know I think the world of you. For you to come here and make such a proposal is indicative of why I feel like I do about you. But how does a man try and love a woman like you?"

"First stop thinking of me as being different from other women. I want you to see me as being your woman, loving you. The rest will work itself out, I promise."

"Huh, you've given me a lot to consider."

She got up from the table, walked over to where he was sitting, straddled his lap and while rubbing her hands along his face.

"Here's something else for you to consider," she whispered.

She then slowly caressed both sides of his face in the palm of her hands and kissed him, gently, but affectionately on his lips. She casually turned it into a French kiss. She wanted him to taste her tongue, feel it moving around in his mouth. She held her kiss just long enough to feel the spontaneity in his body language and his breathing. He reached up and gently caressed her shoulders. She allowed the kiss to last long enough for him to feel her passion then slowly pulled it away from him.

"I know you feel that, I can. That's the passion I feel for you from the debts of my heart," she renounced.

While still holding his face in the palm of her hands, she looked deep into his eyes and smiled.

"I love you, James. I love you more than life itself...You believe me?"

"Well, I do now," he nervously responded.

"You're shaking like a scared little boy," she whispered. "That's good, at least I can feel you want me."

"More than you know," uttered Jenkins.

"I like hearing that...Here's just a reminder to keep that thought in your head."

She kissed him again while still caressing the sides of his face. She slowly grinded her tongue deep into his mouth, then out again, then in again. She had him so worked he could hardly breathe. It was then she realized she had made her point. She ended the kiss, then peered into his eyes again.

"Mmmmmm, I like what I feel. I'll see you tomorrow, huh!" she whispered as she got off him.

"Okay!" sighed Jenkins as he struggled to catch his breathe.

She kissed him again, but not as long. "You're sweet," she whispered as she tapped him on his cheeks.

She stood up and gently rubbed her hand between his legs. He flinched as he let out a quick moan of pleasure. She smiled.

"That's to get even with you for making me wet my panties," she whispered in his ear.

She then walked over to the kitchen doorway, stopped and looked back at him. She could see he was doing all he could to control himself. To add fire to an already burning flame, she reinforced what she had felt by silently gesturing to him.

"I love you!"

She then turned and let herself out. Once she was gone, he continued to sat at the table. She had caught him totally off guard, leaving him completely outdone with what had been said but more so, what had happened. He took a couple of deep breaths, then got up from the table and quickly went to take a cold shower.

Driving home she was beside herself. It was the first time she had any kind of confidence when it came to the two of them getting together.

"Go Menzie! You got it, girl! That man is yours! Ouuuuuuuweee!" she shouted.

But at night fell, it was a different story. The once confident Menzie Ferguson was having a difficult time getting to sleep, as all kinds of thoughts crossed her mind. But more importantly, she started to have second thoughts. Questioning her actions, her motives.

"Ohhhhh! Why did I go and make a fool out of myself? What if he thinks I'm being too forward, too aggressive? Am I really that desperate? What if he thinks I'm just another horny tail broad, Ohhhhhhhh! I wished he would have made a move and I wouldn't have to be going through all this!"

At that moment the phone rang. It startled her, causing her to flinch as she held her hands over her breast. She hoped it was him, yet that made her nervous.

"Oh no, it's too quick," she uttered.

She started to have all kinds of thoughts. 'What if he says no? I would be devastated. How can I face him if he rejects me? She came very close to not answering the phone, but she knew that would be ridiculous, so she did, but very apprehensively and very slowly.

"Hello," she said.

"Hello Miss Ferguson, this is Lynnett Jenkins."

"Oh, hi Mrs. Jenkins. How have you been?"

"I've been better and that's for sure...The reason I called is to thank you for saving my son's life."

"Well, I wouldn't say all that," snickered Ferguson.

"You're being modest Miss Ferguson. From what I've been told, if you hadn't been there when he got sick, he could have died."

"Thanks, I'm just glad I was there for him."

"Look, we've always been honest with one another, so I'll get to the point of my call. Do you still have feelings for my son?"

"Exactly, how are you defining feelings?"

"Look, you know I don't like mind games, so let's keep it real. I'm back to a conversation we had a couple of years ago, you remember that?"

"How can I forget it?"

"Then you know what I mean, just answer my question...Do you still have feelings for my son?"

"Mrs. Jenkins, I love your son. But then, you've always known that."

"Good, because I'm giving you permission to go after him."

"Permission?"

"Yes, and I mean it."

"Why the change of heart?"

"It's the situation that has changed. I don't want my son to be without a wife."

"You mean you want me to marry him?"

"Yes, I would rather see him with you then anybody else. You could be good for him. Good for his kids."

"Thanks for the vote of confidence. But why me and why marriage?"

"Because you are a woman of high class and I know you want the best there is out of life. I don't believe you are the type of woman who would settle for just having a man lying around you. You want love, passion and satisfaction. Besides, my daughter in law told me my son was good in bed. You would like that wouldn't you?

"Isn't that what every woman wants?"

"Well, here's your chance. Show me some of that confidence you showed when you told me you could have him if you wanted to. The hill to climb has just gotten less steep, show me how badly you want to get to the top."

"I'm speechless," responded Ferguson.

"Somehow I doubt that...Consider this, he needs a good women, one good for his children and one who is woman enough for him. I think you're women enough, prove me right."

"You really know how to push my buttons, don't you?"

"Look, I had you pegged right from the moment I even heard about you. You always had deep feelings for him and I knew it and so did his wife. Now the coast is clear, what's your course of action?"

"Have you ever thought that your son may not want me?"

"Well right now, he may not know what he wants. You convince him, charm him, screw him, do--"

"Mrs. Jenkins!" bellowed Ferguson to hear the remark made by the man's mother.

"Look, we are women. And we know how to get a man's nose opened. If all other means fell, then there is always sex to rely on and plenty of it. Come on Miss Actress, act! Do what it takes to make him want you, desire you. I'm sure you can handle that, can't you?"

Menzie chuckled. "You can get right down to it when you really have to, huh?" she asked.

"Yes, and you don't fool me, so do you. We are a lot alike, you and me. We want it all, and we will do what it takes to get it and hold onto it."

"What about Marian? What kind of woman was she?"

"She was a good wife and mother. But not treacherous like you and me."

Ferguson chuckled again.

"I don't know that I like being called treacherous," she said.

"Then call it confidence, call it self assurance, call it what you want. When it comes to what you want, you have shown me you can be relentless. You could look at it as another job that has to be done."

Ferguson chuckled again.

"Well, I really appreciate this call."

"Prove it!" snapped Lynnett Jenkins

"Okay, be advised that I have already charted my course with the man and started my voyage. I'm waiting to see where I'll end up."

"Good, there's no doubt in my mind, you'll get where you want to go...Thank me after you get back from your honeymoon."

"I'll remember to do that."

CHAPTER NINE

PERIOD OF ADJUSTMENTS

Come Monday morning, everything was on the up and up. The along awaited day for Jenkins to come back to work, was here. Except, he didn't show up early like everyone had thought he would. He actually came in about eleven o'clock, which really didn't matter to most of them. They were just glad to see him back.

So much in fact, he couldn't get his work done for the many visitors parading in and out of his office nearly the entire morning. Ferguson was afraid to come by and she really didn't know why. Just another case of that fear of rejection, she told herself as she attempted to get her work done. But by noon, all that was about to change, when Jenkins walked into her office.

"Dr. Jenkins! Welcome back!" bellowed an excited Sara Tillsberge who was standing and talking to the secretary.

"It's good to be back. Is your boss in her office?"

"Sure! Go in!"

Jenkins abruptly rushed into Ferguson's office. The moment she saw him, she got the feeling of a huge lump suddenly growing in her stomach. She took a deep breath and acknowledged him in a way he could not tell how she really felt.

"Hi handsome, welcome back!" she remarked.

"Hey! You hungry? How about lunch?"

"Are we going out? Or to the cafeteria?"

"I prefer going out! I need to talk to you."

"We could talk here if you like!"

"No! What I have to say, I want to say to you in private."

"Sure!" said an apprehensive Menzie Ferguson.

She got up and led Jenkins out of the building. Once outside, she then followed him to his car. He opened the door for her and she got in. He then closed the door and got in. He said nothing while they were in route, and that made her even more nervous. Later as they sat in a local restaurant, he finally broke the ice.

"What are you having for lunch?" he asked.

"You said you had something to talk to me about," said Ferguson "Well, I'm all ears?"

"Menzie, I thought all night about what you asked me. After doing so, I decided to turn down your proposal."

"Oh! I see!" said Ferguson in a disappointing tone of voice. "You mind if I ask you why?" she asked as she peered at Jenkins with a painfully, curious look on her face.

"Menzie, you couldn't have meant everything you said. You couldn't have! You are young, beautiful and I don't think you should waste your time on a ready made family, especially one the size of mine."

"Don't you think that's a decision for me to make?"

"Ahh, yeah! I would think so, yes!"

"James, I've heard your speech before. But I've already made up my mind what I want! If you don't want me, that's okay! That's your decision! But, you know me! And you know I am capable of doing everything I said I would do, don't you?"

"Yeah! And that's why I'm turning your proposal down and making one of my own!" he said.

He reached in his side pocket and pulled out a ring case and sat it on the table. She thought it looked like a ring box, but she wasn't quite sure.

"Is that what I think it is?" she asked.

"Well, pick it up and see!" insisted Jenkins.

She slowly, yet nervously picked up the box and opened it. At first she just sat there with her mouth wide opened.

"Ohhhhhhhhhh!" she bellowed.

He took the box from her, sat it down on the table, and took the ring out. She held out her left hand and he put the ring on her ring finger.

"Menzie, I love you. I would consider it an honor to be your husband. Will you marry me?" he asked.

"Oh! Yes! Yes, I'll marry you!" shouted an excited wife to be as she reached her head across the table hugged and kissed him.

"Well, I like this way better!" said Jenkins.

"Me too! Oh my God! It's beautiful," uttered Ferguson as she held up her hand and looked at her ring.

"I'm glad you like it. Now, you can order anything on the menu you want!"

"There's nothing on the menu I want baby! I've got it all right here! Besides, I couldn't eat now if I wanted to!" she bellowed.

When she got back to her office she walked past the secretary, abruptly rushed by Sara's office, and without saying a word. She went inside her office and slammed the door behind her.

"I guess lunch must have gone bad!" cracked Sara to herself.

"Sara!" shouted Ferguson.

"Yes ma'am!"

"I need you in here, now!" she demanded.

Sara got up and rushed into the office. She could see that Ferguson was sitting at her desk, lip all poked out and her arms crossed.

"Is something wrong, boss?" asked Sara.

"Yes! And I want you to see it for yourself! Come around here!"

"You mean behind your desk?"

"Yes! Come! Now!"

"Couldn't you just tell me what it is from where you're sitting?"

"Are you afraid to come back here?"

"Yes ma'am! I don't think lunch went too well, and I'm scared you might bang my head over your desk."

"You come around here and see, or you're be sorry!" insisted Ferguson.

"Yes ma'am," said a reluctant Sara as she walked behind her boss' desk to see what it was she wanted to show her.

"See! Now you tell me what's wrong with this contract?"

"I can't see it! You've got your hand all over it."

"Look closer."

"Let's see in the...Is that an engagement ring?" asked an excited Sara Tillsberge.

Ferguson didn't say anything, just shook her head in the affirmative. Sara was slow in reacting, but when it hit her, she hugged her boss.

"Ahhhhhhhhhhhh! Congratulations!" she yelled.

"Thank You! You see lunch wasn't so bad after all!" she snickered.

"You were messing with me! Walking in here with your head hanging all down! Had me thinking you got lunch dumped in your lap."

"Yeah, well I didn't!"

"Gladis is going to have a fit when she finds out! Hey, let's mess with her!"

"Yeah, let's!" chuckled Ferguson as she picked up the phone.

"This is Gladis," said the voice on the other end of the telephone.

"Gladis, this is Menzie. I want to talk to you, it's about James Jenkins."

"Honey, I don't have anything to say to you! It's every woman for herself, and God for us all!"

"Well that's, very interesting. But I have the perfect solution to your problem concerning sex and...whatever!"

"Menzie the only solution you could have for my sex problem is to go on vacation and leave James Jenkins on my door step on the way to the airport."

"That's what I'm talking about, me going on vacation,"

"Um um!" Meet you where?"

"It's up to you! Your office, my office, the cafeteria, where ever!"

In lieu of Gladis being suspicious of Ferguson, she came to her office anyway. She walked right past Sara who was sitting at the secretary's desk, and went directly into her inner office. Little did she know, but Ferguson had asked Sara to listen in on the intercom.

"What do you want, Ferguson?" asked an abrupt Gladis Henley.

"I'm wondering if we could come to some arrangement concerning Dr. James Jenkins."

"Arrangement?"

"Yes, it seems the two of us what the same man, but for two entirely different reasons. I want to marry him, have his baby...Do you want to have his baby, Gladis?"

"I might, what's it to you?"

“I don't know. I thought you, just wanted to roll around in the hay with him a few times, then dump him like a hot potato, am I right?"

Sara, although listening to the conversation over the intercom, did all she could to compose herself.

"How do you know I don't want to marry him?" asked Gladis.

"Ahh, well, do you?"

"I might! Smart, good looking man like that, he could be a good catch for a woman like me."

"Ahh! I had no idea you were thinking about marrying him! That being the case, you may as well forget it!"

"Beg your pardon?" asked a surprised Gladis Henley.

"I said, if you were thinking about marrying him, forget it! As a matter of fact, forget about the rolling around in the hay thing too," chuckled Ferguson.

Gladis Henley started to laugh.

"What's so funny?"

"You are! Look heifer, his wife is dead! And that makes him fair game for the first one who serves him up right, if you know what I mean?"

"Serves him up, huh, I think you mean, give him some sex."

"Yeah that's what I mean."

"Well his wife might be dead! But you're already too late."

"Woman! What are you talking about?"

"This!" bellowed Ferguson as she held her ring finger up so Gladis could see her engagement ring.

"Yipessss!" she muttered as she stood there with her mouth wide opened.

At that point, Sara busted into the office. She wanted to personally see the expression on Henley's' face. Henley stood there, eyes and mouth wide open. She looked at Sara.

"She, she, she!"

"Yes, come on! She!" repeated Sara.

"She, she's--"

"She's engaged!" interrupted Sara.

"Engaged!" muttered Henley.

"It took her awhile to get there, but you will have to admit, she's got it!"

"How did you do that? I mean how did you, do that?" repeated Henley. "I mean, who are you engaged to?" she asked in a surprised tone of voice.

"Do I need to call the nurse's office, I think she's in shock!" joked Sara.

"Why you yellow, low life devilish, scheming, no good vamp! I hate you!" said Henley, who then turned and rushed towards the door. "And your little devilish helper too!" she muttered as she passed by Sara on her way out of the door.

"Well, I thought that went rather well, don't you devil helper?" mocked Ferguson.

"Why sho devil and the next time you have one of hell's fallen angels in here in your mist, tell Gabriel to call me!" mocked Sara.

The two of them leaned on Ferguson's desk and laughed.

Within a matter of hours, the entire firm had heard of the engagement of Jenkins to Menzie. To some it was a bit of a shock. To others, it wasn't because some of them believed the rumors circulating of them having an affair. However, most did approve because they were both well liked.

But then there was that little click of Gladis Henley and George Blackshere and the like, who just hated the idea. And they had no problems saying how they felt to Sara, who was standing inline ahead of them while having lunch in the cafeteria the next day.

"Why does he what to get married? Don't he know he could have more fun if he stays single?" asked Blackshere.

"That poor woman! She haven't been dead two years and that hussy is all over her man!" complained Henley.

"Yeah! I bet she is really turning over in her grave right now seeing all this going on!" interjected the co-worker.

"I wonder if that heifer knows witchcraft? She may have put a spell on him and his wife," suggested Henley. "She probably did something to made her die!" suggested the co-worker.

Sara Tillsberge laughed. "You people are crazy, you know that?"

"Put yourself in his wife's shoes! Would you want someone messing with your husband and you've been dead less than two years?" asked the co-worker.

"First of all, he doesn't have a wife. Secondly, the one he had is dead and her only concern from here on is which daisy to push up in the morning," said Sara as she moved up in the line.

"Listen to you! Haven't you no respect for the dead?" asked Henley as she filled her plate with food.

"And exactly what am I suppose to be respecting about dead folks? Surely not their right to be seen or heard," said Sara.

"The dead should be respected just like the living," said Blackshere

"Well, there are a lot of the living around here, I don't respect, present company included," insinuated Sara.

"If you don't like us, then why are you even talking with us?" asked Blackshere.

"Must be my sudden desire to sniff laughing gas," snickered Sara.

"You know you are not funny...Have you ever been to New York?" Henley abruptly asked Sara.

"Yes I have," responded Sara. "What about it?"

"I was wondering if you noticed all those comedians there with no jobs?"

"No I didn't. But I better get away from the likes of you before I get choked on the resentment and envy floating around your empty heads," mocked Sara as she paid for her food and left.

"You know, I can't stand her," commented Henley as she paid for her food.

"So, what's new?" you don't like anybody," chuckled the co-worker as she then paid for her food.

"Well, I like you."

"That's because we are the only friends you have," said Blackshere as he paid for his lunch.

Later the three were sitting and was just finishing up their lunch. But the conversation of Menzie Ferguson, just seemed to consume Gladis Henley.

"I know how she got him. She buttered up his kids," suggested Henley.

"I thought you said she used witchcraft," asked the co-worker.

"Maybe she did them both. You know, maybe she used witchcraft on the kids too," she said.

"I'm still trying to figure out what your problem is. Is it that you want him, or you don't like her?" asked the co-worker.

"It's that I don't want him any more and I never liked her," she responded.

"You know, I just realized how ridiculously that sounded," said Blackshere.

"Me too!" responded the co-worker. "And why are we wasting our time talking about the two of them? Nothing is going to change because we don't like it."

"Well, this is a free country and I can give my opinion about that husband, stealing hussy if I want to."

"You know, I think I better get away from you too. I don't want to throw up my lunch."

Both George Blackshere and the co-worker got up from the table, picked up their trays and started to walk away.

"I know if the shoe was on the other foot, I'd be mad!" shouted Henley.

When she stopped talking and took the time to look around, she could see nearly everybody around her was peering at her. She was so out done, without saying a word. She picked up her tray and hurried out of the cafeteria while attempting to hide her face behind her right shoulder.

The engagement of James Jenkins and Menzie Ferguson had not been an easy one. She had done all she could to prove to him her sincerity about wanting to get married. He on the other hand, still wasn't sure of anything and it was causing him to be up tight and unsure most of the time.

Because of their concerns, they had not told the Jenkins children about their engagement, neither had that told her parents. So again, she decided to take the lead and loosen him up a bit by asking him to take her out to dinner and dancing.

They dressed up and went to an affair being held at the Millennium Crown Hotel, which was known for its Friday night food and dance events. The moment the two of them entered the front door they were recognized by the hotel manager, Mr. Meyers.

"Dr. Jenkins, Miss Ferguson, welcome back," he said. "A table for two?" he asked.

"Yes, please," said Jenkins.

"Let me get you a nice table. Would you like to be close to the dance floor?"

"Yes, we would!" responded Ferguson.

"Charlie, you know Dr. Jenkins and Miss Ferguson?"

"Yes sir I do. Doctor, Miss Ferguson," he acknowledged.

"Put them at table fifteen," instructed Meyers.

Once they had been escorted to their table and sat down, they relaxed to the tone of Sam Cook's version of 'Sentimental Reasoning', which they could hear playing in the background.

"Are you hungry?" asked Jenkins.

"I love that old song, can we dance first?" she responded.

"Okay," he agreed.

The two of them reached the dance floor and started dancing. Ferguson didn't complaint, but he seemed to keep his distance when dancing with her. She pulled him closer more than once, but they would eventuality end up dancing with distance between them. Sitting back and observing all this was a handsome, well dressed Black man calmly smoking a cigarette. They danced a couple of dances, then sat down. Later, the handsome young man walked over to their table.

"May I have this dance?" he asked.

"I'm sorry, but we were about to order," responded Ferguson.

"You can dance if you want to," suggested Jenkins.

"But--"

"You heard what the man said," interrupted the man.

"You sure you don't mind?" she asked.

"No, go head," said James Jenkins.

Ferguson really didn't want to dance, but did so because Jenkins suggested it. He then sat and watched as the two of them danced. He could see the man danced differently from him. Whereas he kept her a comfortable distance away when they danced, the man seemed to enjoy smothering her and she didn't seem to mind as they danced and talked.

As a recording of Sam Cook's 'A Change Is Gonna Come', Jenkins pretended he didn't care how they were dancing, so he did all he could not to watch them while they were on the dance floor. She did glare over at him a couple of times, but assumed he didn't mind, so she didn't say anything. Once the dance had ended and they were back at the table, they didn't talk much until Ferguson initiated the conversation with him.

"I like coming here, don't you?" she asked.

"It's okay," responded Jenkins.

The tension made him nervous, so he excused himself claiming he needed to use the rest room, leaving her sitting and listening to a recording of Marvin Gaye's, 'Let's Get it On'. While he was gone, the man walked over to the table and sat down.

"Excuse me," he said. "My name is Andrew Gray," he continued.

"Oh, hi," she said as she humble the lyrics of the song in the background.

"I see you got rid of the old dude, or is he your father?"

"I'm sorry! Was that a rhetorical question?" she asked.

"Never mind...You know you are one beautiful young woman?"

"Yes, I know!" as she attempted to hear the music. "Look, you know I'm here with somebody!" she snapped.

"Good! Then that tells me he is not your husband. Here's my card, when you get rid of the old goat, give me a call."

Just as she took the man's card, Jenkins saw her. He stood there and watched as she read it. He then turned and walked back to the bench mounted to the floor across from the outside door of the rest room and sat down. He leaned his back up against the wall, crossed his arms and slouched down extending out his legs. His intent was to give her all the time she needed to do what ever it was she needed or wanted to do.

After reading the card, Ferguson looked in the direction of the rest room, but did not see James Jenkins.

"Should I expect a call from you?" asked Gray.

"Huh, oh! I'm sorry did you say something?"

"I asked if I should expect a call from you?" he repeated.

"Look, ah Mr. Gray--"

"Please, call me Andrew!" interrupted Gray.

"Okay, ah, Andrew. My guess is you are looking to get lucky tonight, you know, get yourself a little somin, somin. Well, I'm trying to rack up some points myself, and with the gentle I came in here with. You know, the old dude? Now, here's your card back and I need you to not be here when my friend gets back. He might get the wrong idea."

"So? What is he gonna do, start something?"

"No! But if you mess me up with him, I will! And I don't think you want to get that nice suit all messed up!"

"What are you mean or something?"

"Yeah! And I'm getting meaner by the minute!"

"Well, you don't know what you're missing, baby!" snapped an irate Gray.

"You know, you might be right. That's why I don't want you messing things up for me up in here! So, beat it!" she said in a harsh tone of voice.

Gray stood up and peered back at her. He took out a cigarette, took a lighter from his pocket and lit the cigarette. He took a puff, then blew the smoke in her direction.

"What is your name?" he asked.

"None ya!"

"Nonwa?"

"No! None ya! As in none of your business!"

"Man, you are one cold, sister!" snickered Gray.

"Yeah! Well if you don't mess things up for me, things could get a little hotter any moment now...Hit the road!" she snapped as she peered up at him.

"Tell you what, why don't you keep my card. You might change your mind!" said Gray in a smooth tone of voice.

"I can settle that right now," she said as she tore up his card and threw the pieces on the table. "Did that do it for you, Andrew?" she said as she peered at him with a set of perching, angry eyes.

"I think you're playing hard to get!"

"I'm not playing at all!" she snapped.

Finally Gray took the hint. He walked away angry, as Menzie looked towards the rest rooms again wondering why her date was taking so long. When she still didn't see him, she became a bit concerned. She then looked around until she saw Mr. Meyers and beckoned for him.

"May I help you, Miss Ferguson?" he asked.

"Yes, Dr. Jenkins went to the rest room. He seems to have gotten lost! Would you find him and tell him I'm starving, please!"

"Yes ma'am!" chuckled Meyers.

When he reached where the rest rooms were located, he could see Jenkins sitting with his head hanging down and walked over to him.

"Problem Dr. Jenkins?" he asked.

"Just a little female problem," snickered Jenkins. "You know what I mean?"

"Yes, but if you don't get back to your table and feed Miss Ferguson, your problem is going to get a lot worse," joked Meyers.

When Jenkins walked up to the table, he didn't say anything. Ferguson peered up at him and smiled.

"I thought you had left without feeding me!" she joked.

After dinner, Jenkins was driving her home. On the way, he didn't talk much. And when he wasn't talking, she was peering over at him and that was nearly all the way home. When they walked up to her apartment door, they stopped, while she unlocked the door.

"Would you like to come in for a while?" she asked.

"No, I better let you get some sleep," he responded. "Good night!"

He turned and walked several steps towards the elevator. She reached for him grabbing him by the arm.

"James wait! What's wrong?" she asked.

"Nothing!"

"Okay, now wait a minute! When I did that to you, you didn't like it! I promised I would never do that again. Now, don't do to me! Tell me what's wrong!"

"Menzie, I know we talked about getting married. But ahh, you really don't have to if you don't want to."

"What makes you think I don't want to?"

"It's not that! You are a very pretty, young woman and I know men are attracted to you. If you don't want any strings attached to you, I understand."

At first Ferguson didn't respond to what he had to say. See peered at him for several seconds, then walked closer to him. She stood there looking into his deep, dark brown eyes and smiled.

"James, what are you talking about?"

"I'm just saying, I don't want you not talking to other men because you have made a promised to me."

"Oh, I see...you saw that guy talking to me tonight, didn't you?"

"Ahh, yes I did!" snapped Jenkins.

"Were you jealous!"

"No! It's not like that! Well, maybe I was, a little!" snickered Jenkins.

"So, why didn't you come back to the table and tell that jerk to get lost?"

"Besides I don't blame guys from hitting on you! I mean, look at you. You are more than a desirable woman to any man."

"So, am I the desirable woman you want?"

"Menzie, you're missing my point!"

"I got your point! Answer my question!" she insisted.

"You know you are! But, I also realize you are your own woman!"

"I am your woman! At least I want to be!"

"I hear you. But for a guy like me--." sighed the frustrated father of five. "Well, I don't deserve a women like you. Look at all the baggage I've got."

"James, we've already had this conversation. Let me tell you something. Do you know how hard it is for a woman like me to even get a decent date? It's hard because men fear pretty women. If a woman has principles and morals, it's even worse. Now if a man does ask her out, more then likely he wants sex. When they are rejected, they can justify it by saying we think we are too good for them. Any woman can lower her standard. And when she does, she is almost always the one who ends up disappointed and hurt. So woman like me become careful, sometimes too careful. But it isn't everyday a woman can finds the one man who can make her heart sing with passion, glow with love."

"Are you saying I do that to you?"

"Man, you don't know how my heart flutters when you mention my name. How my very soul becomes enchanted when ever I look into your eyes. How I think of you everyday and dream of you every night. When I think of being with you, I smile. When I dare have the thought of not having you, I cry. It is then I merely existence only to see your face the next day, hear your voice, if only to hear you say my name," she whispered.

"Hearing you say those words, sounds like a song," he uttered.

"That's because of the song I'm hearing in my heart right now."

"Those are beautiful words...I wish I had said them to you."

"What difference does it make, as long as they are said?"

"Are you sure you mean them? I mean are you absolutely sure you mean them?"

"You know what your problem is? You think too much! Now, I want you to hug me, kiss me. Show me those loving words which are in your heart, that you can not put into words. And please, don't handle me like I'm made out of glass. Hold me like I'm made of passion!" she erotically uttered.

Jenkins grabbed her around her waist and pulled her close to him. This was the second time she was this close that she could feel him. At first he just held her there, peering into her intoxicating eyes. He smiled and then gently kissed her, compassionately. She closed her eyes the passion between them was finally being released. How they were close and as she was locked in his embrace, she slowly raised her arms until she could hug him around his neck.

"Mmmmmmmmm," she moaned as he stuck his tongue in her mouth.

It was only the second time they had really kissed, but this was the first time he seemed to really show compassionate and put his heart into it. And they were both feeling it, right then and now. And that wasn't all she felt and for the second time. And what she felt was, what she wanted to feel, him!

First, her eyes popped wide opened, as her body trembled from her losing total control of her breathing. In fact, feeling every thing caused her to abruptly end the most wonderful kiss she had ever felt.

"Wow!" she uttered as she struggle to gain her breath.

"I'm sorry! Was I--?"

"No! That was fine! But you better go! Call me tomorrow."

"Okay! Good night!" said Jenkins as he went for a second kiss.

"I think that's enough for tonight! Good night, James!" she snickered.

She opened the door to her apartment, slowly stepped inside, throw him a final good night kiss and quickly closed the door. Once inside, she stood there for several seconds with her hands over her breasts and attempting to catch her breath.

"I don't believe this," she uttered in disbelief.

Once she had control of her breathing, she realized something. Her body was not only uncontrollable on fire, she could feel it release itself.

"Ohhhhhhhhhh!" she moaned. "Menzie, this is going to be a short engagement," she uttered.

She rushed towards her shower, leaving a trail of her clothes behind her. Once in the shower, the warm water felt good.

"Mmmmmmmmmm," she moaned as the warm water ran down her face, then trickled down her well developed breast and down onto the rest of her body.

She couldn't help but chuckle to herself when she realized he had paid her back for the kiss she had given him when she first asked him to marry her. Later as she lied in her bed, the phone rang. When she picked it up, it was he.

"Hi!" he said.

"Hi!" she reciprocated.

"I just called to tell you I had a wonderful time tonight."

"So did I."

"Menzie, I love you! I love you very much!"

"I sure hope so. If not, my passion for you is really being wasted."

"Well, I do. I think I've been trying to say that all along! It's just been so hard to say to you what I really feel."

"Yes, I know...James, it's okay that you loved Marian. She was your wife and mother of your children. She was a wonderful person and I admired and respected her very much."

"I know you did."

"And I also know you were a close family and I know I've got my work cut out for me with the children. All I'm asking for is a chance, a fair chance to show you how much I sincerely want you and your children."

"You know, you are very special woman and I feel lucky to have you."

"You were lucky to have Marian, please know that. But once we are married, the longer we stay married, the luckier you'll be, trust me."

"Well, I just wanted to talk to you before I went to bed."

"I understand more than you know, Good night sweetheart!"

"Good night."

"And James! I do love you and with all my heart!"

She hung up the phone and just lied there. She pulled the covers up over her breasts and folded her hands across her stomach. A smile came over her face as she thought about her new life, with a man she never expected to be with. She turned over on her side and drifted off to sleep a woman now contented for the first time in her life.

CHAPTER TEN

TRIPLE FAMILY APPROVALS

After being engaged for several weeks, it was time to go to the families and seek their approval. The major problem was getting the Jenkins children to accept Ferguson in the role of a parent and her parents in accepting a parent with five kids and a dead wife for a son in law.

It was just before the Easter of 1976. Marian Jenkins had been dead for over two years. James Jenkins and she had agreed it was time to get married, which also meant going to the families.

One Friday morning, Jenkins had called home and told his children when he got there he wanted to have a family meeting and that because he had something to discuss with them. Being smart children, they discussed the meeting among themselves prior to the family meeting.

"Dad wants to have a family meeting, are we in trouble?" asked Floreese.

"I don't think so. He said Miss Menzie was going to be here!" said Vena.

"How can it be a family meeting, if she going to be here?" asked Javey

"I think he's going to tell us he's going to marry her," responded Vena. "Otherwise, why would he want to talk to us with her here."

"You don't know that for a fact!" said Myron.

"Well, what do you think he wants to talk about, Marcus?" asked Javey.

"I agree with Vena. I think Dad is going to jump the bloom," responded Marcus.

"Why would they want to get married anyway?" asked Javey

"When you get a little older, I'll explain it to you!" insinuated Marcus. "Okay, let's say he is and he ask us what we think. What do we say?" he asked.

"I like Miss Ferguson," interjected Javey.

"I like her too!" insisted Vena. "And she is very nice!"

"Ahh, you only saying that because you have her autograph twice and she been giving you free violin lessons," reminded Javey.

"Here's the deal. Dad isn't getting any younger and he needs somebody to be with, if you know what I mean?" asked Marcus.

"Why does he need somebody? He's got us!" inserted Floreese.

"Bless you my innocent child!" mocked Vena.

"What is that suppose to mean?" asked Floreese.

"Nothing! She trying to be funny," suggested Marcus. "Now, if Dad is going to ask us if it's okay to marry Miss. Ferguson, what do we say?"

"I just don't think she would make a good mother," said Javey.

"I thought you just said you liked her?" asked Marcus.

"I do, but what does that have to do with her being a good mother?"

"Because she's pretty," said Myron.

"It takes more than good looks to be a good mother," said Javey.

"We're forgetting one thing. If Dad wants to talk to us about marrying her, then they are probably already engaged," said Marcus.

"How do you know that?" asked Javey.

"I'm guessing they are."

"Well, I know they are," interjected Vena.

"And just how do you know for sure?" asked Myron.

"Every since she's been giving me violin lessons, she has been wearing this big ring on her finger. My guess is, Dad gave it to her," she surmised.

"Well, then that seals it," said Marcus. "If Dad has made up his mind he wants to marry her, I don't think we should interfere with that," he added.

"I think we should give them our blessing, get on their good side," said Vena.

"Okay, we have to have a vote. If Dad is going to tell us he is going to marry Miss Ferguson, all in favor raise your right hand," requested Marcus.

Every body raised their right hands but Floreese who held out.

"Why aren't you voting?" asked Marcus.

"I don't want a new mamma!" she responded.

"Okay, then don't look at it as you getting a new mamma. Look at it as Dad getting a new wife," suggested Vena.

"Oh, that's different!" bellowed Floreese as she raised her right hand.

Several minutes later, the front door bell rang. Vena opened the door and when she saw it was Miss Ferguson, she let her in and led her to the family room.

"Is your father here yet?" she asked.

"No! But he just called and told us he was running late. Have a seat."

"Okay!" said Ferguson as she sat down on the couch.

She was surprised when Vena left the room, leaving her alone, but it wasn't for long. She had gone to get the rest of her bothers and sister. They walked into the family room and surrounded Ferguson, who had no ideal what was going on. Vena had a tray of chocolate chip cookies she had baked.

"Oh, hi guys!" she bellowed. "What's up?" she asked.

"Would you like to have a cookie?" asked Vena. "I baked them."

"Don't find if I do. They smell good," said Ferguson as she helped herself to a cookie.

"We want to talk to you," said Myron.

"Okay, what about?" asked Ferguson as she took a bit out of the cookie.

"Are you getting ready to marry our father?" asked Javey.

"Shouldn't we wait for your father to come home?" asked Ferguson.

"What we have to say, we don't need him," said Marcus.

"So, this is about the two of you getting hitched, huh?" asked Javey.

"Hitched, that works, I guess!" chuckled Ferguson as she chewed.

"Will we be staying together as a family?" asked Myron.

"Why yes, we will," responded Ferguson as she looked from one child to the next. "I wouldn't have it any other way."

"Are you planning on doing it soon?" asked Marcus.

"Doing what?" asked Ferguson in an attempt to delay them from talking.

"Stay focus, Miss Ferguson, we're talking about you marrying our father and doing it soon," insisted Vena in a serious, yet firm tone of voice.

"Yes ma'am," snickered Ferguson. "Ahh, yes, if that's okay with you."

"How about in June!" asked Vena.

"I've, always wanted to be a June bride!" confessed Ferguson.

"Can we be in the wedding?" asked Myron.

"I'll insist on it!" insured Ferguson.

"Will you still help Vena with her violin lessons?" asked Floreese.

"Of course she will, silly," interjected Vena.

"Well, we think it's a good idea, you two getting married and all," said Marcus.

"Oh, really!" reacted a surprised Menzie Ferguson.

"Really!"

"Well, thank you...I think!" she uttered.

"Now, we have to figure out what to call you. You do understand if we don't call you mother right away, don't you?" asked Marcus.

"Ahh, yes! I do!"

"Good...Let's see...How about Mama Menzie?"

"I don't like that! Sounds too Italian!" said Vena.

"Yeah, it sounds like you're ordering pizza!" interjected Myron.

Ferguson chuckled to see the children having a sense of humor about the entire thing.

"How about Miss Ferguson?" asked Myron.

"If she marries Dad, that won't be her name anymore stupid!" retorted Marcus.

"Oh yeah! You're right!" said Myron. "And it can't be Miss Menzie, either. Can it?"

None of the children responded to the remark made by Myron. They just all peered over at him. Ferguson sat there listening to the children and did all she could to keep from busting out in laughter.

"Why don't we ask her what she wants to be called?" asked Vena.

"That's not a bad idea!" said Marcus. "What do you want us to call you?"

"Well, let's start off with Miss Menzie. The better you get to know me, I am sure you will call me whatever you feel in your heart," she suggested.

"Okay! Then welcome to the family, Miss Menzie!" said Marcus.

He walked over and kissed her on the jaw, followed by Vena. Then the rest of the children followed her, with Floreese barely kissing her and quickly running out of the room.

Several minutes later, Dr. James Jenkins rushed into the front door. When he reached the family room, he could see Menzie Ferguson sitting there with a handkerchief up to her nose.

"Sorry I'm late. I'll get the children," he said to her as he turned to call his children.

"James, don't," she bellowed.

"What?" asked Jenkins as he turned and walked over to where she was. "What's the matter with you?" he asked.

"We've already had our talk!" she sobbed.

"You mean you've talked to the children without me?"

"No, it was more like they talked to me," she sighted as she wiped the tears from her eyes then blew her nose. "They already knew what we were going to talk to them about. Apparently, they got together before I got here. They had everything already worked out. Well, they did ask me what they should call me!" she chuckled as she tapped the tears from her eyes.

"Exactly what are you saying?" he asked as he sat down beside her.

"I'm saying, they think it's a good ideaaaaaaa!" she cried.

"Well, if they thought it was a good idea, why are you crying?"

"You men! You don't know anythingggg, ahhhhhhhh!" she cried.

She cried as she leaned over on Jenkins' chest as he sat there with this complex look on his face.

Later that night, she called her folks in Atlanta to tell them the good news. It was her sister, Tomaia Ferguson, who answered the phone.

"Hello!" she said.

"Tomaia, this is Menzie."

"Oh hi Menz," she said.

"How's school coming along?"

"You know me, just waiting for Spring Break."

"Didn't you just come off Christmas break?"

"Yeah! But you know me--."

"I know, just waiting for Spring break!" chuckled Ferguson. "Look, is Mom and Dad home?"

"Which do you want to talk to, Mom or Dad?"

"I want them both on the phone, silly!" chuckled Menzie.

Tomaia wouldn't get off the phone in the kitchen. So, both of her parents went to the phone in living room, where both of them listened in on the same phone.

"Okay Menz I've got Mom and Dad on the phone," she said.

"Hello Menzie, your mother and I are on the phone together. Tomaia said you had something you wanted to tell us!"

"Yes, I wanted to tell all of you that I'm getting married!"

"Wait! I didn't hear you right Menzie. Did you say you were getting married?" asked Pat Ferguson.

"Yes, you heard right! I am engaged."

"Hey, way to go Menz!" yelled Tomaia.

"Well, that's wonderful!" said Mr. Ferguson.

"Oh Menzie! I am so happy for you! Is he a nice man?" asked Mrs. Ferguson.

"What kind of question is that? Is he a nice man? Of course he's nice man, right Menzie?" asked her father.

"Yes sir! He's a very nice man," expressed Ferguson to her father.

"You see! He's a nice man! My daughter wouldn't marry anything but the best, right baby?"

"Right Daddy!"

"Okay, well, tell us all you can about him!" insisted Mrs. Ferguson.

"He's one of the executives where I work. He has a Ph.D in Management, he's very smart and very handsome."

"Sounds good! Almost too good!" bellowed Thomas Ferguson. "What's the rest of it?" asked a suspicious Mr. Ferguson.

"Well, he's forty-five years old, he's--"

"Forty-five years old?" interrupted Mr. Ferguson.

"Yes Daddy, he's forty-five."

"You couldn't find a younger man, this one is old enough to be your father!"

"Daddy, you're my father and you're almost sixty!"

"You know what I mean!"

"No I don't! I'm thirty. In order for him to be my father, he would have had to have been a father at fifteen!"

"Hush Thomas! I'm eleven years younger than you!" interjected Mrs. Ferguson.

"Forty-five, that's not so bad!" snickered Tomaia.

"Maybe Tomaia shouldn't be listening to this conversation!" insisted Mr. Ferguson.

"Why? Are you going to try and give her your lesson on sex?" asked Tomaia.

"What if I am?"

"I've already heard it! And if what you told me is all you know about sex, Menzie probably knows more about sex than you."

"That did it! Hang up young lady!" shouted Mr. Ferguson.

"Now Thomas, try and remember your blood pressure!" said Mrs. Ferguson.

"Yeah Dad, cool it!" joked Tomaia.

"Cool it! Did she say, cool it?"

"Daddy, you calm down or I'm going to hang up!" insisted Menzie.

"Okay! Okay! I'm calm as a cucumber!" shouted Ferguson.

"Menzie, this is your night to share your news with us. Is there anything else you want to tell us about this man?" asked Pat Ferguson.

"Well...Yes. He's a widower," she said.

"You mean he has a dead wife?"

"Yes Mamma! And before you ask me if he has children, I'll answer that for you. He has five!"

Ms. Ferguson fainted as she fell in Mr. Ferguson's lap, who was still holding the phone to his ear. Ferguson thought she heard something strange, but wasn't quite sure what it was she had heard.

"Dad, did something happen to Mamma?"

"Yes, she fainted! I'm wanting to, but I can't work myself up enough!"

"Oh really? Well, don't bother. You take care of your wife!" said Ferguson as she quickly slammed down the phone.

Later that night, Mrs. Ferguson was lying on her bed with a hot water bottle draped across her forehead. Mr. Ferguson pasted back and forth, while fussing as he did so.

"What is wrong with that daughter of yours? She calls here, she tells us she getting married! Then she tells us she's marrying a man with a dead wife and five kids! That girl was always a little strange."

"Please Thomas! You're making it sound like she's doing something wrong!"

"I'm making it sound like she doing something wrong? Ha!"

"So she's marrying a man who has sowed his oaks a bit."

"If he has five kids, he's done more than sowed his oaks, he's harvesting an entire wheat field!" fussed Mr. Ferguson

Pat Ferguson chuckled a bit. "Well, Thomas it's like you said, she was always a little strange. Remember when she found that half dead bird? She bought it home and tried to nurse it back to health. She stayed up late that entire trying to do so."

"Yeah, she really thought she was going to make it well, didn't she?"

"Yes, remember how she cried when it died anyway?"

"Yeah! I remember that! And I thought she was a little strange then too, "said Ferguson as he continued to walk one way then the other.

"Well, she says she going to marry him, what can we do about it? You know how she can be sometimes when she makes up her mind."

"Yeah! She can be stubborn as a mule, that one!"

"I wonder where she's gets it?" insinuated Pat Ferguson.

"Now, Patricia! This is no time to make sarcasm. What are we going to do?"

"Wait for her to call here and tell us she's going to bring him down here for us to meet and then she'll demand we like him or else!"

"Or else what?"

"Or else, she'll marry him anyway and not invite us to the wedding!"

"Ohhhhhhhh! Now that's just down right ornery!" snapped Mr. Ferguson.

"She did what?" asked Sara once Ferguson told her of the telephone conversation she had with her parents the night before.

"She fainted!" snapped Ferguson as she pranced back and forth in her office. "And Daddy didn't make things any better. He said he would have fainted, but he couldn't get worked up enough! If I had been there, he wouldn't have had to worry about working up to it. I would have hit him over the head with a broom!" she said as she continued to prance the floor.

Sara chuckled. "That was funny!"

"Well, I didn't think so!"

"It was! And if you wasn't so mad, you would think so too!" snickered Sara "Okay, boss! You are known for coming up with solutions. How are you going to handle this one?"

"Oh, I don't have a problem! I'm going to marry James, whether they like it or not!"

"Come on! You know you don't mean that!"

Ferguson didn't respond to Sara's statement. Instead she walked behind her desk sat down, prompted her elbows on her desk then rested her chin in the palms of her hands.

"You know, you could really fight them on this if you wanted to!" hinted Sara.

"I don't see why I have to fight them over a decision I've made about my life. After all, I am a woman, full grown!" she shouted.

"Maybe you won't have to. But of course if you do what I'm thinking, it could be considered dirty pool!"

"When have you ever been concerned about doing anything dirty?"

"Never, but we're not talking about me. We're talking about you."

"Sara, what are you talking about?"

"I'm talking about bringing in the reserves!"

"What reserves?"

"Vena, Marcus, Javey, Myron and Floreese."

"The Kids? How can they help me out in this situation?"

"Take them to Atlanta to fight for you."

"Oh no! That would be low down, dirty. Why that's deceitful, not to mention under handed! I mean how would it look, me using the kids to fight my battles for me?"

"Well! You could look at it as them fighting for their own survival."

"No! No! That's out of the question! I will not stump that low. Using the kids."

"You're going to do what?" asked Mr. Ferguson as he yelled into the phone.

"I'm coming down to Atlanta during Spring Break and I'm bring James and his kids with me."

"Why would you want to do that?"

"Because, I want you to meet my family to be. Isn't that wonderful?"

"Yeah! I can hardly wait!" insinuated Mr. Ferguson.

"Good! Now Daddy, while the kids are there, I want you to behave yourself!"

"I'll do my best. Goodbye, " said Mr. Ferguson as he hung up the phone.

"Did I understand, Menzie is coming here and bringing those five kids?"

"Yes, you understood right! And I don't think it's a good idea!"

"Well, why didn't you tell her that when you had her on the phone?"

"I wanted to, but I was in too much of a shock!"

"You seem calm enough now. Call her back and tell her you don't think it's a good idea."

"I don't think I should do that!" snapped Mr. Ferguson.

"Why not?"

"Because you know your daughter. If I do that she will run out and marry this man tonight, just for spite," he suggested. "Strange that one."

The Ferguson family used the next two weeks getting their minds ready for tolerating the five Jenkins children. However, on the very day they were to arrive in Atlanta, they received a phone call that turned out to be more disturbing news.

"Hell-o, this is Pat."

"Pat how are you?" said the voice on the other end of the phone.

"Who is this?"

"Tillie."

"Aunt Tillie! This you?"

"Yes! It is so nice to hear your voice!" said an excited Aunt Tillie.

"I heard you were over seas somewhere!"

"I was, but now I'm back in the states and on my way there."

"There?"

"Yes, Atlanta."

"Why are you coming to Atlanta?"

"To see you, of course!"

"Me?"

"Yes, you, the family."

"Oh! Tillie, that's not a good idea!"

"Why?"

"Menzie coming here and she's--"

"I think that's great!" interrupted Tillie. "I saw her in a movies while I was in Germany. Just seeing my niece on the big scene, I almost died from excitement."

"Right now, that's not a bad idea," uttered Mrs. Ferguson.

"What was that?"

"I was talking to Thomas and he thinks that a good idea."

"What's a good idea?" asked Mr. Ferguson.

"Aunt Tillie is coming here. And I told her you thought it was a good idea," said Mrs. Ferguson as she covered the phone with her hand so Tillie couldn't hear her.

"I didn't say that!" bellowed Mr. Ferguson

"Shhhh," hissed Mrs. Ferguson in order to quiet her husband.

"At any rate, I'm looking forward to meeting our movie star in person," said an excited Tillie. "Look! I'll see you when I get there, bye, bye."

"Shoot!" bellowed Pat Ferguson as she abruptly hung up the phone.

"Now you went and done it!" bellowed Mr. Ferguson when he saw his wife slammed down the phone.

"If I had any guts, I would have told her to shut her mouth and listen for a change. Then I would have had the guts to tell her not to come here," confessed Pat Ferguson.

"If you had any guts, you would have put her out of her misery the first day you laid eyes on her."

"Oh God! Tillie and Menzie here under the same roof!" hysterically chuckled Mrs. Ferguson.

"Is that your way of laughing instead of crying?" asked Mr. Ferguson.

"No, I would rather faint, but that won't change anything."

"Tillie, why do think that old, devilish heifer is really coming here?"

"Probably to make our lives a living hell."

"Don't you mean my life? Besides, I thought she was in Europe?"

"Well, she was, but now she's on her way here."

"They probably kicked her butt out of Europe for impersonating a woman," chuckled Mr. Ferguson

"Maybe I should call Menzie and ask her not to come."

"Oh no, don't do that. Menzie will raise more hell than the devil. Tillie is the one who should be told she can't come here!" snapped Mr. Ferguson.

"Well, go out on the highway and catch up to her and tell her so. I tried to tell her about Menzie and the kids coming here, but I couldn't get a word in edgewise."

"That's what concerns me, that edgewise she keeps going on. Her always criticizing me and calling me names. Belittling me making me feel useless. And that's on one of her good days."

"I'm worried about how she will treat those kids once she meets them."

"I'd be more concerned about the impression she will leave on those kids!"

"Oh God, what are we going to do about Tillie?"

"Now that's a thought. Ask God to do something to Tillie," joked Mr. Ferguson.

"This in no time to be joking."

"Who said I was joking."

Late that afternoon, a full size van pulled up to the front of the Ferguson's home. Menzie Ferguson got out, opened the door as the Jenkins children piled out, one by one. As they stood on the sidewalk, James Jenkins was not with them.

"They're here!" shouted Tomaia Ferguson as she ran out of the front door to meet them.

"Menzie," she bellowed as she hugged her older sister.

"Hi pee wee," said Menzie.

"Don't call me that in front of the kids," whispered Tomaia in her sister's ear.

"Opps, sorry," uttered Menzie.

Mr. and Mrs. Ferguson rushed out of the house, but stood on the porch as Menzie and the Jenkins children approached them. When they reached the porch, Menzie introduced them.

"Chilren, this is my Mother Mrs. Ferguson, that's my Father Mr. Ferguson. Mom, Dad, this is Vena, the oldest child."

"Please to meet you," she said.

"This young man is Marcus."

"Good afternoon," he said.

"This is Javey," who didn't say anything but waved instead.

"This is Myron."

"Hi," he said.

"And this is the baby girl, Floreese.

"I can curtsy," she said.

"You can?" asked Mrs. Ferguson.

"Yes, you want to see?"

"Why, yes."

Floreese quickly did her rendition of a quick curtsy, much to the delight of Mrs. Ferguson, who then peered over at her husband, then back to the children.

"My, what polite children and good looking too...And the little on is so precious," sighed Pat.

"You have no idea," sighed Menzie as she proudly peered over to the children.

As they stood on the porch getting acquainted, a late model sedan drove up and parked behind the van.

"That couldn't be her already!" bellowed Mr. Ferguson.

"That couldn't be who already?" asked Menzie as she turned and looked towards the sedan.

"That's Aunt Tillie!" said Tomaia Ferguson.

"That's Aunt Tillie? You didn't tell me she was coming here."

"She just called here a few hours ago and told us she was on her way here. I had no idea she was driving her Batmobile here in a hurry!" insinuated Mr. Ferguson.

"You know how she is? Our concern is now she's going to treat the kids!" expressed Mrs. Ferguson.

"Yeah, I know how she is alright! But you better keep her under control or she's going to have me to deal with me while she's here!" snapped Menzie.

"Oh brother! I can see there's going to be trouble!" sighed Mr. Ferguson.

"Too bad you don't have a bat cage to lock her in while she's here."

By the time Tillie was getting out of her car, the children were standing on the front pouch peering at her. She was dressed in men's clothes, and had a case of beer in her hands.

"I see she brought her supply of blood along with her," commented Menzie.

"Good, then maybe she won't have to bite me in the back while she's here," snickered Mr. Ferguson.

He comment got a chuckle from the children. Tillie then stepped up onto the porch while looking at the five children over her gold rim glasses. But it was what she said, which formed their opinion of her and put them on their defensive.

"Oh my!" she said the moment she laid her eyes on the five children. "What do we have here, brats from the neighborhood?" she asked.

"Not quite!" said Pat Ferguson. "We'll explain later," she said as she quickly escorted her aunt into the house with Menzie following close behind.

"Well, tell them to go home! I don't want any mice hanging around me all day!"

The children weren't fond of the reception they received from her. Once she was inside the house and out of their sight, they plotted on how to handle her.

"Who is that?" asked Myron.

"That's Aunt Tillie. She like having a corn on your toe!" insinuated Tomaia.

"I bet she's going to be trouble for us!" said Marcus.

"She might! But you just have to remember her bark is worse then her bite!"

"Well, I don't like her!" bellowed Floreese.

"Don't worry about it too much, it seems she don't care for us either!" said Vena.

"Tillie don't like anybody. I feel sorry for Dad. She'll spend most of her time here picking on him like she always does!" said Tomaia.

"Okay, but she better not make us mad. We can play a pretty good game of hard ball if that's what she wants!" insisted Marcus.

"Well, use your best pitch! She's going to try you, and that's for sure!"

Later, Tillie was sitting at the kitchen table eating a sandwich and drinking a can of beer. Floreese sat across from her, leaned on the table, resting her chin in the palms of her hands and starring at her.

"May I help you, little girl?" asked Tillie in a harsh but proper tone of voice.

"No! I'm just waiting for you to bark."

"What? What, you think I'm a dog or something?"

"Yes!"

"And why is that?"

"Because Tomaia said your bark was worse then your bit!"

"Have you ever had cold beer poured down your back?"

"No!"

"Well, if you don't get away from here, you will!" snapped Tillie.

Floreese got up from the table and passed by Tillie with her lip poked out, and with an angry look on her face.

"You're mean, just like people say!" she bellowed once she was past her.

"Well Merry Christmas to you too!" uttered a sarcastic Tillie.

But Floreese didn't respond to her and kept walking and looking back at her with a look of contempt on her face.

Later at the dinner table, it became obvious to Tillie that the Jenkins children were staying with the Ferguson family much longer then she had hoped. It was at that point that her curiosity got the best of her.

"My, you boys have a real hardy appetite. Don't your mother fix you food at home?"

"Our mother is in heaven!" snapped Floreese.

"Oh, I see!" said Tillie.

"Aunt Tillie, Mom didn't mention to you about the kids you see here," said Menzie.

"Obviously! I thought they would have gone home by now!"

"They came here with me from St. Louis."

"Why, you need to have chaperones when you travel?" snickered Tillie.

Tillie's remark was suppose to have been a joke, but no one sitting at the table snacked as much as a smile. Tillie looked from one person to the next. When none responded to her joke, she cleared her throat. But she did put Menzie on the defensive.

"That was funny Aunt Tillie," she said in a sarcastic tone of voice "I see you are just as corny as you were when you fell through the floor of the out house when you were a teenager!" snapped Menzie.

"I did no such thing! And who told you that?"

"Oh, I'm sorry that was what I hoped would happen to you," snickered Menzie, which also got her a chuckled from the rest of those sitting at the table.

"And I see you and your little sister have the manners of a blind cat. I didn't appreciate your her telling these brats, I was a dog!" argued Tillie.

"I never told them you were a dog!" defended Tomaia. "But now that you mentioned it, you--"

"Tomaia!" interrupted Mrs. Ferguson.

"Never mind that!" insisted Menzie. "The point is I'm marrying their father."

"You're marrying a man who has five kids? Why in the world would you do that?"

"I don't need to explain to a woman like you, why I'm doing anything!"

"Well Pat, what do you think of your precious little girl marrying a man with five kids?"

"Well I--"

"Menzie is a woman full grown! That makes her old enough to make her own decisions!" interrupted Mr. Ferguson.

"Who asked you, you old goat!" yelled Tillie.

"Oh no, don't go there with my Daddy. If you have something to say, you say it to me, right now, right here!" bellowed Menzie.

"I don't know why any woman in her right mind, would marry a man who has five kids," said Tillie.

"That's because you've never been in your right mind," snapped Menzie.

"Well, you're be out of what little mind you have left before they are through with you," reacted Tillie.

"Excuse me!" shouted Marcus. "We'll excuse ourselves while you adult people discuss us!"

He got up from the table and waited for the others to do the same. Once they were all up, they started to leave the room.

"Now see what you've done?" asked Mr. Ferguson.

"If you ask me, I just helped you save on your food bill," chuckled Tillie.

But when the children reached the doorway, those persons sitting at the table, watched Myron rushed back to the table, picked up two pieces of bread, laid them on the table, picked up a poke chop, laid it on the bread and made himself a sandwich.

"I'm ahh, still hungry!" he uttered as he then slowly walked out of the dinning room eating his sandwich.

"Way to go Aunt Tillie, you've hurt their feeling!" uttered Tomaia as she got up from the table and left.

"You keep them away from me, or I'll hurt more than their feeling!" shouted Tillie.

"And what is that suppose to mean?" asked an angry Menzie Ferguson.

The children listened as the argument between Tillie and Menzie went on for sometime. Occasionally, Mrs. Ferguson would try to get a word in but never could. Since Mr. Ferguson was called an old goat and in essence told to shut up, he continued to eat while the others argued among themselves.

On the other hand, Tillie had managed to declared war against Menzie and the Jenkins children. Instead of going directly for her, they made an alliance in the plot to go after her. And it didn't take her long to realize just how hostile they could be when provoked. It all started with Vena and Marcus approaching Mr. Ferguson, who was sitting in his favorite chair, reading the daily news.

"Mr. Ferguson, you got a minute?" asked Marcus.

"Sure, what can I do for you?" he asked as he folded up his paper and laid in on his lap.

"It's about Miss Tillie."

"Look, don't take what she says seriously," he suggested.

"But when she talked nasty to you, you stop talking back to her, why is that?" pointed out Vena.

"Yeah, you're right. I just found it's best not to say too much to her."

"And what is she, a man or a woman?" asked Marcus.

"I would say she's a cross between an old dead cow and a musty skunk," chuckled Mr. Ferguson.

"Yeah, I can smell her breath," said Vena.

"I don't see how you can with all that beer she drinks," said Marcus.

"That's why she drinks deer, to hide the fact that she don't brush her teeth," chuckled Mr. Ferguson.

"Well, my father taught us to respect our elders, don't I would tell her a thing or two," said Vena.

"I get the feeling that won't do much good in her case," said Ferguson.

"That's because she doesn't show you respect. She talks about you, and in your own house. Aren't you the man of this house?" asked Myron.

"Yes, yes I am."

"Then don't let her disrespect you in your won house."

"Huh, you've got a good point there...What would you do if you were me?" asked Mr. Ferguson.

"Put her in her place once and for all!" snapped Marcus.

"Want us to show you how?" asked Vena.

"But wouldn't that be kind of during the same thing she doing," asked Ferguson.

"You wanna know what else our father taught us?"

"Now, so far he's batting a hundred with me."

"You reap what you sow."

"Yeah, my father taught me that too," confirmed Ferguson.

"Tell you what, let us set her up for you. When she starts to get out of line again, you put her in her place," insisted Marcus.

"You know what? You've got a deal," said Mr. Ferguson as he held out his hand to shake on it. Both of them shook hands with him and the Aunt Tillie lesson was in full swing.

It kicked off that Friday night, when Tillie went out and stayed out until the early morning hours. During the day she wanted to sleep, but the Jenkins children and Tomaia played video, so it was hard for her to do so. Myron passed by the family room located in the basement, only to see her sitting and leaning back in a lounge chair with her eyes covered with a blindfold. He could have passed her by, but could not pass up the opportunity to needle her. He walked into the family room and up to her and tapped on the chair. At first she pretended she didn't hear him, so he tapped again. This time she lifted up her left hand and raised the left side of the blind fold so that she could see him.

"What do you want?" she snapped.

"I was just wondering if you were going to sleep all day?" he asked.

"What if I do? What's it to you?"

"My father said your night rest in the best rest for you."

"Well, he's not my father. Besides I like sleeping during the day."

"I saw this movie once and it said bats and vampires sleep during the day. Which one are you, a vampire or a old bat?" he asked.

"Your mama!" snapped Tillie.

"No, my mama is an angel, not an old bat like you," he retorted then quickly walked away from her.

By now she was good and mad. But as if she hadn't had enough, she later had an altercation with Marcus Jenkins as he walked in on her sitting and watching television, while drinking a beer. He didn't say anything at first, just stood peering at her. She didn't like him doing that, so stuck out her tongue at him. It was then he spoke up.

"Why do you drink so much beer?" he asked.

"I happen to like beer, why?"

"My father says if a person drinks all the time, they are an alcoholic and they have a disease."

"You father don't know everything because I am not an alcoholic, and I do not have a disease."

"He also says that's what an alcoholic would say. He said it's called denial."

"Oh he does, does he? You believe everything your father says?"

Yes, he is smart...He has three degrees, how many do you have?"

"I have a degree from the school of hard knocks," chuckled Tillie in an effort to be sarcastic.

"Well, you keeping drinking that beer and you're going to end up being the principle," snickered Marcus.

Now mad, Tillie was hoping one of the other kids smarted off to her, she was ready, or so she thought. This time she had a run in with Javey, who saw her sitting on the porch with her arms crossed. He walked over to her, but didn't say anything. She knew not to say anything, but she couldn't pass up the challenge.

"What the hell are you looking at!" she snapped.

"You, I'm trying to figure out if you are a woman or a man...Are you a woman or a man?" he asked her.

"Look you little brat, why don't you go jump in the lake."

"I could do that because I can swim. But you remind me of one of my teachers from school called brains of steel."

"Oh I do huh?"

"Yes, do you want to know why?"

"Because she's smart huh?" said Tillie in a sarcastic tone of voice.

"First of all, it's not a she it's a he. And being smart is not why you remind me of him you just look like a man because of the way you dress. And the reason we call him brains of steel, is because he acts like he has steel in his head instead of a brain," he said with a serious look on his face.

"Why, you little bastard, get away from me!" snapped Tillie.

"Do you know for a fact who your parents are?"

"What?" snapped Tillie.

"I asked if you knew who your parents are? I do. But I don't think you had parents around, because if you did, they would have taught you the difference between looking like a man and looking like a woman," he said as he walked away.

Now being upset, Tillie could hardy wait to see Menzie to tell her off because of how the children had been abrasive to her. She later saw her in the living room practicing violin lessons with Vena. Mr. Ferguson was sitting in a recliner relaxing and listening to them. She rudely walked over and tapped Menzie on her shoulder.

"I have a bone to pick with you," she snapped.

"Not now Aunt Tillie, can't you see we're practicing?" responded Menzie as she continued to play her violin.

"Well, I've got something to say and it can't wait!" she urged.

"Didn't you hear her, they are practicing," said Mr. Ferguson.

"Nobody is talking to you old man!" she said as she pointed her finger at him.

"I have told you not to talk to my father like that," insisted Menzie as she and Vena stopped playing their violins.

"Okay, I see what's going on around here. So the little brats can talk to me anyway they want to, but I can't say anything to your no good father?"

"You know Tillie, for years you've talked to me like I was dirt or something. I've never said anything to you because of you being Pat's aunt."

"You just using that for an excuse. The truth is you're a little wimp!"

"That did it, I've had it with you. From now on, when you are in my house, you will respect me and my company up in here, or you can pack your duffle bag, drape it around your neck and fly out of here on the same broomstick you flew in here on," said Mr. Ferguson.

"If I leave here, you can bet your life, I'm never coming back here again!" threatened Tillie.

"If I knew for a fact that you have learned to keep your word, I'd fire up your broomstick and take my chance and put you out!" bellowed Mr. Ferguson.

"Go Mr. Ferguson!" shouted Vena.

"Well, I've never," responded Tillie.

"From the way you look and the way you dress, I believe you," snickered Menzie.

At that point Vena, Menzie and her father started to laugh. Tillie was so up set, she turned and stormed out of the living room. On her way out of the room, she past Mrs. Ferguson.

"What's up, Aunt Tillie," she said.

"Go to hell!" snapped Tillie.

"Oh my goodness, what's wrong with her?" she asked.

"I think she's suffering from broomstick jet lag," commented Vena as the three of them kept laughing. Mrs. Ferguson must have caught onto the joke, because she too laughed.

CHAPTER ELEVEN

FAMILY CONFIRMATION

Dr. Jenkins had called that Friday night and advised the family he would be in Atlanta that Saturday afternoon. Bright and early that morning Mrs. Ferguson got up to fix breakfast. When she sleepily strolled into the kitchen she was surprised to see Vena was already there and wearing an apron and frying eggs.

"Good morning," she said.

"Oh, good morning Mrs. Ferguson," she responded. "I hope the family likes scrambled eggs."

"They will eat any eggs they can get around here...What made you fix breakfast?" she asked.

"I get up early every Saturday and fix breakfast for the family at home."

"You do?" asked Mrs. Ferguson as she sat down at the kitchen table.

"Yes ma'am."

"And you don't mind?"

"No ma'am, I like cooking for the family. When my mom was alive, we use to cook together all the time," she said as she continued to nurse her eggs.

"Menzie is the only one of my kids who liked to cook. Tomaia would rather walk thought fire rather that be caught in the kitchen," snickered Mrs. Ferguson.

Vena laughed. "There, the eggs are ready. I found some cherries in the refrigerator and I put them in the pancakes. I hope you don't mind."

"Not at all."

"Have you ever tasted cherries filled pancakes?"

"I don't believe I have, but it sounds good... Did your mother teach you how to cook?"

"Yes, and I also took Home Economics in school...I put cheese on the eggs, do you think that will be okay?"

"I'm sure of it...My everything smells so good."

"Thank you. Would you like to have your breakfast right now?"

"Well, since I'm up, I think I will."

"Okay, you just relax, I'll fix your a plate and bring it to you."

"Okay...I think you are a wonderful young lady...I think I will adopt you," snickered Mrs. Ferguson.

"Wait until you taste my breakfast, then decide that," chuckled Vena.

She fixed Mrs. Ferguson breakfast and brought it to her. Once Mrs. Ferguson started to eat, she fixed her a plate and joined her at the kitchen table.

"Mmmmm, these are good eggs and the pancakes are delicious too. Why don't you have any meat on your plate?"

"I don't eat meat, I'm a vegetarian."

"Really? What made you decide that?"

"If you knew what they put in that stuff, you would probably not be eating it," chuckled Vena.

"I don't know and I'm thinking about it right now," chuckled Mrs. Ferguson.

The two of them sat, ate and talked and got well acquainted. Mr. Ferguson had already told his wife he liked the children. It was then conceded she did too.

Later, when Menzie announced she was picking up Dr. Jenkins at the airport, Vena asked if she could come along, which she did. When they saw him coming through the exit ramp, Vena ran to meet him.

"Daddeeee!" she yelled as the two of them embraced.

"How's my angel?' he asked.

"Fine, I'm so glad to see you," responded as the hugged and walked together.

"Hi handsome," said Menzie as she went to his left side and kissed him of the lips.

"Hi yourself," he reciprocated

They went and picked up his luggage, then left the airport. Once they were in the van, Menzie drove, while he sat in the passenger seat, Vena in the seat directly behind him. As they were headed towards the house, they discussed how things were going.

"Well, how do we stand so far," asked Jenkins.

"Actually, things are going a lot smoother than I thought they would," responded Menzie. "My parents took a wait and see attitude, and that seemed to have worked out."

"What did you tell them? They better behave or else?"

"Something like that," chuckled Menzie.

"Don't forget about Aunt Tillie," remarked Vena."

"Oh yeah, there is Aunt Tillie."

"Who is Aunt Tillie?" asked Jenkins.

"She's my mother's aunt, and she a cross between you having a heart attack and having a knife stuck in your back," snickered Menzie.

"That bad, huh?"

"I don't think she likes us very much," commented Vena.

"Well, don't feel bad, she don't like anybody including Aunt Tillie."

The three of them had a good laugh. Once Menzie was parking the van in front of the house, they could see Tillie sitting on the porch, drinking a beer. It was obvious she was waiting for them too.

"There she is, Daddy, sitting on the porch," said Vena.

"Yeah, there she sits, like a vulture waiting for her lunch to die," uttered Menzie.

"Well, she better not take a bite out of me or she'll bite off more than she can chew," said Jenkins.

"Well, remember she's got fangs, couple that with that filthy, lashing tongue and she'll try to bite your head off in one sweeping gouge."

"And she's got her hourly helping of beer to wash you down with," chuckled Vena.

The three of them laughed as they decided to get out of the van and take their chance with Tillie the Hun. As they stepped up onto the porch, she wasted no time in showing them where she was coming from.

"So, you're the daddy or these ill-mannered brats," she asked of Jenkins.

"I am the Father of the Jenkins children if that's what you mean?"

"Well, why don't you teach them some manners!" she bellowed.

"Funny, they seemed so well adjusted until they came around you."

"What is that suppose to mean?"

"He means, you always seem to bring out the worst in people," signified Menzie Ferguson.

"You see, there's your problem, they been hanging around her too much," instigated Tillie as she took a sip from her beer can.

"Now you have me confused," said Jenkins. "Which is it? I haven't taught them any manners or Miss Ferguson has taught them bad manners?" he asked.

"You know, I don't know why I'm wasting my time trying to talk to you people."

"Well then here's a little motto for you to live by. It says 'It is always best to be thought of as a fool, then to open your mouth and remove all doubt'," said Jenkins as he headed for the door, with Menzie, then Vena following behind him and who was peering at her.

"Mr. Ben Franklin said that," said Vena as she past by the seemly shocked man dressing female who just sat with her mouth hung open.

Sunday the next day, both families went to early morning church service. The only exception being, Tillie, who stayed home alone. Alter service, the Jenkins children got together to do damage control.

"Well, how do you think they like us?" asked Floreese.

"They liked us okay," said Marcus.

"What's there not to like, they are nice people and we are nice kids," responded Vena.

"Miss Tillie don't think so," said Myron.

"Who cares, she's an old, beer drinking, mean old man looking woman," inferred Javey.

"Why do you think she acts like that, Vena?" asked Floreese.

"Because she is not a happy person. She acts like she does to get attention from other people," surmised Vena.

"Why do people act bad, to get attention?" asked Myron

"I think Daddy told me, that's when people have low self esteem," said Vena Jenkins.

"What does low self esteem mean?" asked Myron.

"It's when people don't feel good about themselves," interjected Marcus.

"That's sad," uttered Floreese.

"Well, how did what we did help her?" asked Javey.

"We didn't do what we did to help her. We did what we did to get back at her for what she said about us," said Marcus.

"Do we have low self, ahh, what was that Marcus?" asked Floreese.

"Low self esteem," said Marcus.

"Do we have what, Marcus said?"

"No, why do you ask?" asked Vena.

"Well, if she acted like she acted because she wanted attention, why did we act like we acted?" asked Javey.

"What we did was like cold war. You know, keep the enemy off guard and off your back," said Marcus.

"Did we win?" asked Myron.

None of the children responded just sort of looked among themselves. As dinner was being prepared, Mr. Ferguson and Dr, Jenkins walked unto the porch to have a little talk. Mr. Ferguson sat on the porch steps as he gestured for Dr. Jenkins to set in the porch swing. There they got an understanding of where they stood with one another.

Later the families were enjoying dinner together, Mrs. Ferguson and Vena serviced as hostesses. Again, Tillie was anti-sociable and did not show for dinner. Floreese got up from the table walked over to Vena and signaled for her to put her head down, so she could talk in her ear. Once she did, Vena whispered back to her. She then started to fix a plate of food. The two of them looked for and found Tillie in the basement sitting and watching television and sipping on a beer.

"Miss Tillie, you didn't come to the table, so we brought you something to eat," said Floreese Jenkins.

"You didn't put any poison in it, did you?" asked Tillie.

"Look, if you don't want it, I can take it back upstairs," snapped Vena.

"No, leave it here. I'm hungry."

Vena sat the plate on the coffee table, then went back upstairs, leaving Floreese with her, who laid the napkin on the table, then laid the utensils onto the napkin. The food sat there for about a minute before Floreese said something to her.

"Aren't you going to eat your food?" she asked.

"Yes, I'll eat it later."

"It's going to get cold. Why don't you eat it while it's hot."

"It smells good, who cooked it, Pat?" asked Tillie as she sat down her beer, picked up the utensils, then the plate of food.

"No, Miss Menzie and my sister cooked it."

"Ahh, come on, your sister can't cook," said Tillie as she ate a fork of food.

"She can...Since our Mother went to heaven, she cooks a lot."

"Does your father make her do all of the cooking?"

"No, he cooks sometimes. She likes to cook. She likes to have his dinner ready when he gets home from work. Then Vena brings him his dinner, just like she did you."

"She seems like quite a young lady."

"I heard my Mother and Father talking all the time, and they said how blessed they were to have her. That's why my Daddy calls her angel sometimes."

"Do you miss your mother?"

"Yes, we were all so sad when my mother left us. My Daddy was really sad. Can we change the subject?"

"Sure, what do you want to talk about?" asked Tillie as she ate another fork of food.

"How about you?"

"What about me?"

"Why do you act so mean? Don't you like people?"

"No, because people always treat me bad. So, I make it a point to treat them bad first."

"That's silly!" bellowed Floreese...My Daddy taught us the Gold Rule. Have you ever heard of it?"

"Yes, I've heard of it."

"Can you say it?"

"Why don't you tell me what it says?"

"It says 'Do unto others as you have them do unto you'."

"It does huh? So how does that apply to me?"

"Maybe if you act like you like people, they might act like they like you."

"Did your daddy teach you that too?"

"Yes."

"Do you believe everything your father says?"

"Almost, but he tells us we have a brain of our own and we should learn to think for ourselves."

"Sounds like your father is a smart man."

"I think he's the smartest man in the world," bellowed Floreese.

"Oh my," uttered Tillie as she peered at the young five year old.

"I better get back upstairs. We're going to have a family talk. I guess we'll find out if they like us or not."

"They like you alright."

"How do you know?"

"Trust me, they do."

"Okay, see you later," said Floreese as she headed towards the stairs.

"Floreese," called Tillie.

"Yes," she said as she turned and faced Tillie.

"Thanks for talking to me...and tell your sister I said thanks for the food."

"I will," said Floreese as she smiled, turned and headed up the stairs.

Meanwhile Mr. Ferguson and Dr. Jenkins had finished their dinner and were sitting on the front porch. Ferguson sat on the top step, Jenkins in the porch swing.

"So, you and Menzie are getting married," he insinuated.

"Yes, it looks that way," confirmed Jenkins.

"I understand the two of you work together."

"That's right. We've teamed up on a lot of the firms projects and got a lot done."

"Was a lot of it Menzie's ideas?"

"She has a good business head on her shoulders, but she made it a point to come to me for advice and support. So I guess you could say she came up with great ideas and I confirmed how well they would work. In that, we made a good team."

"Well, prepare yourself for one hell of a ride, my friend."

"I don't quite understand what you mean."

"Menzie is a sweet person, very gentle, a kind person. But make no mistake about it she is smart, very smart. And she is a pusher and she pushes hard. If you haven't prepared yourself to be pushed, you could find that ship hard to sail. Let me tell you about her, she has no limits to what she wants out of life. She is a perfectionist of a strange kind."

"Trust me, I work with her, so I have seen her in action," chuckled Jenkins.

"I hear ya, but that was work. She will work hard and push you hard until everything is perfect, in her life, just like she wants it to be. If you are not prepared to take that ride with her, she will abandon the ship and once she's ashore, she will pulled the pug and make the ship sink. Do you know what I'm trying to say?"

"No, I'm afraid not."

"You are obviously a good man, successful in your own right, but do you have everything you want out of life?"

"I'm sure I don't. Nobody does."

"Then in that lies hope. Neither does she. But she will settle for nothing less. Now I don't know why she picked you to marry. She must see something in you that she needs to get where she wants to get in life. Oh, she loves you and that's for sure. But there has to be something else, deep inside of you that she is convinced she can bring it out. Otherwise, she wouldn't have given you the time of day. In a lot of ways, you are lucky my friend. I just hope you are up for the challenge."

Dr. Jenkins didn't comment to what Mr. Ferguson had to say, but considered it as food for thought. Later and after everyone was finished with dinner, the families gathered in the family room. Even Barbara and her family were there. It was then they found out where they stood with one another, as Mr. Ferguson told it like it was.

"You know my wife and I was worried that Menzie would never get married. We always figured that maybe her standard for a man was too high. When she called us and told us she was getting married, for a few brief moments we were excited. When we asked her about her husband to be, she told us he was a widower and had five kids, we were shocked. In fact, Pat pretended to faint."

"I did not pretend, I really fainted, I did!" bellowed Pat Ferguson.

The families got a good chuckle out of both of their remarks, as he continued to say what it was he was prepared to say.

"Well, we both opposed our objections to this engagement, knowing full well what Menzie would say if we did it too openly. She can be as stubborn as a mule when her mind is made up. So, we decided to wait and see what she was getting herself into. It was then we met these wonderful children. Right away we could see one thing crystal clear. They were so much like her, it was frightening," he chuckled. "They are sweet, very well disciplined, tough, out spoken and would make any adult think twice before they said something around them they didn't like," he chuckled again and which drew a laugh from the families. "Then we met James, Dr. Jenkins. We could see where they got their fighting ways. He's a likeable man, very tough, but smooth with how he handles things. And more then any thing else we liked him right away and we can see where he will be good for her our daughter. Where she lacks in common sense, he seems to make it up."

"Daddy!" bellowed Menzie.

"Just joking sweetheart," he laughed.

Just as he was finishing up, he looked up just as Tillie slowly walked into the family room, wearing a dress and it was obvious, she had shaved the hair from her face, Him watching her, got the attention of everybody, who turned and watched her.

"Why, Tillie, you look decent," commented Ferguson.

"Well, don't let looks fool ya," she chuckled, which got a laugh from both the families.

"Huh," chuckled Ferguson. "Dr. Jenkins, children, we have no idea how all of this happened. But I do know one thing. We love you, all of you and we welcome you with open arms to our family.

"Oh thank you Daddy!" bellowed Menzie.

As she rushed over to him and gave him a big hug, then her Mother, the rest of the Ferguson family was welcoming Dr. Jenkins and the children into the family and vise versa. Tillie was even pleased enough to join them. All and all things were as they should be. But what made it even more the special was when Floreese walked over to Aunt Tillie and yanked on her dress. Once she had her attention they did the unthinkable.

"Aunt Tillie, you look so pretty," she said.

"You know you are something special, you know that? Give me a hug," requested Tillie as she hugged the youngest member of the family. The one she so resented only a few days ago.

CHAPTER TWELVE

THE GRAND WEDDING

How things were settling down. It was now time to prepare for the big event. No one ever thought the wedding was going to be a simple one, but nobody had any inclination of what they were in for. The first hint came when the wedding party reported to practice for the wedding. It was then they realized the wedding was being held in a Cathedral.

"Oh my God!" uttered Barbara, the maid of honor. "I've never even been in a church this big."

"It not called a church, Bobbie. It called a Cathedral," corrected Menzie.

"Why a place so big?"

"Because there are going to be a lot of people here."

"Menzie, are you crazy? There aren't enough people in this whole city to fill up this church."

"Don't be negative, and it's called a Cathedral," repeated Ferguson.

"I think it's cool," said Tomaia, who was one of the bride's maids.

"You would," said Barbara.

Then Mr. and Mrs. Ferguson walked in. At first, they too were surprised to see such a huge place.

"Why is she having a wedding in a place this big?" asked Pat Ferguson.

"She claims there are going to be a lot of people here," responded Barbara.

"Enough to fill up this church?"

"Well she seems to think so. And please, don't let her hear you call it a church. It's a Cathedral," corrected Barbara.

At that point the Jenkins entered the Cathedral. By now Marcus was about six feet, and was one of the escorts, as was Vena one of the bride's maids.

"Wow dad, look at this Chapel!" bellowed Marcus.

"This is nice, that Menzie sure has a lot of class," said Vena.

"I feel important being in a wedding in this place," said Lona Johnson, who was also a maid of honor.

To give the wedding a professional touch and to help practice for the ceremony, Menzie hired a Frenchman by the name of Monsieur Jock Monteier, who had the reputation of conducting some of the most prestigious wedding. Just having him gave the wedding a professional favor, in lieu of him acting a bit feminine. But dealing with her turned out to be more then even he had bargained for.

"Come, come ladies let us line us to practice. I need you to understand I need your full cooperation and you full concentration. We want to make this go rapidly but smoothly," he announced as he clapped his hands.

"Oh brother, what do we have here?" chuckled Lona.

Her remark got a little chuckle from the group as they prepared to practice for the wedding ceremony. Menzie was in the back room getting some final alteration to her dress, so she allowed the practice to go on without her. Monteier lined the couples up on both sides of the back of the church, then explained what he wanted.

"Now here's how it will go ladies and gentleman. The first person down the aisle will be the Maid of Honor. She will come down this aisle. Once she reaches this spot," he indicated by draping a towel over one of the pews "The couple on the opposite side of the church will then start down the aisle. When they reached this on that side of the church, the couple on that side will then start down the aisle. Any questions?"

"I have one," said Tomaia. "Will you have those towels on the pews so we can know when we should start down the aisle?"

"If you like," responded Monsieur Monteier.

"Want that be a little tacky."

"Perhaps, but do you have any suggestions?"

"No."

"Then may I suggest we go with the towels if you don't mind?"

"I have a question," said Vena.

"What?" snapped Monteier.

"Why can't we all come down the same aisle?" she asked.

"Because Mademoiselle, it is the new tradition, that couples alternate aisles. It allows the precession to move along more rapidly.

"You sure Miss Menzie wants it done like that?"

"Well, I am sure she will...Now, may we proceed?"

As Barbara was walking down the aisle, Menzie Ferguson entered the chapel and sat about midways down the aisle. She watched and listened while Monsieur Monteier counted to keep her in step.

"One and two and three and four, and one and two and three and four, good!" he bellowed. “Let's have the first couple, please!" he bellowed.

She watched Lona Johnson and her escort start down the opposite aisle. She turned her head to watch them. When the next couple of Vena and her escort started down the opposite aisle, she turned her head to watch them. It was then she objected.

"No! No! No!" she bellowed as she headed towards Monteier.

After seeing her approaching him, James Jenkins and his son, Marcus peered over at one another, then abruptly sat down on the pew closest to them and crossed their legs and folded their arms.

"Is there something wrong, Mademoiselle?" he asked.

"Yes there's something wrong, Mademoiselle, ahh sir, ahh Monsieur," she baffled, which got a chuckle from the wedding party. "I'm sitting there turning my head from side to side, trying to keep up with the couples."

"And your point?"

"That's too busy. Why aren't all the couples coming down the same aisle?"

"Because Mademoiselle, the traditional wedding now days, alternate the couple's introduction into the sanctuary," he explained.

"Oh, is that so?" mocked Ferguson.

"Yes ma'am."

"Well, Monsieur, this is by no means a traditional wedding. This is my wedding and it is one that is intended to set a standard for all others to follow," Ferguson dramatized. "I am going to run a runner down this aisle. I want all of these couples to have their time in the spotlight. Strolling gracefully like royalty while they savoring every moment as the music reflects them as the grandest of them all. And you my dear Monsieur Monteier, will be forever known as the grandeur of all times!" she gestured by curtsying in the direction where one group stood, then the other.

The wedding party clapped and cheered to show their approval her performance. Afterwards, Monsieur Monteier laughed.

"What funny?" she asked him.

"You are Mademoiselle," he chuckled "You must remember this is a wedding not a Coronation."

"Oh really?" asked Menzie with this sly look on her face.

June 4, 1975, the day of the wedding. The sanctuary was filled to capacity and festively decorated to resemble that of a royal ball. The events, announced as a wedding, did nothing to dispel that appearance of something grand was about to take place. It started when James Jenkins and his best man, Robert Johnson, entered the sanctuary stepping to the trumpet tempo to the introduction to the Coronation March, as played by the St. Louis Symphony Orchestra. Then there was an announcement.

"Ladies and Gentlemen, Mrs. Barbara Ferguson-Ownes, our Maid of Honor.

As the St. Louis Symphony continued to play the Coronation March, Barbara strolled down the aisle to a grand, but smooth tempo of the March. Once she was in place, another announcement was made.

"Mrs. Lona Jenkins-Johnson, escorted by her husband Robert Johnson.

Jenkins' sister and her husband strolled down the isle. Taking their time, savoring the moment. Once they were done, the next announcement was made.

"Tomaia M. Ferguson, escorted by Mr. Rodger Miles.

The two of them started to step to the tempo of the march. Once she was in place, the next announcement was made.

"Miss Vena L. Jenkins, escorted by Mr. Jerry Keen. As she started to stoll down the aisles she smiled. Her smile seemed to light up the room as she stepped gracefully to the tempo of the Coronation March. Once she was in place, the next maid of honor was announced by the announcer, Monsieur Monteier, until they were all in place. Then there was this moment of silence. It lasted for several seconds. Then the St. Louis Symphony Orchestra sounded a roar of trumpets as the introduction of the Wedding March began. Then the doors to the rear of the church slowly opened. There stood Menzie Ferguson, alone. Then Monsieur Monteier proudly announced her.

"Ladies and gentlemen, please stand to receive the bride to be, Miss Menzie Louise Ferguson.

As the attendees stood, Mr. Ferguson joined his daughter, stood there for about a minute, then he escorted his beautiful daughter down the aisle. She wore white as the symbol of purity, the vial pulled down over her face to be revealed to the one man who will have the honor of seeing it for a lifetime. Once she was in place, the minister approached and the ceremony begin as James Jenkins and Menzie Ferguson joined hands.

"Dear beloveth, we have gathered here today to witness the union of this man and this woman in the bonds of holy matrimony. The vowels, which will be taken here are to be binding, ever lasting and should not be taken lightly or the wedding entered into falsely are without full commitment. Who giveth this woman away?" asked the minister.

"I do," said Mr. Ferguson as lifted her vial high enough to kiss her on her cheek.

It was then the marriage, which seemed destined to be, was being fulfilled. But the impact of it being so, was yet to be imagined. Later the reception was held in a ballroom, which just as magnificently decorated as the sanctuary, But as grand as it was, it was not without its admirers as well as its critics.

"Wow, I have never been to a wedding like this before," commented Blackshere's date. It was like going to a real coronation ball for a king and a queen," she continued.

"Yeah, that Menzie always does everything in style," commented Blackshere.

"And she looks so pretty," said a co-worker. “If you ask me, it was too much," criticized Gladis Henley. "And where does she get off wearing white? I bet you that cherry is pushed so far up her butt that it could be mistaken for a stop light," she chuckled.

"Look, I don't want to hear your mouth today. Let's have a good time and wish her well."

"I don't know why you should be so happy for her the way she dogged you out!" snapped Gladis.

"Why do you keep bringing that up?"

"Because."

"Look, me and my woman are here today and we are going to have a good time. And you, I suggest you try and catch the bouquet. And if you do, stuff it in your mouth. Maybe it will help you keep your mouth shut," suggested Blackshere as he walked away from her, as he explained the situation to his date.

"Punk!" snapped Gladis Henley.

"Whateveeeerrrrr!" retorted Blackshere.

The new bride, her husband and the wedding party were standing in line and enjoying the many congratulations and compliments over the magnificence of the wedding ceremony and even from an unlikely source.

"Thank you, Monsieus Monteier, you did a wonderful job," said Menizie.

"Mademoiselle, ahh, pardon shi vous ples. Madame Jenkins, it has been a pleasure working with you," said Monsieus Monteier in his French assent. "Never have I had so much fun during a wedding. May I say, and bon lachance to you, and your handsome husband. I think you make a beautiful couple."

"Oh Menzie, you look so beautiful," said Mrs. Lynnett Jenkins and her husband, hugged her "And welcome to the family," said Mr. John Jenkins.

"Thank you," uttered Menzie as she reciprocated both of their hugs.

"And don't forget what I told you," Mrs. Jenkins whispered in her ear. "Give him plenty of that stuff," she snickered.

"Oh I will, trust me," whispered Menzie with chuckle in her voice.

Later the lovebirds had gone to the ballroom bedroom so that the bride could change clothes. He walked into the bathroom and caught her wearing nothing but her underwear. He walked up to her then wrapped his arms around her.

"I bet you can't guess what I'm thinking?' he asked.

"I can feel what you're thinking," snickered Menzie as she turned around, hugged him and so they could kiss.

It became obvious they enjoyed the kiss. In fact, he started to pull her towards the bed. Once there, he sat down and reached under her slip to take down her panties. But she grabbed his wrists and held them.

"James, wait," she requested.

"Don't you think I've waited long enough," he impatiently uttered as he attempted to get his hands free.

"Wait a minute baby," she said as she sat down next to him. "I want to wait until we get on the honeymoon before we have sex."

"Why?"

"Well, there's a little something I didn't tell you about me."

"You're not going to tell me you're frigid?"

"No, and I know you know better then that," she snickered.

"Well, I'm here to tell you I am a man with a good appetite for sex."

"So I've been told."

"By whom?"

"Let's just say a little birdie told me," she snickered. "Now, I want you to listen to me. I'm going to tell you something and I need you to promise me you won't laugh...promise?" she asked as she took his hands.

"It must be bad, or you wouldn't be playing this little game."

"No it's not bad, I just don't know how you will take it."

"Baby, what is it?"

"James, I'm still a virgin."

"Yeah right!" snapped Jenkins.

"Well, I am."

"Look Menzie, its okay if you're not a virgin. I wasn't expecting you to be."

"I know you weren't that's why I'm telling you now."

"You're serious, aren't you?"

"I'm serious as cancer."

"Menzie, you're telling me you have never been with a man in your whole life?"

"No I haven't, and I swear and hope to die...But you'll find out once you get me on that boat to the Bahamas."

"Man, I would have never thought of you that way."

"Well, you did know that I wasn't a whore?"

"Yeah, I knew that...I'm just surprised."

"Are you disappointed?"

"In what?"

"In finding out I wasn't this worldly woman you thought I was?"

"No, in fact I'm flattered."

"Good, because once you get past this cherry tree, I expect to be giving up plenty of fruit."

"And that I can believe," chuckled Jenkins as the two of them had a good laugh.

Later the happy couple stood on the deck of the cruise ship, which was to take them on a cruise and on to the Bahamas Islands. As they stood and waved to the many who came to see them off. They did so in spite of them desiring to finally be alone. Finally, that night as the ship cruised along, the time for consummation of the marriage vowels was at hand.

James Jenkins was already in the bed patiently waiting for his new bride to come to bed. She stepped out of the bathroom wearing a sexy red negligee, with one hand on her hip, the other extended in the air. His eyes grow twice their size when he saw her.

"You like?" she asked.

"I like what I see very much," he uttered.

"Which are you referring to, the negligee or my body?" she chuckled as she walked over to the bed.

"I like the negligee, but it's the body that making it look good," he said as he grabbed her and laid her on the bed. "You know Mrs. Jenkins, you are a beautiful bride and I love you very much."

"You sure you're not saying that because you want some," she chuckled.

"Oh, I want some alright...but I'm saying it because of what I feel in my heart."

"Well, I'm going to spend the rest of our lives together making sure that feeling stays there, starting tonight," she uttered as initiated their first real compassionate kiss as husband and wife. But like before, she wanted him to taste and feel her tongue, so she gave him plenty of it. Before long, the moment of consummation was at hand. And Menzie Ferguson-Jenkins, feeling the penetration of a man for the first time, said it best.

"Ohhhhhhhhhhhhh!"

CHAPTER THIRTEEN

TROUBLE IN PARADISE

For the newly weds it was heavenly bliss for two whole weeks. Living a life of leisure, a life away from work, seeing such wonderful sights, traveling and making love. It was a welcome change for James Jenkins after going through what he had gone through the last two years. For Mrs. Jenkins this has been the happiest she has ever been. She was now feeling the only thing she was missing in her life was being with the man of her dreams. But all of that took an abrupt change once the reality of the situation started to truly take form.

It was the Jenkins first day back to work. The new Mrs. Jenkins already knew the first obstacle she would have to overcome, and that was a nosy Sara Tilliberge, who wasted no time in finding out how things went.

"Welcome back boss," she said as she entered her boss' office.

"Why hello, you still working here?" chuckled Jenkins.

"I started to quit, but I thought I would wait until you got back so I could see the blush on your face," she joked. "Well, how does it fill being a married woman?"

"Ohhh, I don't feel any different," snickered Jenkins

"Yeah right! Then why do you have this big old grin on your face and that twinkle in your eyes?"

Jenkins laughed. "Everything was wonderful," she said as she warred back in her chair, her fingers locked behind her head.

"How was it, I mean the sex?" asked Sara as she leaned on her boss's desk.

"I not going to tell you that," chuckled Jenkins.

"That good huh?"

Jenkins laughed again. "It was so nice having a man for a change. The only thing that wasn't fun was getting broke in, plus I left some blood on the people's sheets, that was embarrassing. But after that, it was all good, and--."

"Hold it! Back up...What did you just say?"

"I said after I got over the embarrassment, it was all good."

"I mean right before that...the broke in part?"

"Oh, didn't I tell you? I was still a virgin?"

"Since when?"

"Since and up and including the night of June 4th."

"So, you're telling me you were a virgin?"

"Yes I was."

"Well I'll be damned. Now I'm just realizing something you said."

"And what was that?"

"Remember when I asked you when was the last time you had had a man?"

"Yeah, I kind of remember that."

"You said 'If I told you, you won't believe it', remember that?"

"I think so."

"So you were talking about never?"

"Well, yes I was."

Sara laughed.

"See, that's why I didn't tell you, I knew you would laugh."

"That's because it's funny. This tall, good looking woman, kneeing a man in his balls, and to preserve her virginity."

"Oh God! Why do you have to put it like that?"

"Because that was how it was...Man, you wait until I tell Gladis about this."

"See, that's another reason why I didn't tell you, you can't keep a secret. I don't want you telling Gladis what I told you."

"You may not, but remember it was she who said you and the good doctor were screwing around. She believes you were screwing out of both panty legs," chuckled Sara," she chuckled.

"That's just like her to have her mind in the gutter."

"That's because her mind won't fit any place else," snickered Sara

Her remark generated a good laugh between them. While Mrs. Jenikins was getting the third degree from Sara, James Jenkins was about to be tormented by Gladis Henley once she had entered his office unannounced. She then walked behind the desk and sat down, so she could face him. She was wearing a short dress, so she then crossed her legs so that he could get a good look.

"Well, well, well, Dr. Jenkins. And how is the wife?"

"She doing just fine, thank you," he said as he continued to focus on the work he was doing. "How did you get in here?"

"Your secretary was not at her desk...Two weeks on a honeymoon, did she wear you out?"

"Gladis, what do you want?"

"What I want, you won't give me."

"Gladis, don't start," he snapped. "In fact, don't you have some work to do?"

"Now, tell me I was right, you two were screwing around before you got married, even before your wife died?"

"I don't think that's any of your business!" uttered Jenkins.

"Why are you so defensive? I'm just asking you to tell me the truth."

"Okay Gladis, you want to hear the truth. Here it is," said Jenkins as he slammed down the pen he was using. "No! Menzie and I were not sleeping together. The first time we had sex was on our honeymoon. In fact, Menzie was a still virgin until we got married and had sex," he blurted out.

"What?" bellowed Gladis. "She was a what?" she chuckled. "A virgin? Get out of here!" she laughed. "A virgin," she continued to mock.

"That did it," he snapped as he stood and grabbed her by her arm. "I'm putting your butt out of here!"

Just as he grabbed her arm, Mrs. Jenkins walked in his office. She not only saw Gladis sitting on his desk, she saw him holding her arm. To hopefully not give the wrong impression, he quickly snatched his hand away, as Gladis jumped up.

"What the hell is this?" she abruptly asked.

"It not like it seems," chuckled Jenkins.

"I ahh, better be leaving," said Gladis as she intentionally made it seem like more then what it was. "And thanks for that information," she uttered as she walked towards Menzie. "Virgin, right!" she uttered as she past her, as she stood with her arms crossed.

"I asked you what the hell was going on in here?" she snapped.

"You know Gladis, always wanting to start something," said Jenkins as he sat down at his desk.

"Why in the hell was she sitting on your desk with her ass all up in your face?"

"Now Menzie, you got things all wrong."

"I got things all wrong? I walk in here, she sitting on your desk, her ass all up in your face and you holding her by her arm. What the hell could I have wrong?"

"I was about to put her out."

"Couldn't you just ask her to leave?"

"I tried, she wouldn't listen."

"And why in the hell were you discussing me with her? Telling her about me being a virgin?"

"That just sort of slipped out," explained Jenkins.

"Yeah right! Well, you are married to me. I'm your wife! You stay away from that bitch!"

"Now wait a minute here Menzie, I'll stay away from her because I want to, not because you ordered me to."

"Man, you can do what the hell you want to!" scolded Mrs. Jenkins as she turned and stormed out of his office.

"Ahh man!" he gestured as he threw up both of his hands.

Once back at her office she rushed in slamming the door behind her. Sara watched her rush past her and into her office, also slamming the door behind her. Sara then rushed into her office.

"Boss, what's wrong?" she asked as she closed the door behind her.

"I don't feel like talking right now!" she insisted.

"Well I'm not leaving here until you talk to me...What wrong?"

"Suite your self," she snapped.

"Okay, I'll sit right here until we can talk," said Sara as she sat in a chair next to her boss' desk.

"It's that damn Gladis!" she snapped.

"What has that no good heifer done now?" asked Sara as she sat in the chair next to her boss' desk.

"I went to see if my husband wanted to go out for lunch. When I walked into his office, that bitch was sitting on his desk, her butt all up in his face!" she expressed.

"I don't get it. So what are you mad about?"

"He's married to me and he needs to keep the hell away from her!"

"The first thing you need to do is calm down. How you know Gladis. She went after him when he was married to his last wife. What made you think she was going to change, when she don't even like you?"

"If you're suppose to be comforting me, you're doing a bang up job missy," insinuated Jenkins.

"Maybe I'm missing the point here. Who are you made at her or him?"

"I'm mad at him!" snapped his wife.

"Why?"

"Because when I walked in, he had his hand on her arm!" she argued.

"So?"

"First of all, she didn't have any business being in his office!" she scolded.

"So, now we're back to being angry with Gladis?"

"What are you talking about?" asked Jenkins in a harsh tone of voice.

"That's what I'm trying to understand about you, what are you saying?"

"Okay...I walked into his office. She had walked around the back of his desk and was sitting there with her dress all up in her ass."

"So, she was showing him some thigh? What else is new?"

"I caught him with his hand all over her."

"You mean he had his hand up her dress?"

"Well, no, he had his hand on her arm."

"Let me make sure I understand what you just said. She was sitting on his desk, showing him all thighs, but you caught him with his hand on her arm?"

"That's right!"

"I don't get what you are upset about?"

"He shouldn't have had his hands on her, period!" she insisted.

"How do you know he wasn't about to put her ass out?"

"Huh huh, that's what he tried to tell me he was doing."

"And in never donned on you, he may have been telling the truth?"

"Well...no."

"It sounds to me like you jumped to a conclusion before you gave him a chance to explain the facts."

"Yeah, I did...Ah man, I was horrible to him...Sara, what is wrong with me?" she asked as she started to tear.

"If you asking me, I would say you are still a nervous new bride. You've only been married a couple of weeks. You were single a long time. It's going to take some real getting use to being married. You've got a good man. He could have had any woman around here he wanted. Hell, I would have married him if he had ask me," chuckled Sara. "But he married you, and he did it because he loves you. If you love him like you say and you want to keep him, then you're going to have to give your marriage a chance to grow. And you can't run around dogging your man out because it appears he messing around with other women, specially him being a Black man. You piss a brother off, you've got some real hell coming," said Sara as she picked up a box of tissue and held it out to her boss.

"Maybe I should go down there and apologize to him," said Menzie as she pulled a tissue from the box and wiped her eyes.

"No, give him a chance to cool off. Why don't you cook him a good meal. You know the way to a man's heart is through his stomach."

Menzie laughed.

"The last time I said that it went right over that man's head."

"Well, stop aiming at his head and focus more on getting through to his heart," said Sara as she got up and headed towards the door.

"Sara, thanks, again," snickered Jenkins.

After work, Mrs. Jenkins made an assertive effort at grocery shopping to prepare her husband favorite meal. Once done, she rushed home to have things ready by the time he got home from a presentation he was scheduled to make. When she opened the door to the house, she could smell something cooking. When reached the kitchen, Vena had already cooked.

"Oh, you've already cooked?" she asked.

"Yes...Did you want to cook today?" asked Vena.

"Yeah, and I really wanted to."

"Look, I know you guys are busy and kind of still on your honeymoon, so I don't mind cooking for a while."

"You don't understand. It was really important for me to cook this meal."

"Why?"

"Because I'm his wife and it's my job to cook his meals," insisted Menzie.

"Did you say job? Cooking for my Daddy isn't a job," snapped Vena.

"I'm sorry, that was a bad choice of words...I seem to be doing a lot of that lately."

Later that evening Menzie was sitting on the sofa in the living room waiting for her husband to come home from an appointment. Floreese saw her there and approached her.

"Miss Menzie, can I ask you a question?"

"Yes, what is it?" snapped Menzie.

"Nothing," said Floreese as she turned to walk away.

Suddenly she stopped and turned to face Menzie Jenkins. "What were you and Vena fussing about today?" she asked.

"Why do you want to know?" asked Manzie.

"Because you seem to be mad. Why are you taking it out on Vena?"

"I'm not taking anything out of Vena. We'll have to come to some kind of understanding around here."

"You know, you are not like my mamma, she was nice. You are mean," said Floreese, who then turned and abruptly left the room.

"Way to go Menzie," she uttered to herself.

In hopes of getting back in the family's grace, she thought she would start with where the problem started. That night, the newly weds laid in their bed, their backs towards one another. Neither of them could sleep, so she attempted to defuse the situation.

"James...James, I know you're not sleep, please answer me."

"What do you want Menzie?" he snapped.

"I know you're mad with me, but please don't talk to me like that."

"Well, you sure didn't have any problem bitching at me earlier today!"

"James, I'm sorry," she said as she turned, leaned on her elbow while looking at his back.

"Yeah well, don't worry about it."

"I am worried. I'm worried about us."

"Yeah, well don't."

"James, please turn around and talk to me."

"I don't have anything to say."

"Well, I do."

"Then go ahead and talk, you're good at it!" snapped Jenkins.

"James, I am so sorry...I just saw that woman and I just didn't think."

"It was your thinking that caused this problem."

"I know...I want to make it up to you...James, please make love to me."

"I'm not in the mood tonight.

"You're turning me down?"

"Menzie, please!" he snapped.

While the two of them were arguing, Vena heard them and walked into the hall so she could hear what it was all about.

"Man, I make one mistake, and you don't want me...I'm your wife and you better not forget that!" she scolded.

"What is that suppose to mean?"

"I'm just reminding you that's all. And while we're on that subject, I need you to remind your daughter, Vena, of that."

"What does she have to do with this?"

"I wanted to make it up to you, so I was going to fix your favorite meal. I busted my butt shopping and getting home. When I got here, she had already cooked dinner."

"What's your point?"

"The point is, I'm your wife and it is my responsibility to cook for my husband, not hers," she argued.

"Look, Vena is the only one of my kids who seem to be doing all she can do to adjust to losing her mother. I'm not going to make her have a set back by telling her she can't cook, when she feels that's her way of contributing to our situation. If you don't understand that, that's too bad!" snapped Jenkins.

"I understand that, but--"

"I don't think that you do," interrupted James Jenkins.

He abruptly got out of bed and headed towards the bedroom door. Vena heard him, and quickly darted back into her bedroom. Her father rushed down stairs, laid down on the couch and there is where he stayed all night. When he got up the next morning and went to the bedroom, his wife had already left home. Later when he was at work, he went to check on her.

"Hi," he said to Sara when he entered her office.

"Oh hi Dr. Jenkins. If you are looking for your wife, she not here."

"Have you heard from her, today?"

"Yes sir, she came in early and put in for a weeks vacation."

"Thanks," responded Jenkins as he turned and left her office.

Later when he made it home from work, he found Vena sitting on the couch waiting for him.

"Hi angel," he said.

"Hi Daddy, is Miss Menzie with you?"

"No, she isn't."

"She's not coming back is she?"

"It doesn't look like it," he said as he sat down next to his daughter.

"I'm sorry I messed it up for you guys," sniffled Vena.

"You didn't do anything wrong."

"If I hadn't cooked yesterday, she would have and you two would still be together," she said as she and her father hugged one another.

"Sweetheart, one had nothing to do with the other."

"Daddy, I miss Mommy," she sobbed.

"I know you do angel, so do I," he reciprocated as they hugged and sobbed.

Menzie had sent three days at her parent's house. During the time she was there, she had not eaten or slept well. She was sitting in her old room and starring out the window when she received a phone call. When she answered the phone, it was Mrs. Lynnett Jenkins.

"Well, Mrs. Menzie Jenkins, or are you changing your name back to Ferguson?"

"What do you want Mrs. Jenkins?" asked Menzie in disappointed tone of voice.

"It isn't what I want, it's what do you want...I thought you told me you loved my son?"

"Mrs. Jenkins, our situation is complicated."

"What's making it complicated, you?"

"Whatever," snapped Menzie.

"You see that's part of your problem, your attitude."

"What I don't need is somebody telling me what my problem is."

"That's another one of your problems, you don't listen. We talked about what you were getting yourself into when you told me you wanted my son, did we not?"

"Yes we did."

"Were you listening?"

"Apparently not."

"Well you should have...Now you got my grand baby all upset, thinking it was all her fault."

"I don't know why she thinks that."

"She told me you wanted to cook a meal, but she beat you to it. Now she thinks that is why you two broke up and she blaming herself."

"I'm sorry she feels that way."

"If you weren't going to be good for them, then why did you marry my son?"

"I thought it was a good idea at the time," snickered Menzie.

"And now?"

"Right now, I'm not sure of anything."

"If you lack the confidence to be with that family, I wish you had left them alone. Him marrying you made things worse. Now his kids are confused and poor Vena, she thinks the world of her father, now she's upset because he's upset."

"Mrs. Jenkins, I'm am so sorry."

"So, that's all you have to say? After doing all that talk about how you could take him from his wife if you wanted to, that was all talk. That what you are, all talk and no action. You talk about being all woman but you are nothing but a little spoiled brat who wants to have her way all the time. My son loves you. Too bad you don't know the real meaning of love. If you really knew, you would know the compassion that's involved. Have you ever heard of Dr. John Henry Johnson from Florissant, Missouri and not the one from Johnson's Publishing Company?"

"Then I'm afraid I don't know the man."

"He's a writer. I have a poem he wrote called, 'When you know what love is'. Would you like for me to read it to you?"

"Why do I get the feeling you are going to regardless to what I say?"

"No, you see there's where you're wrong," insisted Mrs. Jenkins. "I wouldn't be wasting my time talking to you if I didn't think you were worth it. Would you like to hear it?"

"Yes, I would."

"Now you talking...it goes like this: Love is biding, in that it draws people together. Love is enduring, when all have failed, it lasts. Love is poetic, in that it speaks for itself. Love is emphatic, in that it defines expression. Love is sacred, in that it is an expression of worthiness. But more than these, Love is compromise, in that it is the give and take of the heart and the spirit. When you know what love is, you know and have the essence of the true compassion of life'. Do you understand what that means Menzie?"

"Yes ma'am," said Menzie as tears trickled down her cheeks. "It's the challenge of what love is all about," she responded.

"Right, the very essence of being able to share your love and life with another."

"I never said I didn't love James, I do," she uttered.

"You see, there you go again, talk. I hope you do love him. And if you do, you will take action, do the right thing...But you must know, Vena and her father are close. You have to first make your peace with him, then her. If you do, the rest will work itself out, trust me. Well, good luck on whatever you decide to do, good-bye."

Menzie slowly hung up the phone. She stood there, the tears started to intensify as she pounded over her faith and her love. She rushed back to her room laid across the bed and wept. Later that evening, her mother entered her room carrying a tray of food. She sat in on the nightstand, then sat down on the bed beside her daughter.

"I brought you something to eat," she said.

"Thanks, I'll eat it later."

"Menzie, I know it's none of my business, but what happened? A couple of weeks you were in love, now you seem to be confused about it."

"I don't know what happened Mamma. Sometimes I think I'm going crazy."

"Why do suppose you feel like that?"

"Here's a man I wanted so badly, that when I got him I started to feel I couldn't keep him."

"That doesn't sound like you, having a lack of confidence."

"If it isn't that, then I don't know what else it could be."

"Do you remember seeing the Sound of Music?"

"Yes, I've seen it a couple of times."

"I beg your pardon? How many times?"

"Okay Mamma, I've seen it about ten times," snickered Menzie.

"Maria started to love the Captain when he was trying to give her instructions like she was a domestic, by using his whistle. She then started to work to put his house in a perspective that he had forgotten. That impressed him, to the point that he fell in love with her."

"What's your point, Mamma?"

"In a way, your situation is similar to hers. You took an entire company to a whole new prestigious level. You did it by being smart, using your talent. She used her talent the same as you. James is smart, just like you. But you are competing for his affection with his kids at his level. So, you're never win that battle. But Maria won the Captain's affection and the affection of his kids by using her heart. You're trying to win James with your head, trying to prove you are smart. He already knows that, so at this point in his life, he doesn't care about smart. Use your heart baby. Believe or not, that is your strongest asset."

"You know Mamma, you're right. I love him and I'm going to fight for him on my terms. First thing I need to do, is go shopping."

"And buy what?"

"I'm going to get me a dress that will make his eyes pop out when he sees me. Then I'm going to get me a sexy hairdo. Then I'm getting on a plane and flying to Chicago."

"Why there?"

"Each year our firm has an out of town, three day conference, which starts with a social gathering and dance on Friday. This year it's in Chicago. That's where he'll be. I've got a little surprise for my dear co-workers, and him."

CHAPTER FOURTEEN

WHERE PASSION BEGINS AND BUSINESS ENDS

It was Friday night in Chicago. The night air was rather brisk, but things were about to heat up as a long, white limousine pulls up the Fairview Hotel. A dressed chauffeur got out rushed around to the passenger side back door and opened it. He then helped Mrs. Jenkins, wearing a sexy red dress which reach about midway to her thighs and wearing a waist length white fur coat, and sporting a new sexy hair style, out of the Limousine. He escorted her into the hotel.

Once inside they stood as she attempted to spot her husband. She didn't see him right away, but did spot Gladis Henley and she seemed in a rush. She kept her eyes on her until she could see why she seemed to be in a hurry. She was headed for the table where James Jenkins was sitting. He was listening to and watching the disk jockey as he played, 'Ain't No Mountain High Enough,' by Marvin Gaye and Tammy Terrell.

The chauffeur then escorted her towards them. All heads seemed to turn and focus their attention on her as she strolled along to the beat of the music, her head held high as if she wanted everyone to notice her, and they did. One man looked so hard, his wife slapped the back of his head to show her resentment. But it was a mote point, everyone noticed her as the whispers, compliments and catcalls started to ring throughout the ballroom.

"Well, I'll be damn! Would you look at that!" bellowed one co-worker.

"It's Menzie and she is looking good," chuckled Blackshere.

Just as she and her escort reached the table where her husband was sitting, he saw her, but Gladis was sitting with her back to her, and making her pitch to the woman's husband.

"Look man you know I'm the woman for you. You've ignored me all this time, when you know you should be with me. I mean where is your new wife? Probably back home with her mama," she mocked.

The entire time she was talking James Jenkins had his eye on Menzie. In fact, he was looking so hard, that Gladis finally noticed it.

"No, you look at me, I'm talking to you," she insisted as she kept moving her head in an attempt to block his view. "Notice me...What are you looking at"" she asked as she turned to look behind her.

It was then she saw Mrs. Jenkins standing behind her and listening to every word. Knowing that, she then went of the defensive.

"Ferguson, what are you doing here?" she asked.

"My name is Mrs. Jenkins and you better get your butt away from my husband!" said Menzie in a serious tone of voice.

"I thought you two were separated?"

"Beat it Henley!" she demanded.

"I don't have to leave."

"You better, and right now!" said Jenkins.

"Maybe you should ask James if he wants me to leave," said Gladis as she turned back to look at James Jenkins, who had his eyes fixed on his wife.

"Woman I owe you a butt kicking. If you don't get the hell out of here, you will get it right here, right now!" threaten Mrs. Jenkins.

"You just can't come in here like you all that!" snapped Gladis.

"That's a pretty dress you have on Henley. If you don't move, you're die in it," promised Menzie.

"You know, you two can have each other," uttered Gladis.

Now angry and surprised, Gladis Henley abruptly got up and stormed from the table. While Mrs. Jenkins stood paused with grace, The Chauffeur moved the chair Henley had been sitting in next to Jenkins. Mrs. Jenkins laid her purse on the table, stretched out her arms and waited for the chauffeur to take off her fur coat. Once he did, he left, but she sat down next to her husband then leaned on the table towards him.

"Wow, you look great," bellowed Jenkins.

"Then close your mouth and kiss me like you're glad to see me. And give me some tongue. I want to taste you," she uttered in an erotic tone of voice.

"Jenkins affectionately kissed his wife. It was a long passionate kiss. And anyone seeing them could see he was giving her plenty of tongue and she was enjoying it.

"Oh my God!" uttered Blackshere's date.

"It don' take all that," complaint Henley.

"That Menzie is one classy woman," said Blackshere.

After displaying their show of affection towards one another, they talked. Then started the whole process over again. Things heated up a bit when the disk jockey started to play 'Can't Get Enough Of Your Love, Babe' by Barry White.

"Let's dance," she requested.

"I can't, not right now," responded Jenkins.

"Why not?"

"You don't want to know, trust me," uttered Jenkins.

"Oh my goodness," she snickered I feel what you mean," she whispered after running her hands under the table and feeling him. "Dance with me anyway. And if you show me how much you miss me, I'll take care of that later." she promised.

The two got on the floor and danced. She didn't have to pull him towards her like she had it the past. In fact, they danced so close at times it looked as if they were in the same skin.

"Why don't go get a room," scolded Henley.

"She keep putting it to him like that, they won't need one," chuckled Blackshere.

"That is so disgusting," said Henley as she turned her head away from them.

The now reacquainted couple was excited about being back in each other's arms as they danced nearly all of during the event. It was late and the event was winding down. The disk jockey was closing it out with Al Green's 'Let's Stay Together'. She was whispering the words to the song in her husband's ear as they tightly held onto one another.

"You keep singing in my ear like that, and you're going to get yourself in some big trouble," whispered James Jenkins.

"How much trouble would I be in if I blow in it, like this," she whispered as she blew in her husband's ear.

"That did it...How about we go to my room?" whispered Jenkins.

"I have a better idea, why don't you get your coat and join me at the Rite Star Paramount Lounge. I have a suite there, with a Jacuzzi in my room. And since we didn't take the time to eat, we can order food from my Limousine and they can have it waiting when we get there."

"Sounds like you've thought of everything."

"You're right, including how good I am going to make you feel tonight."

"Well, let's get out of here."

Once they had eaten, they sat naked in the Jacuzzi, just relaxing. Menzie moved over to her husband and started to kiss on his chest. She kissed his chest until she reached his nipples. She started to nibble on one, then the other.

"Mmmmmmmm, that feels good," he uttered.

"I wonder how it feels to make love in a Jacuzzi?" she whispered as she continued to kiss on his stomach.

"Sounds like fun to me," uttered Jenkins.

"Me too," she muttered as she straddled him.

She reached into the water and fumbled until she positioned him like she wanted. Then the couple consummated their marriage for the second time.

"Mmmmmmmmmmmm!" she reacted.

The next afternoon was suppose to have been the business portion of the weekend. But suddenly things took a strange twist. Most of the employees were in place, when a disastrous announcement was made. It was Horence Robinstein who made it.

"Ladies and gentlemen, may I have your attention. My uncle, Mr. Cecil Robinstein has had a heart attack. He is in serious condition," he continued as the crowd started to moan and whisper. "The rest of this weekend's activities have been cancelled. You made enjoy the rest of your stay here. But we do expect you to report to work on Monday, thank you."

Late that night, James Jenkins and his wife returned to their home. Vena, being in her room, heard the cab pull up and rushed over to the window and pulled back the curtain, to make sure it was her father returning home. What she wasn't expecting to see was him returning with his new wife. As they were getting out of the cab, she stood in her window and watched them. She slowly closed the curtain and went to bed and somewhat confused.

"Early the next morning, Mrs. Jenkins had come down to the kitchen to prepare breakfast. At that moment, a sweat soaked and wet Vena walked into the kitchen door. She was wearing a sweat suit, with a towel around her neck.

"Oh, hi Vena," she said

"Hi Miss Menzie," responded Vena as she wiped the wet from her face.

"I see you've been jogging."

"Yes, I jog almost everyday."

"Your father told me...He also told me when you were younger he had to fuss at you for exercising in your room."

"Yeah, I remember that. He said I had my room smelling like a gym," she said as she then wiped her neck. "Why are you here?" she asked.

"Beg your pardon?"

"You heard me! I asked you why you were here?"

"Now wait a minute here!" said Mrs Jenkins in a defensive tone of voice. "I have a right to be here."

"Why, because your twat got hot and you needed my Daddy to cool it down for you? What you went all the way to Chicago, to get some, what!"

"Wait a minute. Just who do you think you are talking to me like that, young lady? I have you to know--"

"That's right Miss Menzie," interrupted Vena. "Fight me! Get me told! Show a young teenager you got some guts, go head show me!"

"Why you disrespectful little--," said Mrs. Jenkins as she walked towards the teen.

"What you gonna hit me now?" she snapped.

Suddenly she stopped and looked at the angry young teen, who peered at her without plinking an eye. She then turned and walked over to the table and sat down. She looked back at the young lady, who was still standing and holding her ground.

"You know I wouldn't hit you. But you are a spicy little thing aren't you?" she asked.

"When I have to be."

"You know I respect that...Come sit down I need to talk to you," she requested.

"No thanks, if you have something to say then say it."

"Please, come and sit down next to me. Let's talk woman to woman."

The young teen was apprehensive, but decided to respect her female elder's request to have a seat. She sat down but didn't change her demeanor much.

"Vena, I'm going to be painful honest with you. When I married your father, I thought things would be different. I'm use to being in charge. I thought I would be the one taking care of your father."

"I can take care of my Father!" snapped Vena.

"I know you can. But I had worked everything out in my mind. What I seemed to forget was what your father told me about you, and how you already had everything under control. In a way, I admire you. You are different then most teenagers today. I consider them as young, foolish and not responsible. It's enlightening to see a good looking, smart young woman like you. Your father says you recycle paper and plastics, give blood at school, even give your personal clothes to the needy, sale Old News Boys in the cold weather. And since your mother been gone, he told me you have become more responsible for things around this household and while still being an honor roll student at school. That's incredible."

"What does all you just said have to do with you being back in this house?"

"I'm saying I'm usually the one who takes charge. I expected to be in charge of him, this household, everything. I underestimated you and the situation here. When it didn't workout like I thought if should have right away, I got scared and I ran. It took me time away from him that I could see the whole picture. I don't want to compete with you. I couldn't win that battle with your father. He loves you too much. But I love him and I want us to be a family. But you and I will have to work together to make it work."

"You're asking me to trust you with my father's welfare. Let me tell you something. My mother was a good woman and I loved her. But there were times she was spoiled rotten. She was a good mother, but she wouldn't go out of her way to do anything for anybody. Not her kids and not her husband. I worked hard to be different from her. My father works hard for us to have a good life. But I want him to be happy. Outside of God, my Father is the most important thing in my life. I want to go on with my life, go to college, get married, have a family. But I can't do any of that until I can be sure he's going to be taken care of. When my Mom died and he married you, I thought you were strong enough to be good for him."

"I am."

"I hear you talking, but you have already did something even my mother never did and that was to break his heart when you left. He pretended not to care, but you really hurt him. Now, you're asking me to trust you with his life. I can't, because I don't trust you that much."

"I understand where you're coming from and I am so sorry for disappointing you, disappointing him. If it's any conciliation, I was disappointed in myself."

"So, where are we on this? Where are you?" asked a concerned Vena.

"I'm asking you to give me a chance. I know this marriage can't work if you and I work together, you helping me out. Help me to work things out with him and the other children, please."

"You really love my Father don't you?"

"With every fiber of my being."

"Whatever that means," chuckled Vena. "Tell you what, everybody desires a second chance, even you."

"Gee, thanks," chuckled Mrs. Jenkins.

"I didn't mean it like it sounded," snickered Vena.

"Yes you did," she chuckled. "But that's all right, I just want the chance to redeem myself."

Suddenly Mrs. Jenkins started to chuckle.

"What's funny?" asked Vena.

"You are. 'Did your twat get hot?'," quoted Mrs. Jenkins as she started to laugh out loud.

"Oh I'm sorry, I just couldn't think of nothing else to say at the time," apologized Vena as she too started to laugh.

"You know, you're right, the twat got hot," she joked.

At that point the two of them leaned on the table and laughed until the two of them started to tear.

Two days later Mrs. Jenkins was just coming in from work. When she walked into the kitchen from the garage, Vena was sitting at the kitchen table, and obviously waiting there for her.

"Oh, hi Vena," she said.

"Hi Miss Menzie...You got a minute?" asked Vena.

"I always have time for you. What's up?" asked Mrs. Jenkins as she sat her purse down on the table.

"I want you to read something," said Vena as she held out a stack of papers.

She took the papers and look through a few of them.

"These look like your father's notes. How did you get them?"

"I was going through the trash, looking for paper to recycle, when I found his notes in there."

"So, he threw them away?"

"Yes."

"Well, he threw them away, he obviously didn't want them."

"But read some of them. The man has the mind, the wisdom of a Prophet. And he is just throwing that away...Go on, read some of it. "

"Okay, she said as she sat down beside her and laid the papers on the table.

"Read this," requested Vena as she thumbed through a few pages, then pick out several of them and handed them to Mrs. Jenkins, who then read the first.

"'Any human being can act irrationally. All they have to do is fail to use the most common of all God's given sense, the ability to think before one acts. When we as human being do not use this most common of sense, then we react instinctively, as if mentally, we are no better than the dog which will lick its own behind or eat it's own bowel'. How disgusting," She remarked.

"Finish it," requested Vena.

"To hate, murder, and not love as God loves, is not common sense. But rather it makes a man an impulsive fool. Why offend God, who has made the likes of man in his own image. Any untamed, wild animal in the jungle could do that. But not a real civilized man. He should know better'. Wow, that's one heck of a statement," responded Mrs. Jenkins.

"That's nothing, read the next to last page," insisted Vena.

Mrs. Jenkins thumbed through the papers until she got to the page Vena wanted her to read.

"'A man's dream is only a shadow of the hope that he has. Without a dream a man's has no hope. Where there is no hope there is no passion for life. A man must have a passion for life to sustain life. For without passion for life, there is no future. When there is no future, one is already socially dead. Once one is socially dead, a physical death is sure to follow. So dream and by all means dream bigger than life. Because the bigger the dream, the more hope is intensified. This kind of hope is the passion of life and will carrying you through to your future knowing full well it will surely be crystallized one day'. Well, the man is a wonder when it comes to words," remarked Menzie as she continued to look at the sheet of paper.

"So, you see what I'm saying? Words lead to books, books lead to knowledge, and knowledge is what we all need. My Daddy should be writing books."

"You know, you make a good point. Plus, it would take him to a whole different level of recognition."

"Exactly," snapped Vena.

"Tell, you know what, let's wait until later tonight. We'll work on him together."

"Well Mrs. Jenkins, you have a way with him. He'll do it if you ask him to."

"Yeah, but you are his daughter and the apple of his eye. Beside, it is your idea and I think you should be the one to tell him how you feel about it."

"What about you?"

"I'll be there with you for morale support."

Later in the day, Vena and her Stepmother entered the den, where her Father was sitting and reading the paper.

"Daddy, you got a minute?" she asked.

"Yes, what's up?" he asked as he laid his paper down on his lap.

"It's about these," she said as she handed him the stack of papers.

"Why these are my old notes...Oh I get it, this is because I should have given them to you to recycle."

"Well, you should have, but that's not what we want to talk to you about. It's about what's in these notes."

"Oh?"

"Daddy I have read these notes and they are filled with good information, things other people need to know about."

"I used a lot of the information in those notes in some of my lectures."

"Well Daddy, that's fine, but what about those who haven't heard you speak?"

"Good point, what did you have in mind?"

"Why don't you put this information in a book?" asked Vena as Menzie stood behind her with her arms crossed.

"A book?"

"Yes, a book. Miss Menzie and I think it's a good idea, don't we Menzie?"

"It's like she said," agreed Mrs. Ferguson.

"I never thought of putting it into a book...But now that you mention it, that's not a bad idea."

"Just think of the prestige and creditability writing a book will give you?"

"You're right."

"You have any more notes?" asked Vena.

"I have plenty of them, why?"

"You go get them and give them to me. Miss Menzie and I will sort through them, organize them in some kind of order and give them to you to type. We can do that can't we Miss Menzie?"

"Yes ma'am, if you say so."

After Dr. Jenkins agreed to write a book, Vena and Menzie left the room headed for the kitchen.

"I thought that went well, didn't you?" she asked Mrs. Jenkins.

"Oh yeah, I think you handled him quite well, and me too," chuckled Mrs Jenkins as the two of them hugged and started to laugh as they walked.

Whereas things seemed to be working out on the home front, something had been bothering Mrs. Jenkins. While they preparing for bed that night, she sat in the bed, her arms crossed, and with a concerned look on her face. When her husband was about to get into bed, he noticed her demeanor. So, instead he sat on the bed so he could face her. It was then she expressed her concern to her husband.

"James, we need to talk," uttered.

"Okay dear, what's on your mind?" he asked.

"With Cecil Robinstein being sick, I'm getting a little concern," said.

"I'm feeling some anxiety about that myself," he responded.

"What do you think is the faith of the firm?"

"I have no idea."

"I think we should be considering a worse case scenario."

"You mean what happens if he dies?"

"Right. So, I've been thinking how we can be prepared should that happen."

"How?"

"Why don't we consider starting our own firm? We could be more then competitive in the market we provide. Besides, it was you and me who built the firm to the financial status it enjoys."

"Good point."

"I'll do you one better. Why don't we consider starting our own firm whether he pulls through or not? You are the one who is in the field spreading and enhancing the firm's reputation. People know you, and they know me. If you went to any of our clients and ask them to name members of our firm, they might name Cecil, but once they get past him, it's us. So, why not do for us what we have done for them?"

"Huh, you know I have thought about stepping out of my own. I never considered it seriously because I never knew how you would feel about it."

"I'm willing to bet, if I told your mother what you just told me, you want to know what she would say?"

"I know what she would say. Follow your first mind."

"I know that is what she would say. So, do it. Hey baby, I got your back and you know that. Let's build a firm that will rival any firm on this planet. Let's build it so we can leave our children, and their children a legacy. Something they can be proud of. Besides, you the man, baby!" she bellowed.

Little did they know at the time, but things at Corrall International Network Incorporated was definitely about to get nasty as the result of old man Cecil Robinstein's death. It started on a Monday's staff meeting when the Robinstein family was announcing to the employees, they were taking over the firm and making it a family business.

The three advocates of the family take over, were Catherine Robinstein. She was Mr. Cecil Robinstein's only sister. Accompanying her was Thomas and Rubin Robinstein his two brothers. It was Thomas who made the announcement, which started a round of in house chaos.

"Quiet! Quiet!" he shouted. "I don't see what the problem is. After all, my bother did own this company."

"If your brother had wanted this to be a family business, don't you think he would have converted it, way before he died," debated George Blackshere, who was Union Steward.

"What difference does that make? He's dead now and we as his family are taking over," said Catherine Robinstein.

Her statement started a bit of chaos among the workers.

"Who then will be appointed the new President?" asked Blackshere.

"I am," announced Thomas Rubinstein. "And we were considering putting Catherine as Vise-President, and Horence in charge of Operations."

"You are? What do you three really know about this business?"

"I'll have you to know, both my sister and I majored in Business in college, and got good grades."

"That's not what I asked you," insisted Blackshere. "I asked what you people, knew about this business?"

"Nothing at the moment. But, I have a good business head. Catherine runs a boutique, and knows business. All I don't know I will learn. Of course, Horence and Catherine will help me with that."

"Horence? Why he couldn't find his way out of a paper bag, even if it had a big hole in it," snickered Blackshere, and which got a chuckle out of the rest of the attendees. "As for Catherine, and her little Boutique, there a big difference in handing out flowers and handing out large contracts," he joked.

"You can make all the jokes you want. But that's the way it going be," insisted Rubin Robnistrein.

"Meanwhile, while you three are playing catch-up, our business will slow down and we will loose clients and money," stated Menzie Jenkins.

"I doubt that!" said Robinstein in a harsh tone of voice. "Everyone here is expected to work just as hard as they have always worked."

"May I make a suggestion?" asked Blackshere.

"I suppose," responded Rubin Robinstein.

"James and Menzie Jenkins, were the two people, who helped elevate this firm to the top 500 companies in America."

"What's your point?" asked Thomas.

"Why not put them in charge. That way, the firm can continue to grow and prosper," suggested Blackshere.

"That's out of the question. We are taking over, and that's that," insisted Rubin. That started more chaos among the rank and file.

"But you haven't taken into consideration, what is best for this company."

"Excuse me," said James Jenkins as he stood, which seemed to calm down the employees and got everyone's attention. "We obviously won't resolve anything here today. Why don't we reconvene this meeting. Make it more private and more professional. Let's pretend we are intelligent and call it a board meeting. Only the Robinstein family, the Union Rep, Menzie and me, need to be there."

"We could do that'" snapped Rubin Robinstein. "Though, I don't see what difference it would make."

"Trust me, you will...By the way, make sure you bring your attorney with you," requested James Jenkins.

"Why?" asked Thomas Robinstein.

"Trust me, you'll find out," remarked James Jenkins.

Three days later, the board meeting was in session. With the exception being James Jenkins, the other attendees were those personnel he had suggested. George Blackshere was addressing the attendees as to the severity of making the decision to make Corrall International Network Incorporated a family enterprise.

"I hope you people realized that making the kind of change you are suggesting is detrimental to the welfare of our firm?" he asked.

"Our firm? You do understand my brother started this company before any of you started to work here?" asked Rubin Robinstein.

"That may be, but it was the Jenkins who made it what it is today. That is why they should have been considered for the top, two positions of this firm."

"We understand the contribution the Jenkins have made to the growth of this company. However, this is now a family business, and we are taking over because we think it is in the best interests of our family," said Thomas Robinstein.

"I'm afraid that best interests you are referring to, has nothing to do with the firm. It has to do with greed, your greed."

"There's no need to be insulting. The decision to make this a family business has been made," said Catherine Robinstein.

"And we already know, there is no way you can stop it," reiterated Thomas. "Now, we are offering the Jenkins a considerable increase in pay to stay on with us, and in the positions they now hold."

"That is so generous of you," said Blackshere with a bit of sarcasm in his voice.

"We thought so," uttered Rubin.

"So, it is final then?" asked Blackshere.

"Yes."

"Well, I would like for Mrs. Menzie Jenkins to have the floor at this time. She has an announcement to make. Menzie."

"Thanks Mr. Blackshere. My husband, Dr. James Jenkins is not here today. He is finalizing the establishing of Consolidation and Data Networking International Incorporated."

"What?" asked Tomas as he lend over and whispered to his sttorney.

"May I continue?" she asked.

"By all means," stated Thomas Robinstein.

This innovative concept of combining data information with aggressive incorporated strategies and updated training provisions, are unique because of its abilities to provide a number of technical as well as professional services and on an international scale."

"What! You're quitting?" asked Thomas Robinstein.

"I'm sorry, but you interrupted me!" snapped Menzie. "Dr. James Jenkins will hold the positions of President and CEO of said firm. I, Mrs. Menzie Jenkins, will therefore hold the position of Vice President. I have here, my husband's resignation to commence today, with an effective date noted two weeks from now. Since he has more than two weeks of vacation coming, he request that the duration of his resignation and his vacation time run concurrently."

"That's fine!" snapped Thomas Robinstein. "We're going to miss Dr. Jen--"

"Excuse me," interrupted Menzie Jenkins. "I am not finished. Since I will be the Vice President, I therefore submit my resignation to commence today and with an effective date to include two weeks from today. I am requesting vacation time, and request that my resignation duration and vacation time run concurrently. Do you have an objections?"

Before answering Mrs. Jenkins' question, Thomas Robinstein conferred to their attorney, then responded to Menzie's question.

"No, we don't," said Thomas.

"Good," responded Menzie. "Now I would like for our attorney, Mr. Steven Thomas to have the floor. Steven."

"Thanks Mrs. Jenkins," said Thomas as he stood before the Robinstein family. "Ladies and gentlemen of the Robinstein family, you have been handed the stock and investment portfolio for this firm...Please refer to page twenty-four."

Thomas waited until the Robinsteins and their attorney picked up their portfolios then turned to page twenty-four.

"As you can see, Dr. James Jenkins has twenty percent stock in this firm. Miss Ferguson, now Mrs. Jenkins, has twenty-five percent. You do see that?"

"Yes we do," responded Thomas.

"Well, since my clients are no longer employed by Corrall International Network Incorporated, they are prepared to sell their stock. Since you are now the principle owners, you are responsible for responding to that scenario. What are you offering?" asked Thomas.

He and Menzie peered over at one another as they watched the Robinsteins conferred with their lawyer as they referred to the portfolios they had been given. Once they seemed to have things worked out, they got back to Steven Thomas.

"Since your clients represent only forty-five percent of the stock in this company, here's what we are proposing," said Thomas

Robinstein. "If your clients desire is to have their stocks remain with our firm, they may. And their new company can be a subordinate to ours. That way we can keep the same working relationship, while sharing in the profits. On the other hand, if your client wants to sell, then we are prepared to buy them out at, let's say forty cents on the dollar."

"Well, if you refer back to your portfolios, page twenty-six, you will see the employees of Corrall International Network Incorporated, own another twenty percent of the stock," pointed out Thomas.

"We know that!" snapped Rubin Robinstein. "What's your point?"

"My point is, if those employees decide to work for my clients, that would be a sixty-five percent of controlling shares. If you decide to leave your stocks in escrow with their new company, your thirty-five percent compared to their combined sixty-five would make them the parent company, and you the subordinate firm, should you choose to stay the course."

"And if we don't?" asked Catherine Robinstein.

"Well, on the other hand if you wish to sell out, my clients are prepared to offer you, let's say, forty cent on the dollar."

"That's impossible!" shouted Catherine Robinstein. "Our employees like working here and the likelihood of all of them leaving at the same time is highly unlikely!" she scolded.

"Oh really!" bellowed Steven Thomas as he peered over at Menzie Jenkins.

The next day, the Robinstein family stood in old man Robinstein's second story office picture window, and with this shocked looks on their faces, as they watched their employees abruptly rushing around, emptying their desks and file cabinets, piling stacks of the firm's paper work on vacant desks. They watched them take their personal items like clocks, pictures and banners off the walls, all in a hurry to get away from them.

"I don't believe this," uttered Catherine Robinstein as she watched in bewilderment.

They continued to watch as a convoy of their employee, who had bought their own chairs were lined up and pushing them out the double doors, with their personal items sitting on them. After it seemed all of the employees had left out, one lone female rushed back into the office, opened one of the desk drawers, took out a pen set and closed the drawer.

"This is mine," she uttered as she held up the pen set so they could see it as she continued to rush out of the firm's doors.

Within a matter of twenty minutes the entire office was void of people. All jumping ship to join the new company started by James and Menzie Jenkins, while all the Robinstein family could do was watched, then peer over at one another as if they no idea what had just happened.

Dr. Jenkins and Mrs. Jenkins worked very hard for themselves just as they did when they worked for someone else. He went out representing the firm. His books and his lecture were good for his reputation as well as the reputation of the firm. Mrs. Jenkins came up with several ideas, which helped the firms draw more clients to her husband and consequently to the firm. Now they were building their own legacy. It didn't take long for the new Consolidation And Data Networking International Incorporated to get a foothold in the business community. In two years, the firm was quickly headed for the top twenty businesses to do business with. Not only did the employees from Corrall International Networking Incorporated enjoyed working for their new firm and the Jenkins, clients unsatisfied with the split, loyalist to Dr. Jenkins and his wife, quickly transferred their business over to them. Eventually other clients not happy with the way the old firm conducted business, transferred their business to the new firm and without hesitation. That made it grow quicker and become more solid. Consequently, the firm became more than the old firm's competitor. It just literately out performed them.

CHAPTER FIFTEEN

THE PRICESS'S SENIOR PROM

More most important occurrence during those two years was now hard Mrs. Jenkins and Vena worked to pull the household together. The more they worked together, the smoother things went. But something else happened. Both had gained a mutual respect for one another. Once her stepmother got to know her, the more she realized she was just like her.

Vena was a honor roll student and had been all of her days in school, so she was obviously smart. She was naive in a way but very mature for her age. Occasionally she showed some interest in boys, but the moment she realized they were not at her maturity level, she would forget the notion and go to something else. Because of her demeanor, she was well liked and well respected every place she went. She stayed on all the family members about recycling papers, plastics. She donated blood at her high school during blood drives, she donated to the Scouts, Salvation Army, even gave her personal clothes to the needy. And every Saturday morning she got up early and cooked breakfast for the entire family. All things she admired about her because that is exactly the kinds of things she would do.

Vena, who was nearing 18 years old, and was about to finish high school. She had been accepted to attend several prestigious universities. So she chose Lincoln University of Missouri, located in Jefferson City, Missouri, mostly because it was where her father had gone. When she came home from school one afternoon, she excitingly looked for her father, but he was not home yet. However, Menzie was there and fixing diner.

"Hi," said Vena when she saw her.

"Hi sweetheart," she responded as she continued to cook.

"Do you know if my Daddy is on his way home?"

"He's meeting with a new client...Are those what I think they are?"

"Yes ma'am, these are my senior pictures."

"Congratulations," she bellowed as she stopped what she was doing, wiped her hands on her apron and walked over to where she was standing. "Let's see them," she requested.

Vena handed them to her then sat down at the table, while Mrs. Jenkins slowly looked at them one at a time.

"You are sure a pretty young woman?"

"Thank you...May I ask you a question?"

"I think you just did," snickered her stepmother.

"Yeah, I guess I did, didn't I," chuckled Vena. "Several of the girls at school want to go to the senior prom. They want to go in together and rent a limousine. You think Dad will go for that?"

"Wouldn't you ladies have dates?"

"I don't want any of these little boys taking me to the prom. For some reason, they think the next stop is the Holiday Inn. I'm not into that, and neither are my friends."

"Now you know you have your father wrapped around your little finger, and you know there isn't anything we wouldn't do for you."

"Yeah, but he'll have to get me a prom dress, he already paid for my pictures. I don't want him spending too much money on me when he has the other kids to worry about."

"I think that is so wonderful. Here your Father and me have all this money and you are worried about him spending too much money on you."

Just as Mrs. Jenkins was finishing her statement, Mr. Jenkins walked into the front door.

"Here he is. You can ask him for yourself," she said.

"She can ask me what for herself?" asked Mr. Jenkins as he walked into the kitchen and joined them.

"Go head sweetheart, ask him."

"Dad, some of the girls graduating with me want to go the Senior Prom. They were talking about chipping in on a limousine to take us there. What do you think?"

"I think that's a wonderful idea."

"You do?"

"Sure, just let me know the dates and I'll arrange that for you."

"Why don't you let me take care of that?" asked Mrs. Jenkins.

"No, I'll do it," insisted Dr. Jenkins.

"Tell you what, I haven't ordered my dress for the Prom yet. Maybe you can help me with my dress, and Dad can help with the limousine."

"Now why didn't I think of that," chuckled Mrs. Jenkins. "Goes to show ya, all you need is a fresh young brain," she snickered.

"Sure you're right!" bellowed Dr. Jenkins.

"What?" asked Vena, as the three of them chuckled as he response.

Weeks passed and the night of the Senior Prom was getting close. But then the reality of talking a good game and putting your money were your mouth is, is quite a different matter as Vena found out. She came home from school on a Friday afternoon a little frustrated. As she entered the house through the garage, Mrs. Jenkins had just gotten home ahead of her and was putting up the groceries. She noticed her demeanor as soon as she closed the kitchen door.

"Hi sweetheart," she said. "Problem?"

"Yes, I want to talk to my Dad about it. Isn't he upstairs?"

"Yes, you mind if I be nosy?"

"No, come on," said Vena as she led her Stepmother up the stairs and into her father's home office, where he was sitting at the computer compiling a book.

"Dad, you got a moment?" she asked.

"Yeah sweetheart," replied Dr. Jenkins.

He stopped what he was doing, turned and faced her.

"What's the matter?" he asked as he then peered over at his wife, then back to her.

"It's these girls at school. When we talked about going to the Prom, they all said they would help out on the money to pay to lease a limousine. Well, tomorrow, we were to have our money to put the down payment on it. Only three of us had our money."

"So how much do you need to confirm the lease?"

"I don't know, but I know this is not enough," she said as she showed him the money she had in her hand as Mrs. Jenkins stood and watched with her arms crossed.

"Vena let me tell you something. You have worked hard to get to where you are and I am very proud of you. Now, I want you to leave that school in style. So, you are going to go to that Prom in a limousine, even if you have to ride in it by yourself.

"You sure?"

"Yes."

"Oh thank you, Daddy!" bellowed Vena as she hugged her Father.

"Tell you what, why don't you and I get on the phone right now and see where we can find you a limousine," suggested Mrs. Jenkins.

"Now about a long white one?" asked Vena.

"Yeah, that sounds great. Plus, Menzie knows all about long white limousines, don't you dear?"

"Come on you two, let's keep it clean," chuckled Vena, as her parents joined her in a good laugh.

To prepare Vena for her Prom, Lynnett Jenkins and Menzie took her shopping to find a Prom dress. They shopped until they helped her find the one grown which made her look extremely elegant. Naturally she fussed that it cost too much. But it didn't take much for the two of them to convince her to take it.

Then came the day of the Prom. All day Menzie Jenkins, her Aunt Lona and Grandmother Lynnett Jenkins pampered her. They took her to have her nails done, to get an expensive pair of shoes to match her grown. They made her get a facial, all to make her feel like the special young lady she was.

That night there was plenty of excitement around the Jenkins' home. It was the night of the Prom. Dr. Jenkins got home early because he was determined to see his daughter before she left for the Prom. When he walked in the door and asked if she was ready, he was told her stepmother was putting on the final touches for her appearance.

Her father was sitting on the sofa anxiously waiting to see her. The doorbell rang. It was the three young ladies who were to ride in the limousine with her. The excitement grew, when this long white limousine pulled up to the Jenkins' home. The chauffeur ranged the doorbell to alert the ladies that their ride was there. All three of the young ladies looked extremely nice in their formal gowns.

Then Menzie Jenkins came down the stairs. The family was waiting in the family room. She stepped just inside the door and made her announcement.

"Ladies and gentlemen, I present to you, Princess Vena L. Jenkins," she said as she gestured towards the bottom of the staircase.

The moment most definitely belonged to Vena Jenkins as she cleared the staircase and stepped into the doorway of the family room.

"Oh, look at my Princess, she looks so pretty," uttered her father.

There she stood, as he looked at the most gracious young woman he had ever seen. To further show her grace, she peered over to her Father and curtsied to him.

"Father," she uttered as she bowed with the grace of royalty.

"Your Highest," he gestured as he tilted his head slightly.

The family and friends all stood as if they were in the presents of a queen. Her friends and family started to take pictures of her. It was as if they all considered this as a very special moment. Her brothers didn't say anything. They just peered at her, then over to one another.

"Oh Vena, you look so pretty," uttered Floreese as she looked at her big sister with a proudly gleam in her eyes.

"Thank you, little sister of mine," she responded.

"May I escort my lady to her waiting cartage?" asked her Father.

"You shall, but only after I have had my picture taken with you, Father."

They all had a big laugh as he escorted his daughter out on the front porch, where they took several pictures together. He then took pictures of her standing by the limousine. He took pictures of her and her friends both inside and beside the long, white limousine. Then finally, he had to let her go. He, his wife and children, her aunt all stood as they watched it pull away from the curb, with her waiving as if she was part of a passing royal review.

"Did you see her?" he asked his wife.

"Yes," said Mrs. Jenkins as she started to tear. "The saga of womanhood is suddenly upon us," she uttered.

"And much too soon for me."

"Yeah, I see what you mean."

It was late when Vena returned home. She was not surprised to see her Father still up waiting for her to come home. She opened the door and could see him sitting on the sofa watching a late movie of the television.

"Hi Daddy," she said as turned and looked the door behind her. "Somehow I knew you would still be up."

"Really?"

"Well, it was more I was hoping you would be up. I'm going to change clothes because we are having an all night dance and sleep over at the school."

"Do you need a ride?"

"No sir, the limousine is still on my time," she chuckled.

She walked over and sat down beside her Father. She looked at him as if she was trying to get his attention, which she finally did.

"Something wrong?" he asked.

"No, I just wanted to thank you for making this a special night for me," she said as she hugged him around his shoulders."

"Well, if anybody deserve a special night, it would be you. I just don't like how you seemed to have grown up to fast."

"Well, Daddy, you know we have to grow up, we can't stay kids for ever you know?"

"Yeah, and just looking at you reminds me of that," he snickered.

"I bet," she chuckled.

"Really. I was just thinking earlier today what a wonderful and bless young lady you have been. I don't think I've ever had to spank you, have I?"

"Yes sir, you did once."

"I did? What did you do?"

"I told you a lie, and you knew it. Even when you spank me, I stuck to it. I felt real bad afterwards."

"Why? Did I hurt you?"

"No sir, that wasn't it. As a matter of fact, the spanking didn't hurt me at all. But I though if I cried hard enough, you would stop, you did."

The two of them laughed.

"Daddy, will you miss me when I'm gone?"

"Sure I will. Why do you ask?"

"Because I'm going to miss everybody, but you most of all. Well, let's make sure we keep in contact."

"You bet, let me go upstairs and change clothes."

Once she was changed and came back downstairs, her Father has sitting in his recliner fast asleep. She walked over to him, stood and watched him for a couple of second, and snickering as she did so. She then bent down and kissed him on his forehead.

"I love you Daddy." She whispered.

"I love you too angel."

She left out of the front door, locking it behind herself. Then got into the long, white limousine and headed back towards the high school. Knowing full well, she had a Father, who regarded her as a very special young lady. And the way he let her have her day of royalty, only proved just how special he really thought she was to him.

To further illustrate just how special she was, she intentionally made it home in time the next morning to get Floreese and Myron up in time to prepare for school, something she had been going every since she was a small child. She made it a point of letting them know they would be on their own from this day forward.

CHAPTER SIXTEEN

DISCOVERY OF A MALE PRODIGY

With all the excitement of Vena graduation from high school and preparing to leave for college, all seemed well. At this point she had full confidence in her new Stepmother's ability to take care of her Father and the family without her. Mrs. Jenkins of course, was waiting for that opportunity. Even though she respected a young woman like Vena taking on that responsibility of caring for the family, she knew the time would come when she would have to consider her owe future and moved on. And now that she was at the helm, it didn't take long for her first real tasking to come forth.

It was right after Vena had left for college. Mrs. Jenkins happened to be passing by Marcus' room when she heard music. Not just any music, it was him singing while playing a gaiter. She stopped and listened as he did so. The song he was signing was very moving. Still it was one she had not heard before. Just as he was finishing up the song, she entered his room, stood and listened to him. He had seen her walk in, but he kept sitting in the chair next to the desk in his room, playing until he was done. Once he did, he peered up at her.

"That was beautiful," she remarked as she stood there, her arms crossed.

"Thank you," responded Marcus.

"I never heard that song before. What was the name of it?"

"It called 'Letter To God' and I made it up."

"You did?"

"Yes, I've written lots of songs," he said as he then started to play another tone on the guitar.

"What's the name of that?" she asked after listening to him play several bars.

"It called 'Teach Me How To Love'."

"The melody sounds great. You write that too?"

"Yes," he said as he then started to sing the lyrics.

Just sitting listening to him playing the guitar and singing like any full man put his stepmother in a sort of transit state of mind. She sat down on his bed and watched him express himself in song. She sat and listened, as she seemed to get caught up in mood of his song, it mesmerized her. She listened until he was finished. She was so over taken she clapped.

"Thank ya, thank ya very much," he recited.

"Man, you have some real talent, you know that...How long have you been writing music?"

"Every since I was five or six, I can't remember."

"Do you know what a Child Prodigy is?" she asked.

"Yes, it a child born with exceptional talent," responded Marcus.

"Of course you know. With this family, why would you assume otherwise," chuckled Mrs. Jenkins.

The two of them laughed a bit.

"Does your father know you write music?"

"No, he doesn't."

"I think we should tell him."

"I don't think we should. He won't like to hear it."

"I think your father would be excited to know he has such a talented son."

"Oh he wouldn't mind that. It's what I want to do with my life he may not understand."

"Maybe you should explain what you mean by that."

"My father is smart, he has three degrees. He expects all of us to go to college like he did."

"So, you can go to college and take up music."

"That's the point, I don't want to go to college. I want to become professional singer. And right now, if it were possible."

"Oh, now I see what you mean...How many songs have you written?"

"About ten, but I've got ideas for a lot more."

"Huh, maybe I can help you out."

"Not if you can't convince Dad that college is not for me, singing is."

"Who says I can't do that?" she uttered as she chuckled a bit.

That Friday night, James Jenkins walked into the bedroom after putting Floreese to bed. When he walked into the bedroom, his wife was already in bed, and with the covers pulled up to her shoulders and holding the spread with both hands. When he looked at her, she was peering back at him this conspicuous look on her face.

"Something wrong?" he asked.

"Huh, huh," she gestured in the positive.

"What?"

"Hot!" she bellowed.

"What?" he asked in a surprise tone of voice.

"Hot!" she repeated as she lifted the cover up so he could see her body.

The moment he saw her naked, he understood and started to quickly get undressed as he kept looking at her body.

"Hurry, the twat is hot!" she uttered.

"What?" he asked as he stopped undressing and peered down at her.

"Trust me, you're know what I mean in a few seconds," she snickered as she started to fan herself with the covers.

Once undressed, Jenkins wasted no time jumping into bed and under the covers. In fact, once there he did state to waste time and his wife made a note of it.

"Mmmmmmmm. You don't have to fire up the skillet, baby. The bacon is already sizzling...Ohhhhhhhhh!" she uttered in passion.

Much later as she lie in her husband's arms attempting to catch a few breaths. Once she was under control, they talked like they always did after making love.

"I am not going to be worth a dime in the morning," she chuckled.

"Menzie, it's already morning," commented her husband.

"See, I'm brain dead already," she snickered.

She then turned and while resting on his chest, she started to nibble on one of his nipples.

"James," she uttered.

"Huh."

"What are you thinking about?"

"You are nibbling on my nipples. If you don't stop you going to find yourself on top of me again," chuckled Jenkins.

"You are one horny old man, you know that?" chuckled Menzie. "But then you are right. I better stop, because if we start up again, we could be here all day," she then chuckled as she laid her head back on his chest. "James, what do you be thinking about when we are making love?"

"Menzie, the only thing I can think about is how good your stuff is," chuckled James Jenkins.

"Yeah right!" chuckled Menzie. "Well, I don't know about you, but every time we make love, I feel like a new bride all over again."

"And why is that?"

"Because you know how to ware out some stuff, just like you did when you first got into it," she chuckled.

"That's because when you give of yourself, you don't hold back. You make love with so much passion. You react with passion, you talk passionately, and what that does is motivate me all the more."

She started to chuckle.

"What's funny?" asked her husband.

"You, when you said I don't hold back...Hell, I held back for over thirty years. I am just glad to be getting me some on a regular basics," she chuckled. "Besides, you do a good job of banging up some stuff," she chuckled.

"How about I bang it out just a little bit more?" asked Jenkins as he rolled over and started to kiss her.

"Mmmmmmmmm, baby!" she moaned. "Just a little bit more...Ohhhhhhhhhh!"

After making love, they finally drifted off to sleep. In fact, they were so worn out they stayed in bed most of the morning. Once they were well awake, they started to talk again.

"Today is one of those days I miss having Vena around to cook breakfast," said Mrs. Jenkins.

"Yeah, I know what you mean. I miss her already."

"James, can we talk seriously about something?" she asked as she turned over on her stomach and faced him

"Is it about good sex?"

"No silly," she chuckled. "It's about Marcus."

"What about him?"

"Did you know he could sing?"

"Of course I knew he could sing. I've heard him sing in church lots of times."

"But did you know he has written several songs?"

"No, I didn't know that."

"He has written ten and has a lot of ideas for some others."

"Huh, I wonder why he hasn't told me about them?

"Because he is no different then the rest of your children. He doesn't want to disappoint you."

"How would him writing songs disappoint me?"

"It isn't what he's done that he feels you will be disappointed about. It's what he doesn't want to do, that bothers him?"

"And what might that be?"

"He is really not interested in going to college."

"So what does he want to do with his life?"

"He wants to pursue a professional singing career."

"Why can't he do them both?"

"I just told you. He isn't interested in going to college."

"Why that's ridicules. He's an honor role student. He knows how important it is for a Black man to have an education!" snapped James Jenkins.

"Now James, he knows how important it is for a Black man to be successful. You have taught all of our children that. But lots of people do real well without a formal education and I know you know that. Now, before you go nuts, let me tell you how I can help."

"You mean to convince him to go to college?"

"No, I mean to help him pursue his dream...Before we got married, I remember hearing you speak. You made a point I have never forgotten. You said, 'Two of the most powerful statements in the human sanity makeup are: (I love you, and I have a dream)', remember that?"

"Yes, in fact it's in the book I'm writing right now. What's your point?"

"In your book aren't you also emphasizing just how important it is to have a dream?"

"Yes."

"Well, he has a dream, a big dream. 'The very essence of life', I believe you said."

Jenkins started to laugh as he sat up and peered over at his wife.

"What's funny?" she asked.

"You are. When you want to make a point, you get a brother in the mood first. That kind of strategy is hard to resist."

"Well you know how to put a woman in the right mood to ask," she chuckled. "You are the only man I know who is equipped enough to try."

"Okay, how do we approach this with Marcus?"

"Leave it to me," said Mrs. Jenkins with this conspicuous look on her face.

That Monday morning and while at work, She made a long distance call to Atlanta, Georgia to talk to an old school mate. The phone rang once and a female answered.

"Good morning, this is Vocal Shines Recording Company, how may I help you?"

"Hello, my name is Menzie Jenkins. May I speak with Timothy Graves?"

"Hold the line please."

"Hello," said a male voice on the other end of the phone.

"Hi Tim, this is Menzie."

"Hey Menzie baby!" How are you?"

"I'm doing just fine and you?"

"Well, right now I'm trying to find that one person, who can help put me back on the charts."

"Ahh come on! I heard you were doing good."

"Menzie, I'm going to be honest with you. I got Rappers up the butt hole and right now they are carrying us, now that's sad. What

I'm looking for are a couple of real, good singers, you know what I mean?"

"Absolutely, that's why I called. I've got one for ya."

"Oh really? Male or female?"

"Male, and he writes his own songs."

"Well, I was really looking for a female vocalist, more sex appeal, you know what I mean?"

"He could be a sex attraction, he's tall and very handsome."

"Hey! I just thought of something," bellowed Graves. "What if I introduced both a male and female vocalists?"

"You have a female in mind?"

"Yes, you."

"Oh no! I'm not interesting in singing right now."

"Listen to me before you turn me down. You already have a reputation as an artist and actress. What if I featured your guy as being discovered by you?"

"How do you know people will remember me?"

"You are a great singer, I remember that from hearing you sing in college. Come in and make an album for me. Shortly after it's released, we'll let you introduce your guy."

"I don't know about that. I mean, here I am trying to get him a break and I end up singing. I don't know how he would take that."

"Menzie, you called me because you needed help. Now this is an opportunity for us to help each other, can't you see that?"

"Sure, but I'm thinking of him and how he will react to me doing like you suggested."

"Menzie, you are a smart woman, and I know you know an opportunity when you hear it."

"Look Timothy, don't try and play me," she snapped. "Let's say, I do as you ask. When do you need me to be there?"

"Menzie, I'm leaving it all up to you. The quicker we can get you on tape, the quicker we can get your guy out there."

"Okay, I'll be there on Wednesday, noonday."

"Do you need me to pick you up at the airport?"

"Now you know I am from Atlanta and can make my own arrangement for transportation."

"Menzie, if I didn't know any better, I would say you still don't have much trust in me."

"Huh, you got it all wrong, I don't trust you one bit. And you know not to try to play me, don't you?"

"What man in his right mind would try and fool you?"

"First of all, you were never in your right mind," chuckled Menzie. "But I do trust your musical instincts and what you suggested is workable.

"Good, then I'll see you on Wednesday."

When she discussed with her husband what had happened in her attempt to get Marcus a try at his music, she was reminded most times people will always promote there own agenda first. However, since she had said she would handled it, he supported whatever she wanted to do. They both agreed however, not to tell Marcus in fear of him not understanding sometimes that's the way life.

Early Wednesday morning, she and her attorney, Steven Thomas, were on a plane to Atlanta. Once there, she got her father's car and they went to the Vocal Shine Recording Company. The moment she walked into the company, she was recognized by several of the females there, well almost.

"Miss Ferguson, welcome to Vocal Shine. May I have your autograph?" requested one of several females who approached her.

"Only if you call me Mrs. Jenkins," insisted Menzie as she watched Graves walk out of his office and towards her.

"Menzie! Baby!" he bellowed as she grabbed her in a bear hug. "You look good enough to eat," he uttered.

"Well, I hope you ate a good lunch before I got here," she chuckled as she worked herself free of him, and as the onlookers also chuckled at her remark.

"That's my Menzie for you, always making with the jokes," he retorted as he let go of her.

"Well, I'm her attorney, Steven Thomas, and if you break a rib, we could have a real, big problem," said Thomas.

"Right," bellowed Tim Graves. "Joe, get your crew together and get studio 6 ready for Miss Ferguson.

"It's Jenkins! Don't you people read the newspaper?" she asked.

Later, she was all set up. The sounds artist had already arranged the music and it was time for her to do her thing. The intro to her song commenced, when she was cued, she started to sing. The tone? 'A House Is Not A Home' previously performed by Miss Dion Warrick.

She was always known for arising to the occasion. This occurrence was no different. As she song, she got everyone's attention. As they watched her put her feeling into the song, just listening to her became a sheer delight to all those around her whether they were involved in the project or not. Even before she was halfway through the song, those who were there could already visualize a woman they could see would no doubt be an instance success.

And when she hit the final note, the entire gathering stood and clapped. The mood could already be felt in the air. Graves was beside himself.

"Now, that's entertainment!" he uttered to coin an old phase.

"Oh God, you were so great," sobbed a female, who was in tears as she hugged her.

"Mrs. Jenkins, that was beautiful," said a second female as she too was in tears.

"Oh, thank you, I'm glad you enjoyed it."

"Menzie baby, great job!" uttered Graves as he grabbed her around her shoulders and kissed her on the lips. "Follow me," he requested as he turned and headed towards his office.

"You wait here. I'll handle this" she advised her attorney.

Once there, he sat down at his desk. She slammed the door behind her, walked over and stood in front of his desk, this angry look on her face.

"What the hell is wrong with you?" she shouted.

"What?" asked Graves, his hands extended out, this look of pure innocence clearly displayed of his face.

"You kissed me, and in front of all those people out there."

"Cool it, they won't make much of it."

"Cool it? Did you say cool it?" she fussed. "We've gone through this in college when you kissed in front of that Malinda gal-"

"Her name was LaMilner," corrected Grave.

"Man! I don't care what her name was, you did that to make her jealous, or so you said."

"Would you keep your voice down?"

"Oh I see, you don't want them to hear me tell your ass off, but it was okay for you to kiss me in front of them?" she scolded as she pointed her finger at him.

"Hey, I'm sorry. But Menzie, you must know how I feel about you. I liked you while we were in grammar school. I've never stopped."

"Well, Timothy, I've always liked you too. But only because you didn't get fresh with me back then. When you tried your little trick in college, I told you then, never to touch me again, remember that?"

"Yeah, I remember. And I swear to you, it won't happen again, okay?"

"It better not! Because the next time you even touch me, I'm going to pop you in your nose so hard, they will need to give you a blood transfusion after it stop bleeding!"

Graves chuckled a bit at her remark. But as he glared at her, he could see she was not in a laughing mood and obviously she meant what she said. But he was determined to have the last say so.

"You know Menzie, you have always had this uppity, better than anyone else attitude."

"Look man, I--"

"Hold up! I'm talking!" snapped Graves. "Remember, you called me because you needed my help. So don't come in here like you run this, I do. Now, this is the contract I have drawn up for you," said Graves as he waved the contract sheet of paper he had in his hand. "You sign it, and we can get things rolling."

"What about my son's contract?"

"We're going to do this my way. After we get you out there, I will listen to your person. If I like him, I will put him under contract," said Graves as Thomas walked in.

"No, let's do this more like professionals. I'm coming back here with my son. You draw up a contract for both of us, and--"

"No! Let's sign you up and get you going. That was our agreement."

"Excuse me," said Thomas. "May I see the contract agreement?" he asked.

He took a couple of minutes and read the contract. He bent over and whispered in her ear. Graves watched as she then whispered in Thomas' ear.

"Let's compromise here," said Thomas. "Mrs. Jenkins, this is a fair contract as far as you are concerned. Since my client's reason for making this contact was to get her son an audition for your record label, we think an addendum should be attracted to this contract indicating, he will get that audition, prior to my client's album being released to the public. That is, if you want to be fair about this thing."

"Fair, we're talking business here," insisted Graves.

"Then good business then," retorted Thomas. "It actually keeps you in the driver seat in this matter," he continued.

"So, what you are proposing, does not obligate me to have to take him, regardless of his talent?"

"My son is good, better then you will ever have around here. He will make your label swore with recognition and popularity."

"Oh really?" bellowed Graves, a bit of sarcasm in his voice.

"Man, he is about to make your name famous, and put you among the best in proving musical entertainment. And he will do it on his own merit," recited Mrs. Jenkins.

"Menzie, Menzie, you and your pipe dream?" chuckled Graves with a sarcastic tone still in his voice.

"That's right! And wipe that smug look off you face," she insisted. "This is business, remember?" she asked in her own sarcastic tone of voice.

"Look, I don't want to fight with you, Menzie. Only a fool would do that. I want this thing to work for us. So, I'll do it as your attorney suggests. You get with my people and figure out the language to make it work. Folks, we have a deal," insisted Graves as he shook hands with Thomas, then Mrs. Jenkins.

Finally they settled down, and worked out the details of the contract. They later went out and had dinner consummate the contractual agreement. The next morning Mrs. Jenkins received a phone call while she was still at the airport in Atlanta. It was from her doctor's office and he wanted to see her the moment she was back in the city. Once she was back home, she dropped in on him.

"Oh hi Mrs. Jenkins," said the receptionist when she walked into the office.

"Hi Gloria, I got a called that Dr. Philips wanted to see me."

"Have a sit, I'll let him know you are here."

After several minutes, Dr. Philips came out, greeted her then escorted her to his office. Once there and she was seated, he explained the reason for his request.

"Well, Mrs. Jenkins, I have the results of your last examination and physical. I have bad news and good. Which would you like to hear first?"

"Oh God! Give me the bad news first," she insisted.

"I'm afraid you are going to be gaining some weight and lose some of that wonderful figure of yours," he started.

"What? You don't mean...I'm pregnant do you?"

"I'm afraid so."

"Oh my God! Oh my God! I'm pregnant? You telling me I'm pregnant?"

"Yes," chuckled her doctor.

"Sceeeeeeeeeeeee!" she screamed from excitement.

On her way out of her doctor's office, she stopped and hugged the receptionist.

"I'm pregnant," she uttered.

"So I heard, congratulation. Is this your first?"

"No, I have five children. No this is my first. On hell, when I got married my husband already had five, and I'm, well, this is my first...Do you know what I mean?"

"I think so," said the receptionist with a blank look on her face.

When she reached the first floor and walked outside of the doctor's office, she stopped, threw up her hands and shouted.

"I'm pregnant!"

At that point her dress flew up and over her head exposing all of her thighs. It was then she realized she was standing over a transit cover and a passenger train was passing underneath her.

"Ohhh!" she uttered as she struggled to pull her dress down as she stepped off it. Little did she know at the time, but there was someone close by and taking pictures of the entire occurrence.

Once she was back at the firm, she did not go directly to her office. Instead she went to Sara Tillsberge's office. She saw her just as she walked in.

"Hi boss, how was your trip?"

"Good afternoon Sara, meet you in your conference room and I'll tell you all about it," she said as she headed directly for the conference room.

Sara followed her there and the two of them sat down.

"You won't believe what happened to me today," she stated.

"Your voice went away and you couldn't sing a lick," guessed Sara.

"No silly," chuckled Mrs. Jenkins "I was told I was pregnant."

"And who was it who told you--. What did you just say?"

"I just left my doctor's office and he told me I was pregnant," she said in an excited tone of voice.

"Oh my God! Congratulations girl!" bellowed Sara as she hugged her boss. "I bet your husband had a fit when you told him."

"I haven't told him yet. I just found out about an hour ago. "Oh my God! I wonder what he's going to say."

"Wait a minute here. You told me you were getting plenty of sex."

"No I didn't...Well, I was," she chuckled.

"Didn't they tell you in sex education, that's how you get pregnant?"

"We knew that, silly. I'm just trying to figure how to let him know. I mean we haven't talked about me having a baby since we've been married."

"So, you don't think he was trying to get you pregnant?"

"I just think the man likes plenty of sex."

"Lucky woman," chuckled Sara.

"You have no idea!" snickered Mrs. Jenkins.

"Okay, okay, here's how you do it. You sat the man down. You sit down next to him. You hold him by the hand and you say, 'Guess what honey, you have screwed yourself upon a baby.' Get it?" chuckled Sara.

"Easy for you to say...If I do it like that, he will faint for sure," she snickered.

"Okay, you tell me how you think you should do it?"

"I'll sat him down and calmly say, dear, remember when we had sex nine times in one week, well one of those days I got pregnant."

"Oh boy, I can see this child is going to have a hard time surviving this pregnancy," said Sara.

The two of them sat and had a good laugh.

CHAPTER SEVENTEEN

THE FAMILY CHALLEGES

Later that night, Mrs. Jenkins was fixing diner when Myron walked into this kitchen this strange look on his face.

"Myron, what wrong," she asked.

"I got a little problem and I don't think that I should tell my Dad about it," he said.

"Would you like to tell me?"

"I guess so."

"Okay, let's sat at the table and you can tell me all about it."

The two of them sat down at the kitchen table. She waited until he was ready to tell her what was on his mind. Finally he did.

"There are these boys at school, they keep picking on me."

"How many are there?"

"There are three of them, but this one kid seems to be like the leader or something. He runs his mouth too much."

"Have you told any of the adults at school about him picking on you?"

"Yeah, I told my teacher and she told the principal. We both talked to the principal, but all that did was make him madder."

"I see...why are you wondering if you should tell your dad?"

"Because he doesn't want me to get in trouble at school."

"I see. So you aren't scared, just afraid to tell your father?" he paused. "Tell, you what. Why don't I come over to the school and alert the principal that the situation hasn't changed?"

"Noh! You do that and I will never hear the last of it."

"Would you like for me to pick you up for a few days? I mean until thing cool down a bit."

"Okay, but please don't tell Dad."

"I promise I won't."

The next day after school, Mrs. Jenkins was on her way to pick up Myron. When she got near the school, she could see a crowd of kids walking behind a group of boys. It was then she realized it was Myron walking and he had these three boys walking behind him. She turned around and parked the car. Once she was out of the car, she rushed towards where the crowd had gathered. She made her what through the crowd in time to see what was going on. It was also when Myron saw her.

"Hi Mom," he said.

"Hi Myron. What's going on here?" she asked.

"I'll tell you what's going on here," said one of the boys. "Your son thinks he is better than everybody else."

"Why because he don't have a big mouth like you?" she snapped.

The other kids started to laugh and tease the big mouth kid, and that made him mad.

"I would punch his lights out. But then I would have to beat up his old lady."

"Hey you! Watch your mouth!" shouted Myron.

"Make me!" challenged the boy as he walked up to Myron.

She didn't comment, just stood watching with her arms crossed.

"Make me!" repeated the boy as he stood in Myron's face. "Make me!" he repeated.

"Noh, you hit me first," said Myron.

"Noh, you hit me first," requested the boy.

"Myron, come over here and let Mamma talk to you," she said as she put her arms around him and walked him away from the crowd.

"See, he's hiding behind his mammy's skirt," mocked the Boy.

"Look, this guy is all talk," she whispered to Myron. "You notice the other boys aren't saying anything?"

"Yeah."

"That's because he's a bully and they are scared of him. Tell you what let's do. Let's walk away from him. Let's get in the car. In the morning I'll go to the Superintendent of the school district, and get this resolved."

"You mean turn my back on him? Yeah, I get it," Myron as he turned and headed towards the car.

"What?" she asked.

She then turned and followed him towards the car. Now with their backs towards the embarrassed big mouth boy, he ran up and pushed Myron in his back. Without hesitation, Myron turned and popped him in the chin. The boy staggered backwards then fell to the ground out cold. A surprised Menzie Jenkins stood with her mouth wide opened. All of the kids started to clap, even the boy's two friends.

On the way home, she was speechless. Myron seemed confused about her demeanor. Finally, he talked to her.

"Mamma," he said. "Did I do something wrong?"

"What do you mean?"

"You told me to turn my back on that kid. Didn't you know he was going to come after me?"

"Why do you ask?"

"Because that's what I thought you wanted him to do so that I could punch him out."

"That wasn't quite what I had in mind. But I've got a feeling he won't be bothering you again."

"That night, Mrs. Jenkins and her husband talked about the incident as they were sitting in their bedroom and watching television. She was in the bed and he was sitting in a chair next to the bed.

"James, I want to tell you something, but I don't want you to get angry."

"What's it about?"

"It about Myron, he had a little trouble at school today."

"Yeah, I know."

"You know?"

"Yeah, he told me about it. He said he tried to avoid this kid, but he kept coming after him. He said he turned to walk away, but this kid pushed him. He then said he knocked the hell out of him."

"He did, I mean pow!" said Mrs. Jenkins as she gestured with fist. "I wonder why he told you after he asked me not to?"

"He seemed to not want to get you in trouble...Look Menzie, I know this is not a perfect world for our kids. Now out of all my kids, Myron is the meanest. But I still have to teach him to practice some self control, otherwise, he will be walking around thinking he is free to pop somebody in the jaw."

"Now I see why your kids love you. And I am so proud of you. Come here, I need a hug.

Other then having a talk with the principal, little was made of the incident. Still, she hadn't told her husband about the baby. She was still waiting for the perfect time. But little did she know, she was about to get another family challenge when she pulled up in the drive way and saw Javey dribbling a basketball. She watched him for a couple of minutes before getting out of the car and approaching him.

"I see you're practicing on your basketball skills. Can you play?" she asked.

"Yes, I can play," he responded as he kept dribbling.

"How good are you?"

"I don't know, but I'm thinking about trying out for the school's freshman team."

"Freshman team? Why not varsity?"

"Because Freshmen don't usually make the varsity."

"You won't make either with an attitude like that."

"What do you mean?" asked Javey as he stopped dribbling and walked over to where she was standing.

"I've heard your father tell you guys to 'Always aim at the heavens, because even if you fall short, you will always find yourself among the stars.', remember him telling you that?"

"Yeah, I remember that. But if I try out and don't make it, it will give him something else to disappointed about. Things with him are positive now and I would like to keep it that way."

"The attitude you guys have about not disappointing your father is amazing. But, sometimes you need to think of doing some things for yourselves."

"I guess so," said Javey as he started back to working on his dribbling.

"You use both hands, that's good. Have you played on a little league team before?"

"No, but I play ball at the center all the time."

"Did you know most kids start playing organized sports when they are seven and eight years old?

"Yeah, I know that," said Javey as he stopped dribbling, and started to spin the ball on his finger. "I've been playing since I was six. A lot of teams have asked me to play on their teams. I even had coaches to ask me," he said as he continued to spin the basketball on his finger.

"That's a neat trick."

"It's not a trick, it's a skill."

"Then, I stand corrected," she chuckled. "You have any other ball handling skills?"

"Yes, watch this," said Javey as he held the basketball on top of hid head, dropped it and caught it behind his back. To show he was good at it, he did it a second and third time, as she watched in amazement.

"Man, that's pretty good. Shows you have good ball handling skills. Tell you what, when you try out, try to make the varsity team. If you don't and you do a good enough job, you could end up as a starter on the freshmen team. That's what happened to me in college."

"You played basketball in college?"

"Oh yeah, and I was pretty good. In fact, I bet you I could still play. Wanna play me a game of one on one?"

"Noh, I don't want to play against a female."

"Why, because I might beat up on you like I use to beat up on all boys in my old neighborhood?"

"There's no way!" bellowed Javey.

"Brother man, I have probably forgotten more things about basketball, then you know right now," she bragged. "Wanna try me? Come on play me a game of one on one," she insisted.

"Miss Menzie, first of all, you are too old. Secondly, I don't think you are in shape enough to even play me."

"Whoa, listen up little brother. I'll have you to know while you were sleeping in your nice warm bed, Vena and I got up early everyday and ran. So don't you worry about me being in shape. As for being too old, you're about to find out I have mellowed with age. You give me a chance to change clothes."

"Okay, but don't say I didn't warn you," warned Javey.

You put up the hoop by yourself?" she asked with a sarcastic tone to her voice

"Don't you worry about the hoop, just get ready to get beat," snapped Javey.

Several minutes after Javey got up the hoop, Mrs. Jenkins came back outside wearing a sweat suit and gym shoes.

"You want to shoot to see who takes it out first?" she asked.

"Noh, ladies first," remarked Javey.

"You going to regret that decision," she said as she took the basketball out of bounds. You want to check me?" she said as she threw him the basketball.

"Noh, play it."

She started to dibble the ball to her right, quickly stopped and hit a jump shot.

"How many point to win?" she asked as she took the ball from him to shoot her free throws.

"Twenty-one," said Javey as he lined up to position himself for a rebound.

But a rebound never came because she hit all three of her free throws.

"That's five," she teased as she took the ball out again.

She inbounds the ball, but this time she took it to her left and drove all the way to the basket and scored.

"That's several. I thought you told me could play?" she asked.

"I can, I'm just taking it easy on you cause you a female."

"Oh, is that right? I just don't think you are as good as you told me you were," she said as she positioned herself to shoot free throws. "I should have warned you I was pretty good around my old hood," she said as she shot her first free throw. "Besides, I learned basketball by playing against the guys. Most of them were older than me." she said as she hit her second free throw. "I have never let a male in my hood beat me...Not once."

She shot her third free throws but missed, giving him a rebound. He took the ball out of bounds, drove right back in took her to the front of the hoop, jumped and scored.

"Take that!" he boosted.

He went to shoot his free throws. He hit his first, but missed the second. But he out rebounded her and quickly scored again.

"That's five to your nine," he said as he lined up to shoot free throws. This time he hit all three, making the score nine to eight.

Once the game was close, they played with a lot of intensity. The game also got a little tough, and had a little ego involved. Him because he was playing a female. It didn't matter she was a woman, grown. Her because of his attitude about thinking he could beat her because she was a female.

He won the first game, but she wasn't happy because the game was close and she thought she should have won it. So she challenged him to a second game. This game was hard fought, was close most of the way. Marcus, Myron and Floreese had joined in as on lookers. They seemed disappointed when she won the second game by two points. In lieu of both of them being tried, they agreed to a winner take all game. She played well, but was no match for the younger male.

The rest of the children cheered for their brother to win.

"Come Javey, beat her!" shouted Floreese

Finally it was over and Javey had won a hard fought game, but by only five points. After the game, they both bent over at the waist all out of breath.

"Good game Miss Menzie," said Javey.

"Well, you're not bad yourself...Tell you what, you try out for that team. Keep in mind that you beat me, knowing I beat every boy in my neighborhood, some of them played varsity ball."

"Really?"

"Yeah, really. You try out for Varsity ball, you might make it," she said as turned to go into the house.

"You okay Miss Menzie?" asked Marcus.

"Oh heck, that was just a little workout for me," she said as she led the others into the house.

The moment she was inside the door, she collapsed from fatigue.

Later her husband came home. The children had told him what had happened and that they had put her to bed. He slowly opened the door to the bedroom and peeped in. She was lying in bed on her back looking up at the ceiling moaning in pain.

"You all right?" he asked as he entered the bedroom, closing the door behind him.

"Man, every muscle in my body hurts, including my eye muscle," she chuckled.

"The kids told me what happened. You mind telling me why were you playing basketball with Javey?" he asked as he sat on the bed beside her.

"It was one of those challenges thing, you know what I mean?"

"Oh yeah, Menzie, always looking for a challenge."

"You mean I'm a sucker for a challenge don't you?" she chuckled.

"They tell me he beat you. Is that right?"

"Oh yeah, in fact he beat me two out of three."

"I didn't know he was that good in basketball."

"Dear Dr. Jenkins. You have some very special kids," she said as she painfully sat up in the bed. "Look at them. Vena is a excellent athlete, in tip top condition. If it had not been for her mother dying and her trying to take care of you, she would have been very good in track. Marcus, not wanting to let you down, would not tell you he didn't want to go to college, and wouldn't tell you about his musical genius. Javey, with all that athletic ability, did not want to take on too much because if he failed, he knows you would worry too much about him, Myron, looks up to all of you. Who knows which one of you he will emulate. Then there is Floreese, the cheer leader for humanity."

"Those are the things I was not aware of about my own children until you came along. They seemed to confide in you."

"That's because they respect you as being the bread winner of the family. And they don't expect the bread winners to have the time to pay attention to those little things in life."

"Well, I'm glad I have you. You seem to bring out the best in everybody."

"In this family, it was very easy to do because there was already so much to work from."

"Remember when the kids caught you rubbing me down?"

"Oh God! How can I forget!" she openly expressed. "I felt so guilty."

"Well, how about I return the favor?"

"Yeah, get use to it because I'm going to have to do some exercise."

"Why, you trying out for the Olympics?"

"Let's just say, I'll have to get use to carrying around some extra weight."

"I don't know what you mean."

"Well, Dr. Jenkins, let me put it a way you can understand. You know how you like to have sex?"

"Shoo you right," he snickered in a bragging tone of voice.

"Well with all that screwing, what did you think was bold to happen?

"I was hoping to knock you up," chuckled Jenkins.

"Ha, ha, ha," she mocked. "Well you can stop hoping, you have."

"What? You trying to tell me you're preg, preg, ahh--"

"Wonders never cease. The man is lost for words," chuckled his wife.

"Menzie, you're having a baby?"

"Well, you recovered quickly," she mocked.

Dr. Jenkins then fainted.

"Or maybe not," she chuckled as she looked at him lying there surprised and out cold.

That next Saturday, Mrs. Jenkins had made arrangements at Vocal Shine Recording Company, to record several songs for her album. But now that predicament had changed, Timothy Graves was about to find out what that meant for him. He watched as she entered the studio. He knew there was going to trouble when he saw she had Steve Thomas and Marcus Jenkins with her.

"Menzie, Mr. Thomas, you here to listen to my star perform today?" he asked.

"No, but we would like to talk to you in your office," responded Thomas.

"Sure, follow me," he insisted.

"You wait right here, mamma will be right back in a minute," said Menzie to Marcus.

The two of them followed Tim Graves to his office. Once there, he sat down at his desk. He had a feeling he was not going to like what was about to happen, so he was rude and did not ask his guests to have a seat. But it didn't matter, for Thomas then stated the purpose for their visit as he sat down his attaché case on his desk and pulled out small stack of folded papers. He then handed them to Graves.

"What is this?" asked Graves as he took the papers.

"You are being sued my man," said Thomas.

"Sued? By who?" he asked in a surprised tone of voice.

"Me," said Mrs. Jenkins as she sat in a chair next to his desk.

"What could you possibly be suing me for?"

"Sexual Harassment," responded Thomas.

"When have I ever sexually harassed you?"

"It was a little over a week ago," she responded.

"Remember?" asked Thomas. "When you openly displayed an unwanted acts of sexual harassment by making obscene remarks, then kissing my client. And in the mouth no doubt, and which I was one of several witnesses," he continued.

"Ahh come on!" bellowed Graves. "That was a kiss between old friends."

"You kissed me in the mouth. Then you told me how much you have wanted to be with me since we were kids. Remember that, Timothy?"

"Menzie, after all we have meant to one another, you would try and do this to me?"

"Don't take it personal, this is business," she stated in a firm tone of voice.

"So, there is apparently something you want," stated Graves as he leaned back in his chair. "What is it?"

"We're going to make life simple for you my friend," said Thomas. "Last week my client signed a contract with you. Since then, things have taken a strange twist. She--"

"I'm having a baby," interrupted Mrs. Jenkins as she rubbed her stomach by circling her hands over it.

"Mrs. Jenkins, please," uttered Thomas.

"Opps, sorry," she snickered.

"As I was saying, circumstances have changed and my client don't feel she will be able to fulfill the physical requirements of that contract. So, we request, you hear what we are asking as a remedy to our litigation."

"I can hardy wait," remarked Graves still trying to be sarcastic.

“Good!" snapped Thomas. "We're proposing you allow her son to audition for recording consideration. If he passes his audition with you, that you put him under a legal contract, which would include Mrs. Jenkins as his manager. I have already drawn up those contractual stipulations...Ahh, page number three, if you care to look."

"So, that's what this is all about? Your boy getting an audition?"

"Well, ahh yes," confirmed Mrs. Jenkins.

"You must think he's awful good to go through all this trouble, Menzie."

"Actually, he is, and it's no trouble at all," she responded.

Graves then started to laugh.

"Menzie, when will I ever learn to never underestimate you," he chuckled.

"Obviously, you have a hard head. As long as you remember which is which, I'm easy to figure out," she chuckled.

"I know, all business," said Graves as he pushed a button on his intercom. "Joe, get studio five ready for a audition. How long will it take you to get some people in there to accompany a vocalist?"

"My son has his own background music prerecorded," interjected Menzie.

"Never mind Joe. The vocalist already has his background music. Call me when you're ready." Graves got off of the intercom, peered over at Menzie, then smiled. "Well, let's go and meet our artist," said Grave as he got up from his desk and led Mrs. Jenkins and her attorney out of his office.

Just before Marcus was to audition, she pulled him aside to give him a pep talk.

"Now, here's the break you've been wanting. You show that idiot how good you are," she said as made sure his clothes were neat. "What are you going to sing first?"

"I thought I would go for the juggler and do 'Letter to God'," responded a chuckling Marcus Jenkins.

"Oh my," she chuckled at his remark. "Don't say that too loud around here, they'll think you got that from me," she whispered to him.

"Then they could be right," chuckled Marcus.

"I just love you," she said as she hugged her son. "Sing that song and make them cry just like you make mamma cry when she heard it."

Marcus confidently walked over to the microphone. Once there, he turned and smiled at his mother.

"What will you be singing?" asked Graves.

"I'm going to sing a song I wrote," responded Marcus.

"Oh really?" asked Graves in a sarcastic tone of voice. "I've got to hear this," he chuckled.

Marcus then signaled for his mother to turn on the background music they had prerecorded. The musical introduction was short and he started to sing. From the moment he started, the song caught the attention of the studio crew.

"What is war? What is peace? And when will be just simply be sat free? What is to live and what is to die? What is this falling from my eye, I want to know.'"

The more he sang, the more attention he got. Mrs. Jenkins kept her eyes on Graves, whom she could see watching through the window of the sound room. She was trying to read him for a reaction to what he was hearing. You could tell Marcus definitely had his undivided attention. She watched him pick up a set of earphones and put them on his ears. When she saw him do that, and as good as Marcus was sounding, she knew things were going to go just as she had planned.

"You go boy!" she uttered to herself.

She knew for sure when she saw Tim Graves pick up her contract, show it to her, then ripped it in half. He then gave her thumbs up. She reciprocated, then confidently turned to hear her son finish his son. The lyrics, the song, the attention it got and the mood it set, could not have been better. And Marcus? Well, you would have thought he was already on stage and in a way he was.

He closed his eyes and finished off the song with the kind of compassion, which affected the entire crowd, and his stepmother could see it as she looked from one person to the next, most of the females were tearing as she watched the handsome young man perform.

"Gone baby, make mamma proud!" she uttered to herself as she too started tearing.

Then Marcus hit that final note. And once he was done, the entire crowd showed their appreciation by standing and applauding. Then they started to clap and cheer words of encouragement.

"Beautiful!" remarked one of the crew as he clapped.

"Way to sing baby!" remarked a female as she wiped tears from her cheeks with her fingers.

"You the man! You the man!" shouted another male as he pointed to Marcus and started to clap again.

Graves was beside himself as he rushed from the sound room and over to where the crowd was standing and clapping.

"Menzie, why didn't you tell me this young man should sing like that?" he asked.

"I tried, I--"

"Young man, you are just marvelous," interrupted Graves. "How old are you? It doesn't matter. I see it now, new teenage idol. Girls will be screaming, crying. Plus, you are very handsome. I understand you wrote that song, right?"

"Right, I have others I have written," remarked Marcus as the crowd stood by listening to what was being said.

"Really now? How many?"

"I've done about ten. But I have a lot of ideas for other songs."

"Great! Menzie, isn't he just marvelous?"

"I've always thought so," she said with a bit of sarcasm to her voice.

"Wonderful. Mr. Thomas, let's go back to my office and talk contract," said Graves as he turned and headed towards his office.

"Good job," said Thomas to Marcus as he touched him on his shoulders.

"Thanks Mr. Thomas." said Marcus.

"Mrs. Jenkins, let's go talk money," said Thomas.

"You go ahead. I want to talk with my son. I'll join you in a couple of minutes."

Thomas headed for Graves' office. Mrs. Jenkins walked over to her son and hugged him. She held him there for several seconds, stopped, then looked into his eyes.

"Marcus, I am so proud of you. You performed like an old pro here today. You wait until I tell your father how well you did. He is really going to be proud too."

"I sure hope so. I really want him to be proud of me, and not be disappointed because I didn't want to go to college."

"Marcus, your father's once told me his main concern was that his kids be able to support themselves. You are about to be a rich and famous young man. That is the one thing your father knows all about."

"Well, thanks Mom. May I call you Mom?"

"Yes, you may. In fact I feel like you are my own son."

"When my mother died, I didn't know what life was going to be like. I guess I was scared. Dad would call that the fear of the unknown."

"Yeah, that's him alright," she chuckled.

"I'm so glad you married my Dad, you have helped him a lot, the whole family a lot."

"Marcus, you have no idea what marrying your father has done for my life. It put around all of you wonderful kids. Gave me something to prove to all of you. Gave me a work to do, a fulfilling work. Can I ask you something?"

"Yes ma'am, what?"

"How do you feel about me having a baby?"

"I think that would be great. Have you talked to Dad about it?"

"It's a little too late for talk."

"You mean you are already having a baby?"

"I'm afraid so."

"Have you told Dad yet?"

"Oh yeah."

"What did he say?"

"Nothing! He fainted," she chuckled.

The two of them had a good laugh as they turned, hugged and headed towards Tim Graves' office.

Once they were home, and had shared all of the news with the family, things started to settle down a bit. It was then that the new mother to be received an unscheduled visit from her new Mother in law.

"Mother Jenkins, she said after letting her in and closing the door behind her.

"Hi," said the elder Jenkins as she kissed her daughter in law on the jaw. "You always look so nice when I see you."

"Than it's a good thing you didn't see me just a few minutes ago," she chuckled.

Mrs. Jenkins walked over and sat down of the sofa. The new Mrs. Jenkins liked seeing her, but did wonder why she had popped in on her.

"Well, I heard about the news," she said.

"What news is that?" she asked.

"Menzie, why are we still playing games?"

"So, you mean about the baby?"

"Yes, I know that was a shock to my son."

"Yeah, I guess you can say that," she chuckled.

"Did you two plan on expanding this family, or did you make that decision?"

"Look wasn't it you who told me he liked having sex?"

"I told you my daughter in law said he was good in bed?"

"Well, he is, and this baby is what it got him," she snickered.

"You are a very cleaver woman," snickered Mrs. Jenkins.

"I think you are giving me too much credit."

"I don't think so...Menzie, what are you?"

"Beg your pardon?"

"I asked what are you? I'm still trying to figure out if you are an saint or a devil."

"And why would you be wondering that about me?"

"You seem to be in control of everything around you."

"Oh, I wouldn't say that," uttered the newer Jenkins family member.

"You wouldn't huh? Well, I would. You seem to get everything you want. You build companies to great wealth. You inspire kids to go beyond their capabilities. You take an ordinary man and you make him a corporate giant. How are you able to do all that?"

"First of all, James is no ordinary man. He was a Diamond in the rough and with great potential, all I did was help him realize that. Secondly, I haven't and can't do anything without help. So give the people around me a lot of the credit. As for his kids, they are smart, well prepared and well behaved and lovable kids. Sometimes they appear to be God sent. But they also came from good stock, good seeds and from both sides of the family."

"Is that right!" snapped Mrs. Jenkins.

"Think about it, a harvest can not be realized unless the seed is planned and cultivated. You are part of the seed from which he was planted. I just cultivated that seed."

Lynnett Jenkins laughed

"What's funny?" asked Menzie Jenkins.

"You are. Not only do you play a good game of cat and mouse, but you talk one too...My family seems to love you. Vena told me she loves you. Now that takes some doing, since you took some of her father's love from her."

"Well, I'm sharing her father's love with her. That's only because I made her have confidence that I wasn't trying to steal all of it. All of his kids feel the same way about him. Trust me, that makes what I do awful easy."

"Well, how is this baby going to fit in?"

"How do you mean?"

"You are bringing it into a situation where there are already five kids. How are you planning on making this one big happy family? You sure won't be able to talk your way through it. And your biggest problem is going to be Floreese. She is use to being his baby. How do think she will take being replaced?"

"Well, she knows I'm having a baby, but she haven't said much. I guess I'll have to cross that bridge when I get to it."

"I see...Menzie is there anything you can't do?"

"I can't live forever. Right now, I'm living a wonderful life. I've been blessed to have a compassionate, loving man in my life, he has introduced me to five wonderful kids, I have all the money I could want, and I'm about to experience motherhood. I don't think life could get any better than this. I wish I could have it all like this forever. But I know I can't. All I can do is pray that God will allow me to enjoy what he has blessed me with for as long as it is humanly possible. I guess I can be content with that?"

"Well," said Mrs. Jenkins as she stood and peered at her. "I guess you are a God sent, so that makes you an angel. And Menzie, I know I haven't said this, but I do appreciate everything you have done for my son and his family. I think my son was blessed twice. His first wife led him to the water, but it was you who made him drink."

"His first wife reminded him that he had a thirst. I led him to the water. Once there, he then quenched his thirst on his own," recited Menzie.

"Touché," uttered Mrs. Jenkins as she hugged Menzie. "You are a remarkable woman. No wonder my family loves you so much. And, well, I do too."

"Thanks, I really needed to hear you say that. And I want us to be close. I'm going to need you to help me pull all of this together once the baby comes."

"Somehow, I doubt that," chuckled Lynnett Jenkins. "But I will be as much of a help as you will allow."

"Thank you, that means a lot to me."

CHAPTER EIGHTEEN

THE HARVEST COMES FORTH

How that Mrs. Jenkins was having the baby, some major changes had to be made at Consolidation And Data Networking International because it came at a time when there was a huge increase in business. To start, the firm started a sub-branch office in Atlanta. This resulted in a lot of opportunities for those loyal to the firm's efforts. Between the two locations, there were plenty of jobs for bright young people, especially Blacks. She stepped down as the main Operations Officer and became the Liaison Officer between the two firms. Sara Tillsberge became the new Operations Officer. George Blackshere became her Administrative Assistant. She persuaded Robert Meyers, the formal General Manager of the Millennium Crown Hotel chain, to take the job of General Manager of the branch office. But her next appointment didn't come without a few wrinkles. But it showed just how much class she really had specially when it came to business.

She had requested Gladis Henley report to her office. Henley apprehensively reported to her office where she and Sara were sitting and waiting for her.

"You ask to see me?" she asked Jenkins.

"Yes, come in and have a seat," she requested.

"What is this all about?" asked Gladis as she sat in a chair next to the desk, this suspicious look on her face.

"Relax, this is a business meeting," insisted Mrs. Jenkins.

"Well with you, one never knows," remarked Gladis.

"This might be a good time for you to keep your big mouth shut and listen for a change!" snapped Sara.

Henley didn't respond to her remark, but sat looking from one of the executives to the other.

"As you know we are doing some major expanding. This presents a lot of opportunities for those employees who have been with this firm a long time, and have done their fair share of work.

We will be depending on those who are in a positioned to take advantage of these opportunities and step up and help us out."

"Yeah, I heard George got your old job, he'll be good at it."

"Well, we thought so...We have an offer for you," said Mrs. Jenkins.

"Oh really?" asked a surprised Henley.

"How mobile are you?" asked Sara Tillsberge.

"I don't know what you mean."

"She's asking you if you would be willing to move to another location for a promotion?" interjected Mrs. Jenkins.

"Where?"

"Atlanta."

"And what's the position?"

"Assistant Branch Manager. Here is the job description and the pay involved," said Mrs. Jenkins as she handed her a sheet of paper.

"Wow, that sounds like a good offer...You're not doing this to keep me away from your man are you?"

"If I was concerned about you bothering my husband, I would fire your ass!" snapped Mrs Jenkins.

"Man! I was just joking," chuckled Henley.

"Well, it's time out for jokes. We are serious," said Tillsberge.

"Okay, I'll take it. How much time do I have to leave?"

"You've got two weeks. We'll give you time off to get packed, go and do some house searching, whatever you need to do to prepare yourself. George will coordinate all your transportation needs," said Mrs. Jenkins.

"Sounds good...Is that all?"

"Do you have any questions?"

"No, no I don't," said Gladis as she got up and walked over to the door, once there, she stopped, turned and looked back at the two ladies. "Menzie, thanks for not holding our past with each other against me."

"Gladis, this is business and has nothing to do with anything else. Beside, we think you will be good at that job for us."

"Thanks, and I appreciate this opportunity. I heard you were having a baby."

"That's right, you mind?"

"No, I think that's great. And Menzie, you have gained my respect. Good luck and I mean that."

"I know you do. And good luck to you too."

Gladis left the office closing the door behind her. Mrs. Jenkins and Sara peered over at one another, then smiled.

"Well, what do you know about that? The woman does have a decent streak," said Mrs. Jenkins.

"Well, don't go around telling everybody, it will mess up her image," chuckled Sara as the two of them then had a good laugh.

Later, as Mrs. Jenkins was finishing up some last minute details before leaving for the weekend, she received an unexpected guest. Her visitor was Marilyn Bash of The Organization Against Male Oppression and who held the position of Chairperson. Her secretary was already gone, so Bash peeked her head into her private office.

"Miss Ferguson, my name is Marilyn Bash. You got a couple of minutes?" she asked as she walked into the office.

"Sure, come in, have a seat," responded Mrs. Jenkins.

"I am sure you have heard of the organization I represent. It's called--"

"I've heard of your organization, and I know who you are."

"Good," said Bash as she sat in a chair located next to her desk. "Then I can get to my reason for being here. It is common knowledge how you helped build up Corrall International Network Incorporated to national prominence and how the Robinstein family gave you the shaft after the original owner died."

"Most of what you've heard is a bit of an over exaggeration."

"Now Miss Ferguson, let us be honest with one another. You and I know you were the backbone of that firm."

"We do?"

"Yes, and I also hear you help start this firm, and again you are not getting your just due."

"Well, if you know all that, then you should know that I am married and that my name is now Mrs. Jenkins.

"Don't you think that is a bit antiquated, using your married name in business? Most professional women continue to use their maiden names. Maybe even a hyphenated name like, Ferguson-Jenkins."

"What is the point of a hyphenated name?"

"Women use hyphenated names in case they get single again, all they have to do is drop the married name."

"That doesn't sound like a woman who is confident she can keep her man. Beside, I pride myself on not being like most women."

"Are you trying to say, you think you are better than most women?"

"I didn't say that, and don't put words into my mouth."

"Obviously, I caught you in a lousy mood," remarked Bash.

"I was doing just fine until you forced your way in here. Now, what is it that you really want, Miss Bash? It is Miss isn't it?"

"Yes it is and I am proud to say so. Now, I'm here to request you be a member of our organization. A powerful woman like you, need our kind of backing to get what you deserve in this male dominated corporate world."

"The world in which I work now involves my husband, is ran by my husband, and I am second in command here."

"You see that's my point. Why second? Why not head of this company?"

"I'm not head of this company because there was a proper protocol to follow and I choose to do that. My husband and I are part owners in this firm. He deserved to be the head of this firm because of his knowledge and education and it is my responsibility as his wife to support him."

"What you are suffering from is male societal brain washing."

"Oh really?" snapped Mrs. Jenkins. "Obviously Bash is not a married name?"

"It's my maiden name."

"Have you ever been married?"

"Yes twice, divorced both times."

"Oh, is that right? Have you ever heard of the Peter Principal?"

"Yes, but what does that have to do with what we're talking about?"

"So, you really don't know what is means. Well, the Peter Principal infers that a man or woman within an institution will advance to his or her highest level of incompetence and stay there."

"What's your point?"

"If you had been more competent as a wife, you most likely would still have a husband and the peace of mind which goes with it. And I would doubt if you would be involved in that ridiculous organization you represent."

"Well!" said Bash as she jumped to her feet. "You are a poor example of a business woman, you know that?" she snapped.

"Oh I don't know about that. I am a content woman, a wealthy woman. I have all the love I need and from a wonderful husband and a beautiful family."

"Well, I wouldn't be too cocky. That can all change over night."

"I doubt that. I know what it takes to please a man. On the other hand, you are a struggling, narrow minded, self serving, man hating bitch."

"If you were a man, I would slap your nose off for what you just said."

"No doubt you would try. But you might find when I have to be, I am the kind of woman who would give you the ass whipping your mamma should have given you."

"You may live to regret talking to me like that," snapped Bash.

"And you need to try and be more of a lady then to waste time pretending to be a woman, while wasting your time acting like a man."

Marilyn Bash didn't comment to her remark. She peered at her for several seconds, turned and stormed out of her office, slamming the door behind her.

Later back at the Jenkins' house the family was preparing for bed. Mrs. Jenkins was sitting in the bed reading a book, when there was a soft tap at the door.

"Come in," she responded.

The door opened slowly and Floreese slowly poked her head inside the room.

"Where is my Daddy?" she asked.

"He's in the bathroom brushing his teeth," said Menzie.

Floreese walked over to the bathroom and tapped on the door.

"Who is it?" asked James Jenkins.

"Me Daddy...You got clothes on?"

"Yes, come in."

Floreese slowly opened the door and could see her father rising out his mouth. She walked in and closed the door behind her. She then walked over and sat down on the side of the tub.

"Daddy, is Miss Menzie having a baby?" she asked.

Dr. Jenkins walked over and sat down on the side of the tub next to his daughter.

"Yes she is," he responded.

"But Daddy, you told me I was going to be your baby forever."

"I know sweetie. When your Mom and I had you, we decided we had enough kids to give all our love to. Then she died. When I married Miss Menzie, she showed all of us that she could step in and take over that love that your Mom couldn't give any more. Now she wants to share that love with a child that she brings into this world. I think that's fair to her, don't you?"

"Well if a new baby comes in here, do you have to share the love you have for me with the baby?"

"Oh no. My love for you will never change. I'll just have to do like Miss Menzie did and reach down inside of me and bring out more love to share with the new baby. Besides, when the new baby gets here, that's going to make you a big sister."

"Yeah, I'll be a big sister just like Vena, right Daddy?"

"Right. And Miss Menzie is going to need your help with the new baby."

"Oh yeah, like Vena helped with me...Have a girl Daddy."

"A girl, why?"

"Then you will have three boys and three girls, silly," she chuckled.

"That's right. Well, we'll pray on that, okay?"

"Daddy you don't pray for a girl, you have to make one," chuckled Floreese.

"Of course, what was I thinking?" chuckled Jenkins.

"When Miss Menzie has a girl, the boys better not touch her, or I'll beat them up."

"Well, if a boy touches her, why don't you come and tell me."

"No sir. If a boy touches her, I'm gonna beat them up," she repeated.

"Okay baby," chuckled Jenkins.

"Goodnight Daddy," said Floreese as she kissed her father.

"Goodnight baby girl," said Jenkins as he hugged her and reciprocated her kiss.

Mrs Jenkins was sitting at the head of the bed, her arms crossed, watched as she came out of the bathroom and headed for the bedroom door. She opened it, then turned and peered over at her.

"Goodnight, Miss Menzie," she said.

"Goodnight sweetheart."

Once prepared for bed, Jenkins came and sat on the side of the bed. His wife moved over to him and hugged him around his neck.

"I liked the way you handled that Dr. Jenkins," she said.

"You heard?" said Jenkins as he peered over at her.

"Yeah, and that just goes to show what a wonderful father you are. No wonder your kids love you so much. I feel so fortunate to have my baby being born into this family. In fact, I want my baby to be just like you. Smart, sensitive, compassionate."

"Whether it was born into this family or not, and if it wasn't like me in the least, it would still have you. No child would go wrong with you as a mother."

"Oh that is so sweet. It lets me know how much you appreciate me."

"Baby, I can't put into words how much I appreciate you."

"Well, you do it by the way you treat me. You make me feel loved and wanted. That's how I know...now there is one other way you could show me."

"And how is that?"

"I'll show you," said Mrs. Jenkins as she let go of his neck.

As she moved to the other side of the bed, and reached down and under it, her husband got a good look at her buttocks.

"Oh yeah, I can see all of that," he chuckled.

She quickly snapped back up and peered over at him.

"Were you looking at my booty?" she snickered.

"I could help it, you had it all up in here," said as he formed his hands in the shape of a frame.

"Well, if you be a good little boy, I'll let you feel on it," she chuckled.

"Then consider me your little angel," he joked.

"Yeah right!" she chuckled. "Now, I need you to get your mind from under my grown and look at something...Now, if you don't want to do this, don't get mad at me for asking, okay?"

"Okay, I promise."

She reached back under the bed, and pulled out a sketch and laid it in her lap.

"Now James, when we got married, I felt honored to move into this house with you and the kids. I know we got all new furniture in here and I appreciated you doing that for me. But I still feel this is Marian's house...I want a house of my own...You mind?" she apprehensively asked.

"I agree with you."

"So, you are not mad that I asked?"

"Don't be ridiculous. Marian and I had a lot of good memories in this house," said Jenkins as he looked around the room. "But now, I am building a lot of new memories of you and me, together. Besides, with the baby coming, we will need the extra room."

"Ahh man, I was so scared you were going to get mad."

"Menzie, when have I ever been mad at you?"

She didn't say anything, just looked at him with this silly look on her face.

"Well, maybe once," he chuckled. "What's that you got?" he asked as he turned so he could look at what she had in her hands.

She moved in closer to him, then folded back the first page of the sketching pad and showed it to him. He looked at it, took it from her so he could get a better look at it.

"Wow, what a beautiful house," he commented.

"It's not a house, it's a home, our home. That's if I can talk you into having it built for me."

"It looks huge. How many rooms?"

"Fifteen."

"Fifteen rooms?"

"Yes, that includes seven bedrooms, one Master Suite with a den and a Jacuzzi. There is a dining room, a kitchen, a breakfast area, a family room and two dens. One down stairs for the guys."

"Huh, I'm surprised you didn't have a gym added on."

"Turn to the next page," she insisted.

"What is this, a separate building?"

"Yes, it's a gym, with a rack room, a Jacuzzi for Vena and I to relax in after we've been jogging. There is also basketball hoops, everything. I figure if I am going to ask the children to leave this house, I have to have some bargaining power with them. Turn the next page."

"This is another house, ahh a home."

"Yeah, I figure I may as well have a home for your mother and father, Jenkins on the same property. You know, have some bargaining power with them too."

"This is all going to be expensive," suggested Jenkins.

"Yes, I know...That's why I'm giving you this to build our home with," said Mrs. Jenkins.

She reached under her pillow, pulled out her bankbook and handed it to him. He took and opened it.

"Man!" he uttered in surprise. "That's a lot of money!" he bellowed.

"It's more than enough to pay for what I want."

"Menzie, you don't have to use your money. I'll do this for you."

"I know you would, but I want to pay for this myself."

"So, you want to pay cash for all of this?"

"Yes, that way I can stay home a while once my baby gets here...You mind?"

Jenkins started to laugh.

"Did I say something funny?"

"No, it's just that you had all of this figured out before you ask me."

"Well, I wanted to make it hard for you to say no. Of course I still had my secret weapon to use in case you were obstinate," she suggested as she moved in closer and wrapped her arms around his neck."

"And what secret weapon was that?"

"This," she uttered as she kissed him very passionately.

After a few seconds, he stopped the kiss and looked deep into her wonderful, brown eyes.

"I should have held out for the secret weapon," he uttered.

"Well, consider it your reward for being so cooperative," she murmured as she started to unbutton his pajama top. Then she pulled him down on top of her. “Mmmmmmmmm…Ohhhhhhhh!”

A couple of months had passed. The Jenkins' family was mostly concentrating on the on coming holidays, when they received some unexpected news. Well, it was for most of the family, but not Mrs. Jenkins.

It all came about when Javey came running through the door after basketball practice. His father and she were sitting and relaxing in the family room.

"Hey you guys, I made the varsity basketball team!" he shouted.

"Hey! That's great!" shouted his father.

"That's my baby," she uttered as she got up and hugged him "What did I tell you? Didn't I tell you that you would?"

"You sure did. Well, the coach said I could still play some of the time on the freshman team, but that I could dress out with the varsity."

"So, what does that mean, you won't be playing much on the varsity?" asked his father.

"Coach said that I wouldn't, but that's okay. When I play with the freshman, I'll start."

"Well, I think you are going to start on the varsity too."

"How do you figure that?" asked Dr. Jenkins.

"Because he is good...Let me ask you, Javey. Those guys already on the varsity, are they real good?"

"Most of them played last year."

"I didn't ask you if they played last year, I asked if they were good?"

"Yeah, pretty good."

"How many games did they win last year?"

"They lost almost half of them."

"You know what that tells me? That says they need help, new talent. The way you play, you can help them win some games. Unless that coach is an idiot and don't want to win, he'll play you as a starter. Any other freshmen make the team?"

"Only one other, the center. But he's six ten."

"Don't you play guard?"

"Yes."

"How tall are you, six feet?"

"Six one."

"That's tall for a guard...Tell you what you work harder than you have ever worked before. If that coach wants to win, he's going to have to play his best players if he wants to win. You just make sure you are one of them. I predict you both will end up starting, and soon, watch."

"Don't worry, I will," responded Javey. "And thanks for the encouragement," he said as he hugged her then turned and left the room.

Dr. Jenkins didn't say anything but peered over at her. He had resigned himself to understand when his wife said something was going to happen, it usually does. So he was anxious to see how this situation was going to play out.

"You watch, my baby is going to start," she uttered.

That next week, the team was involved in a basketball tournament. They had played in it before, but had never won it. On the night of the first game, a very pregnant Mrs. Jenkins, her husband James Jenkins, Myron and Floreese were at the game. It was the forth quarter and the opposing team was winning the game by thirteen points. To make matters worse, the team was in file trouble and the crowd from the school was completely out of it. Javey hadn't seen any action, and it looked as if he never would.

"What is wrong with that coach?" she complained. "He's losing the game, why don't he give the other guys a chance to play?"

"Don't you think the coach knows his job?" asked Jenkins.

"Not if he's losing with talent sitting on his bench."

It was then that the second string Point Guard filed out. The Coach called a time out. After the opposing team hit the two free throws, making the lead fifteen points, he gathered his team on the sideline near their bench.

"Okay, we need someone to go in for Carlson. Any of you coaches have any suggestions?" he asked.

"Put me in coach," requested Javey.

"What?"

"Put me in, we can still win this game."

"Well, I like your confidence, son."

"Oh hell, put him in," said one of the Assistant Coaches.

"Okay, go report to the table," said the coach.

"Well, looks like they are getting ready to put him in," said James Jenkins when they saw him report to the scorer's table.

"Good, now they're getting ready to see some real basketball," commented Mrs. Jenkins.

When he reported back to the huddle, he showed just how prepared he was to play and win.

"Coach, may I make a suggestion?" he asked.

"At this point, I'm opened for anything," said the coach.

"Put Miller in with me. Have him go low post on the left side. When I call out two, have him come to the free-throw line to get the ball. Miller, when I feed it into you, turn around to see how the defense will play you. If you see they don't challenge you, shoot the ball. It will be like shooting free throws. If they come up to defend Miller, Jones you cross over from one side to the other.

Miller, look to give him the ball either in the middle or on the opposite low post."

"You understand what he said to do, Miller?" asked the Coach.

"Yes sir," responded the six ten athlete.

"Good, go to the table report in for Robinson at center."

"That's what I'll talking about," uttered Mrs. Jenkins when she also saw Miller reporting in with Javey. "It' on now, you watch!" she bellowed.

The moment was tense, the crowd for the opposing team was cheering and confident they were going to win the game. The ball was inbound and Javey, who calmly brought it across half court. He dribbled a few seconds then called the play.

"Two."

Miller came to the free throw line, and received the ball from him. He turned and faced the basket. When no one challenged him, he shot and hit two points. Now the lead was thirteen points, with less than three minutes to play. The opposing team in bounded the ball, but Javey quickly stole it. He drove to the basket and scored two points.

"That's my baby!" shouted Mrs. Jenkins. "Come on Javey, show them how to play some ball!" she shouted.

The opposing team in bounded the ball again. Javey attempted to steal another ball, but filed instead. They lined up to shoot free throws. Instead of the home team having four players on the free throw lanes, Javey lined up making it five.

"What is he doing?" asked the Coach.

"Jerry, when he misses this free throw, you take off. Look for the ball," said Javey to his teammate.

When the free throw was missed, he quickly jumped into the lane and got the rebound. He turned up court looking for his teammate, who was heading towards the basket. Showing his speed he quickly got the ball up court and passed it to his teammate, who drove to the basket and scored two points, cutting the lead to nine points.

"Yes! Yes!" shouted Mrs Jenkins as she stood and clapped. Then her husband joined her.

"Way to look Javey!" he shouted.

"Get on the ball! Get on the ball!" shouted Javey.

He and Miller trapped the ball handler in the corner of the court. The ball handler, now having two player on him, both over six feet, panicked and threw the ball away, which was picked up by Javey's team mates. When he saw they had the ball, he took off towards the basket, where his teammate passed him the ball. He drove to the basket and scored, cutting the led down to seven points. In his haste to inbound the ball, the inbound player step on the line for a turnover.

"You got them baby! Keep the pressure on!" shouted Mrs. Jenkins at the top of her voice. She was then joined by several more of the fans.

Now having the ball, and the home crowd getting noisy, Javey in bounded the ball to Miller on the left side on the low post. When he came inbounds, Miller passed him the ball back. He shot, hitting a three pointer and cutting the lead to four points. The opposing team brought the ball over half court, then the Coach called their last time out. Now both teams were out of time outs. That made the game more tensed.

Mrs. Jenkins worked hard to get the home crowd involved in the game. She turned and faced them, then started to clap with excitement.

"Come on people open your mouths, cheer!" she shouted.

During the time out, she continued to work hard to get the crowd into the game. Now with the entire Jenkins family leading the cheering, the crowd started to become part of the game by starting to cheer and have fun just seeing their team come back like they had.

"Okay, we got them where we want them. Let's go man to man. Javey, number twenty-three, he is their best shooter. Play him tight. Keep him from getting the ball, get him tried, that's make him press more. Miller, don't let them penetrate the middle. Don't let them get an easy basket," said the Coach.

Both teams went back into the court. The opposing team went low post. The Center got the ball, turned and scored, making the lead six points again. The ball was in bounded to Javey, who called the play,

"Two."

Miller came high post and received the ball from Javey. He turned to face the basket. But this time he was challenged. The low post forward crossed over from one side to the other. Miller quickly passed him the ball. He shot a quick basket cutting the led again to four points.

"Miller, don't let him get the ball low post!" shouted the Coach.

But Miller couldn't keep the opposing center from getting the ball. But he did force him away from the basket, causing the Center to attempt to dribble the ball. When he put the ball on the floor, Javey tapped it away from him, picked it up and quickly ran up court, stopped at the three point and shot. He scored a another three pointer. Now the opposing team was winning by one point.

"Oh my God! Oh my God!' shouted one of the students.

"I can't believe this! I can't believe this!" shouted another.

"Go! Go! Go! Go!" shouted the crowd.

"Who is that kid, number twenty-one?" asked the Head Coach of the opposing team.

"It says here, his name is Javey Jenkins and he's a freshmen," said one of the Assistant Coaches.

"He a damn one man show out there!" he criticized.

The opposing team in bound the ball. The team worked hard trying to get the ball to their leading scorer, number twenty-three. But Javey worked hard keeping him from getting the ball as the home team crowd cheered them on being led by Mrs. Jenkins and her husband.

"Defense! Defense! Defense! Defense!" they shouted.

The time was under one minute, with the opposing team with the ball. Javey worked hard keeping the ball from the opposing team's leading scorer. Seeing they were running out of time, he filed number twenty-three, sending him to the free throw line."

"Good file Javey!" shouted Mrs. Jenkins, with the entire crowd cheering behind her.

Now there was a lot of tension in the gym. Just about everyone in the gym could feel it. Most of the spectators were so worked up and excited they shouldn't keep their seats. With the pressure on, number Twenty-three hit his first free throw. Now with a two point led, it was looking bad for the home team. Even if he missed the second free throw, it didn't seem like enough time for Javey and his team mates to bring the ball up court, and set up their favorite play. The coach from the opposing team ordered his players off the free throw lanes and made them go up court and set up their defense. This left Javey and his other team mates on the free throw lanes, and the shooter.

"Miller, take the ball out. Give it to me," requested Javey.

Now tried from being chased by Javey, Number twenty-three took the ball to shoot his second free throw, but missed. Miller quickly filled the lane and rebounded the ball. Without hesitation, he passed the ball to Javey. Number twenty-three was hustling up court trying to help set up the defense. After receiving the ball, Javey dribbled until he was just passed half court. He then shot the ball. The entire gym of spectators seemed to hold their breaths as they watched the ball made its long flight towards the basket. Finally, the long awaited three points basket was good and with two seconds left on the clock.

"Oh my God!" shouted several of the fans.

"We win! We win!" shouted several others.

"Sceeeeeeeeeee!" screamed Mrs. Jenkins. "Did you see my baby? Did you see my baby?" she shouted.

"I don't believe it!" shouted Dr. Jenkins.

"Heyyyyyyyyyy!" shouted the Jenkins children.

The opposing team had two seconds left on the clock when the bucket was made. They quickly took the ball out of bounds for an attempt at a last minute shoot. But in their push to get the ball in, they didn't see Javey. They in bounced the ball, but he stole it. He stood there holding the ball as the clock ran out. The entire opposing team seemed in shock. The coach of the opposing team just sat on the bench looking at the clock, seeing his team lose by one point and on a spectacular shoot and defensive play made by a freshmen and one who played less then five minute in the entire game. Meanwhile, Javey was being mobbed by his teammates.

"That's my baby!" shouted Mrs. Jenkins as she gave her husband a high five, then, had to do the same for several other home team spectators.

Once they were home and preparing for bed, both Dr. and Mrs. Jenkins were sitting on opposite sides of the bed.

"Wow, what a night," said Mrs. Jenkins. "I am beat."

"No wonder, all they energy you used up tonight," said her husband.

"Yeah...Wasn't Javey spectacular tonight?"

"He sure was. I had no idea he was that good in basketball."

"Well, I did."

Suddenly Dr. Jenkins started to chuckle.

"What's funny?" asked Mrs. Jenkins.

"You are," he chuckled. "Not only did you inspire him to play a great game, but you got all those people involved."

"Well, I once read something that said 'A prepared mind means a prepared spirit. A prepared spirit is riddled with joy and excitement. When the time arrives, a prepared mind will lift the spirit of a man. It is then that the joy and excitement bottled up in a man will come forth, and lift the spirit of another man. Therefore, the spirit can never be broken again'. My baby was mentally prepared for tonight. The moment he hit the floor, he lifted the spirit of his teammates. Then together they gave the crowd something to feel good about. Then they got excited. Once they got excited and got into the spirit of the game, then they feed off of each other," she said as she laid down and covered herself up

"That seems to be your philosophy on life. Lifting other people's spirits."

"Maybe, but you can only lift the spirit when there is a willing mind."

"Yeah, I see what you mean...Menzie."

"Huh."

"I love you."

"I love you too. And if you want me to keep on loving you, let me get some sleep," she chuckled.

"Good night dear," said Jenkins.

He then laid his head down next to his wife. He peered over to get one last look before he fell asleep.

"Zzzzzzzzzzzzzzzzzzzzzzz," she went.

CHAPTER NINETEEN

THE COST FOR BEING THE BEST

The firm that Dr. James Jenkins and his wife had started became well recognized in the business world. The branch in Atlanta was just as prestigious as the one in Missouri. Suddenly the Jenkins's name was starting to be known all over the United States, with all involved making an impact in their own way. Even when Mrs. Jenkins had her baby, the fact that she went from actress, to a successful business personality, to wife, singer and mother, all made news. Her first, erotic provoking Album, 'Don't Just Give Your Love Away', made the top ten, and remained there for weeks earning her a Platinum Music award.

Dr. Jenkins started not only to be recognized as a powerful and successful businessman, his lectures and his new book, 'A Man's Thought is Worth More Than A Penny', was on the best sellers list for months at a time, earning him an nomination for the Pulitzer Prize.

But the two Jenkins who seemed to dominate the local news was Javey Jenkins with basketball exploits and his older brother Marcus, whose reputation as a songwriter and entertainer was just beginning to make its mark in the music world. But the next five years proved to be the most extraordinary for the Jenkins' name.

Vena had graduated from college and was working as a junior executive at a growing film company in Chicago, Illinois. Marcus was traveling with his band and performing and enjoying fame on his first worldwide tour. Mrs. Jenkins had taken some time off, and she and her daughter, Melody Venus Jenkins, traveled with him on that tour. Of course, she did a lot of singing herself, and between them they put on quite a show.

Javey was now in college and could be seen on national television, still performing his magic in basketball. After making All American three years in high school, it was obvious he was performing at that same level in college.

The one Jenkins who was a bit of a surprise was Myron. After moving into the new estate, he went to the gym nearly every day. The result was a young man, who suddenly became a big person. He went out for high football and made the varsity as a split end. Whereas Javey had help make his high school a winner in basketball, he was now helping the school do the same in football.

Not to be out done, Floreese was now a freshman in the same high school and was a cheerleader. Jealous folks said she got to be a cheerleader because of the reputation on her brothers. Still, when that was all said and done, she was turning out to be one of the best cheerleaders the school has ever had.

The Jenkins's name was starting to be featured in the local media almost as a common place. It was a phone call that Mrs. Jenkins received at the Jenkins' home which seemed to put that name on a path of distraction and embarrassment. It came just as she had returned home and was winding down from the excitement of her traveling. It was she who answered the phone and she could hear stress in her son's voice.

"Hello," she said.

"Hi Miss Mensiz, This is Javey. Is my Dad home?"

"No he hasn't made it home from work yet. Is something wrong?"

"Yeah plenty. I've been arrested."

"What?"

"Yes ma'am, they said this girl said I raped her, but I didn't!" he snapped.

"Where are you?"

"I'm in the county jail here in Chicago.

"Look I know you and you wouldn't do a thing like that. I'll tell your father when he gets home. I'm calling my lawyer. We'll see you sometime tonight."

"Please hurry, I don't like it in here."

"Just hold on baby. Mamma is going to get you out of this."

The moment she got off the phone, she called her attorney.

"Steven, this is Menzie.

"Something wrong?"

"Yes, my son Javey has been arrested for rape."

"That's ridiculous."

"Yeah tell me about it. Look, I need a good criminal lawyer."

"You got it."

"And do you have the name of a good Private Detective?"

"The best."

"Hire him for me. Tell the attorney you hire I need him to be ready to travel. Can you make that happen?"

"For you I can. And if you want to see your son tonight, I can do that too."

"Okay, call and let me know where we stand."

Late that same night, Dr. And Mrs. Jenkins rushed into the county jail. There were two police officers on duty there.

"We're here to see our son," said Dr. Jenkins.

"I'm afraid that's impossible."

"And why is that?" asked Mrs. Jenkins.

"Because we don't keep the jail opened all day for people to run in and out of here," said the one officer. "He raped a girl, and that makes him dangerous."

"First of all, my son didn't rape anybody. And I'm afraid you don't have a choice. Here's a letter from Judge Manchester, and it authorizes us to see our son tonight."

The second officer took the letter and read it. He then handed it to the first officer, who then read it.

"How did you make this happen?" he asked in a harsh tone of voice.

"What does it matter to you? All you have to do is follow orders," said Dr. Jenkins.

"Well, you might tell you son that. He gave me a lot of mouth, and got himself in more trouble. And he scared that poor girl to death."

"If she was so scared, how come she told you my son raped her?" asked Mrs. Jenkins.

"I can't answer that. In fact, I'm not going to try and answer that."

"Yeah, well when I see him, he better be okay." Said Mrs. Jenkins.

Later they sat in a waiting room waiting to see their son. When they did, he was wearing jail clothes, had chains around his wrists and ankle braces around his legs.

"Oh my God! Look at my baby," sighed Mrs. Jenkins as she told with her hands covering her mouth tears trickling down her face.

Javey sat down on one side of the room petition, his parents on the other. They sat next to each other facing him. He had to sit chained, so he was uncomfortable.

"Dad, Miss Menzie."

"Tell me what happened, son? " asked Dr. Jenkins.

"I went to this party last night. There were a lot of students from a lot of different colleges there. I was talking with this nice young lady, when I had to go to the restroom. On the way, I ran into the girl. She was crying, so I asked her if she needed some help. She broke away from me and ran. This morning the police came to the dorm and arrested me for rape."

"That doesn't make any sense."

"Did you tell the police what happened?" asked Mrs. Jenkins.

"I tried, but that didn't seem to make much difference."

"What happened to your face?" asked Dr. Jenkins.

"She scratched me when she broke away from me," Said Javey.

"Then what happened to your lip?" asked Mrs. Jenkins.

Javey seemed to hesitate when he was asked that question. His body language told them something was wrong.

"Javey, I asked you a question. What happened to your lip?"

"I had an accident."

"What kind of an accident?"

"I bumped it."

"Javey, look at your father. Look him in his eyes just like he has taught you to do. Now tell us what happened to your mouth? And don't lie to us," she demanded.

"You don't understand, I've got to be in here until you get me out. I can't say too much."

"One of those cops hit you, didn't they?" she bluntly asked.

"Mamma, please."

"Okay, that's cool," said Dr. Jenkins. "You know the name of the young lady you were talking to?" he asked.

"Yeah, her name was Camille Hudson. She's a freshman at St. Xavier here in Chicago."

"You wouldn't happen to have a number for her?"

"She gave me her number. I tried to give it to this police officer and asked him to call her. But he knocked it out of my hand."

"Is that why he hit you in your mouth?" asked Mrs. Jenkins.

"Yeah, he thought I was trying to tell him what to do, but I wasn't."

"Is there anything else you want to tell us before we leave?" asked Dr. Jenkins.

"Dad, I swear I didn't rape anybody. If you can find this young lady, she can tell you I talked to her just about the whole time I was there."

"Don't worry, we'll find her. I've hired a detective. I'm told he's good," said Mrs. Jenkins.

"We will be here to get you out in the morning," said Dr. Jenkins.

"Please get me out of here, please," pleaded Javey.

The coupled walked out of the police station headed towards their car, when Mrs. Jenkins stopped.

"What's the matter?" asked her husband.

"I left the car keys on the desk in there," she responded.

"Are you sure?"

"Yes, I'll go get them."

"I'll get them for you, dear."

"No, you wait by the car, I'll go and get them," she said as started back towards the entrance.

Once inside she walked over to where the two officers were sitting at their desks.

"I don't know which one of you bastards put your hands on my son. But you better not touch one hair on his head."

"Who do you think you are coming in here talking to us like that?" Shouted the officer. "Your son is in big trouble, he raped a girl."

"Oh so I see. So because he's young, he's guilty. Because he's Black, he's guilty. Because he's a young Black male, he's guilty. Well, in this country you are assumed innocent until proven guilty. Or did they teach you that at the Police Academy, you dipstick. You may have a hard time accepting this, but you are no God's helper. Your job is to serve and protect, not judge and jury. You are a disgrace to the uniform you are wearing. May I suggest you take up grave digging, which is more suited for your personality. You touch my son again, and I'll see to it that you regret it, you red neck bastard."

While Mrs. Jenkins was getting on the officer about their attitude and their action, their supervisor heard the commotion and came to check it out. He heard most of what she had said, and watched while she turned and walked away from them.

"Sawyers, Hampton, come into my office," he requested.

The two officers followed him into his office. He sat down at his desk, the two of them stood.

"What's going on out there?"

"The woman was raising hell because her son was arrested for raping a female. He mouthed off, so I had to pop him in the mouth."

"So you admit you hit him."

"Well, they should have taught him to respect authority."

"Do you know who those two people are?"

"No! And I don't really care."

"Well you should. They are Dr. and Mrs. Jenkins, two of the most affluent people in the business world. Stay away from their kid. If they file a suit against this department, you will be brought up on charges, you understand me?"

The officer didn't respond, but did stand there with this stupid look on his face.

The next day the Jenkins showed up with Steven Thomas and Grey Harmon, who was the Criminal Lawyer recommended by

Thomas. They got Javey out of jail and with the understanding he was under house arrest and he was to have an arraignment that Monday for the charges of rape. They all got together with Jack Brown the Private Investigator. Javey retold his story to include the part about Camille Hudson and where she attended school. Mrs. Jenkins had both of them on the ball because she was determined to have her son cleared before Monday morning. Brown went right to work on finding Hudson, Greg Harmon on the legal aspect of the case. Their hard work paid off when Brown called the hotel where they were staying and told them he had found Hudson. They all met in front of Hudson's house. They all then walked up to the front door. It was Harmon who rang the doorbell. A man opened the door.

"Mr. Hudson, my name is Greg Harmon, I'm Javey Jenkins' attorney," he said as he presented his card.

"That's the young man they say raped that girl," said Mr. Hudson.

"Well, we think we can clear this up, if we could speak to your daughter, Miss Camille Hudson."

"I don't want my daughter involved in this," he responded.

"Mr. Hudson, my client is to be arraigned on Monday. Now we think we can clear this up today. But if we have to go to court, I can request a summons to have your daughter appear in open court, but that's up to you."

"Please Mr. Hudson, we need your daughter's help to clear our son," pleaded Mrs. Jenkins.

"Who is that Daddy?" asked a voice from behind Mr. Hudson.

"It's some people here to see you. If you don't want to talk to them you don't have to."

"Is this about Javey Jenkins?" asked another female voice.

"Yes it is!" shouted Menzie Jenkins.

"I want her to talk with them," she Mrs. Hudson.

Mr. Hudson apprehensively stepped aside and let the party of five into his house. Once inside, Greg Harmon introduced everybody to the Hudson family. "This is Dr. And Mrs. Jenkins,

Javey Jenkins' parents. This is Steve Thomas, their family Attorney. This gentleman is Jack Brown, their Private Detective."

"Good to meet you," said Mrs. Hudson. This is my daughter, Camille, and of course you've met my husband Frank. Have a seat, all of you."

"Is it okay if Mrs. Jenkins talk to your daughter?" asked Harmon.

"Yes, she has already told me what happened. Camille," she said.

"Camille, I understand you met my son on Friday. You mind telling us what you know?"

"Do you mind if I tape her conversation?" asked Harmon.

"Do you have to?" asked Mr. Hudson.

"I want you to," responded Camille Hudson.

"Yes, let them go head. I think what she has to say is very interesting," said Mrs. Hudson.

"I was at this house party on Friday. I saw this tall guy when he walked through the door. I recognized who he was. He helped beat us twice this year in basketball. He was good looking and all these girls were all over him. At first I didn't care. But he seemed uncomfortable with all the attention he was getting. Something told me to rescue him, so I told those hussies I was his girl friend."

"Camille, watch your language," insisted Mrs. Hudson.

"Yes ma'am...anyways, we started to talking. We talked and laughed. I found him to be a very interesting man. Different than any guy I've ever met. After we talked for about an hour or so, he told me he had to go to the restroom and asked me not to leave. He didn't have to ask me that, I wasn't about to leave him there," she chuckled. "No sooner had he left me, I heard this female scream. When I looked to see what was going on, this female ran right past me. When I asked him what happened, he said she had scratched him. His face was bleeding so I got a first aid kit from one of the guys having the party. I fixed him up. Afterwards we talked some more, until the party was over. I gave him my number, and we left."

"How long would you say Javey was away from you?" asked Harmon?"

"Less than a minute. Look, those chicks were all over that brother. If he wanted sex, he could have had any one of them. He sure as hell won't have had to rape any of them."

"Camille," warned Mrs. Hudson.

"It just burns me up that that chick would accuse him of rape. Those two guys who came out of that room may have, but he didn't."

"What two guys are you talking about?" asked Mrs. Jenkins.

"Didn't he tell you about those guys he saw come out of a room near to where he was standing?"

"No he didn't" said Dr. Jenkins.

"Well he told me."

"Did he see the girl come out of that room?" Harmon.

"He told me he didn't. She just sort of ran into him."

"Maybe we need to find out who those two men were," said Brown.

"That's easy. Javey told me one of them had on this red soccer t-shirt. If it's the one I saw, he was one of the guys who had the party."

"How do you know?" asked Menzie.

"I heard him say they were in some kind of trouble before all of this happened."

"What was that address?" asked Harmon.

"10629 Bolen Drive. That's on the Southside," responded Camille.

"Jack," said Harmon.

"I'm on it," said Jack Brown as he got up and left the Hudson home.

As the rest of the party was outside of the Hudson's house and was headed towards their cars, Camille called then ran to catch up to them. Menzie Jenkins waited for her and the two of them talked.

"Look, I thought your son was a real nice guy. I gave him my number. If he loss it and he's still interested, here it is again," she said as she reached inside her blouse and pulled a piece of paper out of her bra and handed to her. Tell him to call me when this is cleared up."

"You are very pretty," said Mrs. Jenkins to Camille.

"Thank you. But you are too. No wonder he talked about you and his father most of the time we talked."

"And I should let you know, he did think you were nice."

"Really? Then you tell him I said he needs a steady girl friend. That will keep him out of trouble with all these flaky females out here," snickered Camille.

"I'll tell him that too," chuckled Mrs. Jenkins.

Later that evening, Dr. Jenkins had gone to get something for his son to eat. While he was out, his wife and his son had a little talk.

"Why is this happening to me?" he asked. "All I want to do is play ball, be the best I can be."

"Well, I'm afraid you are a victim of the times. We live in a time that is riddled with confusion. There is dishonesty, deceit, corruption, hate, jealousy and a tendency to want to get something for nothing. With that kind of attitude these kinds of things are bound to happen."

"What do you mean?"

"Well, take you for instance, your mother and father brought you up in loving, wholesome environment, where you were taught compassion, discipline and self control. Plus you have a Black, educated male as a father and role model. Plus, people can see we are not begging for bread. When you combined all of that, that makes you well bred, the cream of the crop in a country. But instead of people admiring you for that, they hate you for it. When they do, they want to see you taken down. They might even hate you enough to try and take all of that away from you."

"But why? You would think everybody wants the same things out of life?"

"Son, the problem is, some people don't even try."

"So, what are we to do?"

"The only thing I know to do is pray."

"Mom always told us that prayer changes things."

"That's also the best advice I was ever taught."

He reached over and hugged his stepmother, and she returned his hug.

"Miss Menzie thanks for marrying my father. You don't know what it means just to have you here," he sighed as he started to tear.

"I can't put into words what it means for me to be here," she reciprocated as she too started to also tear.

"I love you, Mamma!" he uttered as he held onto her tighter.

"I love you too baby," she whispered as she stoked the back of his head.

A couple of hours later, Brown had located the young man in the red shirt. His name was Kevin Porter, and what he had to say was interesting. And it was at the county police station were he did his talking. The Jenkins were there and so were both attorneys. Brown and the Police supervisor were also there. It was he who asked the questions.

"On Friday night, there was a young lady molested at a house at 10629 Bolen Drive. You know anything about that?" he asked.

"Who says?" asked Kevil Howard.

"She said she was."

"Well, if you are talking about Amanda Hughes, she lied."

"And how do you know that?"

"Because I was one of the people she had sex with that night."

"Did you rape her?"

"Hell no! She got this thing for athletes. When we were having sex my friend Potts walked in on us. We're on the Soccer Team together. When I finished, he asked if he could go a round and she said yes at first. But once he started, she asked him to stop."

"Did he?"

"Well, he didn't want to so I had to pull him off her. She jumped up screaming like a mad woman. We went after her, but she got out of the room."

"She accused another male with raping her. Any ideal why she did that?"

"You talking about that basketball player? Rumor has it he comes from a rich family. Maybe she was after some money or something. Could be she was feeling guilty and tried to cover it up the fact she had sex with two men."

"Did you see this basketball player at your party?"

"Yeah, he was talking to some good looking chick. Then I saw him again when we were trying to catch Amanda. I think she must have run into him or something. Later this chick he was talking to asked my cousin for a first aid kit to fix him up, so she must have scratched him."

"Didn't you know she had accused that young man of raping her?"

"Yeah, I heard about it on T.V."

"Why didn't you come forth and clear this up before now?"

"Look man, my cousin's folks were out of town. We told them we were only going to have a few friends over for a party. When they get back, they are really going to be pissed to know we had a house full of people and that this happened in their crib. So, we decided to stay out of it."

"To stay out of it?"

"Yeah, you know, not get involved," he chuckled.

"You want to know what I think son? I think you are lying. I think you and your cousin raped that girl. What did you do, scare her? Tell her to blame these folk's son for money, what?"

"No way man! She wanted us to do it to her. If she wanted money it had nothing to do with us, me."

"Bull shit!" bellowed the police supervisor as he rang for a couple of his officers to come into his office. "This sounds like one of those blame the Black kid, and I don't like that bull shit not one bit.

"Get his ass out of here!" he ordered. "Book his ass for raped. Put out a warrant for his cousin. Charge that bastard with rape."

They all sat and watched as the officers took the young male out of the office. And the angry supervisor worked to calm himself down.

"Look folks, I'm sorry about all of this. I send someone over to release your son."

"How do we play this now?" asked Thomas.

"We'll have to get with the judge before the hearing on Monday. I'll ask that the charges be dismissed," said Attorney Harmon.

Later that night, the Jenkins entered the room where Javey was lying across the bed. When they walked in, he could see the smiles on their faces.

"What?' he asked with excitement in his voice.

"It's over!" shouted Mrs. Jenkins as she held out her arms to him.

"It's over? You mean I'm cleared?"

"Yes! Bellowed his father as he and his wife rushed over to hug their son.

"Oh thank God! Thank God!" cried their son as he dropped his head and cried, bitterly. "Ahhhhhhhhhhhhhh! I was so scared! I was so scared!"

"We know sweetie. We know," said Mrs. Jenkins in a comforting tone to her voice.

The three of then sat on the bed in a group hug, all crying, all relieved. The family had gone through some crises before. This one threatened everything they had hoped and worked so hard for. But they still held together, showing just how bonded a family must be to withstand the pressures of a sick society. This was the family in which James and Marian Jenkins started with faith in God. And now it is Mrs. Menzie Jenkins who has consummated this family with God's faith in her.

CHAPTER TWENTY

POWER IN THE MAKING

The year was 1990. A lot had changed over the years. Vena was married and had two kids. She was always good with money, so she had financially positioned herself to be a stay home mom. Additionally, she and her husband had bought stock in her families' firm. This meant they were investing in her families' future.

Javey had finished college and had signed a contract for several million dollars and was now playing professional basketball. The season was over but it was the next basket he was about to score, which was to change his life. He surprised his family by bringing, what he described as a special guest, to meet them.

"Hey, what a surprise," said Mrs. Jenkins after opening the front door.

She gave him a good hug when she noticed he had someone with him.

"Camille, how nice to see you again," she said as hugged her. "What's up?" she asked with a suspicious look on her face.

"Can we come in?" he chuckled.

"Oh course you can silly," she snickered.

She stepped aside and let them both in. She noticed Camille seemed a bit nervous so she attempted to calm her.

"Camille, you are a very beautiful young woman, you know that?"

"Well, I do now," chuckled Camille.

"How does it feel to be out of college?"

"I've just completed my undergraduate work and I've already started my graduate work towards my Masters degree."

"I think that is so wonderful. Congratulations," she bellowed as she gave the young lady a second hug.

"Mom, where's Dad?" asked Javey.

"Your father is upstairs in his office. Why don't you let him know you are here," she suggested.

Javey left to go up the stairs to his father's office.

"Well Camille, I've seen you at my son's games, we got the impression you were only friends. I never thought the two of you were going together, or am I assuming too much?"

"No, you're right,"

"How did all of this happen?"

"Well, it did start out with me just liking to see him play. We were friends for a couple of years. I guess we just started to like each other. We started getting serious about a year ago. By the time I was finishing school our relationship just started moving up to the next level."

"What do you mean by that?"

"I think I've better let Jay tell you what's up."

"I see," responded Mrs. Jenkins. "Well, he told us you were friends, and that's all. I had no idea it had gotten this serious."

At that point, Javey and his father walked into the family room. He wasn't told Camille was there, so it did catch him a bit off guard.

"Miss Hudson, how are you?" he said as she shook her hand. "Javey, what's going here?" he asked.

"Have a seat Dad," requested Javey.

"Both Dr. and Mrs. Jenkins sat down on the sofa. They peered over at one another then back to their son.

"Mom, Dad, I know I told you Camille and I were just friends. Well we were, until a years ago. What she didn't know was how much I have always loved her. When I signed up to play pro ball, I told her I was going to ask her to marry me. But we wanted to be sure that's what we both wanted. Doing that time we started getting tight. Then it became obvious we loved each other. So, I asked her to marry me, and she has agreed."

"Really?" asked a shocked Dr. Jenkins.

For a few moments both Dr. and Mrs. Jenkins seemed in shock. It took a while for the message to seek in, but it finally hit them what they had just heard.

"Married? You are getting married?" asked Mrs. Jenkins.

"Yes," responded relieved Javey Jenkins.

"Give me a hug!" shouted Mr. Jenkins as he stood and hugged his son.

"Girl, give me a hug," said Mrs. Jenkins to Camille as she stood and hugged her.

Then Dr. Jenkins hugged Camille, while Mrs. Jenkins hugged her son. Then Venus entered the room just in time to see all the excitement.

"What's going on?" she asked.

"Your brother is getting married," said Dr. Jenkins.

"You getting ready to marry my brother?" she asked of Camille.

"It sure looks like it," she uttered.

"Well, you are getting a good man," she said in her young tender voice.

"Well, aren't you a precious little thing," uttered Camilla as she softly hugged the youngest of the Jenkins' family.

"I'm trying to figure out what she knows about a good man," chuckled Mrs. Jenkins as she and the entire group left the family room preparing to tell the rest of the family.

Later that night, Mrs. Jenkins got a chance to talk to Camille alone.

"So, you guys are getting married. How does your parents feel about you two?"

"When my Mom found out we were seriously dating each other, she assumed we were having sex. Well, we weren't at the time, but she kept asking me if I was considering marrying him? When I told her I might, she seemed somewhat relieved. My mother didn't believe in a woman having sex before marriage."

"How about you?"

"What do you mean, how about me?"

"I'm asking if you believe in sex before marriage."

"I was taught to believe a woman's sexuality is the most important things that she has. Once her virginity is gone, she has to start to weigh what she gained from it. If it's not a life long commitment, then she has wasted it. Then she can never get it back."

"Sounds like your mother had the right idea. What about your father?"

"What do you mean?"

"Well, the last time we talked to him, he didn't approve of my son. When we saw him at the games, he didn't say much to us. How does he feel about this marriage?"

“My father never wanted me to marrying just any old body. He always said I should get me someone very smart and very special. You know a man who can take care of me."

"You mean somebody rich?"

"Not necessarily rich. But I was raised to try and be somebody. You can't be what you want to be if you are dragging dead weight around. When I first met your son, I was hoping he liked me because I knew he was the kind of man I wanted. Once we got close, I knew he was the one."

"That's interesting. But I still remember he weren't too fond of my son when we last talked to them."

"He regrets that. He never apologized to Jay, personally. But once that mess with him was cleared up, he did take the time to get to know him, especially when he realized how I felt about him. He's gained a lot of respect for him. You saw us at just about all of his home games. Man, there were so many of them that were filled with excitement and they were always so tense. My father loved all that drama. Me, I was always too nervous," she chuckled as Mrs. Jenkins starred at her as she listened to her talk. "Now I'm marrying a man who will continue to have that drama as a living. Funny how things turn out sometimes, huh?"

"I guess," agreed Mrs. Jenkins.

“At any rate, I hope you won't hold that against my father, because he has a lot of respect for Jay. He says he like his guts. He was a bit surprised when we told him we were getting married. But he thinks Jay is cool people, and he's happy for us. In fact, he told me he was proud of me. I guess that's good, huh?"

"Yeah I guess so...How are you feeling right about now?"

"Actually, I'm nervous."

"Well that's to be expected."

"Noh, I'm not nervous about getting married. And I know I'm going to be a good wife. And I'm not nervous about Jay. He's a good choice for me and I know he'll make a good husband."

"Then what are you nervous about?"

"It's the standard you women in this family seem to have set. Jay talks about his Grandmother and Vena. Then there's his mother. And or course, he thinks the world of you. Those are hard acts for any woman to follow, you know?"

"I guess so. May I ask you a personal question?"

"Sure."

"So you have already had sex with him?"

"That's too personal of a question."

"Then I have my answer. But you did say your mother thought you were having sex at that time. I'm assuming you did so later. Plus, if you hadn't, you would have given me a definite, no."

"See, that's what I'm talking about, how witty you are. Okay, yes we've had sex, a couple of times. But I was a virgin before we started dating if that's what concerns you."

"I'm just trying to understand where you are coming from."

"Oh, I see. Trying to figure out if I'm good enough for your son."

"Are you?"

"Look, one of the reasons I have never dated is because I was looking for someone special. In fact neither one of us was excited about making any kind of commitment. We started out as friends. We dated, went to the movies, concerts, things like that. And I always liked talking to him."

"Is that when you had sex with him?"

"That really bothers you doesn't it?"

"Not really."

"Oh yes it does. Well that is not when we got together. The more we dated the more I liked him. You won't believe this, but I found myself so in love with the man, I couldn't think straight. When we started seriously dating, I had no idea we would end up having sex. The man just sort of caught me off guard. Just swept me off my feet. That's when we started to have sex and while he was playing pro ball. When we first did it, I got scared."

"And why is that?"

"Because I have always said I wanted to end up with the right man. I wanted to wait until I was married to have sex. And I only want to be married once, have babies and stay with that one man forever. Now here I was having sex with a man with his own apartment and lots of money. I was hoping I was doing it for the right reasons. That sounds silly don't it?"

"No it doesn't."

"I sure hope not, because that's how I felt. That's how I still feel. When he told me he had planes to marry me, I was sure hoping he was serious...Let me ask you a personal question. May I?"

"Sure."

"When you first laid eyes on your husband for the very first time, how did you feel?"

"When I first met my husband he was still married to his first wife."

"But that didn't answer my question. How did you feel when you first saw him?"

"I must as admit, I had this strange feeling in my heart he was going to be important in my life. I had no idea why I felt that way."

"Remember when I told you about me seeing Jay at that party for the first time? He was surrounded by all of these females. I don't really know why I took it upon myself to go rescue him. I just did it. That's because there was something I felt in my heart, and right away."

Mrs. Jenkins couldn't help but chuckle a bit.

"Well, I'll admit, that's something we seem to have in common. Still, I think you lucked out. You gave up that virginity too early. But you gave it to the right men. What you assumed was his high standard of the women in this family, was really the respect he has for woman, period. If you've had sex with him and he still wants to marry you, that means he still respects you. So, that's why I say you were lucky, you picked the right man you."

"Trust me, luck had nothing to do with it. And if I had the slightest doubt he wasn't the man I wanted to spend the rest of my life with, I would not have given up my virginity to him," she snickered.

"I've got the feeling you are going to fit right in with this family."

"Does that mean, I passed your test?"

"What that means is, you are marrying into a family where the females have high morale and solid principles."

"Like I said, women of high standards," retorted Camille Hudson.

"Well, your family has done a good job of bringing you up using some good principles of their own. That means a lot. Welcome to this family. You are going to find this to be an experience of a life time."

"Somehow, I don't doubt that one bit," chuckled Camille as the two of them hugged as they chuckled.

Not to be totally out done, Myron, now coming out of college as a top draft, had also signed a contract for several million dollars, and was playing professional football. Having a background in law, and getting her share of their money was Mrs. Jenkins in that she was the agent for both athletes.

To keep up the productive trend set by their parents, Floreese was a sophomore in college and was a member of the cheer leading squad. Venus was just learning to play the French horn but only after her mother had already taught her to play the piano.

But now the family as well as they were doing was about to get involved in a different phase of life. It happened when Josh Charles the reining Governor of the state was considering retiring after his term was up. He met Mrs. Jenkins at a rally for another candidate considering running for the Mayor's office. Their talk had to do with his replacement. It was then their conversation got very interesting as they sat at and ate at one of the tables.

"What's this I hear about you quitting politics after your term runs out?" she asked him.

"Yeah, I'm getting a little too old."

"Too old?"

"Well, I guess burnt out would be a better diagnosis," chuckled Charles.

"What about the things that need to be done for this state?"

"I've been in politics for over forty years. I've been Governor for two terms. This state needs a fresher face a person with more energy and some innovative ideas," he responded.

"You got anybody in mind?"

"Well, that depends."

"On what?"

"If I can talk you into running."

"Why me?"

"Mrs. Jenkins you and your husband are the most respected business couple in this state. Either one of you could run the politics in this state. A woman Governor would be good for the state."

"Well, I couldn't do it. I've got too many responsibilities now with my son's in sports, being my son's business manager in music, my singing, just too many irons in the fire as it is."

"That's too bad. You would make a good one. How about your husband?"

"James? Other than having his opinions about everything, I don't think he's interested in politics."

"How do you know? Have you ever asked him?"

"No I haven't. But he don't have a lot of respect for politicians."

"Now you've just given him a reason to run for office. If he dislike the way things are, this is a good way to affect change."

"I hear you, but I don't know."

"Look, he is a great public speaker, I've heard him speak. His books are on the best sellers lists, nominated for the Joseph Pulitzer prize, twice. When you think about it, he would be perfect."

"Actually, he would be your best choice and for the reasons you said."

"How would you like for me to ask him?" asked Josh Charles.

"Tel! you what, let me mention it to him, get a feel for what he thinks about the idea. If he seems open minded, I'll call you and maybe we can have you over for dinner."

"Mrs. Jenkins, tell you husband this state really needs his help."

"Once Mrs. Jenkins was home, her husband had left a message we went to pick up Venus. By the time they got home, she was fast sleep, so her father put her right to bed. When he walked into the bedroom, his wife was already in bed. He went into the bathroom and brushed his teeth.

"Hey you!" she shouted.

"Yes," he said as he peeped out of the bathroom.

"I've got an urgent message for you, hurry up!" she insisted.

Once she was finished brushing his teeth, he walked over to his wife, bent down to hear what she had to say. Instead of her saying anything, she pulled his head down to her and gave him a nice long kiss, and with plenty of tongue. Once she stopped the kiss, she still held onto his neck.

"I need your body, husband of mine," she softly whispered in his ear, then started to nibble on it.

"Hold that thought, I want to take a shower," he uttered as he kicked off his shoes.

"Why, I'm only gonna make you work up a sweat," she murmured as she kissed him again, and giving him plenty of tongue. She could feel he was ready.

"You know that tongue of yours has gotten you in more trouble," he uttered.

"Prove it," she challenged then started to unbutton his shirt.

Once she helped him off with his shirt, she then unbuckled his belt, then started unbuttoned his pants and pulled them down to his knees.

"You've got two seconds to get out of those pants," she uttered.

In no time he was undressed. He climbed in bed next to her.

"Now, what was that you were saying?" he asked.

She didn't say anything, just gave him another mouth full of tongue.

He slowly laid her down on her back then rolled over on top of her.

"Ohhhhhhhhhhhhhhhh!" she sighed in pressure.

In the middle of the night, they laid in each other arms.

"Mr. Jenkins, I want to thank you for taking care of my body tonight. I feel so much better," she snickered.

"Anytime you need a turn up, just let me know," he chuckled.

She chuckled at his remark. She then turned so she could lie on his chest and look into his eyes.

"Ummm, I love you Dr. Jenkins," she uttered.

"I love you too dear," he whispered as he lifted his head and kissed her. “By the way, how did things go tonight?"

"I actually had an interesting conversation with the Governor tonight. It seems he is calling it quits."

"Did he say why?"

"Yes, I think he described it as being burnt out," she chuckled. "In fact our conversation turned quite interesting. Would you like to know what he asked me?" How do I get the feeling you are going to tell me regardless to what I say?"

"Okay silly!" she chuckled.

"Okay, you are dying to tell me, so what."

"He was wondering if you would be interesting in running for Governor?"

"He's got to be kidding me," chuckled James Jenkins.

"No, he was quite serious about it."

"Did you tell him I wasn't interested?"

"I sure did. But that didn't change his mind. In fact he was most insisted about it."

"Getting involved in politics isn't something I have given much thought to."

"Well, maybe you should. There isn't a man walking this green earth that could do a better job than you."

"Why do you say that?"

"Give this some thought. How many lives do you think you have changed with your talks and your books?"

"I have no idea."

"Exactly, but I bet you are the most influential man in two states. Look how well you have done in business. You are one of the riches men in this state and the most respected too."

"Sounds to me you have given this some serious consideration."

"I didn't at first. But when Charles made it clear to me he thought you could do it, it's been on my mind every since. Think about it, baby, being the most powerful man in this state. If any man should have that kind of power, it should be you. And that's because you will use it for the betterment of this state."

"Governor huh? You think I should talk to him about it."

"Why are you asking me?"

"Because I value your opinion very much."

"You value my opinion that much to consider politics?"

"Menzie, I value your opinion more than I value life. I want you to listen to me. I never told you the valuable lesson I have learned from you, and that is, a man is only as good as his best thought. But if he has no thoughts of himself and what he can do, then that man has no value in life."

"What does that mean? And how does it apply to me?"

"I had never given much thought as to what I really wanted out of life. All I've ever wanted was to be a good husband and father. Now that's not too bad of a thought to have. But it makes a man have limits as to his abilities in life. It was you, who started to plant these thoughts bigger than life in my heart. They motivated me, and make me reach beyond my limits. Once I understood that, my values changed which consequently change my whole life."

"Man, I did all of that for you?"

"Yes, and you know you have."

"I do, and now here I am planting another thought asking you to take your life, our lives to a different level, right?"

Don't you see that what has also increases my value as a man? I would have be a fool not to even consider what you are asking me now."

"Wow, what you just said helped me realize. You have always had all the love to give coupled with the passion to give. Now you have a chance to gain the power to give. Once you have that, your value as a man will make you immortal. And that will allow you to leave behind a legacy, which will live forever. Man, just thinking about that makes chills run up and down my spine. Yeah baby, you run for the Governor and know that I've got your back all the way."

Several weeks after, Dr. James Jenkins announced his candidacy for Governor of the state of Missouri. The moment he did, three occurrences from his past resurfaced. The first two involved Mrs. Jenkins directly. So she and her husband decided to hold a press conference for her to address those concerns while he sat in the background as she stood before the media. One of the reports showed a picture with her standing in front of a downtown office, her dress covering her head. When she was handed a copy of it, she chuckled.

"What does this picture suggest to you?" she asked the reporter.

"It suggests you were trying to prove you were just as sexy as Marilyn Monroe." Said the reporter with a chuckle in his voice.

"Oh really? Look at the date on that picture. That was the same day my doctor, Dr. Phillips, told me I was pregnant. I was so excited I rushed out of his office to tell the whole world. Being pregnant, the least I had on my mind was being sexy, but I was embarrassed. I just didn't look where I was standing and a draft from the underground terminal got caught my dress. But I do like the thought that you thought I was trying to be sexy," she chuckled.

The entire group laughed at her remark.

Then Marilyn Bash stood and had a few words.

"Do you remember me?" she asked.

"Yes, another Marilyn. There seems to be a lot of that going around," she chuckled.

Her remark got a chuckled from the crowd, but it didn't impress Bash in the least.

"Do you remember a conversation we had in your office?"

"Yes."

"Well, you made a few remarks and I told you then you did not represent today's modern professional woman. So, here you are now, wanting to be the first lady of this state. How can you justify that?"

"Gee Marilyn, I thought I justified it pretty well in my office when we talked. Unlike you, I am a wife and mother first, and a woman of business secondly. My husband is a tremendous leader. What he needed to be success in business and to accomplish what he has done was the love and support of his wife, that's me. I did that and because of that effort, hundreds of lives have been changed. I'm sorry if the business female world didn't think that was proper, but God must have. He blessed us real good!" she emphasized.

Her remark got a round of applauds from the onlookers.

The last issue had to do with her and Dr. Jenkins. It had to do with the rumor they were sleeping together when he was still married.

"Mrs. Jenkins, we understand there were rumors going around the firm where you worked that you and Dr. Jenkins were romantically involved while he was still married to his first wife. How will you respond to that allegation?"

"First I will say, the grapevine is alive and well," she chuckled.

"I'm serious, what's your response to that allegation?" he asked her again.

When Mrs. Jenkins looked around, she could see she had to address the question she was asked. Just as she was prepared to respond to the question a female's voice from the crowd yelled out.

"I'll address that issue!" she said.

The mumbling started to rifle through the conference room until the female making the remark was identified. It was Gladis Henley.

"Give me that mic." She insisted.

A reporter held it out for her to talk, but she snatched it away from him then had her say.

"I worked with Mrs. Jenkins when those rumors were being spread. I was somewhat responsible for those rumors. I did it because I liked him and didn't like her. I thought it was funny people believed me," she chuckled. "But I'm here to tell you the rumors were not true. But more than that, you pick Dr. Jenkins for Governor, and you will get a pair with a proven record of making good thing happen. Mrs. Jenkins, your husband has my vote!" she shouted.

Once she said what she had to say, the crowd went wild. Claps and cheers were so intense so loud one could not hear one think.

Later in the month, the election was about to begin. The convention was held with excitement as Dr. Jenkins and his wife was introduced. They stood there holding hands as the entire audience stood and applauded. Once things settled down, it was his speech, which finally made the difference.

"I was raised to believe that we were all born with a destiny in life. I never paid that much attention. But what I have learned over the years is that we do, all of us. I'll tell you something else I've learned over the years. That most of us spend a lifetime living beneath our Godly privilege. And let me tell you how that happens. When we are young, we take advice from some unwise people who in their own way mean well, but have no idea what they are talking about. How many of you have ever been told as a younger, take your time because you have your whole life ahead of you? The person who gave you that advice, how would they know that? God knows, but how would they know that to be a fact?"

Dr. Jenkins remark got a chuckled from the crowd.

"People who don't know any better might be best served to keep their big mouth shut, if that's all the advice they can give our youth. If they were just a little bit wiser, you know what they would tell you? Work to accomplish your dreams and goals now, then sit back and enjoy the fruits of your labor. The key words here are work and dream or a goal. Our young people do not know the value of work. Therefore their attitude is to always look for the easiest way through life. Get something for nothing. And when that doesn't work for them, they get discouraged and all kinds of difficult things will come into their lives."

The audience was dead silent as he continued his thought.

"That is when they use drugs, start drinking alcohol, being promiscuous and having multi sex partners, stealing, robbing and killing as if nothing else matters. Sometimes they will spend most of their lives trying to prove how tough they are rather than how smart they are. Sometimes they can mess of their lives so bad, they may never be able to recover. They then will spend their life living beneath their privilege, if they manage to live at all. Unfortunately, they will pass that life style down to the next generation, and it goes on and on. Some of you might ask where I'm headed with this? Well, the first things we need to do is get our young people on the right path. They must learn the only way to fight off poverty of life is to understand our systems have rules, they are not hard rules, but they must be followed. And believe it or not, the simplest of these rules is to have a dream or a goal in life. You see having a dream or a goal gives a person something to look forward towards. Let's call it hope. Hope infers a situation is always subject to get better. It infers that a person present situation has nothing to with their destiny in life."

The audience clapped at his remark, and the applauses lasted several minutes.

"Now here is rule number two. We will have to start encouraging our youth to have a dream and a goal early in their lives. Waiting until you think they are of age, can be a big mistake. Now if you are a parent and you know anything about having a dream or a goal, then you must follow rule number three. Get away from the negative people in your life and get around more positive people."

The audience sat silently as if they had been hit with a huge rock.

"Do this," he said. "Get your kids in church. Not just any old church, but one that has not only a Godly concert, but one that can motivate people to focus on more than just going to heaven."

Most of the audience clapped at his remark, whereas some did not. So he addressed that issue too.

"Now, don't get me wrong. Going to heaven is a worth while goal. But you've got to learn how the fight off the pitfalls of hell while you are still living right here on earth first!" he said with a great deal of enthusiasm.

This time the entire stood and clapped, and for a couple of minutes.

"Rule four, we must teach our youth to have a definite plan for their lives, stop taking life as it comes. I once read this, 'Most people don't plan to fail, they just fail to plan'. A plan gives them a road to success, a route that will lead them to their dream of goal. Now this is most difficult rule for them to follow. Rule number five. They need to see us setting the example for them. It is easy to sit back and criticize how bad the youth in this county is. The question is what are we doing to make a change? We must remember either we are part of the problem or part of the solution. When I refer to we, I am talking about we as parents and we as politicians. Oh yeah politicians, we are going to have to clean up our act because right now we are part of the problem and not part of the solution. Those of us who want to make a difference we can start by getting our people out to register to vote and then encourage them to exercise that vote. Those politicians who are not with us are against us, and are not worthy to get paid representing you and me. Now is the time for that kind of leadership, but only if you are ready for it. If you are, then let's get busy!" he shouted as his wife joined him on stage, as they stood holding hands and being held as the next ray of hope. Even Governor Josh Charles was there, standing and clapping as to show to show his support.

Then to show support for his father, Marcus brought his music review to the campaign and they really put on a show. The excitement was in the air as every entertainer who was from Missouri was there. As Marcus Jenkins, super star turned it on and turned if out.

Dr. Jenkins served as Governor for eight years before running for the United State Senate. Once he won that seat, he served until he took sick in 2005. At that point he had given over twenty-five years of public service.

On July 19, 2005, he was hospitalized diagnosed with cancer. That same night his daughter Melody Venus Jenkins performed with the St. Louis Symphony Orchestra. Although he wasn't at the concert, the Jenkins family was well represented.

John and Lynnett Jenkins were up in age as were Thomas and Pat Ferguson, but they were there. Vena, her husband and two kids were there. As was Myron and his Joan and one child. Javey and Camille were there with their three children. Floreese and her husband to be, James, were there. And so was a host of people from politics and from the firm. And Venus' husband to be Jordan Strong was also there.

Dr. James Jenkins laid in a hospital bed watching the concert on television, while his wife of thirty years sat next to him holding his hand. She too watched and listened to the youngest of the Jenkins' family do as so many Jenkins had done before her, be the very best there is. Venus played as a special request to her father, 'Moon Night Sonata'. As she played, the entire Powell Symphony Hall was silent. As he played her father's room was silent as he and his wife listened.

Then Venus hit her last note. And as she did, Mrs. Jenkins watched her husband take his last breath. She held his hand close to her cheek and sobbed. Four day later he was laid to rest.

"So, now Menzie has given us so much," said Jenkins on the tape. "It is time for all of you to rally around her. She loves all of you just as you were her own children. I need you to show her that love back just as she has given it to you. Venus loves you with all of her heart. When it is all said and done, I am her father as I am all of you. Goodbye my little flower and remember Daddy loves you very much...

At that very moment Mrs. Jenkins walked into her son's office. She could see her sitting and crying as the cassette tape had run out.

"Floreese, what's wrong?" she asked as she closed the door behind her and walked over to her.

"Oh Mamma, I miss him so much," she sobbed as she wrapped her arms around her mother's waist, while laying her head on her heart.

"Come on baby," she whispered. "All of us miss him," she said as she hugged her daughter's head. "While he was alive, he gave us all the love he had. Now he's gone, there is still enough from him to last each of us a life's time.

"I know I've never said this to you, but I love you, I really do."

"I know you do, and in your own way you've always shown me that you did. Come on the others are waiting for us. Come on baby," said Mrs. Jenkins as she helped her daughter to her feet.

"I take it your Daddy left you a tape to listen to?"

"Yeah. It's about how you helped him help us."

"Well, he didn't need a lot of help, just a little push now and then."

"It was interesting. I think I'll write it into a book."

"Sounds like that's the part of your father that's in you."

They turned as they hugged and left Myron's office.

"You think you will ever marry again?"

"Noh, I had the man who was perfect for me. Now, I'm just going to enjoy the rest of you and spoil all of my Grandkids rotten," she snickered.

"About this book, Daddy talked about you and his sex life a lot."

"Well, he was a bit of a dirty old man and clean up until he got sick."

"Funny, he blamed you for starting most of it," she chuckled.

"Well, I think we both enjoyed being married. That was only one of the things we had in common, plenty of sex," she then chuckled.

Later the entire family was there for the reading of the will. Steven Thomas did the honors.

"Before reading your father's will, I wanted to say a few words. I've known Menzie Jenkins way before I met your father. She had started to amass a fortune. But never seemed happy. I never said anything because it wasn't my place."

Mrs. Jenkins dropped her head as she reflected back and remembered what that was like.

"When she told me she was getting married, I was really hoping things worked out for her, because she was so deserving. Little did I know how much things were about to change in her life, and that's why I feel so honored to be doing this today. Now, in the reading of your father's will, I don't think I need to tell you he left you all well off. His net worth only, was over sixty-five million dollars. He left fifty percent of his wealth to his six kids to divided up equally, the other fifty percent to his wife. However, she has given fifty percent of her wealth into the pot, so seventy recent of the families' wealth will go to the kids on this day, So, each of you will get over eight million dollars a piece."

The kids seemed overwhelmed as they started to cheer among themselves.

"Now I know to you two athletes that might be chump change because you are already rich. But what your father left behind for you is wealth. To build wealth is to be able to pass on to your families and for generations to come.

The Jenkins children understood where Mr. Thomas was coming from because they all clapped.

"And of course there is the potential to make more with those of you who will be running the firms your parents have built. Man, I would like to be around to witness that," he chuckled again. "Well, good luck to all of you," he said in closing.

He got up and handed the will and all the other papers he had to Mrs. Jenkins. He stood looking back at the Jenkins' children for several second.

"Mrs. Jenkins, this has been one hell of a ride," he chuckled. "I hope you have enjoyed it as much as I have."

"I have, and this is one of those little set backs in life. Nothing last for ever."

"I see what you mean," chuckled Thomas. "Well, it looks like you are going to have plenty of help running the many steams of companies you have. And you've got some tremendous kids. I know you are very proud."

"You have no idea how much."

"Well, goodbye," said Thomas as he hugged Mrs. Jenkins for the last time.

There the entire Jenkins clam sat talking to one another. Floreese and Venus held hands as they talked. Vena, Camille and

Myron talked to their mother, while the rest of them just talked among themselves. When it was all said and done, one man and the two women in his life had given him more than enough fulfillment for any one man. But only one gave him the extraordinary life he lived clean up to when he died. And now that he has passed on, the results of all of their effort now filled the room. There was a retired professional basketball player, now a business executive, with his wife. There was retired professional football player now a Corporate Attorney and his wife. There were two sisters, both female executives and several other professional Business women were also there. There was a R&B professional artist and his wife. There was a professional concert pianist with her husband to be. Not to mention the number of college graduates being the most obvious of them all. And with all that being said, Menzie Ferguson-Jenkins was mostly responsible for their wealth and for them representing one of the most powerful families in the United States of America. Proving that behind every successful man is a great woman.

THE END

ABOUT THE AUTHOR

Dr. John H. Johnson was born and raised in the inner city of St. Louis, Missouri. His mother and father were married for over forty years before they both died. However, most of his young life was spent being raised by his mother from Kinloch Missouri, Vandelia Willie Cunningham-Johnson.

He was the oldest of eight children, five bothers and two sisters. He was educated in the St. Louis Public Schools system, where he played football and ran track. He was also a member of his high school choir. After high school, he spent three years in the service before being honorably discharged.

After the service, he pursued his formal education and obtained BA Degree in Psychology, a MA Degree in Human Relations, and a Ph.D in Psychology. He is retired from the Department of Army, and taught in the Public School in both the city and the counties of Missouri for several years. He has coached High School football and an AAU basketball team and has one National Basketball Championship to his credit. He is currently a Motivational Trainer for a Professional Job Finding Service.

In 1971 he was named 'Whose Who in Colleges and Universities. In 2004, he has been named Marquis's Whose Who in American. In 2005 he was named to the Manchester's Whose Who Among Executives and Professionals, "Honors Edition".

In addition to this novel, Dr. Johnson is also the author of the comedy 'A Man's Rib And A Band Of Gold', which sold over 100 copies in two months. 'Dawn's Bitter Loss Of Innocence', for love story enthusiasts. He is also the author of Sci-Fi thrillers, Adversaries Of God, Opposition to Man, part one and two, and Embryoevolution.

Because of his creative writings, he was named VOICES PUBLISHING COMPANY'S Creative Writer for 2006.

Printed in the United States
52622LVS00004B/181-201

9 780977 937585